PENGUIN CLASSICS

THE STREET OF CROCODILES
AND OTHER STORIES

BRUNO SCHULZ was one of the most gifted writers to have come out of Eastern Europe in the twentieth century. He supported himself by teaching art to high school students in Drohobycz, a small town in southern Poland (now Drohobych, Ukraine) where he spent most of his life. His first book, *Cinnamon Shops* (retitled *The Street of Crocodiles* in its American edition), was published in 1934. *Sanatorium Under the Sign of the Hourglass*, fiction with drawings, followed three years later. Schulz produced his drawings by etching them on spoiled photographic plates he obtained from drugstores; after putting the plate and sensitive paper into a frame, he would expose them to sunlight, and the drawing would be reproduced on paper. A novella, *The Comet* (included in *The Street of Crocodiles*), assorted critical writings, letters, a translation of Franz Kafka's *The Trial*, and a lost work thought to be called *The Messiah* constitute his entire oeuvre. In 1942, at the age of fifty, Schulz, a Jew, ventured into the "Aryan" section of his town and was shot dead in the street by a Gestapo officer.

CELINA WIENIEWSKA was awarded the 1963 Roy Publishers Polish-into-English prize for her translation of *The Street of Crocodiles*.

JONATHAN SAFRAN FOER is the bestselling author of *Everything Is Illuminated* and *Extremely Loud and Incredibly Close*. He lives in Brooklyn, New York.

DAVID A. GOLDFARB taught for eight years in the Slavic department at Barnard College, Columbia University. He has written on a range of writers and subjects, including Bruno Schulz, Witold Gombrowicz, Nikolai Gogol, Mikhail Lermontov, Ivan Turgenev, Leo Tolstoy, and East European cinema.

T0042862

BRUNO SCHULZ

The Street of Crocodiles and Other Stories

Translated by
CELINA WIENIEWSKA

Foreword by
JONATHAN SAFRAN FOER

Introduction by
DAVID A. GOLDFARB

PENGUIN BOOKS

PENGUIN BOOKS
Published by the Penguin Group
Penguin Group (USA) Inc., 375 Hudson Street, New York, New York 10014, U.S.A.
Penguin Group (Canada), 90 Eglinton Avenue East, Suite 700, Toronto, Ontario, Canada M4P 2Y3
(a division of Pearson Penguin Canada Inc.)
Penguin Books Ltd, 80 Strand, London WC2R 0RL, England
Penguin Ireland, 25 St Stephen's Green, Dublin 2, Ireland (a division of Penguin Books Ltd)
Penguin Group (Australia), 250 Camberwell Road, Camberwell, Victoria 3124, Australia
(a division of Pearson Australia Group Pty Ltd)
Penguin Books India Pvt Ltd, 11 Community Centre, Panchsheel Park, New Delhi – 110 017, India
Penguin Group (NZ), 67 Apollo Drive, Rosedale, North Shore 0632, New Zealand
(a division of Pearson New Zealand Ltd)
Penguin Books (South Africa) (Pty) Ltd, 24 Sturdee Avenue, Rosebank, Johannesburg 2196, South Africa

Penguin Books Ltd, Registered Offices:
80 Strand, London WC2R 0RL, England

The Street of Crocodiles first published in the United States of America by Walker and Company 1963
Published in Penguin Books 1977
Sanatorium Under the Sign of the Hourglass first published in the United States of America by
Walker and Company 1978
Published in Penguin Books 1979
Published by arrangement with Walker Publishing Company, Inc.
The Street of Crocodiles and Other Stories with a foreword by Jonathan Safran Foer and an introduction
by David A. Goldfarb published in Penguin Books 2008

The Street of Crocodiles was originally published in Polish under the title *Sklepy cynamonowe (Cinnamon Shops)*, 1934. *Sanatorium Under the Sign of the Hourglass* was published in Polish as *Sanatorium pod klepsydra*, 1937.

"The Republic of Dreams," "Autumn," and "Fatherland" appeared in *The Letters and Drawings of Bruno Schulz: with Selected Prose*, edited by Jerzy Ficowski, translated by Walter Arndt with Victoria Nelson (Harper & Row, 1988). Copyright © 1988 by Harper & Row, Publishers, Inc. By permission of Abner Stein, London.

"Sanatorium under the Sign of the Hourglass," "Loneliness," and "Father's Last Escape" originally appeared in *The New Yorker*.

Grateful acknowledgment is made to Alan Adelson and Jewish Heritage.

CIP data available
978-0-14-310514-5

Printed in the United States of America
Set in Sabon

Contents

SANATORIUM UNDER THE
SIGN OF THE HOURGLASS

Foreword

Bruno Schulz was born in 1892 in Drohobycz, a small town in the Austro-Hungarian province of Galicia. Beneath the surface of his professional life—he taught drawing and handicrafts in a local school—was an explosive creative energy, which expressed itself through fiction, correspondence, drawing, and painting. When the Germans seized Drohobycz in 1941, Schulz, a Jew, distributed his artwork and papers—which are said to have included the manuscript of his masterpiece, *The Messiah*—to gentile friends for safekeeping. These comprised the great bulk of his artistic output, and not a single item among them has been seen since.

Felix Landau, a Gestapo officer in charge of the Jewish labor force in Drohobycz, became aware of Schulz's talents as a draftsman. He directed Schulz to paint murals on the walls of his child's playroom. This relationship brought Schulz certain privileges, most importantly protection. In November 1942, Landau killed a Jew favored by another Gestapo officer, Karl Günther. Soon after, Günther came upon Schulz, on the corner of Czacki and Mickiewicz streets, and shot him in the head. "You killed my Jew," he later boasted to Landau, "I killed yours."

Why was Schulz in the street that afternoon, instead of working on the murals? Perhaps he was putting off the completion of the murals, knowing, like Scheherazade, that it was only his creations that kept him alive. Or had he refused to paint another stroke? More likely, he was finishing preparations for the escape from the ghetto he was planning to attempt that night.

Sixty years later, a documentary filmmaker, Benjamin Geissler, went back to Drohobycz (now Drohobych, Ukraine) in search of the murals. With the help of locals—and despite the hindrances of Ukrainian officialdom—he was able to find Landau's house. It had been converted into apartments, but the structure was otherwise little changed. It was February. White snow blanketed everything. Geissler opened the front door. The hallway's walls were dark. He went from room to room, watching the house unfold through his camera. All of the walls were overpainted with layers of light green.

Geissler was able to find someone who had been in the house decades before and remembered the murals. This person led Geissler to what was once Landau's child's room and had since become a small pantry. The walls were white, but from a few inches away, one could see faint outlines, like shapes deep under ice. Geissler rubbed at one of the walls with the butt of his palm, and colors surfaced. He rubbed more, and forms were released. He rubbed more, like doing the rubbing of a grave, and could make out figures: fairies and nymphs, mushrooms, animals, and royalty . . .

While officials in Drohobych, Ukraine, Poland, Germany, and Israel debated what to do with the murals—"owning" the murals also meant owning some responsibility for Schulz's fate—Yad Vashem, Israel's holocaust museum, came to the apartment and, depending on how one sees things, either stole or rescued them.

The whole story could have been told like this: in Jerusalem there is a wall, under whose surface is an unfinished fairy tale, painted sixty years before and a continent away by the Jewish writer Bruno Schulz, for the pleasure of his captor's child.

In his story "The Book," which some scholars suspect was also part of The Messiah, the narrator recalls a volume—a lost volume—whose pages, when rubbed, reveal plumes of color.

We live on the surface of our planet. Human life happens on a shell as thin, relative to the size of the earth, as an egg's, or as thin as the paint on a wall. We have lifestyles on the surfaces of our lives: habits and culture, clothes, modes of transit, calendars, papers in wallets, ways of killing time, answers to the question "What do you do?" We come home from long days of doing what we do and tuck ourselves under the thin sheets. We read stories printed on even thinner paper. Why, at the end of the day, do we read stories?

There are things, Schulz wrote, "that cannot ever occur with any precision. They are too big and too magnificent to be contained in mere facts. They are merely trying to occur, they are checking whether the ground of reality can carry them. And they quickly withdraw, fearing to lose their integrity in the frailty of realization." Our lives, the big and magnificent lives we can just barely make out beneath the mere facts of our lifestyles, are always *trying to occur*. But save for a few rare occasions—falling in love, the birth of a child, the death of a parent, a revelatory moment in nature— they *don't* occur; the big magnificence is withdrawn. Stories rub at the facts of our lives. They give us access—if only for a few hours, if only in bed at the end of the day—to what's beneath.

But *rub* is too gentle a word for Schulz's writing. And what it uncovers is nothing like a fairy tale. I remember the first time I read *The Street of Crocodiles*. I loved the book but didn't like it. The language was too heightened, the images too magical and precarious, the yearnings too dire, the sense of loss too palpable—everything was comedy or tragedy. The experience was too intense to be pleasant, in large part because it reminded me of how mundane—how unintense—my life was. The fingers of his words rubbed (or scraped or clawed, shoveled, or ripped) and revealed not enough. I took his stories as challenges: do not say the next best thing, do not live in the moment if it is not the right moment, do not withdraw into the frailty of realization. His books still have that effect on me. Good writers are pleasing, very good writers make you feel and think, great writers make you change. "A book must be an ice-axe to break the seas frozen inside of us," Kafka famously wrote. Schulz's two slim books are the sharpest axes I've ever come across. I encourage you to split the chopping block using them.

JONATHAN SAFRAN FOER

Introduction

The town of Drohobych where Bruno Schulz lived—with its magical cinnamon shops, chimeric automobiles, Street of Crocodiles, pockets of suspended time, circus performers, imperious women, and luminous books—was, in reality, alongside the neighboring town of Borysław, a provincial center of the oil industry. From Schulz's birth on July 12, 1892, through his assassination by a Nazi officer on November 19, 1942, and in the years since, Drohobych has had a number of different political affiliations: it was part of the Austro-Hungarian Empire, then belonged to restored Poland after World War I, then became Soviet-occupied territory after the Nazi invasion of Poland, and then Nazi-occupied territory until the end of World War II, ultimately becoming part of Soviet Ukraine after the war, and modern Ukraine today. At the turn of the nineteenth century, it had a population of about 20,000, 40 percent of which was Jewish, and the remainder about evenly split between ethnic Poles and Ukrainians, with a smaller population of Russians as well as a few representatives of Austrian, French, and American oil companies.

The richness of Schulz's symbolic world is a testament to this fecund and diverse cultural environment. Schulz was a secular Jewish writer whose stories began to take shape as letters to the Yiddish modernist poet Debora Vogel, but he wrote them in Polish and was celebrated in Polish avant-garde circles, and the most extensive tradition of Schulz scholarship is in Polish. His work reflects the influence of the German writer Thomas Mann, as well as Franz Kafka and Leopold von Sacher-Masoch (the author of *Venus in Furs*), both German-language writers of non-German cities of the Austro-Hungarian Empire—Prague and Lemberg (Lviv), respectively.

The predominant view of Bruno Schulz is that of an introvert who was so immersed in the imaginative world he had created for himself in Drohobych that he did not seek fame or much in the way of a life outside of his hometown. What we know of Schulz's life and what we have of his letters and drawings comes mainly from the lifetime of tireless searching for artifacts and interviewing of anyone who had contact with Schulz by Schulz's biographer, the poet Jerzy Ficowski. Childhood illnesses necessitated occasional long absences from school. Schulz did spend many hours of his youth reading in the back office of Pilpel's bookstore, so even if he could not afford to travel or to purchase books about the wider world, he did not lack for curiosity. His only significant journeys outside the regions of Galicia, Poland, and what was then German Silesia, were a brief excursion to Stockholm in 1936, and three weeks in Paris in the late summer of 1938, when many Parisians would have been on vacation. It is important to note, however, that on his modest salary as teacher of drawing, art, and occasionally mathematics in the public Gymnasium, Schulz was not really in a position to travel extensively before he had achieved significant recognition as a writer with the publication of his first collection, *Cinnamon Shops* (retitled *The Street of Crocodiles* in U.S. editions). After this, he repeatedly applied for a leave of absence from his teaching duties to pursue his writing, noting the importance of dedicating all of his efforts to this new work, and of spending more time in contact with leading intellectuals and cultural figures in cities such as Warsaw and Lviv. Recent attention, though, to the 1936 period when Schulz was finally granted a semester's leave spent mainly in Warsaw, looks at the book reviews that he wrote for *Wiadomości Literackie* (*Literary News*), and a series of lesser-known political essays about Poland's interwar leader, Józef Piłsudski, that he wrote for *Tygodnik Ilustrowany* (*Illustrated Weekly*), and suggests that perhaps Schulz did seek wider recognition but was thwarted by the outbreak of the war at the height of the fame he had achieved in his lifetime.[1] In a letter to the Board of Education dated November 30, 1936, requesting a transfer to Lviv, which was an important cultural center, Schulz expressed his willingness even to take a position in a vocational or elementary school in order to get out of Drohobych. As it happened, there were no positions available in secondary schools at the time, and he would have had to apply to vocational or primary schools to obtain the transfer, which would likely have been granted. Even in 1938, when modest fame had elevated his status at the Gymnasium to the position of professor, Schulz had to weigh the attractions of three weeks in Paris against the purchase of a new sofa, which he would never have a chance to acquire.

The radiant literary and visual remains of Bruno Schulz's life form a relatively modest corpus that appeared over the course of a mere twenty years, counting from his first visual art exhibition, or only nine years counting from his literary debut. He produced hundreds of drawings, some of which he reproduced using the method of *cliché verre* in the form of a volume entitled *The Booke of Idolatry*. He created a set of illustrations for Witold Gombrowicz's novel *Ferdydurke*. His first exhibition of graphic works took place in 1922, in Warsaw at the Society to Promote Fine Arts, and he continued to show and sell his work through the 1920s. It is known that he painted in oils, and at least one such painting survives. The two collections of stories included in this volume—*The Street of Crocodiles* and *Sanatorium Under the Sign of the Hourglass*—constitute the bulk of Schulz's known fiction. Some stories—"Autumn," "The Republic of Dreams," "The Comet," and "The Fatherland"—appeared separately in various journals. A few critical essays and enough letters to comprise a volume of a few hundred pages have been collected. Murals that Schulz painted during World War II in the apartment of Felix Landau, a Nazi officer who protected him for part of the occupation, have recently been uncovered, with considerable controversy surrounding their ownership. Rumors surface periodically of the lost manuscript of a novel, *The Messiah*, a copy of which he is said to have sent to Thomas Mann.

The Street of Crocodiles, published originally as a collection in December 1933 (with a date of 1934), coalesced as a series of letters—most of which are now lost—to his friend and confidante Debora Vogel. (Schulz and Vogel might have married had her family been amenable, according to Ficowski.) Some of the stories in Schulz's correspondence with Vogel were likely drafted prior to that correspondence, but having been rewritten, and then published as a collection with Vogel's encouragement along with that of important writers like Stanisław Ignacy Witkiewicz, known as Witkacy, and the novelist Zofia Nałkowska—who may be credited with launching Schulz's brief literary career—the work attained greater coherence and might be read as a cycle.

Sanatorium Under the Sign of the Hourglass, published in 1937, contains stories written in the late 1920s, before Schulz's correspondence with Vogel, including most probably "A Night in July," "My Father Joins the Fire Brigade," "A Second Fall," "Sanatorium Under the Sign of the Hourglass," "Dodo," "Eddie," "The Old Age Pensioner," and "Loneliness." This might lead to the conclusion that as a collection, *Sanatorium* constitutes less of a unified act of creation than *The Street of Crocodiles*, assembled from new and old material to fill out a book-length volume in time to take advantage of the publicity resulting from the success of his first volume, but again we might bear in mind the fact that all of Schulz's prose fiction was composed in a very short period of time. Themes and images overlap across works as the product of a single mind.

The interwar period was a time of great literary and artistic experimentation in Poland, as it was in the rest of Europe. It was likely Schulz's success as a graphic artist that led to his acquaintance, around 1925, with Witkacy—the son of Poland's leading modernist painter and critic, Stanisław Witkiewicz, and one of the most radical figures of the interwar avant-garde—a painter, photographer, dramatist, novelist, and philosopher. Witkacy joined the debate over "form" in this period rather stridently with his theory of "Pure Form," which is not so much a way of distinguishing "form" from "content," as one might expect, but a kind of artistic representation that can be taken in whole and without mediation, producing "the metaphysical feeling of the strangeness of existence." This idea is rooted most deeply in the theory of the Sublime, but perhaps more immediately in the aesthetics of Expressionism—the idea that a painting like Edvard Munch's *The Scream* is not a representation of a man screaming into the fjord, but is in fact itself a scream. The key theorist of Expressionism was the Polish writer Stanisław Przybyszewski, of the literary generation before Witkacy and Schulz, who wrote the text for Munch's first Berlin exhibition and is said to have suggested the concrete name *The Scream* for Munch's most famous painting, over Munch's original, emotive title *Despair*. Witkacy argued that poetry, painting, and drama were capable of Pure Form, while prose in general could at best only represent the experience of the individual in the face of Pure Form—the exception being Schulz's prose, which possessed this quality of poetry for Witkacy.

The following frequently quoted passage from Schulz's essay "The Mythicization of Reality" brings into clearer view Schulz's contribution to the debate about form, and illuminates Schulz's understanding of his own art:

> Every fragment of reality lives by virtue of partaking in a universal sense. . . . Poetry happens when short-circuits of Sense occur between words, a sudden regeneration of the primeval myths. . . . Not one scrap of an idea of ours does not originate in myth, isn't transformed, mutilated, denatured mythology. The most fundamental function of the spirit is inventing fables, creating tales. . . . [T]he building materials [that the search for human knowledge] uses were used once before; they come from forgotten, fragmented tales or "histories." Poetry recognizes these lost meanings, restores words to their places, connects them by the old semantics.

Schulz maintains that, when viewed through the "poetic" imagination, any degraded scrap of reality—anything that might be found in the world's *tandeta*, a Polish word describing goods that are shoddy, cast off, second-rate, or trashy—might reveal the qualities of the sublime. *Tandeta* also means "market," in Schulz usually a flea market, but also a stock or commodities market—a chaotic place of haggling and bargaining. In the childlike mind of Schulz's narrator, the trash at a flea market becomes an object of wonder, a key to a whole system of meaning, and a portal to the sublime. Immanuel Kant describes the sublime as awe in the face of what is infinitely great or terrible as opposed to the pleasurable feeling of the free play of the imagination associated with beauty. A tulip inspires the feeling of beauty, but a storm or a mountain range inspires the feeling of the sublime. To offer another point of reference, Roland Barthes has a stronger idea than Schulz of a *mythologie* as a system of meaning, but they both share the notion that the poetic gesture can reveal the mythic potential in everyday phenomena and objects. For Schulz's child narrator, a cheap calendar, a travel guide, or an advertisement for a hair growth formula—in short, "trash" or *tandeta*—can be a work of splendor.

A particularly poignant symbol of the mythic potential of all matter in Schulz is the figure of the *paluba*. *Paluba* is a word so untranslatable that Celina Wieniewska cannot settle on a single English word for it, and sometimes simply passes it over. One scholar of Schulz, Jerzy Jarzębski, has said that *paluba* is a Polish word that must be translated into Polish every time it is used. In the relevant sense, it might be translated as "hag" or "witch," or it could refer to an effigy or doll in the form of a hag. In section two of the story "August," for instance, Schulz describes a garden—"There, those protuberant [*paluby* of] bur clumps spread themselves like resting peasant women, half-enveloped in their own swirling skirts." The untranslated image suggested here is of a rough-hewn folk doll.

The term *paluba* enters the language of Polish modernism as the title of a radically experimental novel first published in 1903 in Lviv by the critic and essayist Karol Irzykowski. The novel begins with a dream sequence, followed by a psychoanalytic biography of the main character, and then layers of notes and pseudo-scholarship amending and correcting the previous text. Irzykowski was not otherwise known for fiction, though he was one of the first European critics to write about cinema in a serious way. While his novel is not well known outside of Poland, it signaled the break with historical and psychological realism that would free writers like Witkacy, Witold Gombrowicz, and Schulz to invent new forms of prose fiction, and Schulz in fact mentions Irzykowski's novel in his review of Gombrowicz's *Ferdydurke*.

The word *paluba* figures most prominently in Schulz in "Treatise on Tailors' Dummies." The waxwork figures that Schulz mentions are *paluby* of a very interesting sort. They are cast from underlying stories. The wax museum might be seen as a form of Schulz's "splendorous book," rendered in three dimensions. Schulz writes: "Demiurge, that great master and artist, made matter invisible, made it disappear under the surface of life. We, on the contrary, love its creaking, its resistance, its [*palubiasta*] clumsiness"—again, the elusive hag, here as an adjective, is lost in translation. A few pages later, the author of the treatise asks, "Can you imagine the pain, the dull imprisoned suffering, hewn into the matter of that dummy [*paluba*] which does not know why it must be what it is, why it must remain in that forcibly imposed form which is no more than a parody?" This characterization of the dummies might just as well apply to the father's birds, since they resemble stuffed museum specimens and also share something in common with the myth of the golem, an artificial creation whose narratives in some versions have been retellings of the Genesis myth of the divine creation of man. These dummies (*paluby*) are not the same as the dummies (*manekin*, "mannequins") of the title, but powerful effigies, commensurate with the inchoate power of matter imprisoned in form.

The idea from Schulz's essay "The Mythicization of Reality" that words have meaning by virtue of their connection to an "all embracing, integral mythology" or "universal sense" resonates with other modernist notions of the primitive in language and art, ranging from T. S. Eliot's concept of the "objective correlative"—the idea that poetry works by means of verbal objects that can evoke a single emotion in the mind of the poet and the reader; to Ezra Pound's fascination with the concrete image as artifact; to J. G. A. Frazer's theory, cataloged in *The Golden Bough*, of universal mythologies shared by cultures that had no historical contact but that had common experiences of nature that led to a common set of mythic master narratives; to C. G. Jung's theory of the collective unconscious, which proposed that common mythic narratives or "archetypes" grounded all mental and social life. Words, fragments of their former mythic selves, "complete [themselves] with sense" for Schulz when they are successfully transformed by the poet's fashioning hand.

Schulz can also be understood in relation to Franz Kafka, another prose writer who dealt in surrealistic metamorphoses and the sense of awe in the face of the infinitely great. Schulz collaborated with Józefina Szelińska, to whom he was formally engaged from 1936 to 1937, on a translation of Kafka's *The Trial*, published in Lviv in 1936. Ficowski argues that the work was mainly Szelińska's—that Schulz lent his name to the project to improve its chances for publication—and goes to some length to differentiate what he reads as Kafka's idealistic absolutism, in contrast to Schulz's rootedness in the "reality-asylum" or a concentrated and heightened sense of the material of life. Ficowski concedes, however, that Schulz admired Kafka's work, and there is plenty of room for interpretation of this connection.

Schulz was also very much inspired by the work of Thomas Mann, who recast biblical narrative in novelistic form in *Joseph and His Brothers*. We might find this influence in Schulz's use of the the Jacob and Joseph story or other images from Genesis and Exodus, but Mann's gesture is to bring epic narrative into the realm of the real and familiar, to imagine the psychological motivations of biblical characters. Schulz's gesture is more one of estrangement and defamiliarization, to take a character embedded in reality, like the eccentric figure of the father, and make him into a mighty prophet or a medieval rabbinic authority on obscure metaphysical questions.

The relatively self-contained quality of Schulz's small body of work, the idea of the creation of a mythic world, and the resonance between the verbal and the visual might invite a comparison to William Blake. As with Blake, at least on Northrop Frye's seminal reading in his book *Fearful Symmetry*, the task of the reader and viewer of Schulz's work might be to make sense of his personal mythology, to reassemble its fragments into so many simultaneous narratives, and then to consider the effect of their fragmentation. A thoroughgoing enumeration of Schulz's mythologies could fill a volume as thick as Frye's. For the sake of an introduction to the mythic imagination of Bruno Schulz, we might limit ourselves to a few predominant leitmotifs and keywords: the Book, the Labyrinth, Franz Joseph and the language of the empire, the dominant woman, and the birds.

The Book: When Schulz writes of books, which are both sources of myth and myths in themselves, he calls them *księgi*, rather than the more common diminutive *książki*. Any ordinary book is a *książka*, but a *księga* is a great sacred ancient book, like the books of the Bible. Schulz would further emphasize this ancient quality in his early graphic work, *The Booke of Idolatry*, by using the archaic spelling, *xięga*, employing the "x" that has been eradicated from modern Polish spelling, perhaps best translated in that instance as "Booke."

The image of The Booke in Schulz's mythic world is like a book of the Talmud—a large folio volume, worn from age and use, where a central text appears in large type at the center surrounded by layers upon layers of commentary and debate among great rabbis and their disciples over centuries, and a wide margin; this inspires his narrator to ask:

> don't I too, surrender to the secret hope that [my words] will merge imperceptibly with the yellowing pages of that most splendid, moldering book, that they will sink into the gentle rustle of its pages and become absorbed there?

But in the childlike mind of Schulz's narrator, recognizing that all poetry is made up of fragments of ancient mythology, virtually any great compendium of arcane mysteries can aspire to the status of The Booke—a calendar, a stamp album, a travel guide, a collection of pornographic images, an ornithological manual.

The Labyrinth: Schulz's Drohobych is a labyrinth of labyrinths. The metaphor applies to the map of Drohobych's streets, the interiors of the "cinnamon shops," the strange time-space of the Sanatorium, or the pages of Schulz's Booke. The town with its central market square and labyrinth of streets around it is itself a kind of sacred text. Each shop represents a story, a mythology, and the streets that wind around the margins offer commentary on the center, and within each labyrinth there may be another labyrinth. "In its multiple labyrinths," Schulz writes of his splendorous town, "nests of brightness were hewn: the shops—large colored lanterns—filled with goods and the bustle of customers."

Schulz's dream time is itself a kind of labyrinth, as in the Sanatorium where Jakub seems somehow suspended as the time of everyday life passes him by. Perhaps Schulz's Drohobych takes on this quality, because it was not exactly the Drohobych of everyday life as it was lived in Schulz's own day, but was also the Drohobych narrated by his ailing father, Jakub, a fabric merchant like the father in Schulz's stories, in his final years. Schulz was the youngest of three children, more than ten years younger than his brother, Izydor, or elder sister, Hania, and he knew his father as an older man in declining health. The extra month of "The Night of the Great Season"—a motif borrowed from the Hebrew lunar calendar, which adds an extra month every three years—is a kind of leftover pocket of time when magical events can happen. Time is described in the original Polish text as having "neighborhoods" like the map of the city, which is like the page of Talmud—a labyrinth along every dimension.

Franz Joseph and the Language of the Empire: A layer of Schulz's prose that is lost in non-Slavic translation is his peculiar Latinism in Polish. Poland has a rich tradition of Latin poetry from the Renaissance, which devolved into macaronic use of Latin in Polish prose in the Baroque period, but Schulz's Latinisms probably derive more from the bureaucratic language of the Austro-Hungarian Empire. The emperor Franz Josef I, mentioned in the story "Spring" as the ubiquitous figure in the stamp album, passed through Schulz's town of Drohobych in

1880, during an extended tour of the Galician oil-producing region, and seems to have left a mark in local legend perhaps as a lesser version of Napoleon Bonaparte, who embodied the *Weltgeist* ("world spirit") for the philosopher G. W. F. Hegel upon passing through Jena after defeating the Prussians. Franz Josef's image was reproduced extensively on stamps and coinage, and Schulz graduated from the Franz Joseph Gymnasium in 1910. He would teach at the same school, rechristened after World War I for the Polish-Lithuanian king Władysław Jagiełło, and renamed again simply for the state during the first Soviet occupation, which began in 1939.

Schulz could draw upon this bureaucratic Latinism as a defamiliarizing gesture, using a word like *kreatura* rather than a more common Slavic term for "creature," or *fluida* rather than the Polish word that is normally applied to things like dishwashing liquid, referring in Schulz's usage alternately to fluids but also to a mystic aura or emanation. The term *panoptikon*, familiar to readers of Michel Foucault as Jeremy Bentham's ideal reformatory where prison cells are arranged in a circle around a central guard tower, but here referring to a circus side show, appears as a word that by virtue of the power of Latin to dignify the object described, in fact degrades its referent. Like P. T. Barnum's famous sign, "This way to the egress," the Latin term is party to a kind of sham, but that sham is just the sort of "degraded reality" that fascinates Schulz. The serious business of petroleum production that was the foundation of Drohobych's economy does not play a major role in Schulz's mythic Drohobych. The fakery at the margins is where the magic is.

The Dominant Woman: Adela, the servant girl and obscure object of desire, is Schulz's "demonic woman." Witkacy, Schulz's elder contemporary and advocate, built a mythology around the idea of the dominant female figure, likely taking the term "demonic woman" from a collection of stories by Leopold von Sacher-Masoch translated into Polish as *Demonic Women*. Sacher-Masoch was a native of Lviv—then Lemberg—not far from Schulz's Drohobych or from Witkacy's Kraków or Zakopane in southern Poland, and he wrote extensively about the local culture even as he became part of the local culture for East Central European modernists.

We might see Adela as the prose version of Undula, the object of worship in *The Booke of Idolatry*. Undula appears nude in high heels and long stockings at the head of a procession of submissive men, as a reclining odalisque with the sole of her foot pressing into the face of a figure who resembles the artist himself (and who also appears in the procession), or in furs like Sacher-Masoch's dominatrix Wanda. In the father's shop in the story "The Night of the Great Season," the assistants chase after Adela as if she were an idol in a scene reminiscent of the worship of the Golden Calf from the book of Exodus. She is often described as "fluttering" like one of the father's birds. Adela is usually recognizable by her broom in theatrical productions and films based on Schulz's writings. When she uses her iconic broom to sweep the attic clean of Father's other birds, she introduces cleanliness and modernity as she puts an end to the old order of the father's "age of genius," the mythic time when wise men could speak the "forgotten language of the birds," a talent attributed to Elijah, Solomon, Orpheus, St. Francis of Assisi, and the Baal Shem Tov, the founder of Hassidism.

The Birds: Schulz's birds come from the pages of another sacred book—the ornithological manual. As Schulz writes in his story "Birds":

> While father pored over his large ornithological textbooks and studied their colored plates, these feathery phantasms seemed to rise from the pages and fill the rooms with colors, with splashes of crimson, strips of sapphire, verdigris, and silver.

The guidebooks that Schulz likely would have known would have been the monumental works of the German ornithologist Anton Reichenow, with their richly colored engravings of birds arranged in unlikely configurations in quasi-naturalistic settings. As a graphic artist himself, Schulz would have admired these engravings after the works of the German wildlife painter Gustav Mützel both for their fine detail and for their flavor of the precursor of the modern natural history museum—the cabinet of curiosities, which was not too distant from the circus side show or *panoptikon*. The composition of these pages was generally like the labyrinth, with the largest, most colorful birds perched at the center, and the lesser ones fluttering at the margins. In the quoted passage from the story "Birds," Schulz moves seamlessly from the book to the fantasy about the birds in Jakub's attic. There are no boundaries between books and the world for Schulz. As the labyrinthine map of Drohobych becomes a page in Schulz's Talmud, the birds on the page inhabit the attic, which becomes a Noah's ark. Following the cycle of "the mythicization of reality," a book becomes a reality, which becomes another book.

The influence of Bruno Schulz's work on later writers might be understood under three main categories. One group consists of Polish and other East European writers whose work is part of a continuous tradition with interwar avant-gardism, who have incorporated Schulz's motifs, compositional techniques, and mythological sense into their own work. These are figures like the Polish visual artist and dramatist Tadeusz Kantor, who plays with Schulz's iconography in his own works for the stage, employing mannequins or an Adela figure with her cleansing broom and chimeric objects like Schulz's camera/car; or the Yugoslav writer Danilo Kiš, who finds common ground with Schulz's myth of the book and the image of the hourglass. Fiction on the other side of the temporal divide created by the Holocaust draws on the element of reassembly of the fragments of a forgotten world that was already part of Schulz's consciousness before the war, and we postwar readers must constantly remind ourselves that this conception of mythology that could so aptly characterize the fragmented and lost world of those who perished under Nazi terror was imagined without any awareness of that terror. The idea we see in Schulz of the writer sifting through the trash—*tandeta*—to find and reassemble mutilated fragments of cast-off mythologies or systems of meaning would become a model for generations of writers following the upheaval of World War II, postcommunism, and even postcolonialism.

Schulz's work and the mysteries of his biography are also the subject of fascination for a second group: mainly Jewish writers who may know Schulz only in translation and do not have access to the wealth of Polish critical writing on Schulz, or most of the rich context of Polish avant-gardism that forms the foundation for Tadeusz Kantor's work, but find in Schulz a connection to the lost world of pre-Holocaust European Jewry, and see Schulz's death as a particularly poignant symbol of that loss. These would be writers like Philip Roth, Cynthia Ozick, and David Grossman, who use characters based on Bruno Schulz himself in "The Prague Orgy," *The Messiah of Stockholm*, and *See Under: Love*, respectively. In some respects, these writers may be more influenced by Schulz's biographer, Jerzy Ficowski, than by Schulz himself. *The Messiah of Stockholm*, for instance, focuses on the mystery of Schulz's lost manuscript, about which little is known. The manuscript of *The Messiah* can thus serve as a vessel for a metaphor of the tragic end to an age of genius. Schulz is also fascinated with a lost age of genius, but the task for Schulz is its restoration through the poetic, rather than lamentation on the loss.

The most recent examples of Schulz's influence recognize the universal significance of his mythic world, assembled from what seem to be deeply personal and esoteric local references. The best case of this phenomenon is a novel that is itself a bricolage of peculiar local references, Salman Rushdie's *The Moor's Last Sigh*.[2] In the last phase of Rushdie's novel, the hero and narrator, Moraes Zogoiby, travels from Cochin, India, to Benengeli, a mountain village in Andalusia, to see Vasco Miranda, a long-lost admirer of his mother's. The village takes on a magical quality not unlike Schulz's Drohobych, particularly in a district called the Street of Parasites, not unlike the "parasitical quarter" that Schulz names the Street of Crocodiles:

> I felt as if I were in some sort of interregnum, in some timeless zone under the sign of an hourglass in which the sand stood motionless, or a clepsydra whose quicksilver had ceased to flow. . . . I wandered down sausage-festooned streets of bakeries and cinnamon shops, smelling, instead, the sweet scents of meat

and pastries and fresh-baked bread, and surrendered myself to the cryptic laws of the town. (Rushdie, 404)

The "hourglass" of the title of Schulz's second collection of stories is *klepsydra* in Polish, which can refer either to a sandglass or a mercury or water clock—"clepsydra" in English. "Under the sign of the hourglass" is a fairly common idiom in Polish for referring to a business establishment, usually a cafe or restaurant, denoted by a distinctive sign or architectural ornament above the door, like the "Club under the sign of the Salamanders" on the Kraków market square. What Rushdie borrows from Schulz, however, is not a particular idiom or scenery or biographical detail, but a kind of metaphysical essence of Schulz's imagined world, a sense of suspended time and a feeling of rootedness in displacement itself, which he transposes onto his own historical and cultural context. Rushdie's ability to find that essence in his own fragmented reality as he sorts through his own version of *tandeta* might attest to Schulz's notion of an underlying "universal sense" that the poet or writer seeks to restore to words that have become separated from their lost mythic meanings.

DAVID A. GOLDFARB

NOTES

1. Thomas Anessi takes this approach in an unpublished paper, "The Great Heresy of the Varsovian Center," presented at the conference *The World of Bruno Schulz/Bruno Schulz and the World: Influences, Similarities, Reception*, Catholic University, Leuven, Belgium, May 2007.
2. Canadian novelist and literature scholar Norman Ravvin discusses this connection between Rushdie and Schulz in his as yet unpublished paper "The Afterlife of Bruno Schulz," presented at the conference *Bruno Schulz: New Readings, New Meanings*, McGill University, Montreal, Canada, May 2007. Ravvin has also written his own novel inspired by the stories and drawings of Bruno Schulz, *Café des Westens* (Red Deer College Press, 1991).

Suggestions for Further Reading

ADDITIONAL WORKS OF BRUNO SCHULZ IN ENGLISH

Ficowski, Jerzy, ed. *The Drawings of Bruno Schulz*. With an essay by Ewa Kuryluk. Adam Kaczkowski, photographer. Evanston, Ill.: Northwestern University Press, 1990.

Schulz, Bruno. *Letters and Drawings of Bruno Schulz with Selected Prose*. Ed. Jerzy Ficowski. Trans. Walter Arndt with Victoria Nelson. New York: Fromm, 1990.

SELECTED CRITICISM AND BIOGRAPHY IN ENGLISH

Błoński, Jan. "On the Jewish Sources of Bruno Schulz." *Cross Currents: A Yearbook of Central European Culture*, 12 (1993): 54–68.

Brown, Russell E. *Myths and Relatives: Seven Essays on Bruno Schulz*. Slavistische Beiträge. Munich: Verlag Otto Sagner, 1991.

Budurowycz, Bohdan. "Galicia in the Work of Bruno Schulz." *Canadian Slavonic Papers*, December 1986, 259–368.

Drozdowski, Piotr J. "Bruno Schulz and the Myth of the Book." *Indiana Slavic Studies*, 5 (1990): 23–30.

Ficowski, Jerzy. *Regions of the Great Heresy. Bruno Schulz, A Biographical Portrait*. Trans. and ed. Theodosia Robertson. New York: W. W. Norton, 2003.

Goldfarb, David A. "A Living Schulz: *The Night of the Great Season*." *Prooftexts*, 14.1 (1994): 25–47.

———. "The Vortex and the Labyrinth: Bruno Schulz and the

Objective Correlative." Bruno Schulz Forum. *East European Politics and Societies*, 11.2 (1997): 257–69.

Iribarne, Louis. "On Bruno Schulz." *Cross Currents: A Yearbook of Central European Culture*, 6 (1987): 172–94.

Kuprel, Diana. "Errant Events on the Branch Tracks of Time: Bruno Schulz and Mythical Consciousness." *Slavic and East European Journal*, 40.1 (1996): 100–17.

Pinsker, Sanford. "Jewish-American Literature's Lost-and-found Department: How Philip Roth and Cynthia Ozick Reimagine Their Significant Dead." *Modern Fiction Studies*, 35.2 (1989): 223–35.

Ravvin, Norman. "Strange Presences on the Family Tree: The Unacknowledged Literary Father in Philip Roth's *The Prague Orgy*." *English Studies in Canada*, 17.2 (1991): 197–207.

Robertson, Theodosia. "Time in Bruno Schulz." *Indiana Slavic Studies* 5 (1990).

———. "Bruno Schulz and Comedy." *Polish Perspectives* 36.2 (1991): 119–26.

Roth, Philip, and Isaac Bashevis Singer. "Roth and Singer on Bruno Schulz." *The New York Times Book Review*, Feb. 15 1977, 5 ff.

Schönle, Andreas. "*Cinnamon Shops* by Bruno Schulz: The Apology of the *tandeta*." *The Polish Review*, 36.2 (1991): 127–44.

———. "Of Sublimity, Shrinkage, and Selfhood in the Works of Bruno Schulz." *Slavic and East European Journal*, 42.3 (1998): 467–82.

Shallcross, Bożena. " 'Fragments of a Broken Mirror': Bruno Schulz's Retextualization of the Kabbalah." Bruno Schulz Forum. *East European Politics and Societies*, 11.2 (1997): 270–81.

———. "Pencil, Pen, and Ink: Bruno Schulz's Art of Interference." Eds. James S. Biskupski, M. B. Napierkowski, and Thomas J. Pula. *Heart of the Nation: Polish Literature and Culture, III*. Selected Essays from the 5th Anniversary International Congress of the PIASA. East European Monographs, 1993: 58–68.

Shmeruk, Chone. "Isaac Bashevis Singer on Bruno Schulz." Trans. Anna Pekal. *Polish Review*, 36.2 (1991): 161–67.

Sokoloff, Naomi. "Reinventing Bruno Schulz: Cynthia Ozick's *The Messiah of Stockholm* and David Grossman's *See Under: Love*." *AJS Review*, 13.1–2 (1988): 171–99.

Spieker, Sven. " 'Stumps Folded Into a Fist': Extra Time, Chance, and Virtual Reality in Bruno Schulz." Bruno Schulz Forum. *East European Politics and Societies* 11.2 (1997): 282–98.

Stala, Krzysztof. *On the Margins of Reality: The Paradoxes of Representation in Bruno Schulz's Fiction*. Stockholm: Almqvist and Wiksell, 1993.

PRIMARY TEXTS IN POLISH

Schulz, Bruno. *Księga listów*. 2nd ed. Ed. and comp. by Jerzy Ficowski. Gdańsk: słowo/obraz terytoria, 2002.

———. *Opowiadania, wybór esejów i listów*. Ed. and introduced by Jerzy Jarzębski. Biblioteka Narodowa, ser. I, nr 264. Wrocław: Ossolineum, 1989.

RECOMMENDED BIBLIOGRAPHIC SOURCES FOR FURTHER RESEARCH IN POLISH

Bolecki, Włodimierz; Jerzy Jarzębski; and Rosiek Stanisław, eds. *Słownik schulzowski*. Gdańsk: słowo/obraz terytoria, 2002. [Includes bibliography of important criticism in Polish through 2002.]

Sulikowski, Andrzej. "Twórczość Brunona Schulza W Krytyce I Badaniach Literackich (1934–1976)." *Pamiętnik Literacki*, 2 (1978): 264–304. [Extensive bibliography of works on Schulz's fiction through 1976.]

The Street of Crocodiles
and Other Stories

THE STREET OF
CROCODILES

AUGUST

I

In July my father went to take the waters and left me, with my mother and elder brother, a prey to the blinding white heat of the summer days. Dizzy with light, we dipped into that enormous book of holidays, its pages blazing with sunshine and scented with the sweet melting pulp of golden pears.

On those luminous mornings Adela returned from the market, like Pomona emerging from the flames of day, spilling from her basket the colorful beauty of the sun—the shiny pink cherries full of juice under their transparent skins, the mysterious black morellos that smelled so much better than they tasted, apricots in whose golden pulp lay the core of long afternoons. And next to that pure poetry of fruit, she unloaded sides of meat with their keyboard of ribs swollen with energy and strength, and seaweeds of vegetables like dead octopuses and squids—the raw material of meals with a yet undefined taste, the vegetative and terrestrial ingredients of dinner, exuding a wild and rustic smell.

The dark second-floor apartment of the house in Market Square was shot through each day by the naked heat of summer: the silence of the shimmering streaks of air, the squares of brightness dreaming their intense dreams on the floor; the sound of a barrel organ rising from the deepest golden vein of day; two or three bars of a chorus, played on a distant piano over and over again, melting in the sun on the white pavement, lost in the fire of high noon.

After tidying up, Adela would plunge the rooms into semi-darkness by drawing down the linen blinds. All colors immediately fell an octave lower, the room filled with shadows, as if it had sunk to the bottom of the sea and the light was reflected in mirrors of green water—and the heat of the day began to breathe on the blinds as they stirred slightly in their daydreams.

On Saturday afternoons I used to go for a walk with my mother. From the dusk of the hallway, we stepped at once into the brightness of the day. The passersby, bathed in melting gold, had their eyes half-closed against the glare, as if they were drenched with honey. Upper lips were drawn back, exposing the teeth. Everyone in this golden day wore that grimace of heat—as if the sun had forced his worshippers to wear identical masks of gold. The old and the young, women and children, greeted each other with these masks, painted on their faces with thick gold paint; they smiled at each other's pagan faces—the barbaric smiles of Bacchus.

Market Square was empty and white hot, swept by hot winds like a biblical desert. The thorny acacias, growing in this emptiness, looked with their bright leaves like the trees on old tapestries. Although there was no breath of wind, they rustled their foliage in a theatrical gesture, as if wanting to display the elegance of the silver lining of their leaves that resembled the fox-fur lining of a nobleman's coat. The old houses, worn smooth by the winds of innumerable days, played tricks with the reflections of the atmosphere, with echoes and memories of colors scattered in the depth of the cloudless sky. It seemed as if whole generations of summer days, like patient stonemasons cleaning the mildewed plaster from old facades, had removed the deceptive varnish revealing more and more clearly the true face of the houses, the features that fate had given them and life had shaped for them from the inside. Now the windows, blinded by the glare of the empty square, had fallen asleep; the balconies declared their emptiness to heaven; the open doorways smelt of coolness and wine.

A bunch of ragamuffins, sheltering in a corner of the square from the flaming broom of the heat, beleaguered a piece of wall, throwing buttons and coins at it over and over again, as if wishing to read in the horoscope of those metal discs the real secret written in the hieroglyphics of cracks and scratched lines. Apart from them, the square was deserted. One expected that, any minute, the Samaritan's donkey, led by the bridle, would stop in front of the wine merchant's vaulted doorway and that two servants would carefully ease a sick man from the red-hot saddle and carry him slowly up the cool stairs to the floor above, already redolent of the Sabbath.

Thus my mother and I ambled along the two sunny sides of Market Square, guiding our broken shadows along the houses as over a keyboard. Under our soft steps the squares of the paving stones slowly filed past—some the pale pink of human skin, some golden, some blue gray, all flat, warm and velvety in the sun, like sundials, trodden to the point of obliteration, into blessed nothingness.

And finally on the corner of Stryjska Street we passed within the shadow of the chemist's shop. A large jar of raspberry juice in the wide window symbolized the coolness of balms which can relieve all kinds of pain. After we passed a few more houses, the street ceased to maintain any pretense of urbanity, like a man returning to his little village who, piece by piece, strips off his Sunday best, slowly changing back into a peasant as he gets closer to his home.

The suburban houses were sinking, windows and all, into the exuberant tangle of blossoms in their little gardens. Overlooked by the light of day, weeds and wildflowers of all kinds luxuriated quietly, glad of the interval for dreams beyond the margin of time on the borders of an endless day. An enormous sunflower, lifted on a powerful stem and suffering from hypertrophy, clad in the yellow mourning of the last sorrowful days of its life, bent under the weight of its monstrous girth. But the naive suburban bluebells and unpretentious dimity flowers stood helpless in their starched pink and white shifts, indifferent to the sunflower's tragedy.

2

A tangled thicket of grasses, weeds, and thistles crackled in the fire of the afternoon. The sleeping garden was resonant with flies. The golden field of stubble shouted in the sun like a tawny cloud of locusts; in the thick rain of fire the crickets screamed; seed pods exploded softly like grasshoppers.

And over by the fence the sheepskin of grass lifted in a hump, as if the garden had turned over in its sleep, its broad, peasant back rising and falling as it breathed on the stillness of the earth. There the untidy, feminine ripeness of August had expanded into enormous, impenetrable clumps of burdocks spreading their sheets of leafy tin, their luxuriant tongues of fleshy greenery. There, those protuberant bur clumps spread themselves, like resting peasant women, half-enveloped in their own swirling skirts. There, the garden offered free of charge the cheapest fruits of wild lilac, the heady aquavit of mint and all kinds of August trash. But on the other side of the fence, behind that jungle of summer in which the stupidity of weeds reigned unchecked, there was a rubbish heap on which thistles grew in wild profusion. No one knew that there, on that refuse dump, the month of August had chosen to hold that year its pagan orgies. There, pushed against the fence and hidden by the elders, stood the bed of the half-wit girl, Touya, as we all called her. On a heap of discarded junk, of old saucepans, abandoned single shoes, and chunks of plaster, stood a bed, painted green, propped up on two bricks where one leg was missing.

The air over that midden, wild with the heat, cut through by the lightning of shiny horseflies, driven mad by the sun, crackled as if filled with invisible rattles, exciting one to frenzy.

Touya sits hunched up among the yellow bedding and odd rags, her large head covered by a mop of tangled black hair. Her face works like the bellows of an accordion. Every now and then a sorrowful grimace folds it into a thousand vertical pleats, but astonishment soon straightens it out again, ironing out the folds, revealing the chinks of small eyes and damp gums with yellow teeth under snoutlike fleshy lips. Hours pass, filled with heat and boredom; Touya chatters in a monotone, dozes, mumbles softly, and coughs. Her immobile frame is covered by a thick cloak of flies. But suddenly the whole heap of dirty rags begins to move, as if stirred by the scratching of a litter of newborn rats. The flies wake up in fright and rise in a huge, furious buzzing cloud, filled with colored light reflected from the sun. And while the rags slip to the ground and spread out over the rubbish heap, like frightened rats, a form emerges and reveals itself: the dark half-naked idiot girl rises slowly to her feet and stands like a pagan idol, on short childish legs; her neck swells with anger, and from her face, red with fury, on which the arabesques of bulging veins stand out as in a primitive painting, comes forth a hoarse animal scream, originating deep in the lungs hidden in that half-animal, half-divine breast. The sun-dried thistles shout, the plantains swell and boast their shameless flesh, the weeds salivate with glistening poison, and the half-wit girl, hoarse with shouting, convulsed with madness, presses her fleshy belly in an excess of lust against the trunk of an elder, which groans softly under the insistent pressure of that libidinous passion, incited by the whole ghastly chorus to hideous unnatural fertility.

Touya's mother, Maria, hired herself to housewives to scrub floors. She was a small saffron-yellow woman, and it was with saffron that she wiped the floors, the deal tables, the benches, and the banisters which she had scrubbed in the homes of the poor.

Once Adela took me to the old woman's house. It was early in the morning when we entered the small blue-walled room, with its mud floor, lying in a patch of bright yellow sunlight in the still of the morning broken only by the frighteningly loud ticking of a cottage clock on the wall. In a straw-filled chest lay the foolish Maria, white as a wafer and motionless like a glove from which a hand had been withdrawn. And, as if taking advantage of her sleep, the silence talked, the yellow, bright, evil silence delivered its monologue, argued, and loudly spoke its vulgar maniacal soliloquy. Maria's time—the time imprisoned in her soul—had left her and—terribly real—filled the room, vociferous and hellish in the bright silence of the morning, rising from the noisy mill of the clock like a cloud of bad flour, powdery flour, the stupid flour of madmen.

3

In one of those cottages, surrounded by brown railings and submerged in the lush green of its garden, lived Aunt Agatha. Coming through the garden to visit her, we passed numerous colored glass balls stuck on flimsy poles. In these pink, green, and violet balls were enclosed bright shining worlds, like the ideally happy pictures contained in the peerless perfection of soap bubbles.

In the gloom of the hall, with its old lithographs, rotten with mildew and blind with age, we rediscovered a well-known smell. In that old familiar smell was contained a marvelously simple synthesis of the life of those people, the distillation of their race, the quality of their blood, and the secret of their fate, imperceptibly mixed day by day with the passage of their own, private time. The old, wise door, the silent witness of the entries and exits of mother, daughters, sons, whose dark sighs accompanied the comings and goings of those people, now opened noiselessly like the door of a wardrobe, and we stepped into their life. They were sitting as if in the shadow of their own destiny and did not fight against it; with their first, clumsy gestures they revealed their secret to us. Besides, were we not related to them by blood and by fate?

The room was dark and velvety from the royal blue wallpaper with its gold pattern, but even here the echo of the flaming day shimmered brassily on the picture frames, on doorknobs and gilded borders, although it came through the filter of the dense greenery of the garden. From her chair against the wall, Aunt Agatha rose to greet us, tall and ample, her round white flesh blotchy with the rust of freckles. We sat down beside them, as on the verge of their lives, rather embarrassed by their defenseless surrender to us, and we drank water with rose syrup, a wonderful drink in which I found the deepest essence of that hot Saturday.

My aunt was complaining. It was the principal burden of her conversation, the voice of that white and fertile flesh, floating as it were outside the boundaries of her person, held only loosely in the fetters of individual form, and despite those fetters, ready to multiply, to scatter, branch out, and divide into a family. It was an almost self-propagating fertility, a femininity without rein, morbidly expansive.

It seemed as if the very whiff of masculinity, the smell of tobacco smoke, or a bachelor's joke, would spark off this feverish femininity and entice it to a lascivious virgin birth. And in fact, all her complaints about her husband or her servants, all her worries about the children were only the caprices of her incompletely satisfied fertility, a logical extension of the rude, angry, lachrymose coquetry with which, to no purpose, she plagued her husband. Uncle Mark, small and hunched, with a face fallow of sex, sat in his gray bankruptcy, reconciled to his fate, in the shadow of a limitless contempt in which he seemed only to relax. His gray eyes reflected the distant glow of the garden, spreading in the window.

Sometimes he tried with a feeble gesture to raise an objection, to resist, but the wave of self-sufficient femininity hurled aside that unimportant gesture, triumphantly passed him by, and drowned the feeble stirrings of male assertiveness under its broad flood.

There was something tragic in that immoderate fertility; the misery of a creature fighting on the borders of nothingness and death, the heroism of womanhood triumphing by fertility over the shortcomings of nature, over the insufficiency of the male. But their offspring showed justification for that panic of maternity, of a passion for childbearing which became exhausted in ill-starred pregnancies, in an ephemeral generation of phantoms without blood or face.

Lucy, the second eldest, now entered the room, her head overdeveloped for her childlike, plump body, her flesh white and delicate. She stretched out to me a small doll-like hand, a hand in bud, and blushed all over her face like a peony. Unhappy because of her blushes, which shamelessly revealed the secrets of menstruation, she closed her eyes and reddened even more deeply under the touch of the most indifferent question, for she saw in each a secret allusion to her most sensitive maidenhood.

Emil, the eldest of the cousins, with a fair mustache in a face from which life seemed to have washed away all expression, was walking up and down the room, his hands in the pockets of his voluminous trousers.

His elegant, expensive clothes bore the imprint of the exotic countries he had visited. His pale flabby face seemed from day to day to lose its outline to become a white blank wall with a pale network of veins, like lines on an old map occasionally stirred by the fading memories of a stormy and wasted life. He was a master of card tricks, he smoked long, noble pipes, and he smelled strangely of distant lands. With his gaze wandering over old memories, he told curious stories, which at some point would suddenly stop, disintegrate, and blow away.

My eyes followed him nostalgically, and I wished he would notice me and liberate me from the tortures of boredom. And indeed, it seemed as if he gave me a wink before going into an adjoining room and I followed him there. He was sitting on a small, low sofa, his crossed knees almost level with his head, which was bald like a billiard ball. It seemed as if it were only his clothes that had been thrown, crumpled and empty, over a chair. His face seemed like the breath of a face—a smudge which an unknown passerby had left in the air. In his white, blue-enameled hands he was holding a wallet and looking at something in it.

From the mist of his face, the protruding white of a pale eye emerged with difficulty, enticing me with a wink. I felt an irresistible sympathy for Emil.

He took me between his knees and, shuffling some photographs in front of my eyes as if they were a pack of cards, he showed me naked women and boys in strange positions. I stood leaning against him looking at those delicate human bodies with distant, unseeing eyes, when all of a sudden the fluid of an obscure excitement with which the air seemed charged, reached me and pierced me with a shiver of uneasiness, a wave of sudden comprehension. But meanwhile that ghost of a smile which had appeared under Emil's soft and beautiful mustache, the seed of desire which had shown in a pulsating vein on his temple, the tenseness which for a moment had kept his features concentrated, all fell away again and his face receded into indifference and became absent and finally faded away altogether.

VISITATION

Already for some time our town had been sinking into the perpetual grayness of dusk, had become affected at the edges by a
rash of shadows, by fluffy mildew, and by moss the dull color
of iron.

Hardly was it freed from the brown smoke and the mists of
the morning than the day turned into a lowering amber afternoon, became for a brief moment transparent, taking the golden
color of ale, only to ascend under the multiple fantastic domes
of vast, color-filled nights.

We lived on Market Square, in one of those dark houses with
empty blind nooks, so difficult to distinguish one from the
other.

This gave endless possibilities for mistakes. For once you had
entered the wrong doorway and set foot on the wrong staircase,
you were liable to find yourself in a real labyrinth of unfamiliar
apartments and balconies, and unexpected doors opening onto
strange empty courtyards, and you forgot the initial object of
the expedition, only to recall it days later after numerous strange
and complicated adventures, on regaining the family home in
the gray light of dawn.

Full of large wardrobes, vast sofas, faded mirrors, and cheap
artificial palms, our apartment sank deeper and deeper into a
state of neglect owing to the indolence of my mother, who spent
most of her time in the shop, and the carelessness of slim-legged
Adela, who, without anyone to supervise her, spent her days in
front of a mirror, endlessly making up and leaving everywhere

tufts of combed-out hair, brushes, odd slippers, and discarded corsets.

No one ever knew exactly how many rooms we had in our apartment, because no one ever remembered how many of them were let to strangers. Often one would by chance open the door to one of these forgotten rooms and find it empty; the lodger had moved out a long time ago. In the drawers, untouched for months, one would make unexpected discoveries.

In the downstairs rooms lived the shop assistants and some-times during the night we were awakened by their nightmares. In winter it would be still deep night when Father went down to these cold and dark rooms, the light of his candle scattering flocks of shadows so that they fled sideways along the floor and up the walls; his task to wake the snoring men from their stone-hard sleep.

In the light of the candle, which Father left with them, they unwound themselves lazily from the dirty bedding, then, sitting on the edge of their beds, stuck out their bare and ugly feet and, with socks in their hands, abandoned themselves for a moment to the delights of yawning—a yawning crossing the borders of sensuous pleasure, leading to a painful cramp of the palate, al-most to nausea.

In the corners, large cockroaches sat immobile, hideously en-larged by their own shadows which the burning candle imposed on them and which remained attached to their flat, headless bodies when they suddenly ran off with weird, spiderlike move-ments.

At that time, my father's health began to fail. Even in the first weeks of this early winter, he would spend whole days in bed, surrounded by bottles of medicine and boxes of pills, and ledgers brought up to him from the shop. The bitter smell of ill-ness settled like a rug in the room and the arabesques on the wallpaper loomed darker.

In the evenings, when Mother returned from the shop, Father was often excited and inclined to argue.

As he reproached her for inaccuracies in the accounts his cheeks became flushed and he became almost insane with anger. I remember more than once waking in the middle of the night to see him in his nightshirt, running in his bare feet up and down the leather sofa to demonstrate his irritation to my baffled mother.

On other days he was calm and composed, completely absorbed in the account books, lost in a maze of complicated calculations.

I can still see him in the light of the smoking lamp, crouched among his pillows under the large carved headboard of the bed, swaying backward and forward in silent meditation, his head making an enormous shadow on the wall.

From time to time, he raised his eyes from the ledgers as if to come up for air, opened his mouth, smacking his lips with distaste as if his tongue were dry and bitter, and looked around helplessly, as if searching for something.

It then sometimes happened that he quietly got out of bed and ran to the corner of the room where an intimate instrument hung on the wall. It was a kind of hourglass-shaped water jar marked in ounces and filled with a dark fluid. My father attached himself to it with a long rubber hose as if with a gnarled, aching umbilical cord and, thus connected with the miserable apparatus, he became tense with concentration, his eyes darkened, and an expression of suffering, or perhaps of forbidden pleasure, spread over his pale face.

Then again came days of quiet, concentrated work, interrupted by lonely monologues. While he sat there in the light of the lamp among the pillows of the large bed, and the room grew enormous as the shadows above the lampshade merged with the deep city night beyond the windows, he felt, without looking, how the pullulating jungle of wallpaper, filled with whispers, lisping and hissing, closed in around him. He heard, without looking, a conspiracy of knowingly winking hidden eyes, of alert ears opening up among the flowers on the wall, of dark, smiling mouths.

He then pretended to become even more engrossed in his work, adding and calculating, trying not to betray the anger which rose in him and overcoming the temptation to throw himself blindly forward with a sudden shout to grab fistfuls of those curly arabesques, or of those sheaves of eyes and ears which swarmed out from the night and grew and multiplied, sprouting, with ever-new ghostlike shoots and branches, from the womb of darkness. And he calmed down only when, in the morning with the ebb of night, the wallpaper wilted, shed its leaves and petals and thinned down autumnally, letting in the distant dawn.

Then, among the twittering of wallpaper birds in the yellow wintry dawn, he would fall, for a few hours, into a heavy black sleep.

For days, even for weeks, while he seemed to be engrossed in the complicated current accounts—his thoughts had been secretly plumbing the depths of his own entrails. He would hold his breath and listen. And when his gaze returned, pale and troubled, from that labyrinth, he calmed it with a smile. He did not wish to believe those assumptions and suggestions which oppressed him, and rejected them as absurd.

In daytime, these were more like arguments and persuasions; long monotonous reasonings, conducted half-aloud and with humorous interludes of teasing and banter. But at night these voices rose with greater passion. The demands were made more clearly and more loudly, and we heard him talk to God, as if begging for something or fighting against someone who made insistent claims and issued orders.

Until one night that voice rose threateningly and irresistibly, demanding that he should bear witness to it with his mouth and with his entrails. And we heard the spirit enter into him as he rose from his bed, tall and growing in prophetic anger, choking with brash words that he emitted like a machine gun. We heard the din of battle and Father's groans, the groans of a Titan with a broken hip, but still capable of wrath.

I have never seen an Old Testament prophet, but at the sight of this man stricken by God's fire, sitting clumsily on an enormous china chamber pot behind a windmill of arms, a screen of desperate wrigglings over which there towered his voice, grown unfamiliar and hard, I understood the divine anger of saintly men.

It was a dialogue as grim as the language of thunder. The jerkings of his arms cut the sky into pieces, and in the cracks there appeared the face of Jehovah swollen with anger and spitting out curses. Without looking, I saw him, the terrible Demiurge, as, resting on darkness as on Sinai, propping his powerful palms on the pelmet of the curtains, he pressed his enormous face against the upper panes of the window which flattened horribly his large fleshy nose.

I heard my father's voice during the intermissions in these prophetic tirades. I heard the windows shake from the powerful growl of the swollen lips, mixed with the explosions of entreaties, laments, and threats uttered by Father.

Sometimes the voices quietened down and grumbled softly, like the nightly chatter of wind in a chimney; then again they exploded with a large, tumultuous noise, in a storm of sobs mixed with curses. Suddenly the window opened with a dark yawn and a sheet of darkness wafted across the room.

In a flash of lightning I could see my father, his nightshirt unbuttoned, as, cursing terribly, he emptied with a masterful gesture the contents of the chamber pot into the darkness below.

2

My father was slowly fading, wilting before our eyes.

Hunched among the enormous pillows, his gray hair standing wildly on end, he talked to himself in undertones, engrossed in some complicated private business. It seemed as if his personality had split into a number of opposing and quarreling selves; he argued loudly with himself, persuading forcibly and passionately, pleading and begging; then again he seemed to be presiding over a meeting of many interested parties whose views he tried to reconcile with a great show of energy and conviction. But every time these noisy meetings, during which tempers would rise violently, dissolved into curses, execrations, maledictions, and insults.

Then came a period of appeasement, of an interior calm, a blessed serenity of spirit. Again the great ledgers were spread on the bed, on the table, on the floor, and an almost monastic calm reigned in the light of the lamp, over the white bedding, over my father's gray, bowed head.

But when Mother returned late at night from the shop, Father became animated, called her and showed her with great pride the wonderful colored decals with which he had laboriously adorned the pages of the main ledger.

About that time we noticed that Father began to shrink from day to day, like a nut drying inside the shell.

This shrinking was not accompanied by any loss of strength. On the contrary: there seemed to be an improvement in his general state of health, in his humor, and in his mobility.

Now he often laughed loudly and gaily; sometimes he was almost overcome with laughter; at others, he would knock on the side of the bed and answer himself, "Come in," in various tones, for hours on end. From time to time, he scrambled down from the bed, climbed on top of the wardrobe, and, crouching under the ceiling, sorted out old dust-covered odds and ends.

Sometimes he put two chairs back-to-back and, taking his weight on them, swung his legs backward and forward, looking with shining eyes for an expression of admiration and encouragement in our faces. It seemed as if he had become completely reconciled with God. Sometimes at night, the face of the bearded Demiurge would appear at the bedroom window, bathed in the dark purple glare of Bengal fire, but it only looked for a moment benevolently on my sleeping father whose melodious snoring seemed to wander far into the unknown regions of the world of sleep.

During the long twilight afternoons of this winter, my father would spend hours rummaging in corners full of old junk, as if he were feverishly searching for something.

And sometimes at dinnertime, when we had all taken our places at the table, Father would be missing. On such occasions, Mother had to call "Jacob!" over and over again and knock her spoon against the table before he emerged from inside a wardrobe, covered with dust and cobwebs, his eyes vacant, his mind on some complicated matter known only to himself which absorbed him completely.

Occasionally he climbed on a pelmet and froze into immobility, a counterpart to the large stuffed vulture which hung on the wall opposite. In this crouching pose, with misty eyes and a sly smile on his lips, he remained for long periods without moving, except to flap his arms like wings and crow like a cock whenever anybody entered the room.

We ceased to pay attention to these oddities in which Father became daily more and more involved. Almost completely rid of bodily needs, not taking any nourishment for weeks, he plunged deeper every day into some strange and complex affairs that were beyond our understanding. To all our persuasions and our entreaties, he answered in fragments of his interior monologue, which nothing from the outside could disturb. Constantly absorbed, morbidly excited, with flushes on his dry cheeks, he did not notice us or even hear us anymore.

We became used to his harmless presence, to his soft babbling, and that childlike self-absorbed twittering, which sounded as if they came from the margin of our own time. During that period he used to disappear for many days into some distant corner of the house and it was difficult to locate him.

Gradually these disappearances ceased to make any impression on us, we became used to them and when, after many days, Father reappeared a few inches shorter and much thinner, we did not stop to think about it. We did not count him as one of us anymore, so very remote had he become from everything that was human and real. Knot by knot, he loosened himself from us; point by point, he gave up the ties joining him to the human community.

What still remained of him—the small shroud of his body and the handful of nonsensical oddities—would finally disappear one day, as unremarked as the gray heap of rubbish swept into a corner, waiting to be taken by Adela to the rubbish dump.

BIRDS

Came the yellow days of winter, filled with boredom. The rust-colored earth was covered with a threadbare, meager tablecloth of snow full of holes. There was not enough of it for some of the roofs and so they stood there, black and brown, shingle and thatch, arks containing the sooty expanses of attics—coal black cathedrals, bristling with ribs of rafters, beams, and spars—the dark lungs of winter winds. Each dawn revealed new chimney stacks and chimney pots which had emerged during the hours of darkness, blown up by the night winds: the black pipes of a devil's organ. The chimney sweeps could not get rid of the crows which in the evening covered the branches of the trees around the church with living black leaves, then took off, fluttering, and came back, each clinging to its own place on its own branch, only to fly away at dawn in large flocks, like gusts of soot, flakes of dirt, undulating and fantastic, blackening with their insistent cawing the musty yellow streaks of light. The days hardened with cold and boredom like last year's loaves of bread. One began to cut them with blunt knives without appetite, with a lazy indifference.

Father had stopped going out. He banked up the stoves, studied the ever-elusive essence of fire, experienced the salty, metallic taste and the smoky smell of wintry salamanders that licked the shiny soot in the throat of the chimney. He applied himself lovingly at that time to all manner of small repairs in the upper regions of the rooms. At all hours of the day one could see him crouched on top of a ladder, working at something under the ceiling, at the cornices over the tall windows, at the counterweights and chains of the hanging lamps. Following the custom of house painters, he used a pair of steps as enormous stilts and he felt perfectly happy in that bird's-eye perspective close to the sky, leaves and birds painted on the ceiling. He grew more and more remote from practical affairs. When my mother, worried and unhappy about his condition, tried to draw him into a conversation about business, about the payments due at the end of the month, he listened to her absentmindedly, anxiety showing in his abstracted look. Sometimes he stopped her with a warning gesture of the hand in order to run to a corner of the room, put his ear to a crack in the floor and, by lifting the index fingers of both hands, emphasize the gravity of the investigation, and begin to listen intently. At that time we did not yet understand the sad origin of these eccentricities, the deplorable complex which had been maturing in him.

Mother had no influence over him, but he gave a lot of respectful attention to Adela. The cleaning of his room was to him a great and important ceremony, of which he always arranged to be a witness, watching all Adela's movements with a mixture of apprehension and pleasurable excitement. He ascribed to all her functions a deeper, symbolic meaning. When, with young firm gestures, the girl pushed a long-handled broom along the floor, Father could hardly bear it. Tears would stream from his eyes, silent laughter transformed his face, and his body was shaken by spasms of delight. He was ticklish to the point of madness. It was enough for Adela to waggle her fingers at him to imitate tickling, for him to rush through all the rooms in a wild panic, banging the doors after him, to fall at last on the bed in the farthest room and wriggle in convulsions of laughter, imagining the tickling which he found irresistible. Because of this, Adela's power over Father was almost limitless.

At that time we noticed for the first time Father's passionate interest in animals. To begin with, it was the passion of the huntsman and the artist rolled into one. It was also perhaps a deeper, biological sympathy of one creature for kindred, yet different, forms of life, a kind of experimenting in the unexplored regions of existence. Only at a later stage did matters take that uncanny, complicated, essentially sinful and unnatural turn, which it is better not to bring into the light of day.

But it all began with the hatching out of birds' eggs.

With a great outlay of effort and money, Father imported from Hamburg, or Holland, or from zoological stations in Africa, birds' eggs on which he set enormous brood hens from Belgium. It was a process which fascinated me as well—this hatching out of the chicks, which were real anomalies of shape and color. It was difficult to anticipate—in these monsters with enormous, fantastic beaks which they opened wide immediately after birth, hissing greedily to show the backs of their throats, in these lizards with frail, naked bodies of hunchbacks—the future peacocks, pheasants, grouse, or condors. Placed in cotton wool, in baskets, this dragon brood lifted blind, walleyed heads on thin necks, croaking voicelessly from their dumb throats. My father would walk along the shelves, dressed in a green baize apron, like a gardener in a hothouse of cacti, and conjure up from nothingness these blind bubbles, pulsating with life, these impotent bellies receiving the outside world only in the form of food, these growths on the surface of life, climbing blindfolded toward the light. A few weeks later, when these blind buds of matter burst open, the rooms were filled with the bright chatter and scintillating chirruping of their new inhabitants. The birds perched on the curtain pelmets, on the tops of wardrobes; they nestled in the tangle of tin branches and the metal scrolls of the hanging lamps.

While Father pored over his large ornithological textbooks and studied their colored plates, these feathery phantasms seemed to rise from the pages and fill the rooms with colors, with splashes of crimson, strips of sapphire, verdigris, and silver. At feeding time they formed a motley, undulating bed on the floor, a living carpet which at the intrusion of a stranger would fall apart, scatter into fragments, flutter in the air, and finally settle high under the ceilings. I remember in particular a certain condor, an enormous bird with a featherless neck, its face wrinkled and knobbly. It was an emaciated ascetic, a Buddhist lama, full of imperturbable dignity in its behavior, guided by the rigid ceremonial of its great species. When it sat facing my father, motionless in the monumental position of ageless Egyptian idols, its eyes covered with a whitish cataract which it

pulled down sideways over its pupil to shut itself up completely
in the contemplation of its dignified solitude—it seemed, with
its stony profile, like an older brother of my father's. Its body
and muscles seemed to be made of the same material, it had
the same hard, wrinkled skin, the same desiccated bony face,
the same horny, deep eye sockets. Even the hands, strong in the
joints, my father's long, thick hands with their rounded nails,
had their counterpart in the condor's claws. I could not resist
the impression, when looking at the sleeping condor, that I was
in the presence of a mummy—a dried-out, shrunken mummy of
my father. I believe that even my mother noticed this strange resemblance, although we never discussed the subject. It is significant that the condor used my father's chamber pot.

Not content with the hatching out of more and more new
specimens, my father arranged the marriages of birds in the attic, he sent out matchmakers, he tied up eager attractive birds in
the holes and crannies under the roof, and soon the roof of our
house, an enormous double-rigged shingle roof, became a real
birds' hostel, a Noah's ark to which all kinds of feathery creatures flew from far afield. Long after the liquidation of the
birds' paradise, this tradition persisted in the avian world and
during the period of spring migration our roof was besieged by
whole flocks of cranes, pelicans, peacocks, and sundry other
birds. However, after a short period of splendor, the whole undertaking took a sorry turn.

It soon became necessary to move my father to two rooms at
the top of the house which had served as storage rooms. We could
hear from there, at dawn, the mixed clangor of birds' voices. The
wooden walls of the attic rooms, helped by the resonance of the
empty space under the gables, sounded with the roar, the flutterings, the crowing, the gurgling, the mating cries. For a few weeks
Father was lost to view. He only rarely came down to the apartment and, when he did, we noticed that he seemed to have
shrunk, to have become smaller and thinner. Occasionally forgetting himself, he would rise from his chair at table, wave his arms
as if they were wings, and emit a long-drawn-out bird's call while
his eyes misted over. Then, rather embarrassed, he would join us
in laughing it off and try to turn the whole incident into a joke.

One day, during spring cleaning, Adela suddenly appeared in Father's bird kingdom. Stopping in the doorway, she wrung her hands at the fetid smell that filled the room, the heaps of droppings covering the floor, the tables, and the chairs. Without hesitation, she flung open the window and, with the help of a long broom, she prodded the whole mass of birds into life. A fiendish cloud of feathers and wings arose screaming, and Adela, like a furious maenad protected by the whirlwind of her thyrsus, danced the dance of destruction. My father, waving his arms in panic, tried to lift himself into the air with his feathered flock. Slowly the winged cloud thinned until at last Adela remained on the battlefield, exhausted and out of breath, along with my father, who now, adopting a worried hangdog expression, was ready to accept complete defeat.

A moment later, my father came downstairs—a broken man, an exiled king who had lost his throne and his kingdom.

TAILORS' DUMMIES

The affair of the birds was the last colorful and splendid counteroffensive of fantasy which my father, that incorrigible improviser, that fencing master of imagination, had led against the trenches and defense works of a sterile and empty winter. Only now do I understand the lonely hero who alone had waged war against the fathomless, elemental boredom that strangled the city. Without any support, without recognition on our part, that strangest of men was defending the lost cause of poetry. He was like a magic mill, into the hoppers of which the bran of empty hours was poured, to reemerge flowering in all the colors and scents of oriental spices. But, used to the splendid showmanship of that metaphysical conjurer, we were inclined to underrate the value of his sovereign magic, which saved us from the lethargy of empty days and nights.

Adela was not rebuked for her thoughtless and brutal vandalism. On the contrary, we felt a vile satisfaction, a disgraceful pleasure that Father's exuberance had been curbed, for although we had enjoyed it to the full, we later ignominiously denied all responsibility for it. Perhaps in our treachery there was secret approval of the victorious Adela to whom we simply ascribed some commission and assignment from forces of a higher order. Betrayed by us all, Father retreated without a fight from the scenes of his recent glory. Without crossing swords, he surrendered to the enemy the kingdom of his former splendor. A voluntary exile, he took himself off to an empty room at the end of the passage and there immured himself in solitude.

We forgot him.

We were beset again from all sides by the mournful grayness

of the city which crept through the windows with the dark rash of dawn, with the mushroom growth of dusk, developing into the shaggy fur of long winter nights. The wallpaper of the rooms, blissfully unconstrained in those former days and accessible to the multicolored flights of the birds, closed in on itself and hardened, becoming engrossed in the monotony of bitter monologues.

The chandeliers blackened and wilted like old thistles; now they hung dejected and ill tempered, their glass pendants ringing softly whenever anybody groped their way through the dimly lit room. In vain did Adela put colored candles in all the holders; they were a poor substitute for, a pale reflection of, those splendid illuminations which had so recently enlivened these hanging gardens. Oh, what a twittering had been there, what swift and fantastic flights cutting the air into packs of magic cards, sprinkling thick flakes of azure, of peacock and parrot green, of metallic sparkle, drawing lines and flourishes in the air, displaying colored fans which remained suspended, long after flight, in the shimmering atmosphere. Even now, in the depth of the grayness, echoes and memories of brightness were hidden but nobody caught them, no clarinet drilled the troubled air.

Those weeks passed under the sign of a strange drowsiness.

Beds unmade for days on end, piled high with bedding crumpled and disordered from the weight of dreams, stood like deep boats waiting to sail into the dank and confusing labyrinths of some dark starless Venice. In the bleakness of dawn, Adela brought us coffee. Lazily we started dressing in the cold rooms, in the light of a single candle reflected many times in black window panes. The mornings were full of aimless bustle, of prolonged searches in endless drawers and cupboards. The clacking of Adela's slippers could be heard all over the apartment. The shop assistants lit the lanterns, took the large shop keys which Mother handed them, and went out into the thick swirling darkness. Mother could not come to terms with her dressing. The candles burned smaller in the candlesticks. Adela disappeared somewhere into the farthest rooms or into the attic where she hung the washing. She was deaf to our calling. A newly lit, dirty, bleak fire in the stove licked at the cold shiny growth of soot in the throat of the chimney. The candle died out, and the room filled with gloom. With our heads on the tablecloth, among the remains of breakfast, we fell asleep, still half-dressed. Lying face downward on the furry lap of darkness, we sailed in its regular breathing into the starless nothingness. We were awakened by Adela's noisy tidying up. Mother could not cope with her dressing. Before she had finished doing her hair, the shop assistants were back for lunch. The half-light in the marketplace was now the color of golden smoke. For a moment it looked as if out of that smoke-colored honey, that opaque amber, a most beautiful afternoon would unfold. But the happy moment passed, the amalgam of dawn withered, the swelling fermentation of the day, almost completed, receded again into a helpless grayness. We assembled again around the table, the shop assistants rubbed their hands, red from the cold, and the prose of their conversation suddenly revealed a full-grown day, a gray and empty Tuesday, a day without tradition and without a face. But it was only when a dish appeared on the table containing two large fish in jelly lying side by side, head-to-tail, like a sign of the zodiac, that we recognized in them the coat of arms of that day, the calendar emblem of the nameless Tuesday: we shared it out quickly among ourselves, thankful that the day had at last achieved an identity.

The shop assistants ate with unction, with the seriousness due to a calendar feast. The smell of pepper filled the room. And when they had used pieces of bread to wipe up the remains of the jelly from their plates, pondering in silence on the heraldry of the following days of the week, and nothing remained on the serving dish but the fish heads with their boiled-out eyes, we all felt that by a communal effort we had conquered the day and that what remained of it did not matter.

And, in fact, Adela made short work of the rest of the day, now surrendered to her mercies. Amid the clatter of saucepans and splashing of cold water, she was energetically liquidating the few hours remaining until dusk, while Mother slept on the sofa. Meanwhile in the dining room the scene was being set for the evening. Polda and Pauline, the seamstresses, spread

themselves out there with the props of their trade. Carried on
their shoulders, a silent immobile lady had entered the room, a
lady of oakum and canvas, with a black wooden knob instead
of a head. But when stood in the corner, between the door and
the stove, that silent woman became mistress of the situation.
Standing motionless in her corner, she supervised the girls' advances and wooings as they knelt before her, fitting fragments
of a dress marked with white basting thread. They waited with
attention and patience on the silent idol, which was difficult to
please. That Moloch was inexorable as only a female Moloch
can be, and sent them back to work again and again, and they,
thin and spindly, like wooden spools from which thread is unwound and as mobile, manipulated with deft fingers the piles of
silk and wool, cut with noisy scissors into its colorful mass,
whirred the sewing machine, treading its pedal with one cheap
patent-leathered foot, while around them there grew a heap of
cuttings, of motley rags and pieces, like husks and chaff spat
out by two fussy and prodigal parrots. The curved jaws of the
scissors tapped open like the beaks of those exotic birds.

The girls trod absentmindedly on the bright shreds of material, wading carelessly in the rubbish of a possible carnival, in
the storeroom for some great unrealized masquerade. They dis-
entangled themselves with nervous giggles from the trimmings,
their eyes laughed into the mirrors. Their hearts, the quick
magic of their fingers were not in the boring dresses which remained on the table, but in the thousand scraps, the frivolous
and fickle trimmings, with the colorful fantastic snowstorm
with which they could smother the whole city.

Suddenly they felt hot and opened the window to see, in the
frustration of their solitude, in their hunger for new faces, at
least one nameless face pressed against the pane. They fanned
their flushed cheeks with the winter night air in which the curtains billowed—they uncovered their burning décolletés, full of
hatred and rivalry for one another, ready to fight for any Pierrot
whom the dark breezes of night might blow in through the window. Ah! how little did they demand from reality! They had
everything within themselves, they had a surfeit of everything in
themselves. Ah! they would be content with a sawdust Pierrot

with the long-awaited word to act as the cue for their well-rehearsed roles, so that they could at last speak the lines, full of a sweet and terrible bitterness, that crowded to their lips exciting them violently, like some novel devoured at night, while the tears streamed down their cheeks.

During one of his nightly wanderings about the apartment, undertaken in Adela's absence, my father stumbled upon such a quiet evening sewing session. For a moment he stood in the dark door of the adjoining room, a lamp in his hand, enchanted by the scene of feverish activity, by the blushes—that synthesis of face powder, red tissue paper, and atropine—to which the winter night, breathing on the waving window curtains, acted as a significant backdrop. Putting on his glasses, he stepped quickly up to the girls and walked twice around them, letting fall on them the light of the lamp he was carrying. The draft from the open door lifted the curtains, the girls let themselves be admired, twisting their hips; the enamel of their eyes glinted like the shiny leather of their shoes and the buckles of their garters, showing from under their skirts lifted by the wind; the scraps began to scamper across the floor like rats toward the half-closed door of the dark room, and my father gazed attentively at the panting girls, whispering softly: "Genus *Avium* . . . If I am not mistaken, *Scansores* or *Psittacus* . . . very remarkable, very remarkable indeed."

This accidental encounter was the beginning of a whole series of meetings, in the course of which my father succeeded in charming both of the young ladies with the magnetism of his strange personality. In return for his witty and elegant conversation, which filled the emptiness of their evenings, the girls permitted the ardent ornithologist to study the structure of their thin and ordinary little bodies. This took place while the conversation was in progress and was done with a seriousness and grace which ensured that even the more risky points of these researches remained completely unequivocal. Pulling Pauline's stocking down from her knee and studying with enraptured eyes the precise and noble structure of the joint, my father would say:

"How delightful and happy is the form of existence which

you ladies have chosen. How beautiful and simple is the truth
which is revealed by your lives. And with what mastery, with
what precision you are performing your task. If, forgetting the
respect due to the Creator, I were to attempt a criticism of creation, I would say, 'Less matter, more form!' Ah, what relief it
would be for the world to lose some of its contents. More
modesty in aspirations, more sobriety in claims, Gentlemen
Demiurges, and the world would be more perfect!" my father
exclaimed, while his hands released Pauline's white calf from
the prison of her stocking.

At that moment Adela appeared in the open door of the dining room, the supper tray in her hands. This was the first meeting of the two enemy powers since the great battle. All of us
who witnessed it felt a moment of terrible fear. We felt extremely uneasy at being present at the further humiliation of the
sorely tried man. My father rose from his knees very disturbed,
blushing more and more deeply in wave after wave of shame.
But Adela found herself unexpectedly equal to the situation.
She walked up to Father with a smile and flipped him on the
nose. At that, Polda and Pauline clapped their hands, stamped
their feet, and each grabbing one of Father's arms, began to
dance with him around the table. Thus, because of the girls'
good nature, the cloud of unpleasantness dispersed in general
hilarity.

That was the beginning of a series of most interesting and
most unusual lectures which my father, inspired by the charm
of that small and innocent audience, delivered during the subsequent weeks of that early winter.

It is worth noting how, in contact with that strange man, all
things reverted, as it were, to the roots of their existence, rebuilt
their outward appearance anew from their metaphysical core,
returned to the primary idea, in order to betray it at some point
and to turn into the doubtful, risky, and equivocal regions
which we shall call for short the Regions of the Great Heresy.
Our Heresiarch walked meanwhile like a mesmerist, infecting
everything with his dangerous charm. Am I to call Pauline his
victim? She became in those days his pupil and disciple, and at
the same time a guinea pig for his experiments.

Next I shall attempt to explain, with due care and without causing offense, this most heretical doctrine that held Father in its sway for many months to come and which during this time prompted all his actions.

TREATISE ON TAILORS' DUMMIES, OR THE SECOND BOOK OF GENESIS

"The Demiurge," said my father, "has had no monopoly of creation, for creation is the privilege of all spirits. Matter has been given infinite fertility, inexhaustible vitality, and, at the same time, a seductive power of temptation which invites us to create as well. In the depth of matter, indistinct smiles are shaped, tensions build up, attempts at form appear. The whole of matter pulsates with infinite possibilities that send dull shivers through it. Waiting for the life-giving breath of the spirit, it is endlessly in motion. It entices us with a thousand sweet, soft, round shapes which it blindly dreams up within itself.

"Deprived of all initiative, indulgently acquiescent, pliable like a woman, submissive to every impulse, it is a territory outside any law, open to all kinds of charlatans and dilettanti, a domain of abuses and of dubious demiurgical manipulations. Matter is the most passive and most defenseless essence in the cosmos. Anyone can mold it and shape it; it obeys everybody. All attempts at organizing matter are transient and temporary, easy to reverse and to dissolve. There is no evil in reducing life to other and newer forms. Homicide is not a sin. It is sometimes a necessary violence on resistant and ossified forms of existence which have ceased to be amusing. In the interests of an important and fascinating experiment, it can even become meritorious. Here is the starting point of a new apologia for sadism."

My father never tired of glorifying this extraordinary element—matter.

"There is no dead matter," he taught us, "lifelessness is only a disguise behind which hide unknown forms of life. The range of these forms is infinite and their shades and nuances limitless.

The Demiurge was in possession of important and interesting creative recipes. Thanks to them, he created a multiplicity of species which renew themselves by their own devices. No one knows whether these recipes will ever be reconstructed. But this is unnecessary, because even if the classical methods of creation should prove inaccessible forevermore, there still remain some illegal methods, an infinity of heretical and criminal methods."

As my father proceeded from these general principles of cosmogony to the more restricted sphere of his private interests, his voice sank to an impressive whisper, the lecture became more and more complicated and difficult to follow, and the conclusions which he reached became more dubious and dangerous. His gestures acquired an esoteric solemnity. He half-closed one eye, put two fingers to his forehead while a look of extraordinary slyness came over his face. He transfixed his listeners with these looks, violated with his cynical expression their most intimate and most private reserve, until he had reached them in the furthest corner whither they had retreated, pressed them against the wall, and tickled them with the finger of irony, finally producing a glimmer of understanding laughter, the laughter of agreement and admission, the visible sign of capitulation.

The girls sat perfectly still, the lamp smoked, the piece of material under the needle of the sewing machine had long since slipped to the floor, and the machine ran empty, stitching only the black, starless cloth unwinding from the bale of winter darkness outside the window.

"We have lived for too long under the terror of the matchless perfection of the Demiurge," my father said. "For too long the perfection of his creation has paralyzed our own creative instinct. We don't wish to compete with him. We have no ambition to emulate him. We wish to be creators in our own, lower sphere; we want to have the privilege of creation, we want creative delights, we want—in one word—Demiurgy." I don't know on whose behalf my father was proclaiming these demands, what community or corporation, sect or order supported him loyally and lent the necessary weight to his words. As for us, we did not share these demiurgical aspirations.

But Father had meanwhile developed the program of this second Demiurgy, the picture of the second Genesis of creatures which was to stand in open opposition to the present era.

"We are not concerned," he said, "with long-winded creations, with long-term beings. Our creatures will not be heroes of romances in many volumes. Their roles will be short, concise; their characters—without a background. Sometimes, for one gesture, for one word alone, we shall make the effort to bring them to life. We openly admit: we shall not insist either on durability or solidity of workmanship; our creations will be temporary, to serve for a single occasion. If they be human beings, we shall give them, for example, only one profile, one hand, one leg, the one limb needed for their role. It would be pedantic to bother about the other, unnecessary, leg. Their backs can be made of canvas or simply whitewashed. We shall have this proud slogan as our aim: a different actor for every gesture. For each action, each word, we shall call to life a different human being. Such is our whim, and the world will be run according to our pleasure. The Demiurge was in love with consummate, superb, and complicated materials; we shall give priority to trash. We are simply entranced and enchanted by the cheapness, shabbiness, and inferiority of material.

"Can you understand," asked my father, "the deep meaning of that weakness, that passion for colored tissue, for papier-mâché, for distemper, for oakum and sawdust? This is," he continued with a pained smile, "the proof of our love for matter as such, for its fluffiness or porosity, for its unique mystical consistency. Demiurge, that great master and artist, made matter invisible, made it disappear under the surface of life. We, on the contrary, love its creaking, its resistance, its clumsiness. We like to see behind each gesture, behind each move, its inertia, its heavy effort, its bearlike awkwardness."

The girls sat motionless, with glazed eyes. Their faces were long and stultified by listening, their cheeks flushed, and it would have been difficult to decide at that moment whether they belonged to the first or the second Genesis of Creation.

"In one word," Father concluded, "we wish to create man a second time—in the shape and semblance of a tailors' dummy."

Here, for reasons of accuracy, we must describe an insignificant small incident which occurred at that point of the lecture and to which we do not attach much importance. The incident, completely nonsensical and incomprehensible in the sequence of events, could probably be explained as vestigial automatism, without cause and effect, as an instance of the malice of inanimate objects transferred into the region of psychology. We advise the reader to treat it as lightly as we are doing. Here is what happened:

Just as my father pronounced the word "dummy," Adela looked at her wristwatch and exchanged a knowing look with Polda. She then moved her chair forward and, without getting up from it, lifted her dress to reveal her foot tightly covered in black silk, and then stretched it out stiffly like a serpent's head.

She sat thus throughout that scene, upright, her large eyes shining from atropine, fluttering, while Polda and Pauline sat at her sides. All three looked at Father with wide-open eyes. My father coughed nervously, fell silent, and suddenly became very red in the face. Within a minute the lines of his face, so expressive and vibrant a moment before, became still and his expression became humble.

He—the inspired Heresiarch, just emerging from the clouds of exaltation—suddenly collapsed and folded up. Or perhaps he had been exchanged for another man? That other man now sat stiffly, very flushed, with downcast eyes. Polda went up to him and bent over him. Patting him lightly on the back, she spoke in the tone of gentle encouragement: "Jacob must be sensible. Jacob must obey. Jacob must not be obstinate. Please, Jacob . . . Please . . . ."

Adela's outstretched slipper trembled slightly and shone like a serpent's tongue. My father rose slowly, still looking down, took a step forward like an automaton, and fell to his knees. The lamp hissed in the silence of the room, eloquent looks ran up and down in the thicket of wallpaper patterns, whispers of venomous tongues floated in the air, zigzags of thought . . .

TREATISE ON TAILORS' DUMMIES, CONTINUATION

The next evening Father reverted with renewed enthusiasm to his dark and complex subject. Each wrinkle of his deeply lined face expressed incredible cunning. In each fold of skin, a missile of irony lay hidden. But occasionally inspiration widened the spirals of his wrinkles and they swelled horribly and sank in silent whorls into the depths of the winter night.

"Figures in a waxwork museum," he began, "even fairground parodies of dummies, must not be treated lightly. Matter never makes jokes: it is always full of the tragically serious. Who dares to think that you can play with matter, that you can shape it for a joke, that the joke will not be built in, will not eat into it like fate, like destiny? Can you imagine the pain, the dull imprisoned suffering, hewn into the matter of that dummy which does not know why it must be what it is, why it must remain in that forcibly imposed form which is no more than a parody? Do you understand the power of form, of expression, of pretense, the arbitrary tyranny imposed on a helpless block, and ruling it like its own, tyrannical, despotic soul? You give a head of canvas and oakum an expression of anger and leave it with it, with the convulsion, the tension enclosed once and for all, with a blind fury for which there is no outlet. The crowd laughs at the parody. Weep, ladies, over your own fate, when you see the misery of imprisoned matter, of tortured matter which does not know what it is and why it is, nor where the gesture may lead that has been imposed on it forever.

"The crowd laughs. Do you understand the terrible sadism, the exhilarating, demiurgical cruelty of that laughter? Yet we should weep, ladies, at our own fate, when we see that misery of violated matter, against which a terrible wrong has been committed. Hence the frightening sadness of all those jesting golems, of all effigies which brood tragically over their comic grimaces.

"Look at the anarchist Luccheni, the murderer of the Empress Elizabeth of Austria; look at Draga, the diabolical and unhappy Queen of Serbia; look at that youth of genius, the hope and pride of his ancient family, ruined by the unfortunate habit of masturbation. Oh, the irony of those names, of those pretensions!

"Is there anything left of Queen Draga in the wax figure's likeness, any similarity, even the most remote shadow of her being? But the resemblance, the pretense, the name reassures us and stops us from asking what that unfortunate figure is in itself and by itself. And yet it must be somebody, somebody anonymous, menacing, and unhappy, some being that in its dumb existence had never heard of Queen Draga . . .

"Have you heard at night the terrible howling of these wax figures, shut in the fair booths; the pitiful chorus of those forms of wood or porcelain, banging their fists against the walls of their prisons?"

In my father's face, convulsed by the horror of the visions which he had conjured up from darkness, a spiral of wrinkles appeared, a maelstrom growing deeper and deeper, at the bottom of which there flared the terrible eye of a prophet. His beard bristled grotesquely, the tufts of hair growing from warts and moles and from his nostrils stood on end. He became rigid and stood with flaming eyes, trembling from an internal conflict like an automaton of which the mechanism has broken down.

Adela rose from her chair and asked us to avert our eyes from what was to follow. Then she went up to Father and, with her hands on her hips in a pose of great determination, she spoke very clearly.

The two other girls sat stiffly, with downcast eyes, strangely numb . . .

TREATISE ON TAILORS' DUMMIES,
CONCLUSION

On one of the following evenings, my father continued his lecture thus: "When I announced my talk about lay figures, I had not really wanted to speak about those incarnate misunderstandings, those sad parodies that are the fruits of a common and vulgar lack of restraint. I had something else in mind."

Here my father began to set before our eyes the picture of that *generatio aequivoca* which he had dreamed up, a species of beings only half-organic, a kind of pseudofauna and pseudoflora, the result of a fantastic fermentation of matter.

They were creations resembling, in appearance only, living creatures such as crustaceans, vertebrates, cephalopods. In reality the appearance was misleading—they were amorphous creatures, with no internal structure, products of the imitative tendency of matter which, equipped with memory, repeats from force of habit the forms already accepted. The morphological scope of matter is limited on the whole and a certain quota of forms is repeated over and over again on various levels of existence.

These creatures—mobile, sensitive to stimuli, and yet outside the pale of real life—could be brought forth by suspending certain complex colloids in solutions of kitchen salt. These colloids, after a number of days, would form and organize themselves in precipitations of substance resembling lower forms of fauna.

In creatures conceived in this way, one could observe the processes of respiration and metabolism, but chemical analysis revealed in them traces neither of albumen nor of carbon compounds.

Yet these primitive forms were unremarkable compared with the richness of shapes and the splendor of the pseudofauna and pseudoflora, which sometimes appeared in certain strictly defined environments, such as old apartments saturated with the emanations of numerous existences and events; used-up atmospheres, rich in the specific ingredients of human dreams; rubbish heaps, abounding in the humus of memories, of nostalgia, and of sterile boredom. On such a soil, this pseudovegetation sprouted abundantly yet ephemerally, brought forth short-lived generations which flourished suddenly and splendidly, only to wilt and perish.

In flats of that kind, wallpapers must be very weary and

bored with the incessant changes in all the cadenzas of rhythm;
no wonder that they are susceptible to distant, dangerous
dreams. The essence of furniture is unstable, degenerate, and
receptive to abnormal temptations: it is then that on this sick,
tired, and wasted soil colorful and exuberant mildew can flourish in a fantastic growth, like a beautiful rash.

"As you will no doubt know," said my father, "in old apartments there are rooms which are sometimes forgotten. Unvis-
ited for months on end, they wilt neglected between the old
walls and it happens that they close in on themselves, become
overgrown with bricks, and, lost once and for all to our memory, forfeit their only claim to existence. The doors, leading to
them from some backstairs landing, have been overlooked by
people living in the apartment for so long that they merge with
the wall, grow into it, and all trace of them is obliterated in a
complicated design of lines and cracks.

"Once, early in the morning toward the end of winter," my
father continued, "after many months of absence, I entered such
a forgotten passage, and I was amazed at the appearance of the
rooms.

"From all the crevices in the floor, from all the moldings,
from every recess, there grew slim shoots filling the gray air
with a scintillating filigree lace of leaves: a hothouse jungle, full
of whispers and flickering lights—a false and blissful spring.
Around the bed, under the lamp, along the wardrobes, grew
clumps of delicate trees which, high above, spread their luminous crowns and fountains of lacy leaves, spraying chlorophyll,
and thrusting up to the painted heaven of the ceiling. In the
rapid process of blossoming, enormous white and pink flowers
opened among the leaves, bursting from bud under your very
eyes, displaying their pink pulp and spilling over to shed their
petals and fall apart in quick decay.

"I was happy," said my father, "to see that unexpected flowering which filled the air with a soft rustle, a gentle murmur,
falling like colored confetti through the thin rods of the twigs.

"I could see the trembling of the air, the fermentation of too
rich an atmosphere which provoked that precocious blossoming, luxuriation, and wilting of the fantastic oleanders which

had filled the room with a rare, lazy snowstorm of large pink clusters of flowers.

"Before nightfall," concluded my father, "there was no trace left of that splendid flowering. The whole elusive sight was a fata morgana, an example of the strange make-believe of matter which had created a semblance of life."

My father was strangely animated that day; the expression in his eyes—a sly, ironic expression—was vivid and humorous. Later he suddenly became more serious and again analyzed the infinite diversity of forms which the multifarious matter could adopt. He was fascinated by doubtful and problematic forms, like the ectoplasm of a medium, by pseudomatter, the cataleptic emanations of the brain which in some instances spread from the mouth of the person in a trance over the whole table, filled the whole room, a floating, rarefied tissue, an astral dough, on the borderline between body and soul.

"Who knows," he said, "how many suffering, crippled, fragmentary forms of life there are, such as the artificially created life of chests and tables quickly nailed together, crucified timbers, silent martyrs to cruel human inventiveness? The terrible transplantation of incompatible and hostile races of wood, their merging into one misbegotten personality.

"How much ancient suffering is there in the varnished grain, in the veins and knots of our old familiar wardrobes? Who would recognize in them the old features, smiles, and glances, almost planed and polished out of all recognition?"

My father's face, when he said that, dissolved into a thoughtful net of wrinkles, began to resemble an old plank full of knots and veins, from which all memories had been planed away. For a moment we thought that Father would fall into a state of apathy, which sometimes took hold of him, but all of a sudden he recovered himself and continued to speak:

"Ancient, mythical tribes used to embalm their dead. The walls of their houses were filled with bodies and heads immured in them: a father would stand in a corner of the living room—stuffed, the tanned skin of a deceased wife would serve as a mat under the table. I knew a certain sea captain who had in his cabin a lamp, made by Malayan embalmers from the body of his murdered mistress. On her head, she wore enormous antlers. In the stillness of the cabin, the face stretched between the antlers at the ceiling, slowly lifted its eyelids: on the half-opened lips a bubble of saliva would glint, then burst with the softest of whispers. Octopuses, tortoises, and enormous crabs, hanging from the rafters in place of chandeliers, moving their legs endlessly in that stillness, walking, walking, walking without moving . . ."

My father's face suddenly assumed a worried, sad expression when his thoughts, stirred by who knows what associations, prompted him to new examples:

"Am I to conceal from you," he said in a low tone, "that my own brother, as a result of a long and incurable illness, has been gradually transformed into a bundle of rubber tubing, and that my poor cousin had to carry him day and night on his cushion, singing to the luckless creature endless lullabies on winter nights? Can there be anything sadder than a human being changed into the rubber tube of an enema? What disappointment for his parents, what confusion for their feelings, what frustration of the hopes centered around the promising youth! And yet, the faithful love of my poor cousin was not denied him even during that transformation."

"Oh, please, I cannot, I really cannot listen to this any longer!" groaned Polda leaning over her chair. "Make him stop, Adela . . ."

The girls got up, Adela went up to my father with an outstretched finger, made as if to tickle him. Father lost countenance, immediately stopped talking and, very frightened, began to back away from Adela's moving finger. She followed him, however, threatening him with her finger, driving him, step-by-step, out of the room. Pauline yawned and stretched herself. She and Polda, leaning against one another, exchanged a look and a smile.

NIMROD

I spent the whole of August of that year playing with a splendid little dog that appeared one day on the kitchen floor, awkward and squeaking, still smelling of milk and infancy, with a round, still unformed, and trembling head, paws like a mole's, spreading to the sides, and the most delicate, silky-soft coat.

From the moment I first saw it, that crumb of life won the whole enthusiasm and admiration of which I was capable.

From what heavens had that favorite of the gods descended, to become closer to my heart than all the most beautiful toys? To think that an old, completely uninteresting charwoman could have had the wonderful idea to bring from her home in the suburbs—at a very early, transcendental hour—such a lovely dog to our kitchen!

Ah! one had still been absent—alas—not yet brought back from the dark bosom of sleep, when that happiness had been fulfilled and was waiting for us, lying awkwardly on the cool floor of the kitchen, unappreciated by Adela and the other members of the household. Why had I not been wakened earlier? The saucer of milk on the floor bore witness to Adela's maternal instincts, bore witness, too, unfortunately, to moments lost to me forever from the joys of parenthood.

But before me all the future lay open. What a prospect of new experiences, experiments, and discoveries! The most essential secret of life, reduced to this simple, handy, toylike form was revealed here to my insatiable curiosity. It was overwhelmingly interesting to have as one's own that scrap of life, that particle of the eternal mystery in a new and amusing shape, which by its very strangeness, by the unexpected transposition of the spark of life, present in us human beings, into a different, animal form, awoke in me an infinite curiosity.

Animals! the object of insatiable interest, examples of the riddle of life, created, as it were, to reveal the human being to man himself, displaying his richness and complexity in a thousand kaleidoscopic possibilities, each of them brought to some curious end, to some characteristic exuberance. Still unburdened by the complications of eccentric interests which spoil relationships between people, my heart was filled with sympathy for that manifestation of the eternity of life, with a loving tender curiosity that was identical with self-revelation.

The dog was warm and as soft as velvet and had a small quick heartbeat. He had two petal-soft ears, opaque blue eyes, a pink mouth into which one could put one's finger with impunity, delicate and innocent paws with enchanting pink warts on the outside, over the foretoes. He crept with these paws right into a bowl of milk, greedy and impatient, lapping it up with his pale red tongue. When he had had enough he would sadly lift his small muzzle, with drops of milk hanging from it, and retreat clumsily from the milky bath.

He walked with an awkward oblique roll in an undecided direction, along a shaky and uncertain line. His usual mood was one of indefinite basic sadness. He had the dejected helplessness of an orphan—an inability to fill the emptiness of life between the sensational events of meals. This was reflected in the aimlessness of his movements, in his irrational fits of melancholia, his sad whimpering, and his inability to settle down in any one place. Even in the depths of sleep, in which he had to satisfy his need for protection and love by curling himself up into a trembling ball, he could not rid himself of the feeling of loneliness and homelessness. Oh, how a young and meager life, brought forth from familiar darkness, from the homely warmth of a mother's womb into a large, foreign, bright world, shrinks and retreats and recoils from accepting the undertaking—and with what aversion and disappointment!

But slowly, little Nimrod (for that was the proud and martial name we gave him) began to like life better. His exclusive preoccupation with longing for a return to the maternal womb gave way before the charms of plurality.

The world began to set traps for him: the unknown and tantalizing taste of various foods, the square patch of morning sunlight on the floor in which it was so pleasant to rest, the movements of his own limbs, his own paws, his tail roguishly inviting him to play, the fondling of human hands which induced a certain playfulness, the gaiety that filled him with a need for completely new, violent, and risky movements—all this tickled and encouraged him to the acceptance of the experiment of life and to submission to it.

One more thing: Nimrod began to understand that what he was experiencing was, in spite of its appearance of novelty, something which had existed before—many times before. His body began to recognize situations, impressions, and objects. In reality, none of these astonished him very much. Faced with new circumstances, he would dip into the fount of his memory, the deep-seated memory of the body, would search blindly and feverishly, and often find ready made within himself a suitable reaction: the wisdom of generations, deposited in his plasma, in his nerves. He found actions and decisions of which he had not been aware but which had been lying in wait, ready to emerge.

The backdrop of his young life, the kitchen with its buckets and cloths full of complicated and intriguing smells, the clacking of Adela's slippers and her noisy bustle, ceased to frighten him. He got used to considering it his domain, began to feel at home in it and to develop a vague feeling of belonging to it, almost of patriotism.

Unless of course there was a sudden cataclysm in the shape of floor scrubbing—an abolition of the laws of nature—the splashing of warm lye, flooding all the furniture and the loud scraping of Adela's brushes.

But the danger passed; the brush, now calm and immobile, returned to its corner, the floor smelled sweetly of damp wood. Nimrod, restored again to his normal rights and to the freedom of his own territory, would have a sudden urge to grab an old rug between his teeth and to tear at it with all his strength, pulling it to the left and to the right. The pacification of the elements filled him with indescribable joy.

Suddenly he stopped still: in front of him, some three puppy steps away, there appeared a black monster, a scarecrow moving quickly on the rods of many entangled legs. Deeply shaken, Nimrod's eyes followed the course of the shiny insect, observing tensely the flat, apparently headless torso, carried with uncanny speed by the spidery legs.

Something stirred in him at that sight, a feeling which he could not yet understand, a mixture of anger and fear, rather pleasurable and combined with a shiver of strength, of self-assertion, of aggression.

And suddenly he dropped onto his forepaws and uttered a sound unfamiliar to him, a strange noise, completely different from his usual whimpering. He uttered it once, then again and again, in a thin faltering descant.

But in vain did he apostrophize the insect in this new language, born of sudden inspiration, as a cockroach's understanding is not equal to such a tirade: the insect continued on its journey to a corner of the room, with movements sanctified by an ageless ritual of the cockroach world.

The feeling of loathing had as yet no permanence or strength in the dog's soul. The newly awakened joy of life transformed every sensation into a great joke, into gaiety. Nimrod kept on barking, but the tone of it had changed imperceptibly, had become a parody of what it had been—an attempt to express the incredible wonder of that capital enterprise, life, so full of unexpected encounters, pleasures, and thrills.

PAN

In a corner between the backs of sheds and outbuildings was a blind alley leading from the courtyard; the farthest, ultimate cul-de-sac, hemmed in between the privy and the wall of the chicken run—a dismal spot, beyond which one could see no farther.

This was the land's end, the Gibraltar of the courtyard, desperately knocking its head against the blind fence of horizontal planks, enclosing that little world with finality.

From under the fence ran a rivulet of black stinking water, a vein of rotting greasy mud which never dried out—the only road which led across the border of the fence into the wider world. The despair of the fetid alleyway had pushed for so long against the obstacle of the fence that it had loosened one of its planks. We boys did the rest and prized the plank free. In this way we made a breach, opening a window to the sun. Putting a foot on the plank which we had thrown as a bridge across the puddle, the prisoner of the courtyard could squeeze through the crack and let himself out into a new, wider world of fresh breezes. There, spread out before him, was a large, overgrown garden. Tall pear trees, broad apple trees, grew there in profusion, covered with silvery rustling leaves, with a foaming white glinting net. Thick tangled grass, never cut, covered the undulating ground with a fluffy carpet. Common meadow grasses with feathery heads grew there; wild parsley with its delicate filigrees; ground ivy with rough wrinkled leaves, and dead nettles smelling of mint. Shiny sinewy plantains spotted with rust shot up to display bunches of thick red seeds. The whole of this jungle was soaked in the gentle air and filled with blue breezes. When you lay in the grass you were under the azure map of clouds and sailing continents, you inhaled the whole geography of the sky. From that communion with the air, the leaves and blades became covered with delicate hair, with a soft layer of down, a rough bristle of hooks made, it seemed, to grasp and hold the waves of oxygen. That delicate and whitish layer related the vegetation to the atmosphere, gave it the silvery gray-ish tint of the air, of shadowy silences between two glimpses of the sun. And one of the plants, yellow, inflated with air, its pale stems full of milky juice, brought forth from its empty shoots only pure air, pure down in the shape of fluffy dandelion balls scattered by the wind to dissolve noiselessly into the blue silence.

The garden was vast with a number of extensions, and had various zones and climates. From one side it was open to the sky and air, and there it offered the softest, most delicate bed of fluffy green. But where the ground extended into a low-lying isthmus and dropped into the shadow of the back wall of a deserted soda factory, it became grimmer, overgrown and wild with neglect, untidy, fierce with thistles, bristling with nettles, covered with a rash of weeds, until, at the very end between the walls, in an open rectangular bay, it lost all moderation and became insane. There, it was an orchard no more, but a paroxysm of madness, an outbreak of fury, of cynical shamelessness and lust. There, bestially liberated, giving full rein to their passion, ruled the empty, overgrown, cabbage heads of burs—enormous witches, shedding their voluminous skirts in broad daylight, throwing them down, one by one, until their swollen, rustling, hole-riddled rags buried the whole quarrelsome bastard breed under their crazy expanse. And still the skirts swelled and pushed, piling up one on top of another, spreading and growing all the time—a mass of tinny leaves reaching up to the low eaves of a shed.

It was there that I saw him first and for the only time in my life, at a noon hour crazy with heat. It was at a moment when time, demented and wild, breaks away from the treadmill of events and like an escaping vagabond, runs shouting across the fields. Then the summer grows out of control, spreads at all points all over space with a wild impetus, doubling and trebling itself into an unknown, lunatic dimension.

At that hour, I submitted to the frenzy of chasing butterflies, to the passion of pursuing these shimmering spots, these errant white flakes, trembling in awkward zigzags in the burning air. And it so happened that one of these spots of light divided during flight into two, then into three—and the shining, blindingly white triangle of spots led me, like a will-o'-the-wisp, through the jungle of thistles, scorched by the sun.

I stopped at the edge of the burs, not daring to advance into that hollow abyss.

And then, suddenly, I saw him.

Submerged up to his armpits in the thicket of burs, he crouched in front of me.

I saw his broad back in a dirty shirt and the grubby side of his jacket. He sat there, as if ready to leap, his shoulders hunched as under a great burden. His body panted with tension, and perspiration streamed down his copper brown face, glinting in the sun. Immobile, he seemed to be working very hard, struggling under some enormous weight.

I stood, nailed to the spot by his look, held captive by it.

It was the face of a tramp or a drunkard. A tuft of filthy hair bristled over his broad forehead, rounded like a stone washed by a stream. That forehead was now creased into deep furrows. I did not know whether it was the pain, the burning heat of the sun, or that superhuman effort that had eaten into his face and stretched those features near to cracking. His dark eyes bored into me with the fixedness of supreme despair or of suffering. He both looked at me and did not, he saw me and did not see. His eyes were like bursting shells, strained in a transport of pain or the wild delights of inspiration.

And suddenly on those taut features there slowly spread a terrible grimace. The grimace intensified, taking in the previous madness and tension, swelling, becoming broader and broader, until it broke into a roaring, hoarse shout of laughter.

Deeply shaken, I saw how, still roaring with laughter, he slowly lifted himself up from his crouching position and, hunched like a gorilla, his hands in the torn pockets of his ragged trousers, began to run, cutting in great leaps and bounds through the rustling tinfoil of the burs—a Pan without a pipe, retreating in flight to his familiar haunts.

MR. CHARLES

Early on Saturday afternoon my Uncle Charles, a grass widower, set out for a holiday resort, an hour's walk from the city, to visit his wife and children, who were spending the summer there.

Since his wife's departure, the house had not been cleaned, the bed not made. Charles returned home late at night, battered and bruised by the nightly revels to which he succumbed under the pressure of the hot empty days. The crushed, cool, disordered bedclothes seemed like a blissful haven, an island of safety on which he succeeded in landing with the last ounce of his strength like a castaway, tossed for many days and nights on a stormy sea.

Groping blindly in the darkness, he sank between the white mounds of cool feathers and slept as he fell, across the bed or with his head downward, pushing deep into the softness of the pillows, as if in sleep he wanted to drill through, to explore completely, that powerful massif of feather bedding rising out of the night. He fought in his sleep against the bed like a bather swimming against the current, he kneaded it and molded it with his body like an enormous bowl of dough, and woke up at dawn panting, covered with sweat, thrown up on the shores of that pile of bedding which he could not master in the nightly struggle. Half-landed from the depths of unconsciousness, he still hung on to the verge of night, gasping for breath, while the bedding grew around him, swelled and fermented—and again engulfed him in a mountain of heavy, whitish dough.

He slept thus until late morning, while the pillows arranged themselves into a large flat plain on which his now quieter sleep would wander. On these white roads, he slowly returned to his senses, to daylight, to reality—and at last he opened his eyes as does a sleeping passenger when the train stops at a station.

Stale dusk filled the room with the dregs of many days of solitude and quietness. The window buzzed with the morning swarms of flies and only the curtains shone brightly. Charles yawned out of his body, out of the depth of all its cavities the remains of yesterday. The yawning was convulsive as if his body wanted to turn itself inside out. In this way he got rid of the sand and ballast, the undigested remains of the previous day.

Having thus eased himself, he wrote down his expenses in a notebook, calculated something, added it all up, and became pensive. Then he lay immobile for a long time, with glazed eyes which were the color of water, protuberant and moist. In the diffused dusk of the room, brightened by the glare of the hot day behind the curtains, his eyes, like minuscule mirrors, reflected all the shining objects: the white light of the sun in the cracks of the window, the golden rectangle of the curtains, and enclosed, like a drop of water, all the room with the stillness of its carpets and its empty chairs.

Meanwhile, the day behind the blinds resounded more and more violently with the buzzing of flies frenzied by the sun. The window could not contain this white fire and the curtains went faint from the bright undulations.

At last Charles dragged himself from the bed and sat on it for some time, groaning. Past thirty, his body was beginning to thicken. His system, swelling with fat, harassed by sexual indulgence, but still flowing with seminal juices, seemed slowly to shape, in that silence, its future destiny.

While Charles sat there in a thoughtless, vegetative stupor, completely surrendered to circulation, respiration, and the deep pulsation of his natural juices, there formed inside his perspiring body an unknown, unformulated future, like a terrible growth, pushing forth in an unknown direction. He was not afraid of it, because he already felt at one with that unknown and enormous thing which was to come, and he was growing together with it without protest, in a strange unison, numb with resigned awe, recognizing his future self in those colossal exuberances, those fantastic tumors which were maturing before his inward-turned sight. One of his eyes would then slightly squint to the outside, as if leaving for another dimension.

Afterward, he awoke from those hopeless musings, returning to the reality of the moment. He looked at his feet on the carpet, plump and delicate like a woman's, and slowly removed his gold cuff links from the cuffs of his shirt. Then he went to the kitchen and in a shady corner found a bucket of water, a round, silent, watchful mirror waiting for him—the only living and knowing thing in that empty apartment. He poured water into the basin and tasted with his skin its young, sweet, stale moisture.

He dressed with care, but without haste, with long pauses between the separate manipulations.

The rooms, empty and neglected, did not approve of him, the furniture and the walls watched him in silent criticism.

He felt, entering that stillness, like an intruder in an underwater kingdom with a different, separate notion of time.

Opening his own drawers, he felt like a thief and could not help moving on tiptoe, afraid to arouse noisy and excessive echoes that waited irritably for the chance to explode on the slightest provocation.

And finally, when after sneaking from dresser to closet, he had found piece by piece all he needed and had finished his dressing among the furniture which bore with him in silence, and was ready at last, he stood, hat in hand, feeling rather embarrassed that even at the last moment he could not find a word which would dispel that hostile silence; he then walked toward the door slowly, resignedly, hanging his head, while someone else, someone forever turning his back, walked at the same pace in the opposite direction into the depths of the mirror, through the row of empty rooms which did not exist.

CINNAMON SHOPS

At the time of the shortest, sleepy winter days, edged on both sides with the furry dusk of mornings and evenings, when the city reached out deeper and deeper into the labyrinth of winter nights, and was shaken reluctantly into consciousness by the short dawn, my father was already lost, sold and surrendered to the other sphere.

His face and head became overgrown with a wild and recalcitrant shock of gray hair, bristling in irregular tufts and spikes, shooting out from warts, from his eyebrows, from the openings of his nostrils and giving him the appearance of an old ill-tempered fox.

His sense of smell and his hearing sharpened extraordinarily and one could see from the expression of his tense silent face that through the intermediary of these two senses he remained in permanent contact with the unseen world of mouse holes, dark corners, chimney vents, and dusty spaces under the floor.

He was a vigilant and attentive observer, a prying fellow conspirator, of the rustlings, the nightly creakings, the secret gnawing life of the floor. He was so engrossed in it that he became completely submerged in an inaccessible sphere and one which he did not even attempt to discuss with us.

He often used to flip his fingers and laugh softly to himself when the manifestations of the unseen became too absurd; he then exchanged knowing looks with our cat, which, also initiated in these mysteries, would lift its cynical cold striped face, closing the slanting chinks of its eyes with an air of indifference and boredom.

It sometimes happened that, during a meal, my father would

suddenly put aside his knife and fork and, with his napkin still
tied around his neck, would rise from the table with a feline
movement, tiptoe to the door of the adjoining room, and peer
through the keyhole with the utmost caution. Then, with a
bashful smile, he would return to the table slightly embarrassed, murmuring and whispering indistinctly in tune with the
interior monologue that wholly preoccupied him.

To provide some distraction for him and to tear him away
from these morbid speculations, my mother would force him to
go out for a walk in the evenings. He went in silence, without
protest but also without enthusiasm, distrait and absent in
spirit. Once we even went all together to the theater.

We found ourselves again in that large, badly lit, dirty hall,
full of somnolent human chatter and aimless confusion. But
when we had made our way through the crowd, there emerged
before us an enormous pale blue curtain, like the sky of another
firmament. Large painted pink masks with puffed-up cheeks
floated in a huge expanse of canvas. The artificial sky spread
out in both directions, swelling with the powerful breath of
pathos and of great gestures, with the atmosphere of that fictitious floodlit world created on the echoing scaffolding of the
stage. The tremor sailing across the large area of that sky, the
breath of the vast canvas which made the masks revive and
grow, revealed the illusory character of that firmament, caused
that vibration of reality which, in metaphysical moments, we
experience as the glimmer of revelation.

The masks fluttered their red eyelids, their colored lips whispered voicelessly, and I knew that the moment was imminent
when the tension of mystery would reach its zenith and the
swollen skies of the curtain would really burst open to reveal
incredible and dazzling events.

But I was not allowed to experience that moment, because in
the meantime my father had begun to betray a certain anxiety.
He was feeling in all his pockets and at last declared that he had
left behind at home a wallet containing money and certain most
important documents.

After a short conference with my father, during which
Adela's honesty was submitted to a hasty assessment, it was

suggested that I should go home to look for the wallet. According to my mother, there was still plenty of time before the curtain rose, and, fleet-footed as I was, I had every chance of returning in time.

I stepped into a winter night bright from the illuminations of the sky. It was one of those clear nights when the starry firmament is so wide and spreads so far that it seems to be divided and broken up into a mass of separate skies, sufficient for a whole month of winter nights and providing silver and painted globes to cover all the nightly phenomena, adventures, occurrences, and carnivals.

It is exceedingly thoughtless to send a young boy out on an urgent and important errand into a night like that, because in its semiobscurity the streets multiply, becoming confused and interchanged. There open up, deep inside a city, reflected streets, streets which are doubles, make-believe streets. One's imagination, bewitched and misled, creates illusory maps of the apparently familiar districts, maps in which streets have their proper places and usual names but are provided with new and fictitious configurations by the inexhaustible inventiveness of the night. The temptations of such winter nights begin usually with the innocent desire to take a shortcut, to use a quicker but less familiar way. Attractive possibilities arise of shortening a complicated walk by taking some never-used side street. But on that occasion things began differently.

Having taken a few steps, I realized that I was not wearing my overcoat. I wanted to turn back, but after a moment that seemed to me an unnecessary waste of time, especially as the night was not cold at all; on the contrary, I could feel waves of an unseasonal warmth, like breezes of a spring night. The snow shrank into a white fluff, into a harmless fleece smelling sweetly of violets. Similar white fluffs were sailing across the sky on which the moon was doubled and trebled, showing all its phases and positions at once.

On that night the sky laid bare its internal construction in many sections, which, like quasi-anatomical exhibits, showed the spirals and whorls of light, the pale green solids of darkness, the plasma of space, the tissue of dreams.

On such a night, it was impossible to walk along Rampart Street, or any other of the dark streets which are the obverse, the lining as it were, of the four sides of Market Square, and not to remember that at that late hour the strange and most attractive shops were sometimes open, the shops which on ordinary days one tended to overlook. I used to call them cinnamon shops because of the dark paneling of their walls.

These truly noble shops, open late at night, have always been the objects of my ardent interest. Dimly lit, their dark and solemn interiors were redolent of the smell of paint, varnish, and incense; of the aroma of distant countries and rare commodities. You could find in them Bengal lights, magic boxes, the stamps of long-forgotten countries, Chinese decals, indigo, calaphony from Malabar, the eggs of exotic insects, parrots, toucans, live salamanders and basilisks, mandrake roots, mechanical toys from Nuremberg, homunculi in jars, microscopes, binoculars, and, most especially, strange and rare books, old folio volumes full of astonishing engravings and amazing stories.

I remember those old dignified merchants who served their customers with downcast eyes, in discreet silence, and who were full of wisdom and tolerance for their customers' most secret whims. But most of all, I remember a bookshop in which I once glanced at some rare and forbidden pamphlets, the publications of secret societies lifting the veil on tantalizing and unknown mysteries.

I so rarely had the occasion to visit these shops—especially with a small but sufficient amount of money in my pocket— that I could not forgo the opportunity I had now, in spite of the important mission entrusted to me.

According to my calculations I ought to turn into a narrow lane and pass two or three side streets in order to reach the street of the night shops. This would take me even farther from home, but by cutting across Saltworks Street I could make good the delay.

Lent wings by my desire to visit the cinnamon shops, I turned into a street I knew and ran rather than walked, anxious not to lose my way. I passed three or four streets, but still there was no sign of the turning I wanted. What is more, the appearance of the street was different from what I had expected. Nor was there any sign of the shops. I was in a street of houses with no doors and of which the tightly shut windows were blind from reflected moonlight. On the other side of those houses—I thought—must run the street from which they were accessible. I was walking faster now, rather disturbed, beginning to give up the idea of visiting the cinnamon shops. All I wanted now was to get out of there quickly into some part of the city I knew better. I reached the end of the street, unsure where it would lead me. I found myself in a broad, sparsely built-up avenue, very long and straight. I felt on me the breath of a wide-open space. Close to the pavement or in the midst of their gardens, picturesque villas stood there, the private houses of the rich. In the gaps between them were parks and walls of orchards. The whole area looked like Lesznianska Street in its lower and rarely visited part. The moonlight filtered through a thousand feathery clouds, like silver scales on the sky. It was pale and bright as daylight—only the parks and gardens stood black in that silvery landscape.

Looking more closely at one of the buildings, I realized that what I saw was the back of the high school, which I had never seen from that side. I was just approaching the gate which, to my surprise, was open; the entrance hall was lit. I walked in and found myself on the red carpet of the passage. I hoped to be able to slip through unobserved and come out through the front gate, thus taking a splendid shortcut.

I remembered that at that late hour there might be, in Professor Arendt's classroom, one of the voluntary classes which in winter were always held in the late evenings and to which we all flocked, fired by the enthusiasm for art which that excellent teacher had awakened in us.

A small group of industrious pupils was almost lost in the large dark hall on whose walls the enormous shadows of our heads broke abruptly, thrown by the light of two small candles set in bottles.

To be truthful, we did not draw very much during these classes and the professor was not very exacting. Some boys brought cushions from home and stretched themselves out on benches for a short nap. Only the most diligent of us gathered around the candle, in the golden circle of its light.

We usually had to wait a long while for the professor's arrival, filling the time with sleepy conversation. At last the door from his room would open and he would enter—short, bearded, given to esoteric smiles and discreet silences and exuding an aroma of secrecy. He shut the door of his study carefully behind him: through it for a brief moment we could see over his head a crowd of plaster shadows, the classical fragments of suffering. Niobides, Danaïdes, and Tantalides, the whole sad and sterile Olympus, wilting for years on end in that plaster-cast museum. The light in his room was opaque even in daytime, thick from the dreams of plaster-cast heads, from empty looks, ashen profiles, and meditations dissolving into nothingness. We liked to listen sometimes in front of that door—listen to the silence laden with the sighs and whispers of the crumbling gods withering in the boredom and monotony of their twilight.

The professor walked with great dignity and unction up and down among the half-empty benches on which, in small groups, we were drawing amidst the gray reflections of a winter night. Everything was quiet and cozy. Some of my classmates were asleep. The candles were burning low in their bottles. The professor delved into a deep bookcase, full of old folios, unfashionable engravings, woodcuts, and prints. He showed us, with his esoteric gestures, old lithographs of night landscapes, of tree clumps in moonlight, of avenues in wintry parks outlined black on the white moonlit background.

Amid sleepy talk, time passed unnoticed. It ran by unevenly, as if making knots in the passage of hours, swallowing somewhere whole empty periods. Without transition, our whole gang found ourselves on the way home long after midnight on the garden path white with snow, flanked by the black, dry thicket of bushes. We walked alongside that hairy rim of darkness, brushing against the furry bushes, their lower branches snapping under our feet in the bright night, in a false milky brightness. The diffuse whiteness of light filtered by the snow, by the pale air, by the milky space, was like the gray paper of an engraving on which the thick bushes corresponded to the deep black lines of decoration. The night was copying now, at that late hour, the nightly landscapes of Professor Arendt's engravings, reenacting his fantasies.

In the black thickets of the park, in the hairy coat of bushes, in the mass of crusty twigs there were nooks, niches, nests of deepest fluffy blackness, full of confusion, secret gestures, conniving looks. It was warm and quiet there. We sat on the soft snow in our heavy coats, cracking hazelnuts of which there was a profusion in that springlike winter. Through the copse, weasels wandered silently, martens and ichneumons, furry, ferreting elongated animals on short legs, stinking of sheepskin. We suspected that among them were the exhibits from the school cabinets which, although degutted and molting, felt on that white night in their empty bowels the voice of the eternal instinct, the mating urge, and returned to the thickets for short moments of illusory life.

But slowly the phosphorescence of the springlike snow became dulled: it vanished then, giving way to a thick black darkness preceding dawn. Some of us fell asleep in the warm snow, others went groping in the dark for the doors of their houses and walked blindly into the sleep of their parents and brothers, into a continuation of deep snoring which caught up with them on their late return.

These nightly drawing sessions held a secret charm for me, so that now I could not forgo the opportunity of looking for a moment into the art room. I decided, however, that I would not stop for more than a little while. But walking up the back stairs, their cedar wood resounding under my steps, I realized that I was in a wing of the school building completely unknown to me.

Not even a murmur interrupted the solemn silence. The passages were broader in this wing, covered with a thick carpet and most elegant. Small, darkly glowing lamps were hung at each corner. Turning the first of these, I found myself in an even wider, more sumptuous hall. In one of its walls there was a wide glass arcade leading to the interior of an apartment. I could see a long enfilade of rooms, furnished with great magnificence. The eye wandered over silk hangings, gilded mirrors, costly furniture, and crystal chandeliers and into the velvety softness of the luxurious interiors, shimmering with lights, entangled garlands, and budding flowers. The profound stillness of these empty rooms was filled with the secret glances ex-

changed by mirrors and the panic of friezes running high along
the walls and disappearing into the stucco of the white ceilings.

I faced all that magnificence with admiration and awe, guessing that my nightly escapade had brought me unexpectedly into
the headmaster's wing, to his private apartment. I stood there
with a beating heart, rooted to the spot by curiosity, ready to escape at the slightest noise. How would I justify, if surprised, that
nocturnal visit, that impudent prying? In one of those deep
plush armchairs there might sit, unobserved and still, the young
daughter of the headmaster. She might lift her eyes to mine—
black, sibylline, quiet eyes, the gaze of which none could hold.
But to retreat halfway, not having carried through the plan I
had, would be cowardly. Besides, deep silence reigned in those
magnificent interiors, lit by the hazy light of an undefined hour.
Through the arcades of the passage, I saw on the far side of the
living room a large glass door leading to the terrace. It was so
still everywhere that I felt suddenly emboldened. It did not strike
me as too risky to walk down the short steps leading to the level
of the living room, to take a few quick steps across the large,
costly carpet and to find myself on the terrace from which I
could get back without any difficulty to the familiar street.

This is what I did. When I found myself on the parquet floor
under the potted palms that reached up to the frieze of the ceiling, I noticed that now I really was on neutral ground, because
the living room did not have a front wall. It was a kind of large
loggia, connected by a few steps with a city square, an enclosed
part of the square, because some of the garden furniture stood
directly on the pavement. I ran down the short flight of stone
steps and found myself at street level once more.

The constellations in the sky stood steeply on their heads, all
the stars had made an about-turn, but the moon, buried under
the featherbed of clouds which were lit by its unseen presence,
seemed still to have before her an endless journey and, absorbed
in her complicated heavenly procedures, did not think of dawn.

A few horse-drawn cabs loomed black in the street, half-
broken and loose jointed like crippled, dozing crabs or cockroaches. A driver leaned down toward me from his high box.
He had a small red kindly face. "Shall we go, master?" he

asked. The cab shook in all the joints and ligatures of its many-limbed body and made a start on its light wheels.

But who would entrust oneself on such a night to the whims of an unpredictable cabby? Amid the click of the axles, amid the thud of the box and the roof, I could not agree with him on my destination. He nodded indulgently at everything I said and sang to himself. We drove in a circle around the city.

In front of an inn stood a group of cabbies who waved friendly hands to him. He answered gaily and then, without stopping the carriage, he threw the reins on my knees, jumped down from the box, and joined the group of his colleagues. The horse, an old wise cab horse, looked round cursorily and went on in a monotonous regular trot. In fact, that horse inspired confidence—it seemed smarter than its driver. But I myself could not drive, so I had to rely on the horse's will. We turned into a suburban street, bordered on both sides by gardens. As we advanced, these gardens slowly changed into parks with tall trees and the parks in turn into forests.

I shall never forget that luminous journey on that brightest of winter nights. The colored map of the heavens expanded into an immense dome, on which there loomed fantastic lands, oceans and seas, marked with the lines of stellar currents and eddies, with the brilliant streaks of heavenly geography. The air became light to breathe and shimmered like silver gauze. One could smell violets. From under the white woolly lambskin of snow, trembling anemones appeared with a speck of moonlight in each delicate cup. The whole forest seemed to be illuminated by thousands of lights and by the stars falling in profusion from the December sky. The air pulsated with a secret spring, with the matchless purity of snow and violets. We entered a hilly landscape. The lines of hills, bristling with the bare spikes of trees, rose like sighs of bliss. I saw on these happy slopes groups of wanderers, gathering among the moss and the bushes the fallen stars which now were damp from snow. The road became steep, the horse began to slip on it and pulled the creaking cab only with an effort. I was happy. My lungs soaked up the blissful spring in the air, the freshness of snow and stars. Before the horse's breast the rampart of white snowy foam grew

higher and higher, and it could hardly wade through that pure
fresh mass. At last we stopped. I got out of the cab. The horse
was panting, hanging its head. I hugged its head to my breast
and saw that there were tears in its large eyes. I noticed a
round black wound on its belly. "Why did not you tell me?" I
whispered, crying. "My dearest, I did it for you," the horse
said and became very small, like a wooden toy. I left him and
felt wonderfully light and happy. I was debating whether to
wait for the small local train which passed through here or to
walk back to the city. I began to walk down a steep path,
winding like a serpent amid the forest; at first in a light elastic
step; later, passing into a brisk happy run which became gradually faster, until it resembled a gliding descent on skis. I could
regulate my speed at will and change course by light movements of my body.

On the outskirts of the city, I slowed this triumphal run and
changed it into a sedate walk. The moon still rode high in the
sky. The transformations of the sky, the metamorphoses of its
multiple domes into more and more complicated configurations
were endless. Like a silver astrolabe the sky disclosed on that
magic night its internal mechanism and showed in infinite evo-
lutions the mathematics of its cogs and wheels.

In Market Square I met some people enjoying a walk. All of
them, enchanted by the displays of that night, walked with uplifted faces, silvery from the magic of the sky. I completely
stopped worrying about Father's wallet. My father, absorbed by
his manias, had probably forgotten its loss by now, and as for
my mother, I did not much care.

On such a night, unique in the year, one has happy thoughts
and inspirations, one feels touched by the divine finger of poetry. Full of ideas and projects, I wanted to walk toward my
home, but met some school friends with books under their
arms. They were on their way to school already, having been
wakened by the brightness of that night that would not end.

We went for a walk all together along a steeply falling street,
pervaded by the scent of violets; uncertain whether it was the
magic of the night which lay like silver on the snow or whether
it was the light of dawn . . .

THE STREET OF
CROCODILES

My father kept in the lower drawer of his large desk an old and beautiful map of our city. It was a whole folio sheaf of parchment pages which, originally fastened with strips of linen, formed an enormous wall map, a bird's-eye panorama.

Hung on the wall, the map covered it almost entirely and opened a wide view on the valley of the River Tysmienica, which wound itself like a wavy ribbon of pale gold, on the maze of widely spreading ponds and marshes, on the high ground rising toward the south, gently at first, then in ever tighter ranges, in a chessboard of rounded hills, smaller and paler as they receded toward the misty yellow fog of the horizon. From that faded distance of the periphery, the city rose and grew toward the center of the map, an undifferentiated mass at first, a dense complex of blocks and houses, cut by deep canyons of streets, to become on the first plan a group of single houses, etched with the sharp clarity of a landscape seen through binoculars. In that section of the map, the engraver concentrated on the complicated and manifold profusion of streets and alleyways, the sharp lines of cornices, architraves, archivolts, and pilasters, lit by the dark gold of a late and cloudy afternoon which steeped all corners and recesses in the deep sepia of shade. The solids and prisms of that shade darkly honeycombed the ravines of streets, drowning in a warm color here half a street, there a gap between houses. They dramatized and orchestrated in a bleak romantic chiaroscuro the complex architectural polyphony.

On that map, made in the style of baroque panoramas, the area of the Street of Crocodiles shone with the empty whiteness that usually marks polar regions or unexplored countries of which almost nothing is known. The lines of only a few streets were marked in black and their names given in simple, unadorned lettering, different from the noble script of the other captions. The cartographer must have been loath to include that district in the city and his reservations found expression in the typographical treatment.

In order to understand these reservations, we must draw attention to the equivocal and doubtful character of that peculiar area, so unlike the rest of the city.

It was an industrial and commercial district, its soberly utilitarian character glaringly underlined. The spirit of the times, the mechanism of economics, had not spared our city and had taken root in a sector of its periphery which then developed into a parasitical quarter.

While in the old city a nightly semiclandestine trade prevailed, marked by ceremonious solemnity, in the new district modern, sober forms of commercial endeavor had flourished at once. The pseudo-Americanism, grafted on the old, crumbling core of the city, shot up here in a rich but empty and colorless vegetation of pretentious vulgarity. One could see there cheap jerry-built houses with grotesque facades, covered with a monstrous stucco of cracked plaster. The old, shaky suburban houses had large hastily constructed portals grafted onto them which only on close inspection revealed themselves as miserable imitations of metropolitan splendor. Dull, dirty, and faulty glass panes in which dark pictures of the street were wavily reflected, the badly planed wood of the doors, the gray atmosphere of those sterile interiors where the high shelves were cracked and the crumbling walls were covered with cobwebs and thick dust, gave these shops the stigma of some wild Klondike. In row upon row there spread tailors' shops, general outfitters, china shops, drugstores, and barbers' saloons. Their large gray display windows bore slanting semicircular inscriptions in thick gilt letters:

CONFISERIE, MANUCURE, KING OF ENGLAND.

The old established inhabitants of the city kept away from that area where the scum, the lowest orders had settled—creatures without character, without background, moral dregs, that inferior species of human being which is born in such ephemeral communities. But on days of defeat, in hours of moral weakness, it would happen that one or another of the city dwellers would venture half by chance into that dubious district. The best among them were not entirely free from the temptation of voluntary degradation, of breaking down the barriers of hierarchy, of immersion in that shallow mud of companionship, of easy intimacy, of dirty intermingling. The district was an El Dorado for such moral deserters. Everything seemed suspect and equivocal there, everything promised with secret winks, cynical stressed gestures, raised eyebrows, the fulfillment of impure hopes, everything helped to release the lowest instincts from their shackles.

Only a few people noticed the peculiar characteristics of that district: the fatal lack of color, as if that shoddy, quickly growing area could not afford the luxury of it. Everything was gray there, as in black-and-white photographs or in cheap illustrated catalogs. This similarity was real rather than metaphorical because at times, when wandering in those parts, one in fact gained the impression that one was turning the pages of a prospectus, looking at columns of boring commercial advertisements, among which suspect announcements nestled like parasites, together with dubious notices and illustrations with a double meaning. And one's wandering proved as sterile and pointless as the excitement produced by a close study of pornographic albums.

If one entered, for example, a tailor's shop to order a suit—a suit of cheap elegance characteristic of the district—one found that the premises were large and empty, the rooms high and colorless. Enormous shelves rose in tiers into the undefined height of the room and drew one's eyes toward the ceiling which might be the sky—the shoddy, faded sky of that quarter. On the other hand, the storerooms, which could be seen through the open door, were stacked high with boxes and crates—an enormous filing cabinet rising to the attic to disintegrate into the geometry of emptiness, into the timbers of a void. The large gray windows, ruled like the pages of a ledger, did not admit daylight yet the shop was filled with a watery anonymous gray light which did not throw shadows and did not stress anything. Soon, a slender young man appeared, astonishingly servile, agile, and compliant, to satisfy one's requirements and to drown one in the smooth flow of his cheap sales talk. But when, talking all the time, he unrolled an enormous piece of cloth, fitting, folding, and draping the stream of material, forming it into imaginary jackets and trousers, that whole manipulation seemed suddenly unreal, a sham comedy, a screen ironically placed to hide the true meaning of things.

The tall dark salesgirls, each with a flaw in her beauty (appropriately for that district of remaindered goods), came and went, stood in the doorways watching to see whether the business entrusted to the experienced care of the salesman had reached a suitable point. The salesman simpered and pranced around like a transvestite. One wanted to lift up his receding chin or pinch his pale powdered cheek as with a stealthy meaningful look he discreetly pointed to the trademark on the material, a trademark of transparent symbolism.

Slowly the selection of the suit gave place to the second stage of the plan. The effeminate and corrupted youth, receptive to the client's most intimate stirrings, now put before him a selection of the most peculiar trademarks, a whole library of labels, a cabinet displaying the collection of a sophisticated connoisseur. It then appeared that the outfitter's shop was only a facade behind which there was an antique shop with a collection of highly questionable books and private editions. The servile salesman opened further storerooms, filled to the ceiling with books, drawings, and photographs. These engravings and etchings were beyond our boldest expectations: not even in our dreams had we anticipated such depths of corruption, such varieties of licentiousness.

The salesgirls now walked up and down between the rows of books, their faces, like gray parchment, marked with the dark greasy pigment spots of brunettes, their shiny dark eyes shooting out sudden zigzag cockroachy looks. But even their dark blushes, the piquant beauty spots, the traces of down on their upper lips betrayed their thick, black blood. Their overintense coloring, like that of an aromatic coffee, seemed to stain the books which they took into their olive hands, their touch seemed to run on the pages and leave in the air a dark trail of freckles, a smudge of tobacco, as does a truffle with its exciting, animal smell.

In the meantime, lasciviousness had become general. The salesman, exhausted by his eager importuning, slowly withdrew into feminine passivity. He now lay on one of the many sofas which stood between the bookshelves, wearing a pair of deeply cut silk pajamas. Some of the girls demonstrated to one another the poses and postures of the drawings on the book jackets, while others settled down to sleep on makeshift beds. The pressure on the client had eased. He was now released from the circle of eager interest and left more or less alone. The salesgirls, busy talking, ceased to pay any attention to him. Turning their backs on him they adopted arrogant poses, shifting their weight from foot to foot, making play with their frivolous footwear, abandoning their slim bodies to the serpentine movements of their limbs and thus laid siege to the excited onlooker whom they pretended to ignore behind a show of assumed indifference. This retreat was calculated to involve the guest more deeply, while appearing to leave him a free hand for his own initiative.

But let us take advantage of that moment of inattention to escape from these unexpected consequences of an innocent call at the tailor's, and slip back into the street.

No one stops us. Through the corridors of books, from between the long shelves filled with magazines and prints, we make our way out of the shop and find ourselves in that part of the Street of Crocodiles where from the higher level one can see almost its whole length down to the distant, as yet unfinished buildings of the railway station. It is, as usual in that district, a gray day, and the whole scene seems at times like a photograph in an illustrated magazine, so gray, so one-dimensional are the houses, the people, and the vehicles. Reality is as thin as paper and betrays with all its cracks its imitative character. At times one has the impression that it is only the small section immediately before us that falls into the expected pointillistic picture of a city thoroughfare, while on either side the improvised masquerade is already disintegrating and, unable to endure, crumbles behind us into plaster and sawdust, into the storeroom of an enormous empty theater. The tenseness of an artificial pose, the assumed earnestness of a mask, an ironical pathos tremble on this facade.

But far be it from us to wish to expose this sham. Despite our better judgment we are attracted by the tawdry charm of the district. Besides, that pretense of a city has some of the features of self-parody. Rows of small one-story suburban houses alternate with many-storied buildings which, looking as if made of cardboard, are a mixture of blind office windows, of gray-glassed display windows, of fasciae of advertisements and numbers. Among the houses the crowds stream by. The street is as broad as a city boulevard, but the roadway is made, like village squares, of beaten clay, full of puddles and overgrown with grass. The street traffic of that area is a byword in the city; all its inhabitants speak about it with pride and a knowing look. That gray, impersonal crowd is rather self-conscious of its role, eager to live up to its metropolitan aspirations. All the same, despite the bustle and sense of purpose, one has the impression of a monotonous aimless wandering, of a sleepy procession of puppets. An atmosphere of strange insignificance pervades the scene. The crowd flows lazily by and, strange to say, one can see it only indistinctly; the figures pass in gentle disarray, never reaching complete sharpness of outline. Only at times do we catch among the turmoil of many heads a dark vivacious look, a black bowler hat worn at an angle, half a face split by a smile formed by lips which had just finished speaking, a foot thrust forward to take a step and fixed forever in that position.

A peculiarity of that district are the cabs, without coachmen, driving along unattended. It is not as if there were no cabbies, but mingling with the crowd and busy with a thousand affairs of their own, they do not bother about their carriages. In that area of sham and empty gestures no one pays much attention to the precise purpose of a cab ride and the passengers entrust

themselves to these erratic conveyances with the thoughtlessness which characterizes everything here. From time to time
one can see them at dangerous corners, leaning far out from under the broken roof of a cab as, with the reins in their hands,
they perform with some difficulty the tricky maneuver of over-
taking.

There are also trams here. In them the ambition of the city
councillors has achieved its greatest triumph. The appearance of
these trams, though, is pitiful, for they are made of papier-
mâché with warped sides dented from the misuse of many years.
They often have no fronts, so that in passing one can see the passengers, sitting stiffly and behaving with great decorum. These
trams are pushed by the town porters. The strangest thing of all
is, however, the railway system in the Street of Crocodiles.

Occasionally, at different times of day toward the end of the
week, one can see groups of people waiting at a crossroads for
a train. One is never sure whether the train will come at all or
where it will stop if it does. It often happens, therefore, that
people wait in two different places, unable to agree where the
stop is. They wait for a long time standing in a black, silent
bunch alongside the barely visible lines of the track, their faces
in profile: a row of pale cutout paper figures, fixed in an expression of anxious peering.

At last the train suddenly appears: one can see it coming
from the expected side street, low like a snake, a miniature
train with a squat puffing locomotive. It enters the black corridor, and the street darkens from the coal dust scattered by the
line of carriages. The heavy breathing of the engine and the
wave of a strange sad seriousness, the suppressed hurry and excitement transform the street for a moment into the hall of a
railway station in the quickly falling winter dusk.

A black market in railway tickets and bribery in general are
the special plagues of our city.

At the last moment, when the train is already in the station, negotiations are conducted in nervous haste with corrupt railway
officials. Before these are completed, the train starts, followed
slowly by a crowd of disappointed passengers who accompany
it a long way down the line before finally dispersing.

The street, reduced for a moment to form an improvised station filled with gloom and the breath of distant travel, widens out again, becomes lighter and again allows the carefree crowds of chattering passersby to stroll past the shop windows—those dirty gray squares filled with shoddy goods, tall wax dummies, and barber's dolls.

Showily dressed in long lace-trimmed gowns, prostitutes have begun to circulate. They might even be the wives of hairdressers or restaurant bandleaders. They advance with a brisk rapacious step, each with some small flaw in her evil corrupted face; their eyes have a black, crooked squint, or they have harelips, or the tips of their noses are missing.

The inhabitants of the city are quite proud of the odor of corruption emanating from the Street of Crocodiles. "There is no need for us to go short of anything," they say proudly to themselves, "we even have truly metropolitan vices." They maintain that every woman in that district is a tart. In fact, it is enough to stare at any of them, and at once you meet an insistent clinging look which freezes you with the certainty of fulfillment. Even the schoolgirls wear their hair ribbons in a characteristic way and walk on their slim legs with a peculiar step, an impure expression in their eyes that foreshadows their future corruption.

And yet, and yet—are we to betray the last secret of that district, the carefully concealed secret of the Street of Crocodiles?

Several times during our account we have given warning signals, we have intimated delicately our reservations. An attentive reader will therefore not be unprepared for what is to follow. We spoke of the imitative, illusory character of that area, but these words have too precise and definite a meaning to describe its half-baked and undecided reality.

Our language has no definitions which would weigh, so to speak, the grade of reality, or define its suppleness. Let us say it bluntly: the misfortune of that area is that nothing ever succeeds there, nothing can ever reach a definite conclusion. Gestures hang in the air, movements are prematurely exhausted and cannot overcome a certain point of inertia. We have already noticed the great bravura and prodigality in intentions, projects, and anticipations which are one of the characteristics of the district. It is in fact no more than a fermentation of desires, prematurely aroused and therefore impotent and empty. It is an atmosphere of excessive facility, every whim flies high, a passing excitement swells into an empty parasitic growth; a light gray vegetation of fluffy weeds, of colorless poppies sprouts forth, made from a weightless fabric of nightmares and hashish. Over the whole area there floats the lazy licentious smell of sin, and the houses, the shops, the people seem sometimes no more than a shiver on its feverish body, the gooseflesh of its febrile dreams. Nowhere as much as there do we feel threatened by possibilities, shaken by the nearness of fulfillment, pale and faint with the delightful rigidity of realization. And that is as far as it goes.

Having exceeded a certain point of tension, the tide stops and begins to ebb, the atmosphere becomes unclear and troubled, possibilities fade and decline into a void, the crazy gray poppies of excitement scatter into ashes.

We shall always regret that, at a given moment, we have left the slightly dubious tailor's shop. We shall never be able to find it again. We shall wander from shop sign to shop sign and make a thousand mistakes. We shall enter scores of shops, see many which are similar. We shall wander along shelves upon shelves of books, look through magazines and prints, confer intimately and at length with young women of imperfect beauty, with an excessive pigmentation who yet would not be able to understand our requirements.

We shall get involved in misunderstandings until all our fever and excitement have spent themselves in unnecessary effort, in futile pursuit.

Our hopes were a fallacy, the suspicious appearance of the premises and of the staff were a sham, the clothes were real clothes, and the salesman had no ulterior motives. The women of the Street of Crocodiles are depraved to only a modest extent, stifled by thick layers of moral prejudice and ordinary banality. In that city of cheap human material no instincts can flourish, no dark and unusual passions can be aroused.

The Street of Crocodiles was a concession of our city to modernity and metropolitan corruption. Obviously, we were unable to afford anything better than a paper imitation, a montage of illustrations cut out from last year's moldering newspapers.

COCKROACHES

It happened during the period of gray days that followed the splendid colorfulness of my father's heroic era. These were long weeks of depression, heavy weeks without Sundays or holidays, under closed skies in an impoverished landscape. Father was then no more with us. The rooms on the upper floor had been tidied up and let to a lady telephone operator. From the bird estate only one specimen remained, the stuffed condor that now stood on a shelf in the living room. In the cool twilight of drawn curtains, it stood there as it did when it was alive, on one foot, in the pose of a Buddhist sage, its bitter dried-up ascetic face petrified in an expression of extreme indifference and abnegation. Its eyes had fallen out and sawdust scattered from the washed-out tear-stained sockets. Only the pale blue horny Egyptian protuberances on the powerful beak and the bald neck gave that senile head a solemnly hieratic air.

Its coat of feathers was in many places moth-eaten and it shed soft, gray down, which Adela swept away once a week together with the anonymous dust of the room. Under the bald patches one could see thick canvas sacking from which tufts of hemp were coming out.

I had a hidden resentment against my mother for the ease with which she had recovered from Father's death. She had never loved him, I thought, and as Father had not been rooted in any woman's heart, he could not merge with any reality and was therefore condemned to float eternally on the periphery of life, in half-real regions, on the margins of existence. He could not even earn an honest citizen's death, everything about him had to be odd and dubious. I decided at an appropriate moment to force my mother into a frank conversation. On that day (it was a heavy winter day and from early morning the light had been dusky and diffused) Mother was suffering from a migraine and was lying down on the sofa in the drawing room.

In that rarely visited, festive room exemplary order had reigned since Father's death, maintained by Adela with the help of wax and polish. The chairs all had antimacassars; all the objects had submitted to the iron discipline which Adela exercised over them. Only a sheaf of peacock's feathers standing in a vase on a chest of drawers did not submit to regimentation. These feathers were a dangerous, frivolous element, hiding rebelliousness, like a class of naughty schoolgirls who are quiet and composed in appearance, but full of mischief when no longer watched. The eyes of those feathers never stopped staring; they made holes in the walls, winking, fluttering their eyelashes, smiling to one another, giggling and full of mirth. They filled the room with whispers and chatter; they scattered like butterflies around the many-armed lamps; like a motley crowd they pushed against the matted, elderly mirrors, unused to such bustle and gaiety; they peeped through the keyholes. Even in the presence of my mother, lying on the sofa with a bandage round her head, they could not restrain themselves; they made signs, speaking to each other in a deaf-and-dumb language full of secret meaning. I was irritated by that mocking conspiracy hatched behind my back. With my knees pressed against Mother's sofa, absentmindedly touching with two fingers the delicate fabric of her housecoat, I said lightly:

"I have been wanting to ask you for a long time: it is he, isn't it?"

And, although I did not point to the condor even with my eyes, Mother guessed at once, became embarrassed and cast down her eyes. I let the silence drag on for a long moment in order to savor her confusion, and then very calmly, controlling my rising anger, I asked her:

"What is the meaning then of all the stories and the lies which you are spreading about Father?"

But her features, which at first contracted in panic, composed themselves again.

"What lies?" she asked, blinking her eyes, which were empty, filled with dark azure without any white.

"I heard about them from Adela," I said, "but I know that they come from you; and I want to know the truth."

Her lips trembled lightly, she avoided looking me in the eye, her pupils wandering into the corners of her eyes.

"I was not lying," she said and her lips swelled but at the same time became smaller. I felt she was being coy, like a woman with a strange man. "What I said about the cockroaches is true; you yourself must remember . . . ."

I was disconcerted. I did remember the invasion of cockroaches, the black swarm which had nightly filled the darkness with a spidery running. All cracks in the floors were full of moving whispers, each crevice suddenly produced a cockroach, from every chink would shoot a crazy black zigzag of lightning. Ah, that wild lunacy of panic, traced in a shiny black line on the floor! Ah, those screams of horror which my father emitted, leaping from one chair to another with a javelin in his hand!

Refusing all food and drink, with fever patches on his cheeks, with a grimace of revulsion permanently fixed around his mouth, my father had grown completely wild. It was clear that no human body could bear for long such a pitch of hatred. A terrible loathing had transformed his face into a petrified tragic mask, in which the pupils, hidden behind the lower lids, lay in wait, tense as bows, in a frenzy of permanent suspicion. With a wild scream he would suddenly jump up from his seat, run blindly to a corner of the room and stab downward with the javelin, then lift it, having impaled an enormous cockroach that desperately wriggled its tangle of legs. Adela would then come to the rescue and take the lance with its trophy from Father, now pale and faint with horror, and shake it off into a bucket. But even at the time, I could not tell whether these pictures were implanted in my mind by Adela's tales or whether I had witnessed them myself. My father at the time no longer possessed that power of resistance which protects healthy people from the fascination of loathing. Instead of fighting against the terrible attraction of that fascination, my father, a prey to madness, became completely subjected to it. The fatal consequences were quick to follow. Soon, the first suspicious symptoms appeared, filling us with fear and sadness. Father's behavior changed. His madness, the euphoria of his excitement wore off. In his gestures and expressions signs of a bad conscience began to show. He took to avoiding us. He hid, for days on end, in corners, in wardrobes, under the eiderdowns. I saw him sometimes looking pensively at his own hands, examining the consistency of skin and nails, on which black spots began to appear like the scales of a cockroach.

In daytime he was still able to resist with such strength as remained in him, and fought his obsession, but during the night it took hold of him completely. I once saw him late at night, in the light of a candle set on the floor. He lay on the floor naked, stained with black totem spots, the lines of his ribs heavily outlined, the fantastic structure of his anatomy visible through the skin; he lay on his face, in the grip of the obsession of loathing which dragged him into the abyss of its complex paths. He moved with the many-limbed, complicated movements of a strange ritual in which I recognized with horror an imitation of the ceremonial crawl of a cockroach.

From that day on we gave Father up for lost. His resemblance to a cockroach became daily more pronounced—he was being transformed into one.

We got used to it. We saw him ever more rarely, as he would disappear for weeks on end on his cockroachy paths. We ceased to recognize him; he merged completely with that black, uncanny tribe. Who could say whether he continued to live in some crack in the floor, whether he ran through the rooms at night absorbed in cockroachy affairs, or whether perhaps he was one of those dead insects which Adela found every morning lying on their backs with their legs in the air and which she swept up into a dustpan to burn later with disgust?

"And yet," I said, disconcerted, "I am sure that this condor is he."

My mother looked at me from under her eyelashes.

"Don't torture me, darling; I have told you already that Father is away, traveling all over the country: he now has a job as a commercial traveler. You know that he sometimes comes home at night and goes away again before dawn."

THE GALE

During that long and empty winter, darkness in our city reaped an enormous, hundredfold harvest. The attics and storage rooms had been left cluttered up for too long, with old pots and pans stacked one on top of another, and batteries of discarded empty bottles.

There, in those charred, many-raftered forests of attics, darkness began to degenerate and ferment wildly. There began the black parliaments of saucepans, those verbose and inconclusive meetings, those gurglings of bottles, those stammerings of flagons. Until one night the regiments of saucepans and bottles rose under the empty roofs and marched in a great bulging mass against the city.

The attics, now freed from their clutter, opened up their expanses; through their echoing black aisles ran cavalcades of beams, formations of wooden trestles, kneeling on their knees of pine, now at last freed to fill the night with a clatter of rafters and the crash of purlins and crossbeams.

Then the black rivers of tubs and watercans overflowed and swept through the night. Their black, shining, noisy concourse beseiged the city. In the darkness that mob of receptacles swarmed and pressed forward like an army of talkative fishes, a boundless invasion of garrulous pails and voluble buckets.

Drumming on their sides, the barrels, buckets, and watercans rose in stacks, the earthenware jars gadded about, the old bowlers and opera hats climbed one on top of another, growing toward the sky in pillars only to collapse at last.

And all the while their wooden tongues rattled clumsily, while they ground out curses from their wooden mouths, and spread blasphemies of mud over the whole area of the night, until at last these blasphemies achieved their object.

Summoned by the creaking of utensils, by their fulsome chatter, there arrived the powerful caravans of wind and dominated the night. An enormous black moving amphitheater formed high above the city and began to descend in powerful spirals. The darkness exploded in a great stormy gale and raged for three days and three nights . . .

"You won't go to school today," said my mother in the morning, "there's a gale blowing."

A delicate veil of resin-scented smoke filled the room. The stove roared and whistled, as if a whole pack of hounds or demons were held captive in it. The large face painted on its protruding belly made colorful grimaces and its cheeks swelled dramatically.

I ran barefoot to the window. The sky was swept lengthwise by the gusts of the wind. Vast and silvery white, it was cut into lines of energy tensed to breaking point, into awesome furrows like strata of tin and lead. Divided into magnetic fields and trembling with discharges, it was full of concealed electricity. The diagrams of the gale were traced on it which, itself unseen and elusive, loaded the landscape with its power.

One could not see the gale. One could recognize its effect on the houses, on the roofs under which its fury penetrated. One after the other, the attics seemed to loom larger and to explode in madness when touched by its finger.

It swept the squares clean, leaving behind it a white emptiness in the streets; it denuded the whole area of the marketplace. Only here and there a lonely man, bent under the force of the wind, could be seen clinging to the corner of a house. The whole market square seemed to shine like a bald head under the powerful gusts of wind.

The gale blew cold and dead colors onto the sky—streaks of green, yellow, and violet—the distant vaults and arcades of its spirals. The roofs loomed black and crooked, apprehensive and expectant. Those under which the wind had already penetrated rose in inspiration, outgrew the neighboring roofs, and prophesied doom under the unkempt sky. Then they fell and expired, unable to hold any longer the powerful breath which then moved further along and filled the whole space with noise and terror. And yet more houses rose with a scream, in a paroxysm of prediction, and howled disaster.

The enormous beech trees around the church stood with their arms upraised, like witnesses of terrifying visions, and screamed and screamed.

Farther along, beyond the roofs of Market Square, I saw the gable ends and the naked walls of suburban houses. They climbed one over the other and grew, paralyzed with fear. The distant cold red glare painted them in autumnal colors.

We did not have our midday meal that day because the fire in the range belched circles of smoke into the kitchen. All the rooms were cold and smelled of wind. About two o'clock in the afternoon a fire broke out in the suburbs and spread rapidly. My mother and Adela began to pack our bedding, fur coats, and valuables.

Night came. The wind intensified in force and violence, grew immeasurably and filled the whole area. It had now stopped visiting the houses and roofs, and had started to build a many-storied multilevel spiral over the city, a black maze, growing relentlessly upward. From that maze it shot out along galleries of rooms, raced amid claps of thunder through long corridors and then allowed all those imaginary structures to collapse, spreading out and rising into the formless stratosphere.

Our rooms trembled gently, the pictures rattled on the walls, the windowpanes shone with the greasy reflection of the lamp. The curtains swelled with the breath of that stormy night. We suddenly remembered that we had not seen Father since the morning. He must have gone out very early to the shop, where the gale had probably surprised him and cut him off from home.

"He will not have had anything to eat all day," Mother wailed. The senior shop assistant, Theodore, volunteered to venture into the windswept night, to take some food to Father. My brother decided to go with him.

Wrapped in large bearskin coats, they filled their pockets

with flat irons and brass pestles, metal ballast to prevent them from being blown away by the gale. The door leading into the night was opened cautiously. No sooner had Theodore and my brother taken one step into the darkness, than they were swallowed up by the night on the very threshold of the house. The wind immediately washed away all traces of their departure. From the window one could not see the light of the lantern which they had taken.

Having swallowed them, the wind quietened down for a while. Adela and Mother again tried to light a fire in the kitchen range. All the matches went out and through the opened access door ashes and soot were blown all over the room. We stood behind the front door of the house and listened. In the lament of the gale one could hear all kinds of voices, questions, calls and cries. We imagined that we could hear Father, lost in the gale, calling for help, or else that it was my brother and Theodore chatting unconcernedly outside the door. The sounds were so deceptive that Adela opened the door at one point and in fact saw Theodore and my brother just emerging, with great effort, from the gale in which they had sunk up to their armpits.

They came in panting and closed the door with difficulty behind them. For a moment they had to lean against it, so strong was the storming of the wind at the entrance. At last they got the door bolted and the wind continued its chase elsewhere.

They spoke almost incoherently of the terrible darkness, of the gale. Their fur coats, soaked with wind, now smelled of the open air. They blinked in the light; their eyes, still full of night, spilled darkness at each flutter of the eyelids. They could not reach the shop, they said; they had lost their way and hardly knew how to get back; the city was unrecognizable and all the streets looked as if they had been displaced.

My mother suspected that they were not telling the truth. In fact we all had the impression that they had perhaps stood under our windows for a few minutes without attempting to go anywhere. Or perhaps the city and the marketplace had ceased to exist, and the gale and the night had surrounded our house with dark stage props and some machinery to imitate the howling, whistling, and groaning? Perhaps these enormous and mournful spaces suggested by the wind did not exist, perhaps there were no vast labyrinths, nor spirals, no windowed corridors to form a long black flute on which the wind played its tunes? We were increasingly inclined to think that the gale was only an invention of the night, a poor representation on a confined stage of the tragic immensity, the cosmic homelessness and loneliness of the wind.

Our front door now opened time after time to admit visitors wrapped tightly in capes and shawls. A breathless neighbor or friend would slowly shed his outer wrappings and throw out confused and unconnected words which fantastically exaggerated the dangers of the night.

We all sat together in the brightly lit kitchen. Behind the kitchen range and the black broad eaves of the chimney, a few steps led to the attic door. On these steps Theodore now sat, listening to the attic shaking in the wind. He heard how, during the pauses between gusts, the bellows of the rafters folded themselves into pleats and the roof hung limply like an enormous lung from which air had escaped; then again how it inhaled, stretched out the rafters, grew like a Gothic vault and resounded like the box of an enormous double bass.

And then we forgot the gale. Adela started pounding cinnamon in a mortar. Aunt Perasia had come to call. Small, vivacious, and very active, with the lace of her black shawl on her head, she began to bustle about the kitchen, helping Adela, who by then had plucked a cockerel. Aunt Perasia put a handful of paper in the grate and lit it. Adela grasped the cockerel by its neck, and held it over the flames to scorch off the remaining feathers. The bird suddenly spread its wings in the fire, crowed once and was burned. At that Aunt Perasia began to shout and curse. Trembling with anger, she shook her fists at Adela and at Mother. I could not understand what it was all about, but she persisted in her anger and became one small bundle of gestures and imprecations. It seemed that in her paroxysm of fury she might disintegrate into separate gestures, that she would divide into a hundred spiders, would spread out over the floor in a black, shimmering net of crazy running cockroaches. Instead,

she began suddenly to shrink and dwindle, still shaking and
spitting curses. And then she trotted off, hunched and small,
into a corner of the kitchen where we stacked the firewood and,
cursing and coughing, began feverishly to rummage among the
sonorous wood until she found two thin, yellow splinters. She
grabbed them with trembling hands, measured them against her
legs, then raised herself on them as if they were stilts and began
to walk about, clattering on the floor, jumping here and there
across the slanting lines of the floorboards, quicker and quicker,
until she finished up on a pine bench, whence she climbed on
the shelf with the crockery, a tinkling wooden shelf running the
whole length of the kitchen wall. She ran along it on her stilts
and shrank away into a corner. She became smaller and smaller,
black and folded like a wilted, charred sheet of paper, oxidized
into a petal of ash, disintegrating into dust and nothingness.

We all stood helpless in the face of this display of self-
destructive fury. With regret we observed the sad course of the
paroxysm and with some relief returned to our occupations
when the lamentable process had spent itself.

Adela clanked the mortar again, pounding cinnamon; Mother
returned to her interrupted conversation; and Theodore, listening to the prophecies in the attic, made comical faces, lifting his
eyebrows and softly chuckling to himself.

THE NIGHT OF THE
GREAT SEASON

Everyone knows that in a run of normal uneventful years that great eccentric, Time, begets sometimes other years, different, prodigal years which—like a sixth, smallest toe—grow a thirteenth freak month.

We use the word "freak" deliberately, because the thirteenth month only rarely reaches maturity, and like a child conceived late in its mother's life, it lags behind in growth; it is a hunchback month, a half-witted shoot, more tentative than real.

What is at fault is the senile intemperance of the summer, its lustful and belated spurt of vitality. It sometimes happens that August has passed, and yet the old thick trunk of summer continues by force of habit to produce and from its moldered wood grows those crablike weed days, sterile and stupid, added as an afterthought; stunted, empty, useless days—white days, permanently astonished and quite unnecessary. They sprout, irregular and uneven, formless and joined like the fingers of a monster's hand, stumps folded into a fist.

There are people who liken these days to an apocrypha, put secretly between the chapters of the great book of the year; to palimpsests, covertly included between its pages; to those white, unprinted sheets on which eyes, replete with reading and the remembered shapes of words, can imagine colors and pictures, which gradually become paler and paler from the blankness of the pages, or can rest on their neutrality before continuing the quest for new adventures in new chapters.

Ah, that old, yellowed romance of the year, that large, crumbling book of the calendar! It lies forgotten somewhere in the archives of Time, and its content continues to increase between the boards, swelling incessantly from the garrulity of months, from the quick self-perpetuation of lies, of drivel, and of dreams which multiply in it. Ah, when writing down these tales, revising the stories about my father on the used margins of its text, don't I, too, surrender to the secret hope that they will merge imperceptibly with the yellowing pages of that most splendid, moldering book, that they will sink into the gentle rustle of its pages and become absorbed there?

The events I am now going to relate happened in that thirteenth, supernumerary, freak month of that year, on those blank pages of the great chronicles of the calendar.

The mornings were strangely refreshing and tart. From the quietened and cooler flow of time, from the completely new smell in the air, from the different consistency of the light, one could recognize that one had entered a new series of days, a new era of the Lord's Year.

Voices trembled under these new skies resonantly and lightly, as in a new and still-empty house which smells of varnish and paint, of things begun and not yet used. With a strange emotion one tried out new echoes, one bit into them with curiosity as, on a cool and sober morning on the eve of a journey, one bites into a fresh, still warm currant loaf.

My father was again sitting at the back of his shop, in a small, low room divided like a beehive into many cells of file boxes from which endless layers of paper, letters and invoices, overflowed. From the rustle of sheets, from the ceaseless turning over of pages, arose the squared empty existence of that room; the constant moving of files of innumerable letters with business headings created in the stuffy air an apotheosis, a bird's-eye mirage of an industrial city, bristling with smoky chimneys, surrounded by a row of medals, and with a clasp formed from the curves and flourishes of a proud "& Co."

There my father would sit, as if in an aviary, on a high stool; and the lofts of filing cabinets rustled with piles of paper and all the pigeonholes filled with the twitter of figures.

The depth of the large shop became, from day to day, darker and richer, with stocks of cloth, serge, velvet, and cord. On the somber shelves, those granaries and silos, the cool, felted fabrics matured and yielded interest. The powerful capital of autumn multiplied and mellowed. It grew and ripened and spread, ever wider, until the shelves resembled the rows of some great amphitheater. It was augmented daily by new loads of goods brought in crates and bales in the cool of the morning on the broad, bearlike shoulders of groaning, bearded porters who exuded an aura of autumn freshness mixed with vodka. The shop assistants unpacked these new supplies and filled with their rich, drapery colors, as with putty, all the holes and cracks of the tall cupboards. They ran the gamut of all the autumn shades and went up and down through the octaves of color. Beginning at the bottom, they tried shyly and plaintively the contralto semitones, passed on to the washed-out grays of distance, to tapestry blues and, going upward in ever-broader chords, reached deep, royal blues, the indigo of distant forests and the plush of rustling parks, in order to enter, through the ochers, reds, tans, and sepias, the whispering shadows of wilting gardens, and to reach finally the dark smell of fungi, the waft of mold in the depth of autumn nights and the dull accompaniment of the darkest basses.

My father walked along these arsenals of autumn goods and calmed and soothed the rising force of these masses of cloth, the power of the season. He wanted to keep intact for as long as possible those reserves of stored color. He was afraid to break into that iron fund of autumn, to change it into cash. Yet, at the same time, he knew and felt that soon an autumn wind would come, a devastating wind which would blow through the cupboards; that they would give way; that nothing would check the flood, and that the streams of color would engulf the whole city.

The time of the Great Season was approaching. The streets were getting busy. At six in the evening the city became feverish, the houses stood flushed, and people walked about made up in bright colors, illuminated by some interior fire, their eyes shining with a festive fever, beautiful yet evil.

In the side streets, in quiet backwaters fleeing into the night, the city was empty. Only children were out under the balconies of the small squares, playing breathlessly, noisily, and nonsensically.

They put small balloons to their lips and filled them with air, in order to transform themselves into red and crowing cockerels, colored autumnal masks fantastic and absurd. It seemed that thus swollen and crowing, they would begin to float in the air in long colored chains and fly over the city like migrating birds—fantastic flotillas of tissue paper and autumn weather. Or else they pushed one another on small clattering carts, which played tunes with their little rattling wheels, axles and shafts. Filled with their happy cries the carts rolled down the street to the broadly spreading, evening yellow river where they disintegrated into a jumble of discs, pegs, and sticks.

And while the children's games became increasingly noisier and more complicated, while the city's flushes darkened into purple, the whole world suddenly began to wilt and blacken and exude an uncertain dusk which contaminated everything. Treacherous and poisonous, the plague of dusk spread, passed from one object to another, and everything it touched became black and rotten and scattered into dust. People fled before it in silent panic, but the disease always caught up with them and spread in a dark rash on their foreheads. Their faces disappeared under large, shapeless spots. They continued on their way, now featureless, without eyes, shedding as they walked one mask after another, so that the dusk became filled with the discarded larvae dropped in their flight. Then a black, rotting bark began to cover everything in large putrid scabs of darkness. And while down below everything disintegrated and changed into nothingness in that silent panic of quick dissolution, above there grew and endured the alarum of sunset, vibrating with the tinkling of a million tiny bells set in motion by the rise of a million unseen larks flying together into the enormous silvery infinite. Then suddenly night came, a vast night, growing vaster from the pressure of great gusts of wind. In its multiple labyrinths nests of brightness were hewn: the shops—large colored lanterns—filled with goods and the bustle of customers. Through the bright glass of these lanterns the noisy and strangely ceremonial rites of autumn shopping could be observed.

The great undulating autumn night, with the shadows rising

in it and the winds broadening it, hid in its folds pockets of brightness, the motley wares of street traders—chocolates, biscuits, exotic sweets. Their kiosks and barrows, made from empty boxes, papered with advertisements, full of soap, of gay trash, of gilded nothings, of tinfoil, trumpets, wafers, and colored mints, were stations of lightheartedness, outposts of gaiety, scattered on the hangings of the enormous, labyrinthine, wind-shaken night.

The dense crowd sailed in darkness, in loud confusion, with the shuffle of a thousand feet, in the chatter of a thousand mouths—a disorderly, entangled migration proceeding along the arteries of the autumnal city. Thus flowed that river, full of noise, of dark looks, of sly winks, intersected by conversations, chopped up by laughter, an enormous babel of gossip, tumult, and chatter.

It seemed as if a mob of dry poppy heads, scattering their seeds—rattleheads—was on the march.

My father, his cheeks flushed, his eyes shining, walked up and down his festively lit shop; excited, listening intently.

Through the glass panes of the shop window and of the door the distant hubbub of the city, the drone of wandering crowds could be heard. Above the stillness of the shop, an oil lamp hung from the high ceiling, expelling the shadows from all the remote nooks and crannies. The empty floor cracked in the silence and added up in the light, crosswise and lengthwise, its shining parquet squares. The large tiles of this chessboard talked to each other in tiny dry crackles, and answered here and there with a louder knock. The pieces of cloth lay quiet and still in their felty fluffiness and exchanged looks along the walls behind my father's back, passing silent signs of agreement from cupboard to cupboard.

Father was listening. In the silence of the night his ear seemed to grow larger and to reach out beyond the window: a fantastic coral, a red polypus watching the chaos of the night.

He listened and heard with growing anxiety the distant tide of the approaching crowds. Fearfully he looked around the empty shop, searching for his assistants. Unfortunately those dark and red-haired administering angels had flown away somewhere. Father was alone, terrified of the crowd which was soon to flood the calm of the shop in a plundering, noisy mob; to divide among themselves and put up to auction the whole rich autumn which he had collected over the years and stored in his large secluded silo.

Where were the shop assistants? Where were those handsome cherubs who had been entrusted with the defense of the dark bastions of cloth? My father thought with painful suspicion that perhaps they were somewhere in the depths of the building with other men's daughters. Standing immobile and anxious, his eyes shining in the lamplit silence of the shop, he heard with his inner ear what was happening inside the house, in the back chambers of that large colored lantern. The house opened before him, room after room, chamber after chamber, like a house of cards, and he saw the shop assistants chasing Adela through all the empty brightly lit rooms, upstairs and downstairs, until she escaped them and reached the kitchen to barricade herself there behind the kitchen dresser.

There Adela stood, panting, amused, smiling to herself, her long lashes fluttering. The shop assistants were giggling, crouched behind the door. The kitchen window was open onto the black night, saturated with dreams and complications. The dark, half-opened panes shone with the reflections of a distant illumination. The gleaming saucepans and jars stood immobile on all sides and glinted with their thick glaze. Adela leaned cautiously from the window her brightly made-up face with the fluttering eyes. She looked for the shop assistants in the dark courtyard, sensing an ambush. And then she saw them, advancing slowly and carefully toward her in single file, along the narrow ledge under the window which ran the length of the wall, now red from the glare of distant lights. My father shouted in anger and desperation, but at that very moment the hubbub of voices drew much nearer and the shop window became peopled with faces crooked with laughter, with chattering mouths, with noses flattened on the shining panes. My father grew purple with anger and jumped on the counter. And while the crowd stormed his fortress and entered his shop in a noisy mass, Father, in one leap, reached the shelves of fabrics and, hanging high above the crowd, began to blow with all his strength a large shofar, sounding the alert. But the ceiling did not resound with the rustle of angels' wings speeding to his rescue: instead, each plaint of the shofar was answered by the loud, sneering choir of the crowd.

"Jacob, start trading! Jacob, start selling!" they called and the chant, repeated over and over again, became rhythmical, transforming itself into the melody of a chorus, sung by them all. My father saw that resistance would be useless, jumped down from his ledge, and moved with a shout toward the barricades of cloth. Grown tall with fury, his head swollen into a purple fist, he rushed like a fighting prophet on the ramparts of cloth and began to storm against them. He leaned with his whole strength against the enormous bales, heaving them from their places. He put his shoulders under the great lengths of cloth and made them fall on the counter with a dull thud. The bales overturned, unfolding in the air like enormous flags, the shelves exploded with bursts of draperies, with waterfalls of fabrics as if touched by the wand of Moses.

The reserves from the cupboard poured out and flowed in a broad relentless stream. The colorful contents of the shelves spread and multiplied, covering all the counters and tables.

The walls of the shop disappeared under the powerful formations of that cosmogony of cloth, under its mountain ranges that rose in imposing massifs. Wide valleys opened up between the slopes, and lines of continents loomed up from the pathos of broad plains. The interior of the shop formed itself into the panorama of an autumn landscape, full of lakes and distance. Against that backdrop my father wandered among the folds and valleys of a fantastic Canaan. He strode about, his hands spread out prophetically to touch the clouds, and shaped the land with strokes of inspiration.

And down below, at the bottom of that Sinai which rose from my father's anger, stood the gesticulating crowd, cursing, worshipping Baal, and bargaining. They dipped their hands into the soft folds of fabric, they draped themselves into colored cloth, they wrapped improvised cloaks around themselves, and talked incoherently and without cease.

My father would suddenly appear over a group of customers, increased in stature by his anger, to thunder against the idolaters with great and powerful words. Then, driven to despair, he would climb again on the high galleries of the cupboards, and run crazily along the ledges and shelves, on the resounding boards of the bare scaffolding, pursued by visions of the shameless lust which, he felt, was being given full rein behind his back. The shop assistants had just reached the iron balcony, level with the window and, clinging to the railings, they grabbed Adela by the waist and pulled her away from the window. She still fluttered her eyelids and dragged her slim, silk-stockinged legs behind her.

When my father, horrified by the hideousness of sin, merged his angry gestures with the awe-inspiring landscape, the carefree worshippers of Baal below him gave themselves up to unbridled mirth. An epidemic of laughter took hold of that mob. How could one expect seriousness from that race of rattles and nutcrackers! How could one demand understanding for my father's stupendous worries from these windmills, incessantly grinding words to a colored pulp! Deaf to the thunder of Father's prophetic wrath, those traders in silk kaftans crouched in small groups around the piles of folded material gaily discussing, amid bursts of laughter, the qualities of the goods. These black-clad merchants with their rapid tongues obscured the noble essence of the landscape, diminished it by the hash of words, almost engulfed it.

In other places in front of the waterfalls of light fabrics stood groups of Jews in colored gaberdines and tall fur hats. These were the gentlemen of the Great Congregation, distinguished and solemn men, stroking their long well-groomed beards and holding sober and diplomatic discourse. But even in those ceremonial conversations, in the looks which they exchanged, glimmers of smiling irony could be detected. Around these groups milled the common crowd, a shapeless mob without face or individuality. It somehow filled the gaps in the landscape, it littered the background with the bells and rattles of its thoughtless chatter. These were the jesters, the dancing crowd of Harlequins and Pulcinellas who, without any serious business intentions themselves, made by their clownish tricks a mockery of the negotiations starting here and there.

Gradually, however, tired of jokes, this merry mob scattered to the farthest points of the landscape and there slowly lost itself among the rocky crags and valleys. Probably one by one those jesters sank into the cracks and folds of the terrain, like children tired of playing who disappear during a party into the corners and back rooms of the festive house.

Meanwhile, the fathers of the city, members of the Great Sanhedrin, walked up and down in dignified and serious groups, and led earnest discussion in undertones. Having spread themselves over the whole extensive mountain country, they wandered in twos and threes on distant and circuitous roads. Their short dark silhouettes peopled the desert plateau over which hung a dark and heavy sky, full of clouds, cut into long parallel furrows, into silvery white streaks, showing in its depth ever more distant strata of air.

The lamplight created an artificial day in that region—a strange day, a day without dawn or dusk.

My father slowly quietened down. His anger composed itself and cooled under the calming influence of the landscape. He was now sitting in a gallery of high shelves and looking at the vast autumnal country. He saw people fishing in distant lakes. In their tiny shell-like boats fishermen, two to a boat, dipped their nets in the water. On the banks, boys were carrying on their heads baskets full of flapping silvery catches.

And then he noticed that groups of wanderers in the distance were lifting their faces to the sky, pointing to something with upraised hands.

And soon the sky came out in a colored rash, in blotches which grew and spread, and was filled with a strange tribe of birds, circling and revolving in great crisscrossing spirals. Their lofty flight, the movement of their wings, formed majestic scrolls that filled the silent sky. Some of them, enormous storks, floated almost immobile on calmly spread wings; others, resembling colored plumes or barbarous trophies, had to flap their wings heavily and clumsily to maintain height upon the current of warm air; still others, formless conglomerations of wings, of powerful legs and bare necks, were like badly stuffed vultures and condors from which the sawdust was spilling.

There were among them two-headed birds and birds with many wings, there were cripples too, limping through the air in one-winged, awkward flight. The sky now resembled those in old murals, full of monsters and fantastic beasts, which circled around, passing and eluding each other in elliptical maneuvers.

My father rose on his perch and, in a sudden glare of light, stretched out his hands, summoning the birds with an old incantation. He recognized them with deep emotion. They were the distant, forgotten progeny of that generation of birds which at one time Adela had chased away to all four points of the sky. That brood of freaks, that malformed, wasted tribe of birds, was now returning degenerated or overgrown. Nonsensically large, stupidly developed, the birds were empty and lifeless inside. All their vitality went into their plumage, into external adornment. They were like exhibits of extinct species in a museum, the lumber room of a birds' paradise.

Some of them were flying on their backs, had heavy misshapen beaks like padlocks, were blind, or were covered with curiously colored lumps. How moved my father was by this unexpected return, how he marveled at the instinct of these birds, at their attachment to the Master, whom that expelled tribe had preserved in their soul like a legend, in order to return to their ancient motherland after numerous generations, on the last day before the extinction of the tribe.

But these blind birds made of paper could not recognize my father. In vain did he call them with the old formulas, in the forgotten language of the birds—they did not hear him nor see him.

All of a sudden, stones began to whistle through the air. The merrymakers, the stupid, thoughtless people had begun to throw them into the fantastic bird-filled sky.

In vain did Father warn them, in vain did he entreat them with magical gestures—he was not heard, nor heeded. The birds began to fall. Hit by stones, they hung heavily and waited while still in the air. Even before they crashed to the ground, they were a formless heap of feathers.

In a moment, the plateau was strewn with strange, fantastic carrion. Before my father could reach the place of slaughter, the once-splendid birds were dead, scattered all over the rocks.

Once now, from nearby, did Father notice the wretchedness of that wasted generation, the nonsense of its second-rate anatomy. They had been nothing but enormous bunches of feathers, stuffed carelessly with old carrion. In many of them one could not recognize where the heads had been, for that misshapen part of their bodies was unmarked by the presence of a soul. Some were covered with a curly matted fur, like bison, and stank horribly. Others reminded one of hunchbacked, bald, dead camels. Others still must have been made of a kind of cardboard, empty inside but splendidly colored on the outside. Some of them proved at close quarters to be nothing more than large peacocks' tails, colorful fans, into which by some obscure process a semblance of life had been breathed.

I saw my father's unhappy return. The artificial day became slowly tinted with the colors of an ordinary morning. In the deserted shop, the highest shelves were bathed in the reflections of the morning sky. Amid the fragments of the extinct landscape, among the ruined background of scenery of the night, Father saw his shop assistants awakening from sleep. They rose from among the bales of cloth and yawned toward the sun. In the kitchen, on the floor above, Adela, warm from sleep and with unkempt hair, was grinding coffee in a mill which she pressed to her white bosom, imparting her warmth to the broken beans. The cat was washing itself in the sunlight.

THE COMET

That year the end of the winter stood under the sign of particularly favorable astronomical aspects. The predictions in the calendar flourished in red in the snowy margins of the mornings. The brighter red of Sundays and holy days cast its reflection on half the week and these weekdays burned coldly, with a freak, rapid flame. Human hearts beat more quickly for a moment, misled and blinded by the redness, which, in fact, announced nothing—being merely a premature alert, a colorful lie of the calendar, painted in bright cinnabar on the jacket of the week. From Twelfth Night onward, we sat night after night over the white parade ground of the table gleaming with candlesticks and silver, and played endless games of patience. Every hour, the night beyond the windows became lighter, sugar-coated and shiny, filled with sprouting almonds and sweetmeats. The moon, that most inventive transmogrifier, wholly engrossed in her lunar practices, accomplished her successive phases and grew continually brighter and brighter. Already by day, the moon stood in the wings, prematurely ready for her cue, brassy and lusterless. Meanwhile whole flocks of feather clouds passed like sheep across her profile on their silent white extensive wandering, barely covering her with the shimmering mother-of-pearl scales into which the firmament froze toward the evening.

Later on, the pages of days turned emptily. The wind roared over the roofs, blew through the cold chimneys to the very hearths, built over the city imaginary scaffoldings and grandstands, and then destroyed these resounding air-filled structures with a clatter of planks and beams. Sometimes, a fire would start in a distant suburb. The chimney sweeps explored the city at roof level among the gables under a gaping verdigris sky. Climbing from one foothold to another, on the weather vanes and flagpoles, they dreamed that the wind would open for them for a moment the lids of roofs over the alcoves of young girls and close them again immediately on the great stormy book of the city—providing them with breathtaking reading matter for many days and nights.

Then the wind grew weary and blew itself out. The shop assistants dressed the shop window with spring fabrics and soon the air became milder from the soft colors of these woolens. It turned lavender blue, it flowered with pale reseda. The snow shrank, folded itself up into an infant fleece, evaporated drily into the air, drunk by the cobalt breezes, and was absorbed again by the vast sunless and cloudless sky. Oleanders in pots began to flower here and there inside the houses, windows remained open for longer, and the thoughtless chirping of sparrows filled the room, dreaming in the dull blue day. Over the cleanly swept squares, tomtits and chaffinches clashed for a moment in violent skirmishes with an alarming twittering, and then scattered in all directions, blown away by the breeze, erased, annihilated in the empty azure. For a second, the eyes held the memory of colored speckles—a handful of confetti flung blindly into the air—then they dissolved in the fundus of the eye.

The premature spring season began. The lawyers' apprentices twirled their mustaches, turning up the ends, wore high stiff collars, and were paragons of elegance and fashion. On days hollowed out by winds as by a flood, when gales roared high above the city, the young lawyers greeted the ladies of their acquaintance from a distance, doffing their somber-colored bowler hats and leaning their backs against the wind so that their coattails opened wide. They then immediately averted their eyes, with a show of self-denial and delicacy so as not to expose their beloved to unnecessary gossip. The ladies momentarily lost the ground under their feet, exclaimed with alarm amid their billowing skirts, and, regaining their balance, returned the greeting with a smile.

In the afternoon the wind would sometimes calm down. On the balcony Adela began to clean the large brass saucepans that clattered metallically under her touch. The sky stood immobile over the shingle roofs, stock-still, then folded itself into blue streaks. The shop assistants, sent over from the shop on errands, lingered endlessly by Adela on the threshold of the kitchen, propped against the balcony rails, drunk from the day-long wind, confused by the deafening twitter of sparrows. From the distance, the breeze brought the faint chorus of a barrel organ. One could not hear the soft words which the young men sang in undertones, with an innocent expression but which in fact were meant to shock Adela. Stung to the quick, she would react violently, and, most indignant, scold them angrily, while her face, gray and dulled from early spring dreams, would flush with anger and amusement. The men lowered their eyes with assumed innocence and wicked satisfaction at having succeeded in upsetting her.

Days and afternoons came and went, everyday events streamed in confusion over the city seen from the level of our balcony, over the labyrinth of roofs and houses bathed in the opaque light of those gray weeks. The tinkers rushed around, shouting their wares. Sometimes Abraham's powerful sneeze gave comical emphasis to the distant, scattered tumult of the city. In a faraway square the mad Touya, driven to despair by the nagging of small boys, would dance her wild saraband, lifting high her skirt to the amusement of the crowd. A gust of wind smoothed down and leveled out these sounds, melted them into the monotonous, gray din, spreading uniformly over the sea of shingle roofs in the milky, smoky air of the afternoon. Adela, leaning against the balcony rails, bent over the distant, stormy roar of the city, caught from it all the louder accents and, with a smile, put together the lost syllables of a song, trying to join them, to read some sense into the rising and falling gray monotony of the day.

It was the age of electricity and mechanics and a whole swarm of inventions was showered on the world by the resourcefulness of human genius. In middle-class homes cigar sets appeared equipped with an electric lighter: you pressed a switch and a sheaf of electric sparks lit a wick soaked in petrol. The inventions gave rise to exaggerated hopes. A musical box in the shape of a Chinese pagoda would, when wound, begin to play a little rondo while turning like a merry-go-round. Bells tinkled at intervals, the doors flapped wide to show the turning barrel playing a snuffbox triolet. In every house electric bells were installed. Domestic life stood under the sign of galvanism. A spool of insulated wire became the symbol of the times. Young dandies demonstrated Galvani's invention in living rooms and were rewarded with radiant looks from the ladies. An electric conductor opened the way to women's hearts. After an experiment had succeeded, the heroes of the day blew kisses all round, amid the applause of the living rooms.

It was not long before the city filled with velocipedes of various sizes and shapes. An outlook based on philosophy became obligatory. Whoever admitted to a belief in progress had to draw the logical conclusion and ride a velocipede. The first to do so were of course the lawyers' apprentices, that vanguard of new ideas, with their waxed mustaches and their bowler hats, the hope and flower of youth. Pushing through the noisy mob, they rode through the traffic on enormous bicycles and tricycles which displayed their wire spokes. Placing their hands on wide handlebars, they maneuvered from the high saddle the enormous hoop of the wheel and cut into the amused mob in a wavy line. Some of them succumbed to apostolic zeal. Lifting themselves on their moving pedals, as if on stirrups, they addressed the crowd from on high, forecasting a new happy era for mankind—salvation through the bicycle . . . And they rode on amid the applause of the public, bowing in all directions.

And yet there was something grievously embarrassing in those splendid and triumphal rides, something painful and unpleasant, which even at the summit of their success threatened to disintegrate into parody. They must have felt it themselves when, hanging like spiders among the delicate machinery, straddled on their pedals like great jumping frogs, they performed ducklike movements above the wide turning wheels. Only a step divided them from ridicule and they took it with despair, leaning over the handlebars and redoubling the speed of their ride, in a tangle of violent head-over-heels gymnastics. Can one wonder? Man was entering under false pretenses the sphere of incredible facilities, acquired too cheaply, below cost price, almost for nothing, and the disproportion between outlay and gain, the obvious fraud on nature, the excessive payment for a trick of genius, had to be offset by self-parody. The cyclist rode on among elemental outbursts of laughter—miserable victors, martyrs to their genius—so great was the comic appeal of these wonders of technology.

When my brother brought an electromagnet for the first time home from school, when with a shiver we all sensed by touch the vibrations of the mysterious life enclosed in an electric circuit, my father smiled a superior smile. A long-range idea was maturing in his mind; there merged and forged a chain of ideas he had had for a long time. Why did Father smile to himself, why did his eyes turn up, misty, in a parody of mock admiration? Who can tell? Did he foresee the coarse trick, the vulgar intrigue, the transparent machinations behind the amazing manifestations of the secret force? Yet that moment marked a turning point: it was then that Father began his laboratory experiments.

Father's laboratory equipment was simple: a few spools of wire, a few bottles of acid, zinc, lead, and carbon—these constituted the workshop of that very strange esoterist. "Matter," he said, modestly lowering his eyes and stifling a cough, "Matter, gentlemen—" He did not finish his sentence, he left his listeners guessing that he was about to expose a big swindle, that all we who sat there were being taken for a ride. With downcast eyes my father quietly sneered at that agelong fetish. "*Panta rei!*" he exclaimed, and indicated with a movement of his hands the eternal circling of substance. For a long time he had wanted to mobilize the forces hidden in it, to make its stiffness melt, to pave its way to universal penetration, to transfusion, to universal circulation in accordance with its true nature.

"*Principium individuationis*—my foot," he used to say, thus expressing his limitless contempt for that guiding human principle. He threw out these words in passing, while running from wire to wire. He half-closed his eyes and touched delicately

various points of the circuit, feeling for the slight differences in
potential. He made incisions in the wire, leaned over it, listening, and immediately moved ten steps farther, to repeat the
same gestures at another point of the circuit. He seemed to have
a dozen hands and twenty senses. His brittle attention wandered to a hundred places at once. No point in space was free
from his suspicions. He leaned over to pierce the wire at some
place and then, with a sudden jump backward, he pounced at
another like a cat on its prey and, missing, became confused. "I
am sorry," he would say, addressing himself unexpectedly to
the astonished onlooker. "I am sorry, I am concerned with that
section of space which you are filling. Couldn't you move a little to one side for a minute?" And he quickly made some lightning measurements, agile and nimble as a canary twitching
efficiently under the impulses of its sympathetic system.

The metals dipped in acid solutions, salty and rusting in that
painful bath, began to conduct in darkness. Awakened from
their stiff lifelessness, they hummed monotonously, sang metallically, shone molecularly in the incessant dusk of those mournful and late days. Invisible charges rose in the poles and
swamped them, escaping into the circling darkness. An imper-
ceptible tickling, a blind prickly current traversed the space po-
larized into concentric lines of energy, into circles and spirals of
a magnetic field. Here and there an awakened apparatus would
give out signals, another would reply a moment later, out of
turn, in hopeless monosyllables, dash-dot-dash in the intervals
of a dull lethargy. My father stood among those wandering currents, a smile of suffering on his face, impressed by that stam-
mering articulation, by the misery, shut in once and for all,
irrevocably, which was monotonously signaling in crippled half
syllables from the unliberated depths.

As a consequence of these researches, my father achieved
amazing results. He proved, for instance, that an electric bell,
built on the principle of Neeff's hammer, is an ordinary mystification. It was not man who had broken into the laboratory of
nature, but nature that had drawn him into its machinations,
achieving through his experiments its own obscure aims. During dinner my father would touch the nail of his thumb with the

handle of a spoon dipped in soup, and suddenly Neeff's bell would begin to rattle inside the lamp. The whole apparatus was quite superfluous, quite unnecessary: Neef's bell was the point of convergence of certain impulses of matter, which used man's ingenuity for its own purposes. It was nature that willed and worked, man was nothing more than an oscillating arrow, the shuttle of a loom, darting here or there according to nature's will. He was himself only a component, a part of Neeff's hammer.

Somebody once mentioned "mesmerism" and my father took this up too, immediately. The circle of his theories had closed, he had found the missing link. According to his theory, man was only a transit station, a temporary junction of mesmeric currents, wandering hither and thither within the lap of eternal matter. All the inventions in which he took such pride were traps into which nature had enticed him, were snares of the unknown. Father's experiments began to acquire the character of magic and legerdemain, of a parody of juggling. I won't mention the numerous experiments with pigeons, which, by manipulating a wand, he multiplied into two, four, or ten, only to enclose them, with visible effort, back again into the wand. He would raise his hat and out they flew fluttering, one by one, returning to reality in their full complement and settling on the table in a wavy, mobile, cooing heap. Sometimes Father interrupted himself at an unexpected point of the experiment, stood up undecided, eyes half-closed, and, after a second, ran with tiny steps to the entrance hall where he put his head into the chimney shaft. It was dark there, bleak from soot, cozy as in the very center of nothingness, and warm currents of air streamed up and down. Father closed his eyes and stayed there for a time in that warm, black void. We all felt that the incident had little to do with the matters at hand, that it somehow occurred at the backstage of things; we inwardly shut our eyes to that marginal fact which belonged to quite a different dimension.

My father had in his repertoire some really depressing tricks that filled one with true melancholy. We had in our dining room a set of chairs with tall backs, beautifully carved in the realistic manner into garlands of leaves and flowers; it was enough for

Father to flip the carvings and they suddenly acquired an exceptionally witty physiognomy; they began to grimace and wink significantly. This could become extremely embarrassing, almost unbearable, for the winking took on a wholly definite direction, an irresistible inevitability, and one or another of those present would suddenly exclaim: "Aunt Wanda, by God, Aunt Wanda!" The ladies began to scream for it really was Aunt Wanda's true image; it was more than that—it was she herself on a visit, sitting at table and engaging in never-ending discourses during which one could never get a word in edgewise. Father's miracles canceled themselves out automatically, for he did not produce a ghost but the real Aunt Wanda in all her ordinariness and commonness, which excluded any thought of a possible miracle.

Before we relate the other events of that memorable winter, we might shortly mention a certain incident which has been always hushed up in our family. What exactly had happened to Uncle Edward? He came at that time to stay with us, unsuspecting, in sparkling good health and full of plans, having left his wife and small daughter in the country. He just came in the highest of spirits, to have a little change and some fun away from his family. And what happened? Father's experiments made a tremendous impression on him. After the first few tricks, he got up, took off his coat, and placed himself entirely at Father's disposal. Without reservations! He said this with a piercing direct look and stressed it with a strong and earnest handshake. My father understood. He made sure that Uncle had no traditional prejudices regarding *principium individuationis*. It appeared that he had none, none at all. Uncle had a progressive mind and no prejudices. His only passion was to serve Science.

At first Father left him a degree of freedom. He was making preparations for a decisive experiment. Uncle Edward took advantage of his leisure to explore the city. He bought himself a bicycle of imposing dimensions and rode it around Market Square, looking from the height of his saddle into the windows of first-floor apartments. Passing our house, he would elegantly lift his hat to the ladies standing in the window. He had a twirled, upturned mustache and a small pointed beard. Soon, however, Uncle discovered that a bicycle could not introduce him into the deeper secrets of mechanics, that that astonishing machine was unable to provide lasting metaphysical thrills. And then the experiments began, based on the *principium individuationis*. Uncle Edward had no objections at all to being physically reduced, for the benefit of Science, to the bare principle of Neeff's hammer. He agreed without regret to a gradual shedding of all his characteristics in order to lay bare his deepest self, in harmony, as he had felt for a long time, with that very principle.

Having shut himself in his study, Father began the gradual penetration into Uncle Edward's complicated essence by a tiring psychoanalysis that lasted for many days and nights. The table of the study began to fill with the isolated complexes of Edward's ego. At first Uncle, although much reduced, turned up for meals and tried to take part in our conversations. He also went once more for a ride on his bicycle, but soon gave it up as he felt rather incomplete. A kind of shame took hold of him, characteristic for the stage at which he found himself. He began to shun people. At the same time, Father was getting ever nearer to his objective. He had reduced Uncle to the indispensable minimum, by removing from him one by one all the inessentials. He placed him high in a wall recess in the staircase, arranging his elements in accordance with the principle of Leclanche's reaction. The wall in that place was moldy and white mildew showed on it. Without any scruples Father took advantage of the entire stock of Uncle's enthusiasm, he spread his flex along the length of the entrance hall and the left wing of the house. Armed with a pair of steps he drove small nails into the wall of the dark passage, along the whole path of Uncle's present existence. Those smoky, yellow afternoons were almost completely dark. Father used a lighted candle with which he illuminated the mildewy wall at close quarters, inch by inch. I have heard it said that at the last moment Uncle Edward, until then heroically composed, showed a certain impatience. They say that there was even a violent, although belated, explosion that very nearly ruined the almost completed work. But the installation was ready and Uncle Edward, who all his life had been a model husband, father, and businessman, eventually submitted with dignity to his final role.

Uncle functioned excellently. There was no instance of his refusal to obey. Having discarded his complicated personality, in which at one time he had lost himself, he found at last the purity of a uniform and straightforward guiding principle to which he was subjected from now on. At the cost of his complexity, which he could manage only with difficulty, he had now achieved a simple problem-free immortality. Was he happy? One would ask that question in vain. A question like this makes sense only when applied to creatures who are rich in alternative possibilities, so that the actual truth can be contrasted with partly real probabilities and reflect itself in them. But Uncle Edward had no alternatives; the dichotomy "happy/unhappy" did not exist for him because he had been completely integrated. One had to admit to a grudging approval when one saw how punctually, how accurately he was functioning. Even his wife, Aunt Teresa, who followed him to our city, could not stop herself from pressing the button quite often, in order to hear that loud and sonorous sound in which she recognized the former timbre of her husband's voice in moments of irritation. As to their daughter, Edy, one might say that she was fascinated by her father's career. Later, it is true, she took it out on me, avenging my father's action, but that is part of a different story.

2

The days passed, the afternoons grew longer: there was nothing to do in them. The excess of time, still raw, still sterile and without use, lengthened the evenings with empty dusks. Adela, after washing up early and clearing the kitchen, stood idly on the balcony looking vacantly at the pale redness of the evening distance. Her beautiful eyes, so expressive at other times, were blank from dull reveries, protruding, large, and shining. Her complexion, at the end of winter matted and gray from kitchen smells, now, under the influence of the springward gravitation

of the moon, which was waxing from quarter to quarter, became younger, acquired milky reflexes, opaline shades, and the
glaze of enamel. She now had the whip hand over the shop assistants, who cringed under her dark looks, discarded the role
of would-be cynics, frequenters of city taverns and other places
of ill repute and, enraptured by her new beauty, sought a different method of approach, ready to make concessions toward
putting the relationship on a new basis and to recognize positive facts.

Father's experiments did not, in spite of expectations, produce any revolution in the life of the community. The grafting
of mesmerism on the body of modern physics did not prove fertile. It was not because there was no grain of truth in Father's
discoveries. But truth is not a decisive factor for the success of
an idea. Our metaphysical hunger is limited and can be satisfied
quickly. Father was just standing on the threshold of new revelations when we, the ranks of his adherents and followers, began to succumb to discouragement and anarchy. The signs of
impatience became more and more frequent: there were even
open protestations. Our nature rebelled against the relaxation
of fundamental laws; we were fed up with miracles and wished
to return to the old, familiar, solid prose of the eternal order.
And Father understood this. He understood that he had gone
too far, and put a rein on the flight of his fancies. The circle of
elegant female disciples and male followers with waxed mustaches began to melt away day by day. Father, wishing to withdraw with honor, was intending to give a final concluding
lecture, when suddenly a new event turned everybody's attention in a completely unexpected direction.

One day my brother, on his return from school, brought the
improbable and yet true news of the imminent end of the world.
We asked him to repeat it, thinking that we had misheard. We
hadn't. This is what that incredible, that completely baffling
piece of news was: unready and unfinished, just as it was, at a
random point in time and space, without closing its accounts,
without having reached any goal, in midsentence as it were,
without a period or exclamation mark, without a last judgment
or God's wrath—in an atmosphere of friendly understanding,

loyally, by mutual agreement and in accordance with rules observed by both parties—the world was to be hit on the head, simply and irrevocably. No. It was not to be an eschatological, tragic finale as forecast long ago by the prophets, nor the last act of the *Divine Comedy*. No. It was to be a trick cyclist's, a prestidigitator's, end of the world, splendidly hocus-pocus and bogus experimental—accompanied by the plaudits of all the spirits of Progress. There was almost no one to whom the idea would not appeal. The frightened, the protesters, were immediately hushed up. Why did not they understand that this was a simply incredible chance, the most progressive, freethinking end of the world imaginable, in line with the spirit of the times, an honorable end, a credit to the Supreme Wisdom? People discussed it with enthusiasm, drew pictures *ad oculos* on pages torn from pocket notebooks, provided irrefutable proofs, knocking their opponents and the skeptics out of the ring. In illustrated journals whole-page pictures began to appear, drawings of the anticipated catastrophe with effective staging. These usually represented panic-stricken populous cities under a night sky resplendent with lights and astronomical phenomena. One saw already the astonishing action of the distant comet, whose parabolic summit remained in the sky in immobile flight, still pointing toward the earth, and approaching it at a speed of many miles per second. As in a circus farce, hats and bowlers rose into the air, hair stood on end, umbrellas opened by themselves, and bald patches were disclosed under escaping wigs— and above it all there spread a black enormous sky, shimmering with the simultaneous alert of all the stars.

Something festive had entered our lives, an eager enthusiasm. An importance permeated our gestures and swelled our chests with cosmic sighs. The earthy globe seethed at night with a solemn uproar from the unanimous ecstasy of thousands. The nights were black and vast. The nebulae of stars around the earth became more numerous and denser. In the dark interplanetary spaces these stars appeared in different positions, strewing the dust of meteors from abyss to abyss. Lost in the infinite, we had almost forsaken the earthy globe under our feet; we were disoriented, losing our bearings; we hung head down like antipodes over the upturned zenith and wandered over the starry heaps, moving a wetted finger across maps of the sky, from star to star. Thus we meandered in extended, disorderly, single file, scattering in all directions on the rungs of the infinite ladders of the night—emigrants from the abandoned globe, plundering the immense ant heap of stars. The last barriers fell, the cyclists rode into stellar space, rearing on their vehicles, and were perpetuated in an immobile flight in the interplanetary vacuum, which revealed ever new constellations. Thus circling on an endless track, they marked the paths or a sleepless cosmography, while in reality, black as soot, they succumbed to a planetary lethargy, as if they had put their heads into the fireplace, the final goal of all those blind flights.

After short, incoherent days, partly spent in sleeping, the nights opened up like an enormous, populated motherland. Crowds filled the streets, turned out in public squares, head close to head, as if the top of a barrel of caviar had been removed and it was now flowing out in a stream of shiny buckshot, a dark river under a pitch black night noisy with stars. The stairs broke under the weight of thousands, at all the upper floor windows little figures appeared, matchstick people jumping over the rails in a moonstruck fervor, making living chains, like ants, living structures and columns—one astride another's shoulders—flowing down from windows to the platforms of squares lit by the glare of burning tar barrels.

I must beg forgiveness if in describing these scenes of enormous crowds and general uproar I tend to exaggerate, modeling myself unwittingly on certain old engravings in the great book of disasters and catastrophes of the human species. But they all create a pre-image and the megalomanic exaggeration, the enormous pathos of all these scenes proved that we had removed the bottom of the eternal barrel of memories, of an ultrabarrel of myth, and had broken into a prehuman night of untamed elements, of incoherent anamnesis, and could not hold back the swelling flood. Ah, these nights filled with stars shimmering like fish scales! Ah, these banks of mouths incessantly swallowing in small gulps, in hungry drafts, the swelling undrunk streams of those dark rain-drenched nights! In what fatal

nets, in what miserable trammels did those multiplicated generations end?

O skies of those days, skies of luminous signals and meteors,
covered by the calculations of astronomers, copied a thousand
times, numbered, marked with the watermarks of algebra!
With faces blue from the glory of those nights, we wandered
through space pulsating from the explosions of distant suns, in
a sidereal brightness—human ants, spreading in a broad heap
on the sandbanks of the Milky Way spilled over the whole
sky—a human river overshadowed by the cyclists on their spidery machines. O stellar arena of night, scarred by the evolu-
tions, spirals and leaps of those nimble riders; O cycloids and
epicycloids executed in inspiration along the diagonals of the
sky, amid lost wire spokes, hoops shed with indifference, to
reach the bright goal denuded, with nothing but the pure idea
of cycling! From these days dates a new constellation, the thirteenth group of stars, included forever in the zodiac and resplendent since then in the firmament of our nights: THE
CYCLIST.

The houses, wide open at night during that time, remained
empty in the light of violently flickering lamps. The curtains
blew out far into the night and the rows of rooms stood in an
all-embracing, incessant draft, which shot through them in violent, relentless alarm. It was Uncle Edward sounding the alert.
Yes, at last he had lost patience, cut off his bonds, trod down
the categorical imperative, broken away from the rigors of high
morals, and sounded the alarm. One tried to silence him with
the help of a long stick, one put kitchen rags to stop the violent
explosions of sound. But even gagged in this way he never
stopped agitating, he rang madly, without respite, without heed
that his life was flowing away from him in the continuous rattling, that he was bleeding white in everybody's sight, beyond
help, in a fatal frenzy.

Occasionally someone would rush into the empty rooms
pierced by that devilish ringing under the glowing lamps, take a
few hesitant steps on tiptoe, and stop abruptly as if looking for
something. The mirrors took him speechlessly into their transparent depths and divided him in silence between themselves.

Uncle Edward was ringing to high heaven through all these bright and empty rooms. The lonely deserter from the stars, conscience stricken, as if he had come to commit an evil deed, retreated stealthily from the apartment, deafened by the constant ringing. He went to the front door accompanied by the vigilant mirrors which let him through their shiny ranks, while into their depth there tiptoed a swarm of doubles with fingers to their lips.

Again the sky opened above us with its vastness strewn with stellar dust. In that sky, at an early hour of each night appeared that fatal comet, hanging aslant, at the apex of its parabola, aiming unerringly at the earth and swallowing many miles per second. All eyes were directed at him, while he, shining metallically, oblong in shape, slightly brighter in his protuberant middle, performed his daily work with mathematical precision. How difficult it was to believe that that small worm, innocently glowing among the innumerable swarms of stars, was the fiery finger from Belshazzar's feast, writing on the blackboard of the sky the perdition of our globe. But every child knew by heart the fatal formula expressed in the logarithm of a multiple integer, from which our inescapable destruction would result. What was there to save us?

While the mob scattered in the open, losing itself under the starry lights and celestial phenomena, my father remained stealthily at home. He was the only one who knew a secret escape from our trap, the back door of cosmology. He smiled secretly to himself. While Uncle Edward, choked with rags, was desperately sounding the alarm, Father silently put his head into the chimney shaft of the stove. It was black and quiet there. It smelled of warm air, of soot, of silence, of stillness. Father made himself comfortable and sat blissfully, his eyes closed. Into that black carapace of the house, emerging over the roof into the starry night, there entered the frail light of a star and breaking as if in the glass of a telescope lit a spark in the hearth, a tiny seed in the dark retort of the chimney. Father was slowly turning the screw of a microscope and the fatal creation, bright like the moon, brought near to arm's length by the lens, plastic and shining with a limestone relief in the silent blackness of planetary

emptiness, moved into the field of vision. It was slightly scrofu-
lous, somewhat pockmarked—that brother of the moon, his
lost double, returning after a thousand years of wandering to
the motherland of the earth. My father moved it closer to his
protruding eye: it was like a slice of Gruyère cheese riddled
with holes, pale yellow, sharply lit, covered with white, leprous
spots. His hand on the screw of the microscope, his gaze
blinded by the light of the oculars, my father moved his cold
eyes on the limestone globe, he saw on its surface the complicated print of the disease gnawing at it from inside, the curved
channels of the bookworm, burrowing under the cheesy, unhealthy surface. Father shivered and saw his mistake: no, this
was not Gruyère cheese, this was obviously a human brain, an
anatomical crosscut preparation of the brain in all its complicated structure. Concentrating his gaze, he could even decipher
the tiny letters of captions running in all directions on the complicated map of the hemisphere. The brain seemed to have been
chloroformed, deeply asleep, and blissfully smiling in its sleep.
Intrigued by its expression, my father saw the essence of the
phenomenon through the complex surface print and again
smiled to himself. There is no telling what one can discover in
one's own familiar chimney, black like tobacco ash. Through
the coils of gray substance, through the minute granulations,
Father saw the clearly visible contours of an embryo in a characteristic head-over-heels position, with fists next to its face,
sleeping upside down its blissful sleep in the light waters of am-
nion. Father left it in that position. He rose with relief and shut
the trap door of the flue.

   Thus far and no further. But what has become of the end of
the world, that splendid finale, after the magnificently developed introduction? Downcast eyes and a smile. Was there a slip
in calculation, a small mistake in addition, a printer's error
when the figures were being printed? Nothing of the sort. The
calculations were correct, there was no fault in the column of
figures. What had happened, then? Please listen. The comet
proceeded bravely; rode fast like an ambitious horse in order to
reach the finish line on time. The fashion of the season ran with
him. For a time, he took the lead of the era, to which he lent his

shape and name. Then the two gallant mounts drew even and ran neck-to-neck in a strained gallop, our hearts beating in fellow feeling with them. Later on, fashion overtook by a nose and outstripped the indefatigable bolide. That millimeter decided the fate of the comet. It was doomed, it has been outdistanced forever. Our hearts now ran along with fashion, leaving the splendid comet behind. We looked on indifferently as he became paler, smaller, and finally sank resignedly to a point just above the horizon, leaned over to one side, trying in vain to take the last bend of its parabolic course, distant and blue, rendered harmless forever. He was unplaced in the race, the force of novelty was exhausted, nobody cared anymore for a thing that had been outstripped so badly. Left to itself, it quietly withered away amid universal indifference.

With heads hung low we reverted to our daily tasks, richer by one more disappointment. The cosmic perspectives were hurriedly rolled down, life returned to its normal course. We rested at that time by day and by night, making good for the lost time of sleep. We lay flat on our backs in already dark houses, heavy with sleep, lifted up by our breathing to the blind paths of starless dreams. Thus floating, we undulated—squeaky bellies, bagpipes and flutes, snoring our way through the pathless tracts of the starless nights. Uncle Edward had been silenced forever. There still remained in the air the echo of his alarmed despair, but he himself was alive no more. Life had flowed out of him in that paroxysm of frenzy, the circuit had opened, and he himself stepped out unhindered onto the higher rungs of immortality.

In the dark apartment my father alone was awake, wandering silently through the rooms filled with the singsong of sleep. Sometimes he opened the door of the flue and looked grinning into its dark abyss, where a smiling homunculus slept forever its luminous sleep, enclosed in a glass capsule, bathed in fluorescent light, already adjudged, erased, filed away, another record card in the immense archives of the sky.

SANATORIUM UNDER THE SIGN OF THE HOURGLASS

THE BOOK

I am simply calling it The Book without any epithets or qualifi-
cations, and in this sobriety there is a shade of helplessness, a
silent capitulation before the vastness of the transcendental, for
no word, no allusion, can adequately suggest the shiver of fear,
the presentiment of a thing without name that exceeds all our
capacity for wonder. How could an accumulation of adjectives
or a richness of epithets help when one is faced with that splen-
diferous thing? Besides, any true reader—and this story is only
addressed to him—will understand me anyway when I look him
straight in the eye and try to communicate my meaning. A short
sharp look or a light clasp of his hand will stir him into awareness, and he will blink in rapture at the brilliance of The Book.
For, under the imaginary table that separates me from my readers, don't we secretly clasp each other's hands?

The Book . . . Somewhere in the dawn of childhood, at the
first daybreak of life, the horizon had brightened with its gentle
glow. The Book lay in all its glory on my father's desk, and he,
quietly engrossed in it, patiently rubbed with a wet fingertip the
top of transfers until the blank pages grew opaque and ghostly
with a delightful foreboding and, suddenly flaking off in bits of
tissue, disclosed a peacock-eyed fragment; blurred with emotion, one's eyes turned toward a virgin dawn of divine colors,
toward a miraculous moistness of purest azure.

O that shedding of the film, O that invasion of brightness,
that blissful spring, O Father . . .

Sometimes my father would wander off and leave me alone

with The Book; the wind would rustle through its pages and the pictures would rise. And as the windswept pages were turned, merging the colors and shapes, a shiver ran through the columns of text, freeing from among the letters flocks of swallows and larks. Page after page floated in the air and gently saturated the landscape with brightness. At other times, The Book lay still and the wind opened it softly like a huge cabbage rose; the petals, one by one, eyelid under eyelid, all blind, velvety, and dreamy, slowly disclosed a blue pupil, a colored peacock's heart, or a chattering nest of hummingbirds.

This was a very long time ago. My mother had not appeared yet. I spent my days alone with my father in our room, which at that time was as large as the world.

The crystals hanging from the lamp filled the room with diffused colors, a rainbow splashed into all the corners, and, when the lamp swayed on its chains, the whole room revolved in fragments of the rainbow, as if the spheres of all nine planets had shifted, one turning around the other. I liked to stand between my father's legs, clasping them from each side like columns. Sometimes he wrote letters. I sat on his desk and watched, entranced, the squiggles of his signature, crabbed and awhirl like the trills of a coloratura singer. Smiles were budding in the wallpaper, eyes hatched, somersaults turned. To amuse me, my father blew soap bubbles through a long straw; they burst in the iridescent space or hit the walls, their colors still hanging in the air.

Then my mother materialized, and that early, bright idyll came to an end. Seduced by my mother's caresses, I forgot my father, and my life began to run along a new and different track with no holidays and no miracles. I might even have forgotten The Book forever, had it not been for a certain night and a certain dream.

2

On a dark wintry morning I woke up early (under the banks of darkness a grim dawn shone in the depths below) and while a multitude of misty figures and signs still crowded under my eyelids, I began to dream confusedly, tormented by various regrets about the old, forgotten Book.

No one could understand me and, vexed by their obtuseness, I began to nag more urgently, molesting my parents with angry impatience.

Barefoot, wearing only my nightshirt and trembling with excitement, I riffled the books on Father's bookshelves, and, angry and disappointed, I tried to describe to a stunned audience that indescribable thing, which no words, no pictures drawn with a trembling and elongated finger, could evoke. I exhausted myself in endless explanations, complicated and contradictory, and cried in helpless despair.

My parents towered over me, perplexed, ashamed of their helplessness. They could not help feeling uneasy. My vehemence, the impatient and feverish urgency of my tone, made me appear to be in the right, to have a well-founded grievance. They came up to me with various books and pressed them into my hands. I threw them away indignantly.

One of them, a thick and heavy tome, was again and again pushed toward me by my father. I opened it. It was the Bible. I saw in its pages a great wandering of animals, filling the roads, branching off into processions heading for distant lands. I saw a sky filled with flocks of birds in flight, and an enormous, upturned pyramid on whose flat top rested the Ark.

I raised my reproachful eyes to Father.

"You must know, Father," I cried, "you must. Don't pretend, don't quibble! This book has given you away. Why do you give me that fake copy, that reproduction, a clumsy falsification? What have you done with The Book?"

My father averted his eyes.

3

Weeks went by. My excitement abated, then passed, but the image of The Book continued to burn in my memory with a bright flame; a large, rustling Codex, a tempestuous Bible, the wind blowing through its pages, plundering it like an enormous, petal-shedding rose.

My father, seeing that I had become calmer, approached me cautiously one day and said in a tone of gentle suggestion:

"As a matter of fact, there are many books. The Book is a myth in which we believe when we are young, but which we cease to take seriously as we get older."

At that time I already held quite a different opinion. I knew then that The Book is a postulate, that it is a goal. I carried upon my shoulders the burden of a great mission. I did not answer; I was scornful and filled with bitter, dogged pride.

In fact, I was already in possession of some tattered remnants of The Book, a few pitiful shreds that by a freak of fate had fallen into my hands. I hid my treasure carefully from everybody, distressed by the utter downfall of that Book and knowing that I could not expect anyone to appreciate those mutilated pages. It happened like this:

One day during that winter I surprised Adela tidying up a room. A long-handled brush in her hand, she was leaning against a reading desk, on which lay some papers. I looked over her shoulder, not so much from curiosity as to be close to her and enjoy the smell of her body whose youthful charms had just revealed themselves to my recently awakened senses.

"Look," she said, submitting without protest to my pressing against her. "Is it possible for anyone to have hair reaching down to the ground? I should like to have hair like that."

I looked at the picture. On a large folio page there was a photograph of a rather squat and short woman with a face expressing energy and experience. From her head flowed an enormous stole of hair, which fell heavily down her back, trailing its thick ends on the ground. It was an unbelievable freak of nature, a full and ample cloak spun out of the tendrils of hair. It was hard to imagine that its burden was not painful to carry, that it did not paralyze the head from which it grew. But the owner of this magnificence seemed to bear it proudly, and the caption printed under the picture told the history of that miracle, beginning with the words: "I, Anna Csillag, born at Karlovice in Moravia, had a poor growth of hair . . ."

It was a long story, similar in construction to the story of Job. By divine will, Anna Csillag had been struck with a poor growth of hair. All her village pitied her for this disability, which they tolerated because of the exemplary life she led, although they suspected it could not have been entirely undeserved. But, lo and behold, her ardent prayers were heard, the curse was removed from her head, and Anna Csillag was graced with the blessing of enlightenment. She received signs and portents and concocted a mixture, a miraculous nostrum that restored fertility to her scalp. She began to grow hair, and what is more, her husband, brothers, even cousins were covered overnight with a tough, healthy black coating of hair growth. On the reverse of the page, Anna Csillag was shown six weeks after the prescription was revealed to her, surrounded by her brothers, brothers-in-law, and nephews, bewhiskered men with beards down to their waists, exposed to the admiration of beholders in an eruption of unfalsified, bearlike masculinity. Anna Csillag became the benefactress of her village, on which the blessing of wavy heads of hair and of enormous fringes had descended, and whose male inhabitants, henceforth, could sweep the ground with their beards like broad besoms. Anna Csillag became the apostle of hairiness. Having brought happiness to her native village, she now wanted to make the whole world happy and asked, begged, and urged everyone to accept for their salvation the gift of the gods, the wonderful mixture of which she alone knew the secret.

I read that story over Adela's arm and was struck by a sudden overwhelming thought. This was The Book, its last pages, the unofficial supplement, the tradesmen's entrance full of refuse and trash! Fragments of rainbow suddenly danced on the wallpaper. I snatched the sheaf of paper out of Adela's hands, and in a faltering voice I breathed:

"Where did you find this Book?"

"You silly boy," she answered shrugging her shoulders. "It has been lying here all the time; we tear a few pages from it every day and take them to the butcher's for packing meat for your father's lunch . . ."

4

I rushed to my room. Deeply perturbed, with burning cheeks I began to turn the pages of the old Book with trembling fingers. Alas, not many remained. Not a single page of the real text, nothing but advertisements and personal announcements. Immediately following the prophecies of the long-haired Sibyl was a page devoted to a miraculous nostrum for all illnesses and infirmities. Elsa—the Liquid with a Swan—was a balm that worked wonders. The page was full of authenticated, touching testimonials from people who had experienced its effects.

The enthusiastic convalescents from Transylvania, Slavonia, and Bucovina hurried to bear witness and to relate their stories in warm and moving words. They came bandaged and bent, shaking their now superfluous crutches, tearing plasters from their eyes and bandages from their sores.

Beyond these processions of cripples one imagined distant, mournful villages under skies white as paper, hardened by the prose of daily drudgery. They were villages forgotten in the depth of time, peopled by creatures chained forever to their tiny destinies. A cobbler was a total cobbler: he smelled of hide; he had a small and haggard face, pale myopic eyes, and a colorless, sniffing mustache; he felt a cobbler through and through. And when their abscesses did not worry them and their bones did not creak, when dropsy did not force them onto their pallets, these people plunged into a lifeless, gray happiness, smoking cheap yellow imperial-and-royal tobacco or dully daydreaming in front of kiosks where lottery tickets were sold.

Cats crossed their paths, both from the left and from the right; they dreamed of black dogs, and their palms frequently itched. Once in a while, they wrote a letter copied from a letter-writing manual, carefully stuck a stamp on the envelope, and entrusted it reluctantly to a letter box, which they then struck with their fists, as if to wake it up. And afterward they dreamed of white pigeons that carried letters in their beaks before disappearing in the clouds.

The pages that followed rose over the sphere of daily affairs into the region of pure poetry.

There were harmoniums, zithers, and harps, once played by consorts of angels; now, thanks to the progress of industry, they were accessible at popular prices to ordinary people—to all God-fearing people for their suitable entertainment and for the gladdening of their hearts.

There were barrel organs, real miracles of technology, full of flutes, stops, and pipes, trilling sweetly like nests of sobbing nightingales: priceless treasures for crippled veterans, a source of lucrative income for the disabled, and generally indispensable in every musical family. One imagined these barrel organs, beautifully painted, carried on the backs of little gray old men, whose indistinct faces, corroded by life, seemed covered by cobwebs—faces with watery, immobile eyes slowly leaking away, emaciated faces as discolored and innocent as the cracked and weathered bark of trees, and now like bark smelling only of rain and sky.

These old men had long forgotten their names and identities, and, lost in themselves, their feet encased in enormous heavy boots, they shuffled on bent knees with small, even steps along a straight monotonous line, disregarding the winding and tortuous paths of others who passed them by.

On white, sunless mornings, mornings stale with cold and steeped in the daily business of life, they would disentangle themselves imperceptibly from the crowd and stand the barrel organ on a trestle at street corners, under the yellow smudge of a sky cut by lines of telegraph wires. As people hurried aimlessly by with their collars upturned, they would begin their tune—not from the start but from where it had stopped the day before—and play "Daisy, Daisy, give me your answer, do . . ." while from the chimneys above, white plumes of steam would billow. And—strange thing—that tune, hardly begun, fell at once into its place at that hour and in that landscape as if it had belonged by right to that dreamlike inward-looking day. The thoughts and gray cares of the people hurrying past kept time with the tune.

And when, after a time, the tune ended in a long expansive whizz ripped from the insides of the barrel organ, which now started on something quite else, the thoughts and cares stopped for a moment, like in a dance, to change step, and then at once turned in the opposite direction in time to a new tune now emerging from the pipes of the barrel organ: "Margaretta, treasure of my soul . . ."

And in the dull indifference of that morning nobody noticed that the sense of the world had completely changed, that it now ran in time not with "Daisy, Daisy . . ." but with "Mar-ga-ret-ta . . ."

I turned another page . . . What might this be? A spring downpour? No, it was the chirping of birds, which landed like gray shot on open umbrellas, for here I was offered real German canaries from the Harz Mountains, cageloads of goldfinches and starlings, basketfuls of winged talkers and singers. Spindle-shaped and light, as if stuffed with cotton wool; jumping jerkily, agile as if running on smooth ball bearings; chattering like cuckoos in clocks—they were destined to sweeten the life of the lonely, to give bachelors a substitute for family life, to squeeze from the hardest of hearts the semblance of maternal warmth brought forth by their touching helplessness. Even when the page was almost turned, their collective, alluring chirping still seemed to persist.

But later on, the miserable remains of The Book became ever more depressing. The pages were now given over to a display of boring quackery. In a long coat, with a smile half-hidden by his black beard, who was it who presented his services to the public? Signor Bosco of Milan, a master of black magic, was making a long and obscure appeal, demonstrating something on the tips of his fingers without clarifying anything. And, although in his own estimation he reached amazing conclusions, which he seemed to weigh for a moment before they dissolved into thin air, although he pointed to the dialectical subtleties of his oratory by raising his eyebrows and preparing one for something unexpected, he remained misunderstood, and, what is worse, one did not care to understand him and left him with his gestures, his soft voice, and the whole gamut of his dark smiles, to turn quickly the last, almost disintegrated pages.

These pages quite obviously had slipped into a maniacal babble, into nonsense: a gentleman offered an infallible method of

achieving decisiveness and determination and spoke at length of
high principles and character. But to turn another page was
enough for me to become completely disoriented as far as principles and firmness were concerned.

A certain Mme Magda Wang, tethered by the train of her
gown, declared above a modest décolletage that she frowned on
manly determination and principles and that she specialized in
breaking the strongest characters. (Here, with a slight kick of her
small foot, she rearranged the train of her gown.) There were
methods, she continued through clenched teeth, infallible methods she could not divulge here, referring the readers to her mem-
oirs, entitled *The Purple Days* (published by the Institute of
Anthroposophy in Budapest); in them she listed the results of her
experiences in the Colonies with the "dressage" of men (this last
word underlined by an ironic flash of her eyes). And strangely
enough, that slovenly and loose-tongued lady seemed to be sure
of the approval of those about whom she spoke so cynically, and
in the peculiar confusion of her words one felt that their meaning
had mysteriously shifted and that we had moved to a totally different sphere, where the compass worked back to front.

This was the last page of The Book, and it left me peculiarly
dizzy, filled with a mixture of longing and excitement.

5

Leaning over that Book, my face glowing like a rainbow, I
burned in quiet ecstasy. Engrossed in reading, I forgot my mealtimes. My intuition was right: this was the authentic Book, the
holy original, however degraded and humiliated at present. And
when late in the evening, smiling blissfully, I put the script away
in the bottom of a drawer and hid it under a pile of other books,
I felt as if I were putting to sleep the dawn that emits a self-
igniting purple flame.

How dull all my other books now seemed!

For ordinary books are like meteors. Each of them has only
one moment, a moment when it soars screaming like the
phoenix, all its pages aflame. For that single moment we love

them ever after, although they soon turn to ashes. With bitter resignation we sometimes wander late at night through the extinct pages that tell their stone-dead messages like wooden rosary beads.

The exegetes of The Book maintain that all books aim at being authentic. That they live only a borrowed life, which at the moment of inspiration returns to its ancient source. This means that as the number of books decreases, the Authentic must increase. However, we don't wish to tire the reader with an exposition of doctrine. We should only like to draw his attention to one thing: the Authentic lives and grows. What does this mean? Well, perhaps next time, when we open our old script, we may not find Anna Csillag and her devotees in their old place. Perhaps we shall see her, the long-haired pilgrim, sweeping with her cloak the roads of Moravia, wandering in a distant land,

through white villages steeped in prose and drabness, and distributing samples of Elsa's balm to God's simpletons who suffer from sores and itches. Ah, and what about the worthy village beavers, immobilized by their enormous beards? What will that loyal commune do, condemned to the care and administration of their excessive growths? Who knows, perhaps they will all purchase the genuine Black Forest barrel organs and follow their lady apostle into the world, looking for her everywhere while playing "Daisy, Daisy"?

O Odyssey of beavers, roaming from town to town with barrel organs in pursuit of your spiritual mother! Is there a bard equal to this epic subject, who has been left in their village and is now wielding the spiritual power in Anna Csillag's birthplace? Couldn't they foresee that, deprived of their elite, of their splendid patriarchs, the village will fall into doubt and apostasy and will open its gates—to whom? Whom but the cynical and perverse Magda Wang (published by the Anthroposophical Institute of Budapest), who will open there a school of human dressage and breaking of character?

But let us return to our pilgrims.

We all know that old guard of wandering Cumbrians, those black-haired men with apparently powerful bodies, made of tissue without brawn or vigor. Their whole strength, their whole power, has gone into their hair. Anthropologists have been pondering for a long time over that peculiar tribe of men always clad in dark suits, with thick silver chains dangling on their stomachs, with fingers adorned with brass signet rings.

I like them, these Caspars or Balthazars; I like their deep seriousness, their funereal decorativeness; I like those magnificent male specimens with beautiful glossy eyes like burnt coffee beans; I like the noble lack of vitality in their overblown and spongy bodies, the *morbidezza* of decadence, the wheezing breath that comes from their powerful lungs, and even the smell of valerian emanating from their beards.

Like angels of the Presence, they sometimes appear suddenly in the door of our kitchen, enormous and short of breath, and, quickly tired, they wipe off perspiration from their damp brows while rolling the bluish whites of their eyes; for a moment they forget the object of their mission, and, astonished, looking for an excuse, a pretext for their arrival, they stretch out a hand and beg for alms.

Let's return to the Authentic. We have never forsaken it. And here we must stress a strange characteristic of the script, which by now no doubt has become clear to the reader: it unfolds while being read, its boundaries open to all currents and fluctuations.

Now, for instance, no one is offering goldfinches from the Harz Mountains, for from the barrel organs of those dark men the feathery little singers fly out at irregular intervals, and the market square is covered with them as with colored twigs. Ah, what a multiplication of shimmering chattering birds! . . . On all the cornices and flagpoles, colorful bottlenecks are formed by birds fluttering and fighting for position. If you push out of the window the crook of a walking stick, it will be covered with a chirping, heavy bunch of birds before you can draw it back into your room.

We are now quickly approaching the magnificent and catastrophic part of our story, which in our biography is known as the Age of Genius.

Here we must for a moment go completely esoteric, like Signor Bosco of Milan, and lower our voices to a penetrating whisper. By meaningful smiles we must give point to our exposition and grind the delicate substance of imponderables between the tips of our fingers. It won't be our fault if sometimes we shall look like those merchants of invisible fabrics, who display their fake goods with elaborate gestures.

Well then, did the Age of Genius ever occur? It is difficult to answer this question. Yes and no. There are things that cannot ever occur with any precision. They are too big and too magnificent to be contained in mere facts. They are merely trying to occur, they are checking whether the ground of reality can carry them. And they quickly withdraw, fearing to lose their integrity in the frailty of realization. And if they break into their capital, lose a thing or two in these attempts at incarnation, then soon, jealously, they retrieve their possessions, call them in, reintegrate: as a result, white spots appear in our biography—scented stigmata, the faded silvery imprints of the bare feet of angels, scattered footmarks on our nights and days—while the fullness of life waxes, incessantly supplements itself, and towers over us in wonder after wonder.

And yet, in a certain sense, the fullness is contained wholly and integrally in each of its crippled and fragmentary incarnations. This is the phenomenon of imagination and vicarious being. An event may be small and insignificant in its origins and yet, when drawn close to one's eye, it may open in its center an infinite and radiant perspective because a higher order of being is trying to express itself in it and irradiates it violently.

Thus we shall collect these allusions, these earthly approximations, these stations and stages on the paths of our life, like the fragments of a broken mirror. We shall re-create piece by piece what is one and indivisible—the great era, the Age of Genius of our life.

Perhaps in an attempt at diminution, overawed by the immensity of the transcendental, we have circumscribed, questioned, and doubted too much. Yet, despite all reservations: it did occur.

It was a fact, and nothing can shake our certainty of it: we can still feel its taste on our tongue, its cold fire on our palate, the width of its breath fresh like a draft of pure ultramarine.

Have we to some extent prepared the reader for the things that will follow? Can we risk a return journey into our Age of Genius?

The reader may have caught some of our stage fright: we can feel his anxiety. In spite of appearances our heart is heavy, and we are full of fear.

In God's name, then—let's embark and go!

THE AGE OF GENIUS

Ordinary facts are arranged within time, strung along its length as on a thread. There they have their antecedents and their consequences, which crowd tightly together and press hard one upon the other without any pause. This has its importance for any narrative, of which continuity and successiveness are the soul.

Yet what is to be done with events that have no place of their own in time; events that have occurred too late, after the whole of time has been distributed, divided, and allotted; events that have been left in the cold, unregistered, hanging in the air, homeless, and errant?

Could it be that time is too narrow for all events? Could it happen that all the seats within time might have been sold? Worried, we run along the train of events, preparing ourselves for the journey.

For heaven's sake, is there perhaps some kind of bidding for time? Conductor, where are you?

Don't let's get excited. Don't let's panic; we can settle it all calmly within our own terms of reference.

Have you ever heard of parallel streams of time within a two-track time? Yes, there are such branchlines of time, somewhat illegal and suspect, but when, like us, one is burdened with contraband of supernumerary events that cannot be registered, one cannot be too fussy. Let us try to find at some point of history such a branchline, a blind track onto which to shunt these illegal events. There is nothing to fear. It will all happen imperceptibly: the reader won't feel any shock. Who knows? Perhaps even now, while we mention it, the doubtful maneuver is already behind us and we are, in fact, proceeding into a cul-de-sac.

2

My mother rushed in, frightened, and enfolded my screams with her arms, wanting to stifle them like flames and choke them in the warmth of her love. She closed my mouth with hers and screamed together with me.

But I pushed her away, and, pointing to the column of fire, a golden bar that shot through the air like a splinter and would not disappear—full of brightness and spiraling dust specks—I cried: "Tear it out, tear it out!"

The large colored picture painted on the front of the stove grew bloodred; it puffed itself up like a turkey, and in the convulsions of its veins, sinews, and all its swollen anatomy, it seemed to be bursting open, trying to liberate itself with a piercing crowing scream.

I stood rigid like a signpost, with outstretched, elongated fingers, pointing in anger, in fierce concentration, hand trembling in ecstasy.

My hand guided me, alien and pale, and pulled me after it, a stiff, waxen hand, like the large votive hands in churches, like angels' palms raised for an oath.

It was toward the end of winter. The world had dissolved in puddles, but sudden waves of heat seemed full of fire and pepper. The honey-sweet pulp of day was cut into silvery furrows, into prisms filled with colors and spicy piquancies. Noonday collected within a short space the whole fire of these days and all the moments that glowed.

At that hour, unable to contain the heat, the day shed its scales of silvery tinplate, of crunchy tinfoil, and, layer after layer, disclosed its core of solid brightness. And as if this were not enough, chimneys smoked and billowed with lustrous steam. The bright flanks of the sky exploded into white plumes, banks of clouds dispersed under the shellfire of an invisible artillery.

The window facing the sky swelled with those endless ascents, the curtains stood in flames, smoking in the fire, spilling golden shadows and shimmering spirals of air. Askew on the carpet lay a quadrilateral of brightness that could not detach itself from the floor. That bar of fire disturbed me deeply. I stood transfixed, legs astride, and barked short, hard curses at it in an alien voice.

In the doorway and in the hall stood frightened, perplexed people: relatives, neighbors, overdressed aunts. They approached on tiptoe and turned away, their curiosity unsatisfied. And I screamed:

"Don't you remember?" I shouted to my mother, to my brother. "I have been telling you that everything is held back, tamed, walled in by boredom, unliberated! And now look at that flood, at that flowering, at that bliss . . . ."

And I shed tears of happiness and helplessness.

"Wake up," I shouted, "come and help me! How can I face this flood alone, how can I deal with this inundation? How can I, all alone, answer the million dazzling questions that God is swamping me with?"

And as they remained silent, I cried in anger: "Hurry up, collect bucketfuls of these riches, store them up!"

But nobody could assist me; bewildered, they looked over their shoulders, hiding behind the backs of neighbors.

Then I realized what I had to do; I began to pull from the cupboards old Bibles and my father's half-filled and disintegrating ledgers, throwing them on the floor under that column of fire that glowed and brightened the air. I wanted more and more sheaves of paper. My mother and brother rushed in with ever-new handfuls of old newspapers and magazines and threw them in stacks on the floor. And I sat among the piles of paper, blinded by the glare, my eyes full of explosions, rockets, and colors, and I drew wildly, feverishly, across the paper, over the printed or figure-covered pages. My colored pencils rushed in inspiration across columns of illegible text in masterly squiggles, in breakneck zigzags that knotted themselves suddenly into anagrams of vision, into enigmas of bright revelation, and then dissolved into empty, shiny flashes of lightning, following imaginary tracks.

Oh, those luminous drawings, made as if by a foreign hand. Oh, those transparent colors and shadows. How often, now, do I dream about them, then rediscover them after so many years at the bottom of old drawers, glimmering and fresh like dawn—still damp from the first dew of the day: figures, landscapes, faces!

Oh, those blues that stop your breath with the pang of fear. Oh, those greens greener than wonder. Oh, those preludes of anticipated colors waiting to be given a name!

Why did I squander them at the time with such wanton carelessness in the richness of surfeit? I allowed the neighbors to rummage about and plunder these stacks of drawings. They carried away whole sheaves of them. In what houses did they finally land, which rubbish heaps did they fill? Adela hung them up in the kitchen like wallpaper until the room became light and bright as if snow had fallen during the night.

The drawings were full of cruelty, pitfalls, and aggression. While I sat on the floor taut as a bow, immobile and lurking, the papers around me glowed brightly in the sun. It was enough if a drawing, pinned down by the tip of my pencil, made the slightest move toward escape, for my hand, trembling with new impulses and ideas, to attack it like a cat. Fierce and rapacious, I would, with lightning bites, savage the creation that tried to escape from under my crayon. And that crayon only left the paper when the now dead and immobile corpse displayed its colorful and fantastic anatomy on the page, like a plant in an herbal.

It was a murderous pursuit, a fight to the death. Who could tell the attacker from the attacked in that tangle that spluttered with rage, with squeaks and fears? At times my hand would start to attack twice or three times in vain, only to reach its victim on the fourth or fifth attempt. Often it winced in pain and fear in the fangs and pincers of the monsters writhing under my scalpel.

From hour to hour the visions became more crowded, bottlenecks arose, until one day all roads and byways swarmed with processions and the whole land was divided by meandering or marching columns—endless pilgrimages of beasts and animals.

As in Noah's day, colorful processions would flow, rivers of hair and manes, of wavy backs and tails, of heads nodding monotonously in time with their steps.

My room was the frontier and the tollgate. Here they stopped, tightly packed, bleating imploringly. They wriggled, shuffling their feet anxiously: humped and horned creatures, encased in the varied costumes and armors of zoology and frightened of each other, scared by their own disguises, looking with fearful and astonished eyes through the camouflage of their hairy hides and mooing mournfully, as if gagged under their attires.

Did they expect me to name them and solve their riddle? Or did they ask to be christened so that they could enter into their names and fill them with their being? Strange monsters, question-mark apparitions, blueprint creatures appeared, and I had to scream and wave my hands to chase them away.

They withdrew backward lowering their heads, looking askance, lost within themselves; then they returned, dissolving into chaos, a rubbish dump of forms. How many straight or humped backs passed at that time under my hand, how many heads did my hand touch with a velvety caress!

I understood then why animals have horns: perhaps to introduce an element of strangeness into their lives, a whimsical or irrational joke. An idée fixe, transgressing the limits of their being, reaching high above their heads and emerging suddenly into light, frozen into matter palpable and hard. It then acquired a wild, incredible, and unpredictable shape, an arabesque, invisible to their eyes yet frightening, an unknown cipher under the threat of which they are forced to live. I understood why these animals are given to irrational and wild panic, to the frenzy of a stampede: pushed into madness, they are unable to extricate themselves from the tangle of these horns, between which—when they lower their heads—they peer wildly or sadly, as if trying to find a passage between the branches. These horned animals have no hope of deliverance and carry on their heads the stigma of their sin with sadness and resignation.

The cats were even further removed from light. Their perfection was frightening. Enclosed in the precision and efficiency of their bodies, they did not know either fault or deviation. They would descend for a moment into the depths of their being, then become immobile within their soft fur, solemnly and threateningly serious, while their eyes became round like moons, sucking the visible into their fiery craters. But a moment later, thrown back to the surface, they would yawn away their vacuity, disenchanted and without illusions. In their lives full of self-sufficient grace, there was no place for any alternative. Bored by this prison of perfection, seized with spleen, they spat with their wrinkled lips, while their broad, striped faces expressed an abstract cruelty.

Lower down martens, polecats, and foxes sneaked stealthily by, thieves among animals, creatures with a bad conscience. They had reached their place in life by cunning, intrigue, and trickery, against the intent of their Creator and, pursued by hatred, always threatened, always on their guard, always in fear for that place, they passionately loved their furtive, stealthy existence and prepared to be torn to pieces in its defense.

At last, all the processions had filed past, and silence fell on my room once more. I again began to draw, engrossed in my papers that breathed brightness. The window was open, and on the windowsill doves and pigeons shivered in the spring breeze. Turning their heads to one side, they showed their round and glassy eyes in profile, as if afraid and full of flight. The days toward their end became soft, opaline, and translucent, then again pearly and full of a misty sweetness.

Easter came, and my parents went away for a week to visit my married sister. I was left alone in the apartment, a prey to my inspirations. Adela brought me breakfast and dinner on a tray. I did not notice her presence when she stopped in the doorway in her Sunday best, smelling of spring in her tulles and silks.

Through the open window gentle breezes entered the room, filling it with the reflections of distant landscapes. For a moment the colors of distance stayed in the air, but not for long; they soon dispersed, dissolving into blue shadows; tender and gentle. The flood of paintings receded a little, the waters of imagination quieted and abated.

I sat on the floor. Spread out around me were my crayons and buttons of paint: godly colors, azures breathing freshness, greens straying to the limits of the possible. And when I took a red crayon in my hand, happy fanfares of crimson marched out into the world, all balconies brightened with red waving flags, and whole houses arranged themselves along streets into a triumphant lane. Processions of city firemen in cherry red uniforms paraded in brightly lit happy streets, and gentlemen lifted their strawberry-colored bowlers in greeting. Cherry red sweetness and cherry red chirping of finches filled the air scented with lavender.

And when I reached for blue paint, the reflection of a cobalt spring fell on all the windows along the street; the panes trembled, one after the other, full of azure and heavenly fire; curtains waved as if alerted; and a joyful draft rose in that lane between muslin curtains and oleanders on the empty balconies, as if somebody distant had appeared from the other side of a long and bright avenue and was now approaching, somebody luminous, preceded by good tidings, by premonitions, announced by the flight of swallows, by beacons of fire spreading mile after mile.

3

At Easter time, usually at the end of March or the beginning of April, Shloma, the son of Tobias, was released from prison, where he had been locked up for the winter after the brawls and follies he had been involved in during the summer and autumn. One afternoon that spring I saw him from the window leaving the barber who in our town combined the functions of hairdresser and surgeon; I watched him carefully open the shining glass-paned door of the shop and descend the three wooden steps. He looked fresh and somehow younger, his hair carefully cut. He was wearing a jacket that was too short and too tight for him and a pair of checked trousers; slim and youthful in spite of his forty years.

Trinity Square was at that time empty and tidy. After the spring thaw the slush had been rinsed away by torrential rains that had left the pavements washed clean. The thaw was followed by many days of quiet, discreet fine weather, with long spacious days stretching beyond measure into evenings when dusk seemed endless, empty, and fallow in its enormous expectations. When Shloma had shut the glass door of the barber's after himself, the sky filled it at once, just as it filled all the small windows of the one-story house.

Having come down the steps, he found himself completely alone on the edge of the large, empty square, which that afternoon seemed shaped like a gourd; like a new, unopened year. Shloma stood on its threshold, gray and extinguished, steeped in blueness and incapable of making a decision that would break the perfect roundness of an unused day.

Only once a year, on his discharge from prison, did Shloma feel so clean, unburdened, and new. Then the day received him unto itself, washed from sin, renewed, reconciled with the world, and with a sigh it opened before him the spotless orbs of its horizons.

Shloma did not hurry. He stood at the edge of the day and did not dare cross it, or advance with his small, youthful, slightly limping steps into the gently vaulted conch of the afternoon.

A translucent shadow lay over the city. The silence of that third hour after midday extracted from the walls of houses the pure whiteness of chalk and spread it voicelessly, like a pack of cards. Having dealt one round, it began a second, drawing reserves of whiteness from the large baroque facade of the Church of the Holy Trinity, which, like an enormous divine shift fallen from heaven, folded itself into pilasters, projections, and embrasures and puffed itself up into the pathos of volutes and archvolutes before coming to rest on the ground.

Shloma lifted his face and sniffed the air. The gentle breeze carried the scent of oleanders, of cinnamon, and of festive interiors. Then he sneezed noisily, and his famous powerful sneeze frightened the pigeons on the roof of the police station so that they panicked and flew away. Shloma smiled to himself: by the explosion of his nostrils God must have given him a sign that spring was here. This was a surer sign than the arrival of storks, and from then on days would be interrupted by these detonations, which, lost in the hubbub of the city, would punctuate its events from various directions like a witty commentary.

"Shloma," I called out from our low first-floor window.

Shloma noticed me, smiled his pleasant smile, and saluted.

"We are alone in the whole square, you and I," I said softly, because the inflated globe of the sky resounded like a barrel.

"You and I," he repeated with a sad smile. "How empty is the world today!"

We could have divided it between us and renamed it, so open, unprotected, and unattached was the world. On such a day the Messiah advances to the edge of the horizon and looks down on the earth. And when He sees it, white, silent, surrounded by azure and contemplation, He may lose sight of the boundary of clouds that arrange themselves into a passage, and, not knowing what He is doing, He may descend upon earth. And in its reverie the earth won't even notice Him, who has descended onto its roads, and people will wake up from their afternoon nap remembering nothing. The whole event will be rubbed out, and everything will be as it has been for centuries, as it was before history began.

"Is Adela in?" Shloma asked with a smile.

"There is no one at home, come up for a moment and I'll show you my drawings."

"If there is no one in, I shall do so with pleasure if you will open the door."

And looking left and right in the gateway, with the gait of a sneak thief he entered the house.

4

"These are wonderful drawings," Shloma said, stretching out his arm with the gesture of an art connoisseur. His face lit up with the reflection of color and light. Then he folded his hand round his eye and looked through this improvised spyglass, screwing up his features in a grimace of earnest appreciation.

"One might say," he said, "that the world has passed through your hands in order to renew itself, in order to molt in them and shed its scales like a wonderful lizard. Ah, do you think I would be stealing and committing a thousand follies if the world weren't so outworn and decayed, with everything in it without its gilding, without the distant reflection of divine hands? What can one do in such a world? How can one not succumb and allow one's courage to fail when everything is shut tight, when all meaningful things are walled up, and when you constantly knock against bricks, as against the walls of a prison? Ah, Joseph, you should have been born earlier."

We stood in the semidarkness of my vast room, elongated in perspective toward the window opening on the square. Waves of air reached us in gentle pulsations, settling down on the silence. Each wave brought a new load of silence, seasoned with the colors of distance, as if the previous load had already been used up and exhausted. That dark room came to life only by the reflections of the houses far beyond the window, showing their colors in its depth as in a camera obscura. Through the window one could see, as through a telescope, the pigeons on the roof of the police station, puffed up and walking along the cornice of the attic. At times they rose up all at once and flew in a semicircle over the square. The room brightened for a moment with their fluttering wings, broadened with the echo of their flight, and then darkened when they settled down again.

"To you, Shloma," I said, "I can reveal the secret of these drawings. From the very start I had some doubts whether it was really I who made them. Sometimes they seem to me unintentional plagiarism, something that has been suggested to me or remembered . . . As if something outside me had used my inspiration for an unknown purpose. For I must confess to you," I added softly, looking into his eyes, "I have found the great Original . . ."

"The Original?" he asked, and his face lit up.

"Yes indeed, look for yourself," I said, kneeling in front of a chest of drawers. I first took out from it Adela's silk dress, then a box of her ribbons, and finally her new shoes with high heels. The smell of powder and scent filled the air. I took out some books: in the bottom of the drawer lay the long unseen, precious, beloved script.

"Shloma," I said trembling with emotion, "look, here it is . . ."

But he was deep in thought, with one of Adela's shoes in his hand, looking at it meditatively.

"God did not say anything of the kind," he said, "and yet my conviction is total. I cannot find any arguments to the contrary. These lines are irresistible, amazingly accurate, and final, and like lightning illuminate the very center of things. How can you plead innocence, how can you resist when you yourself have been bribed, outvoted, and betrayed by your most loyal allies? The six days of Creation were divine and bright. But on the seventh day God broke down. On the seventh day He felt an unknown texture under His fingers, and frightened, He withdrew His hands from the world, although His creative fervor might have lasted for many more days and nights. Oh, Joseph, beware the seventh day . . ."

And lifting up with awe Adela's slim shoe, he spoke as if seduced by the lustrous eloquence of that empty shell of patent leather.

"Do you understand the horrible cynicism of this symbol on a woman's foot, the provocation of her licentious walk on such elaborate heels? How can I leave you under the sway of that symbol? God forbid that I should do it . . ."

Saying this, his skillful fingers stuffed Adela's shoes, dress, and beads into his pockets.

"What are you doing, Shloma?"

But he was already moving quickly toward the door, limping slightly, his checked trousers flapping round his legs. In the doorway he turned his gray, already indistinct face toward me and lifted his hand in a reassuring gesture. And then he was gone.

SPRING

I

This is the story of a certain spring that was more real, more dazzling and brighter than any other spring, a spring that took its
text seriously: an inspired script, written in the festive red of sealing wax and of calendar print, the red of colored pencils and of
enthusiasm, the amaranth of happy telegrams from far away . . .

Each spring begins like this, with stunning horoscopes reaching beyond the expectations of a single season. In each spring
there is everything: processions and manifestations, revolutions
and barricades. Each brings with it, at a given moment, the hot
wind of frenzy, an infinity of sadnesses and delights that seek in
vain their equivalents in reality.

Later on, these exaggerations, culminations, and ecstasies are
transformed into blossoming, into the trembling of cool leaves,

and are absorbed by the tumultuous rustling of gardens. In this way springs betray their promise; each of them, engrossed in the breathless murmur of flowering parks, forgets its pledges and sheds, one by one, the leaves of its testament.

But that particular spring had the courage to endure, to keep its promise and bond. After many unsuccessful efforts, it succeeded in acquiring a permanent shape and burst upon the world as the ultimate all-embracing spring.

Oh that winds of events, that hurricane of happenings: the successful coups d'état, those grandiose, triumphant, highfalutin days! How I wish that the pace of this story would catch their entrancing, inspired beat, the heroic tone of that epic, the marching rhythm of that springlike "Marseillaise"!

How boundless is the horoscope of spring! One can read it in a thousand different ways, interpret it blindly, spell it out at will, happy to be able to decipher anything at all amid the misleading divination of birds. The text can be read forward or backward, lose its sense and find it again in many versions, in a thousand alternatives. Because the text of spring is marked by hints, ellipses, lines dotted on an empty azure, and because the gaps between the syllables are filled by the frivolous guesses and surmises of birds, my story, like that test, will follow many different tracks and will be punctuated by springlike dashes, sighs, and dots.

2

During those wild spacious nights that preceded the spring, when the sky was vast, still raw and unscented, and aerial byways led into the starry infinite, my father sometimes took me out to supper in a small garden restaurant hidden between the back walls of the farthest houses of the market square.

We walked in the damp light of streetlamps hissing in the wind, cutting across the large expanse of the square, forlorn, crushed by the immensity of the sky, lost and disoriented by its empty vastness. My father lifted his face bathed in the scanty light and looked anxiously at the starry grit scattered among the shallows of heavenly eddies. Their irregular and countless agglomerations were not yet ordered into constellations, and no figures emerged from the sterile pools.

The sadness of the starlit space lay heavily over the town, the lamps pierced the night below with beams of light, tying them haphazardly into knots. Under these lamps, passersby stopped in groups of two or three in the circle of light which for a short moment looked like the glow of a lamp over a dining table, although the night was indifferent and unfriendly, dividing the sky into wild airscapes, exposed to the blows of a homeless wind. Conversations faltered; under the deep shadow of their

hats people smiled with their eyes and listened dreamily to the
distant hum of the stars.

The paths in the restaurant garden were covered with gravel.
Two standard lamps hissed gently. Gentlemen in black frock
coats sat in twos or threes at tables covered with white cloths,
looking dully at the polished plates. Sitting thus, they calculated
mentally the moves on the great chessboard of the sky, each seeing with his mind's eye the jumping knights and lost pawns of
which new constellations immediately took the place.

Musicians on the rostrum dipped their mustaches in mugs of
bitter beer and sat around idly, deep in thought. Their violins
and nobly shaped cellos lay neglected under the voiceless downpour of the stars. From time to time one of them would reach
for his instrument and try it, tuning it plaintively to harmonize
with his discreet coughing. Then he would put it aside as if it
were not yet ready, not yet measuring up to the night, which
flowed along unheeding. And then as the knives and forks began
to clank softly above the white tablecloths, the violins would rise
alone, now suddenly mature although tentative and unsure just a

short while before; slim and narrow-waisted, they eloquently proceeded with their task, took up again the lost human cause, and pleaded before the indifferent tribunal of stars, now set in a sky on which the shapes of the instruments floated like water signs or fragments of keys, unfinished lyres or swans, an imitatory, thoughtless starry commentary on the margin of music.

The town photographer, who had for some time been casting meaningful glances at us from a neighboring table, joined us at last and sat down, putting his mug of beer on the table. He smiled equivocally, fought with his own thoughts, snapped his fingers, losing again and again some elusive point. We had felt for some time that our improvised restaurant encampment under the auspices of distant stars was doomed to collapse miserably, unequal to the ever-increasing demands of the night. What could we set against these bottomless wastes? The night simply canceled our human undertaking, even though it was supported by the sound of the violins, and moved into the gap, shifting its constellations to their rightful positions.

We looked at the disintegrating camp of tables, the battlefield of half-folded tablecloths and crumpled napkins, across which the night trod in triumph, luminous and immense. We got up as well, and our thoughts, forestalling our bodies, followed the movements of starry carts on their great and shiny paths.

And so we walked off under the stars, anticipating with half-closed eyes the ever more splendid illuminations. Ah, the cynicism of such a triumphant night! Having taken possession of the whole sky, it now played dominoes in space, lazily and without calculation, indifferently losing or winning millions. Then, bored, it traced on the battlefield of overturned tiles transparent squiggles, smiling faces, the same smile in a thousand copies, which a moment later rose toward the stars, already eternal, and dispersed into starry indifference.

On our way home we stopped at a pastry shop to get cakes. No sooner had we entered the white icing-sugar room than the night suddenly tensed up and became watchful lest we should escape. It waited for us patiently, outside the door, showing the unmoving stars through the window panes of the shop while we were inside selecting our cakes with great deliberation.

It was then that I saw Bianca for the first time. She stood side-ways in front of the counter with her governess; she was slim and linear in a white dress as if she had just left the zodiac. She did not turn her head but stood with the perfect poise of a young girl, eating a cream bun. I could not see her clearly, for the zigzags of starry lines still lingered under my eyelids. It was the first time that our still confused horoscopes had crossed, met, and dissolved in indifference. We did not anticipate our fate from that early aspect of the stars, and we left the shop ca-sually, making the glass-fronted door rattle.

The photographer, my father, and I walked home in a round-about way, through distant suburbs. The few houses there were small, and eventually houses disappeared altogether. We entered a climate of gentle warm spring; the silvery reflection of a young, violet moon just risen crept on the muddy path. That pre-spring night antedated itself, feverishly anticipating its later phases. The air, a short while before seasoned with the usual tartness of the time of year, became sweetly insipid, filled with the smell of rain, of damp loam, and of the first snowdrops that bloomed spec-trally in the white, magic light. And it was strange that under that benevolent moon frog spawn did not spread on the silvery mud, that the night did not resound with a thousand gossiping mouths on those graveled riverbanks saturated with shiny drops of sweet water. And one had to imagine the croaking of frogs in the night, which was filled with the murmur of subterranean springs, so that—after a moment of stillness—the moon might continue on its way and climb higher in the sky, spreading wide its whiteness, ever more luminous, more magical and transcendental.

We walked thus under the waxing moon. My father and the photographer half-carried me between them, for I was stum-bling with tiredness and hardly able to walk. Our steps crunched in the moist sand. It had been a long time since I had slept while walking, and under my eyelids I now saw the whole phosphorescence of the sky, full of luminous signs, of signals and starry phenomena. At last we reached an open field. My father laid me down on a coat spread on the ground. With closed eyes I saw the sun, the moon, and eleven stars aligned in the sky and parading before me.

"Bravo, Joseph!" my father exclaimed and clapped his hands in praise. I committed an unconscious plagiarism of another Joseph and the circumstances were not the same, but no one held it against me. My father, Jacob, shook his head and smacked his lips, and the photographer stood his tripod on the sand, pulled out his camera like a concertina, and hid himself entirely in the folds of its black cloth: he was photographing the strange phenomenon, a shining horoscope in the sky, while I, my head swimming in brightness, lay blinded on the ground and limply held up my dream to exposure.

3

The days became long, light, and spacious—maybe too spacious for their content, which was still poor and tenuous. They were days with an allowance for growth, days pale with boredom and impatience and full of waiting. A light, bright breeze cut their emptiness, yet untroubled by the exhalations of the bare and sunny gardens; it blew the streets clean, and they looked long and festively swept, as if waiting for someone's announced but uncertain arrival. The sun headed for the equinoctial position, then braked and almost reached the point at which it would seem to stand immobile, keeping an ideal balance and throwing out streams of fire, wave after wave, onto the empty and receptive earth.

A continuous draft blew through the whole breadth of the horizon, creating avenues and lanes. It calmed itself while blowing and stopped at last, breathless, enormous and glassy as if wishing to enclose in its all-embracing mirror the ideal picture of the city, a fata morgana magnified in the depth of its luminous concavity. Then the world stood motionless for a while, holding its breath, blinded, wanting to enter whole into that illusory picture, into that provisional eternity that opened up before it. But the enticing offer passed, the wind broke its mirror, and Time took us into his possession once again.

The Easter holidays came, long and opaque. Free from school, we young scholars wandered about the town without

aim or necessity, not knowing how to make use of our empty, undefined leisure. Undefined ourselves, we expected something from Time, which was unable to provide a definition and wasted itself in a thousand subterfuges.

In front of the café, tables were already put out on the pavement. Ladies sat at them in brightly colored dresses, and in small gulps they swallowed the breezes as if they were ice cream. Their skirts rustled, the wind worried them from below like a small angry dog. The ladies became flushed, their faces burned from the dry wind, and their lips were parched. This was still an interval with its customary boredom, while the world moved slowly and tremulously toward some boundary.

In those days we all ate like wolves. Dried out by the wind, we rushed home to eat in dull silence enormous chunks of bread and butter, or else we would buy on street corners large cracknels smelling of freshness, or we would sit in a row without a single thought in our heads in the vast vaulted porch of a house in the market square. Through the low arcades we could see the white and clean expanse of the square. Empty, strong-smelling wine barrels stood under the walls of the hall. We sat on a long bench, on which colored peasants' kerchiefs were displayed on market days, and we thumped the planks with our heels in listlessness and boredom.

Suddenly Rudolph, his mouth still full of cracknel, produced from his pocket a stamp album and spread it before me.

4

I realized in a flash why that spring had until then been so empty and dull. Not knowing why, it had been introverted and silent—retreating, melting into space, into an empty azure without meaning or definition—a questioning empty shell for the admission of an unknown content. Hence that blue (as if just awakened) neutrality, that great and indifferent readiness for everything. That spring was holding itself ready: deserted and roomy, it was simply awaiting a revelation. Who could foresee that this would emerge—ready, fully armed, and dazzling—from Rudolph's stamp album?

In it were strange abbreviations and formulae, recipes for civilizations, handy amulets that allowed one to hold his thumb and finger between the essence of climates and provinces. These were bank drafts on empires and republics, on archipelagoes and continents. Emperors and usurpers, conquerors and dictators could not possess anything greater. I suddenly anticipated the sweetness of domination over lands and peoples, the thorn of that frustration that can only be healed by power. With Alexander of Macedonia, I wanted to conquer the whole world and not a square inch of ground less.

5

Ignorant, eager, full of chafing desire, I took the march-past of creation, the parade of countries, shining processions I could see only at intervals, between crimson eclipses, caused by the rush of blood from my heart beating in time with the universal march of all the races. Rudolph paraded before my eyes those battalions and regiments; he took the salute fully absorbed and diligent. He, the owner of the album, degraded himself voluntarily to the role of an aide, reported to me solemnly, somewhat disoriented by his equivocal part. At last, very excited in a rush of fierce generosity, he pinned on me, like a medal, a pink Tasmania, glowing like May, and a Hyderabad swarming with a gypsy babble of entangled lettering.

6

It is then that the revelation took place: the vision of the fiery beauty of the world suddenly appeared, the secret message of good tidings, the special announcement of the limitless possibilities of being. Bright, fierce, and breathtaking horizons opened wide, the world trembled and shook in its joints, leaning dangerously, threatening to break out from its rules and habits.

What attraction, dear reader, has a postage stamp for you? What do you make of the profile of Emperor Franz Josef with his bald patch crowned by a laurel crown? Is it a symbol of ordinariness, or is it the ultimate within the bounds of possibility, the guarantee of unpassable frontiers within which the world is enclosed once and for all?

At that time, the world was totally encompassed by Franz Josef I. On all the horizons there loomed this omnipresent and inevitable profile, shutting the world off, like a prison. And just when we had given up hope and bitterly resigned ourselves inwardly to the uniformity of the world—the powerful guarantor of whose narrow immutability was Franz Josef I—then suddenly O God, unaware of the importance of it, You opened before me that stamp album, You allowed me to cast a look on its glimmering colors, on the pages that shed their treasures, one after another, ever more glaring and more frightening . . . Who will hold it against me that I stood blinded, weak with emotion,

and that tears flowed from my eyes? What a dazzling rela-
tivism, what a Copernican deed, what flux of all categories and
concepts! O God, so there were uncounted varieties of existence, so Your world was indeed vast and infinite! This was
more than I had ever imagined in my boldest dreams. So my
early anticipation that, in spite of all evidence to the contrary,
continued to nag at me and insist that the world was immeasur-
able in its variety had been proven right at last!

7

The world at that time was circumscribed by Franz Josef I. On
each stamp, on every coin, and on every postmark his likeness
confirmed its stability and the dogma of its oneness. This was
the world, and there were no other worlds besides, the effigies of
the imperial and royal old man proclaimed. Everything else was
make-believe, wild pretense, and usurpation. Franz Josef I rested
on top of everything and checked the world in its growth.

By inclination we tend to be loyal, dear reader. Being also af-
fable and easygoing, we are not insensitive to the attractions of
authority. Franz Josef I was the embodiment of the highest authority. If that authoritarian old man threw all his prestige on
the scales, one could do nothing but give up all one's aspirations
and longings, manage as well as one could in the only possible
world—that is, a world without illusions and romanticism—and
forget.

But when the prison seemed to be irrevocably shut, when the
last bolt-hole was bricked up, when everything had conspired
to keep silent about You, O God, when Franz Josef had barred
and sealed even the last chink so that one should not be able to
see You, then You rose wearing a flowing cloak of seas and continents and gave him the lie. You, God, took upon Yourself the
odium of heresy and revealed this enormous, magnificent, colorful blasphemy to the world. O splendid Heresiarch! You
struck me with the burning book, with that explosive stamp album from Rudolph's pocket. I did not know at that time that
stamp albums could be pocket size; in my blindness I at first

took it for a paper pistol with which we sometimes pretended
to fire at school, from under the seats, to the annoyance of
teachers. Yet this little album symbolized God's fervent tirade, a
fiery and splendid philippic against Franz Josef and his estate of
prose. It was the book of truth and splendor.

I opened it, and the glamour of colorful worlds, of becalmed
spaces, spread before me. God walked through it, page after
page, pulling behind Him a train woven from all the zones and
climates. Canada, Honduras, Nicaragua, Abracadabra, Hip-
porabundia . . . I at last understood You, O God. These were the
disguises for Your riches, these were the first random words that
came to Your mind. You reached into Your pocket and showed
me, like a handful of marbles, the possibilities that Your world
contained. You did not attempt to be precise; You said whatever
came into Your mind. You might equally well have said Panphi-
brass or Halleleevah, and the air among palms would flutter
with motley parrot wings, and the sky, like an enormous sapphire cabbage rose, blown open to its core, would show in its
dazzling center Your frightening peacock eye, would shine with
the glare of Your wisdom, and would spread a superscent. You
wanted to dazzle me, O God, to seduce me, perhaps to boast,
for even You have moments of vanity when You succumb to self-
congratulation. Oh, how I love these moments!

How greatly diminished you have become, Franz Josef, and
your gospel of prose! I looked for you in vain. At last I found
you. You were among the crowd, but how small, unimportant,
and gray. You were marching with some others in the dust of the
highway, immediately following South America, but preceding
Australia, and singing together with the others: Hosanna!

8

I became a disciple of the new gospel. I struck up a friendship
with Rudolph. I admired him, feeling vaguely that he was only
a tool, that the album was destined for somebody else. In fact,
he seemed to me only its guardian. He cataloged, he stuck in
and unstuck the stamps, he put the album away and locked the

drawer. In reality he was sad, like a man who guesses that he is waning while I am waxing. He was like the man who came to straighten the Lord's paths.

9

I had reasons to believe that the album was predestined for me. Many signs seemed to point to its holding a message and a personal commission for me. There was, for instance, the fact that no one felt himself to be the owner of the album, not even Rudolph, who acted more like its servant, an unwilling and lazy servant in the bond of duty. Sometimes envy would flood his heart with bitterness. He rebelled inwardly against the role of keeper of a treasure that did not really belong to him. He looked with envy on the reflection of distant worlds that flooded my face with a gamut of color. Only in that reflection did he notice the glow of these pages. His own feelings were not really engaged.

10

I once saw a prestidigitator. He stood in the center of the stage, slim and visible to everybody, and demonstrated his top hat, showing its empty white bottom. Thus having assured us that his art was above suspicion of fraudulent manipulation, he traced with his wand a complicated magic sign and at once, with exaggerated precision and openness, began to produce from the top hat paper strips, colored ribbons by the foot, by the yard, finally by the mile. The room filled with the rustling mass of color, became bright from the heaps of light tissue, while the artist still pulled at the endless weft, despite the spectators' protests, their cries of ecstasy and spasmodic sobs, until it became clear that all this effort was nothing to him, that he was drawing this plenty, not from his own, but from supernatural resources that had been opened to him and that were beyond human measures and calculations.

But some people who could perceive the real sense of this demonstration went home deep in thought and enchanted, having had a glimpse of the truth that God is boundless.

I I

Now perhaps is the time for drawing a parallel between Alexander the Great and my modest self. Alexander was susceptible to the aroma of countries. His nostrils anticipated untold possibilities. He was one of those men on whose head God lays His hand while they are asleep so that they get to know what they don't know, so that they are filled with intuitions and conjectures, while the reflections of distant worlds pass across their closed eyelids. Alexander, however, took divine allusions too literally. As a man of action—that is to say, of a shallow spirit—he interpreted his mission as that of conqueror of the world. He felt as unfulfilled as I was, his breast heaved with the same kind of sighs, and he hungered after ever-new horizons and landscapes. There was no one who could point out his mistake. Not even Aristotle could understand him. Thus, although he had conquered the whole world, he died disappointed, doubting the God who kept eluding him and doubting God's miracles. His likeness adorned the coins and seals of many lands. In the end, he became the Franz Josef of his age.

I 2

I should like to give the reader at least an approximate idea of that album in which the events of that spring were adumbrated, then finally arranged. An indescribable, alarming wind blew through the avenue of these stamps, the decorated street of crests and standards, and unfurled these emblems in an ominous silence, under the shadow of clouds that loomed threateningly over the horizon. Then the first heralds appeared in the empty street, in dress uniforms with red brassards, perspiring, perplexed, full of the sense of their mission. They gestured silently, preoccupied and solemn, the street immediately darkened from the advancing procession, and all the side streets were obscured by the steps of the demonstrating throngs. It was an enormous manifestation of countries, a universal May Day, a march-past of the world. The world was demonstrating with thousands of hands raised as for an oath, it averred in a thousand voices that it was *not* behind Franz Josef but behind somebody infinitely greater. The demonstration was bathed in a pale red, almost pink light, the liberating color of enthusiasm. From Santo Domingo, from San Salvador, from Florida came hot and panting delegations, clothed in raspberry red, who waved cherry pink bowler hats from which chattering goldfinches escaped in twos and threes. Happy breezes sharpened the glare of trumpets, brushed softly against the surface of the instruments, and brought forth tiny sparks of electricity. In spite of the large numbers taking part in the march-past, everything was orderly, the enormous parade unfolded itself in silence and according to plan. There were moments when the flags, waving violently from balconies, writhing in amaranthine spasms, in violent silent flutters, in frustrated bursts of enthusiasm, became still as for a roll call: the whole street then turned red and full of a silent threat, while in the darkened distance the carefully counted salvos of artillery resounded dully, all forty-nine of them in the dusk-filled air.

And then the horizon suddenly clouded over as before a spring storm, with only the instruments of the bands brassily shining, and in the silence one could hear the murmur of the darkening sky, the rustle of distant spaces, while from nearby gardens the scent of bird cherry floated in concentrated doses and dissolved imperceptibly in the air.

13

One day toward the end of April the morning was warm and gray; people walking in the streets and looking ahead did not notice that the trees in the park were splitting in many places and showing sweet, festering wounds.

Enmeshed in the black net of tree branches, the gray, sultry sky lay heavily on human shoulders. People scrambled from under its weight like june bugs in a warm dampness or, without a thought in their heads, sat hunched on the benches of the park, a sheet of faded newspaper on their laps.

Then at about ten o'clock the sun appeared like a luminous smudge from under the swollen body of a cloud, and suddenly among the tree branches all the fat buds began to shine and a veil of chirruping uncovered the now pale golden face of the day. Spring had come.

And at once the avenue of the park, empty a moment before, filled with people hurrying in all directions, as if this were the hub of the city, and blossomed with women's frocks. Quick and shapely girls were hurrying—some to work in shops and offices, others to assignations—but for a few moments, while they passed the openwork basket of the avenue, which now exuded the moisture of a greenhouse and was filled with birds' trills, they seemed to belong to that avenue and to that hour, to be the extras in a scene of the theater of spring, as if they had been reborn in the park together with the delicate branches and leaves. The park avenue seemed crowded with their refreshing hurry and the rustle of their underskirts. Ah, these airy, freshly starched shifts, led for a walk under the openwork shadow of the spring corridor, shifts damp under the armpits, now drying in the violet breezes of distance! Ah, these young, rhythmical steps, those legs hot from exercise in their new crunchy silk stockings that covered red spots and pimples, the healthy spring rash of hot-blooded bodies! The whole park became shamelessly pimply, and all the trees came out in buddy spots, which burst with the voices of birds.

And then the avenue became empty, and under the vaults of trees one could hear the soft squeaks of a perambulator on high wheels. In the small varnished canoe, engulfed in highly starched bands of linen, like in a bouquet, slept something more precious than a flower. The girl who slowly pushed the pram would lean over it from time to time, tilt to its back wheels the swinging, squeaking basket that bloomed with white freshness, and blow caressingly into the bouquet of tulle until she had reached its sweet sleepy core, across whose dreams tides of cloud and light floated like a fairy tale.

At noon the paths of the park were crisscrossed with light and shadow, and the song of birds hung continuously in the air, but the women passing on the edge of the promenade were already tired, their hair matted with migraine, and their faces fatigued by the spring. Later still, the avenue emptied completely, and in the silence of the early afternoon smells began slowly to drift across from the park restaurant.

14

Every day at the same time, accompanied by her governess, Bianca could be seen walking in the park. What can I say about Bianca, how can I describe her? I only know that she is marvelously true to herself, that she fulfills her program completely. My heart tight with pleasure, I notice again and again how with every step, light as a dancer, she enters into her being and how with each of her movements she unconsciously hits the target.

Her walk is ordinary, without excessive grace, but its simplicity is touching, and my heart fills with gladness that Bianca can be herself so simply, without any strain or artifice.

Once she slowly lifted her eyes to me, and the seriousness of that look pierced me like an arrow. Since then, I have known that I can hide nothing from her, that she knows all my thoughts. At that moment, I put myself at her disposal, completely and without reservation. She accepted this by almost imperceptibly closing her eyes. It happened without a word, in passing, in one single look.

When I want to imagine her, I can only evoke one meaningless detail: the chapped skin on her knees, like a boy's; this is deeply touching and guides my thoughts into tantalizing regions of contradiction, into blissful antinomies. Everything else, above and below her knees, is transcendental and defies my imagination.

1 5

Today I delved again into Rudolph's stamp album. What a
marvelous study! The text is full of cross-references and allusions. But all the lines converge toward Bianca. What blissful
conjectures! My expectations and hopes are ever more dazzling. Ah, how I suffer, how heavy is my heart with the mysteries that I anticipate!

1 6

A band is now playing every evening in the city park, and people
on their spring outings fill the avenues. They walk up and down,
pass one another, and meet again in symmetrical, continuously
repeated patterns. The young men are wearing new spring hats
and nonchalantly carrying gloves in their hands. Through the
hedges and between the tree trunks the dresses of girls walking
in parallel avenues glow. The girls walk in pairs, swinging their
hips, strutting like swans under the foam of their ribbons and
flounces; sometimes they land on garden seats, as if tired by the
idle parade, and the bells of their flowered muslin skirts expand
on the seats, like roses beginning to shed their petals. And then
they disclose their crossed legs—white irresistibly expressive
shapes—and the young men, passing them, grow speechless and
pale, hit by the accuracy of the argument, completely convinced
and conquered.

    At a particular moment before dusk all the colors of the
world become more beautiful than ever, festive, ardent yet sad.
The park quickly fills with pink varnish, with shining lacquer
that makes every other color glow deeper; and at the same time
the beauty of the colors becomes too glaring and somewhat suspect. In another instant the thickets of the park strewn with
young greenery, still naked and twiggy, fill with the pinkness of
dusk, shot with coolness, spilling the indescribable sadness of
things supremely beautiful but mortal.

Then the whole park becomes an enormous, silent orchestra, solemn and composed, waiting under the raised baton of the conductor for its music to ripen and rise; and over that potential, earnest symphony a quick theatrical dusk spreads suddenly as if brought down by the sounds swelling in the instruments. Above, the young greenness of the leaves is pierced by the tones of an invisible oriole, and at once everything turns somber, lonely, and late, like an evening forest.

A hardly perceptible breeze sails through the treetops, from which dry petals of cherry blossom fall in a shower. A tart scent drifts high under the dusky sky and floats like a premonition of death, and the first stars shed their tears like lilac blooms picked from pale, purple bushes.

It is then that a strange desperation grips the youths and young girls walking up and down and meeting at regular intervals. Each man transcends himself, becomes handsome and irresistible like a Don Juan, and his eyes express a murderous strength that chills a woman's heart. The girls' eyes sink deeper and reveal dark labyrinthine pools. Their pupils distend, open without resistance, and admit those conquerors who stare into their opaque darkness. Hidden paths of the park reveal themselves and lead to thickets, ever deeper and more rustling, in which they lose themselves, as in a backstage tangle of velvet curtains and secluded corners. And no one knows how they reach, through the coolness of these completely forgotten darkened gardens, the strange spots where darkness ferments and degenerates, and vegetation emits a smell like the sediment in long-forgotten wine barrels.

Wandering blindly in the dark plush of the gardens, the young people meet at last in an empty clearing, under the last purple glow of the setting sun, over a pond that has been growing muddy for years; on a rotting balustrade, somewhere at the back gate of the world, they find themselves again in preexistence, a life long past, in attitudes of a distant age; they sob and plead, rise to promises never to be fulfilled, and, climbing up the steps of exaltation, reach summits and climaxes beyond which there is only death and the numbness of nameless delight.

17

What is a spring dusk?

Have we now reached the crux of the matter, and is this the end of the road? We are beginning to be at a loss for words: they become confused, meandering, and raving. And yet it is beyond these words that the description of that unbelievable, immense spring must begin. The miracle of dusk! Again, the power of our magic has failed and the dark element that cannot be embraced is roaring somewhere beyond it. Words are split into their components and dissolved, they return to their etymology, reenter their depths and distant obscure roots. This process is to be taken literally. For it is getting dark, our words lose themselves among unclear associations: Acheron, Orcus, the Underworld . . . Do you feel darkness seeping out of these words, molehills crumbling, the smell of cellars, of graves slowly opening? What is a spring dusk? We ask this question once more, the fervent refrain of our quest that must remain unrewarded.

When the tree roots want to speak, when under the turf a great many old tales and ancient sagas have been collected, when too many whispers have been gathered underground, inarticulate pulp and dark nameless things that existed before words—then the bark of trees blackens and disintegrates into thick rough scales which form deep furrows. You dip your face into that fluffy fur of dusk, and everything becomes impenetrable and airless like under the lid of a coffin. Then you must screw up your eyes and bully them, squeeze your sight through the impenetrable, push across the dull humus—and suddenly you are at your goal, on the other side; you are in the Deep, in the Underworld. And you can see . . .

It is not quite as dark here as we thought. On the contrary, the interior is pulsating with light. It is, of course, the internal light of roots, a wandering phosphorescence, tiny veins of light marbling the darkness, an evanescent shimmer of nightmarish substances. Likewise, when we sleep, severed from the world, straying into deep introversion, on a return journey into ourselves, we can see clearly through our closed eyelids, because thoughts are kindled in us by internal tapers and smolder erratically. This is how total regressions occur, retreats into self, journeys to the roots. This is how we branch out into anamnesis and are shaken by underground subcutaneous shivers. For it is only above ground, in the light of day, that we are a trembling, articulate bundle of tunes; in the depth we disintegrate again into black murmurs, confused purring, a multitude of unfinished stories.

It is only now that we realize what the soil is on which spring thrives and why spring is so unspeakably sad and heavy with knowledge. Oh, we would not have believed it had we not seen it with our own eyes! Here are labyrinths of depth, warehouses and silos of things, graves that are still warm, the litter, and the rot. Age-old tales. Seven layers (like in ancient Troy), corridors, chambers, treasure chests. Numerous golden masks—one next to another—flattened smiles, faces eaten out, mummies, empty cocoons . . . Here are columbaria, the drawers for the dead, in which they lie desiccated, blackened like roots, awaiting their moment. Here are great apothecary storerooms where they are displayed in lachrymatories, crucibles, and jars. They have been standing on the shelves for years in a long, solemn row, although no one has been there to buy them. Perhaps they have come alive in their pigeonholes, completely healed, clean as incense, and scented—chirruping specifics, awakened impatient drugs, balms, and morning unguents—balancing their early taste on the tip of the tongue. These walled-in pigeon perches are full of chicks hatching out and making their first attempts at chirping. How dew-fresh and time-anticipating are these long, empty lanes where the dead wake up in rows, deeply rested—to a completely new dawn!

But we have not finished yet; we can go deeper. There is nothing to fear. Give me your hand, take another step: we are at the roots now, and at once everything becomes dark, spicy, and tangled like in the depth of a forest. There is a smell of turf and tree rot; roots wander about, entwined, full with juices that rise as if sucked up by pumps. We are on the nether side, at the lining of things, in gloom stitched with phosphorescence. There is a lot of movement and traffic, pulp and rot, tribes and generations, a brood of Bibles and *Iliads* multiplied a thousand times! Wanderings and tumult, the tangle and hubbub of history! That road leads no farther. We are here at the very bottom, in the dark foundations, among the Mothers. Here are the bottomless infernos, the hopeless Ossianic spaces, all those lamentable Nibelungs. Here are the great breeding grounds of history, factories of plots, hazy smoking rooms of fables and tales. Now at last one can understand the great and sad machinery of spring. Ah, how it thrives on stories, on events, on chronicles, on destinies! Everything we have ever read, all the stories we have heard and those we have never heard before but have been dreaming since childhood—here and nowhere else is their home and their motherland. Where would writers find their ideas, how would they muster the courage for invention, had they not been aware of these reserves, this frozen capital, these funds salted away in the underworld? What a buzz of whispers, what persistent purr of the earth! Continuous persuasions are throbbing in your ears. You walk with half-closed eyes in a warmth of whispers, smiles, and suggestions, importuned endlessly, pinpricked a thousand times by questions as though by delicate insect proboscides. They would like you to take something from them, anything, a pinch at least of these disembodied, timeless stories, absorb it into your young life, into your bloodstream; save it, and try to live with it. For what is spring if not a resurrection of history? It alone among these disembodied things is alive, real, cool, and unknowing. Oh, how attracted are these specters and phantoms, larvae and lemurs, to its young green blood, to its vegetative ignorance! And spring, helpless and naive, takes them into its slumber, sleeps with them, wakes half-conscious at dawn, and remembers nothing. This is why it is heavy with the sum of all that is forgotten and sorrowful, for it alone must live vicariously on these rejected lives, and must be beautiful to embody all that has been lost . . . And to make up for all this, it has only the heady smell of cherry blossom to offer, streaming in one eternal, infinite flood in which everything is contained . . . What does forgetting mean? New greenery has grown overnight on old stories, a soft green tuft, a bright, dense mass of buds has sprouted from all the pores in a uniform growth like the hair on a boy's head on the day after a haircut. How green with oblivion spring becomes: old trees regain their sweet nescience and wake up with twigs, unburdened by memories although their roots are steeped in old chronicles. That greenness will once more make them new and fresh as in the beginning, and stories will become rejuvenated and start their plots once again, as if they had never been.

There are so many unborn tales. O those sad lamenting choruses among the roots, those stories outbidding one another, those inexhaustible monologues among suddenly exploding improvisations! Have we the patience to listen to them? Before the oldest known legend there were others no one has ever heard; there were nameless forerunners; novels without a title; enormous, pale, and monotonous epics; shapeless bardic tales; formless plots; giants without a face; dark texts written for the drama of evening clouds. And behind these lays, sagas, unwritten books, books—eternal pretenders, and lost books *in partibus infidelium.*

Among all the stories that crowd at the roots of spring, there is one that long ago passed into the ownership of the night and settled down forever at the bottom of the firmament as an eternal accompaniment and background to the starry spaces. During every spring night, whatever might happen in it, that story unfolds itself above the croaking of frogs and the endless working of mills. A man walks under the milky stars strewn by the hand mills of night; he walks hugging a child in the folds of his cloak; he walks across the sky, constantly on his way, a perpetual wanderer through the endless spaces. O the sadness of loneliness, the pathos of orphanhood in the vastness of night. O glare of distant stars! In that story time can never change anything. The story appears on the starry horizons and will do so forever, always afresh, for once derailed from the tracks of time, it has become unfathomable, never to be exhausted by repetition. There goes that man who hugs the child in his arms—we are repeating on purpose that refrain, that pitiful motto of the night, in order to express the intermittent continuity of walking, sometimes obstructed by the tangle of stars, sometimes completely invisible during long, silent intervals in which one can feel the breeze of eternity. The distant worlds come within reach, glaring frighteningly, they send violent signals through eternity in an unspoken, mute language—while he walks on and on and soothes the little girl endlessly, monotonously, and without hope, helpless against the whispers and sweet persuasions of the night, against the only word formed on the lips of silence, when no one is listening to it . . .

The story is about a princess kidnapped and changed for another child.

18

When late at night they return to the spacious villa among gardens, to a low white room where a black shining piano stands with all its strings silent, when through the wide glass wall, as if through the panes of a greenhouse, the spring night looks in, pale and blinking with stars, and the scent of cherry blossom floats from bottles and containers over the cool white bedding—then anxious listening fills the sleepless night and the heart speaks in sleep, sobs, races, and stumbles through the long, dewy, moth-swarming night, luminous and scented with bird cherry . . . Ah, it is the bird cherry that gives depth to the limitless night; hearts aching from flights, tired from happy pursuits, would like to rest awhile on some airy narrow ridge, but from that endless pale night a new night is born, even paler and more disembodied, cut into luminous lines and zigzags, into spirals of stars and pale flights, pierced a thousand times by the suckers of invisible gnats bloated with the blood of maidens; the tireless heart must again stumble through sleep, mad, engaged in starry and complex affairs, in breathless hurry, in moonlit panics, ascending and enlarged, entangled in pale fascinations, in comatose lunar dreams and lethargic shivers.

Ah, all these rapes and pursuits of that night, the treacheries and whispers, Negroes and helmsmen, balcony railings and night blinds, muslin frocks and veils trailing behind hurried escapes! . . . Until at last, after a sudden blackout, a dull black pause, a moment comes when all the puppets are back in their boxes, all the curtains are drawn, and all the bated breaths are quietly exhaled, while on the vast calm sky dawn is building noiselessly its distant pink and white cities, its delicate, lofty pagodas and minarets.

19

Only now will the nature of that spring become clear and legible to an attentive reader of The Book. All these morning preparations, all the day's early ablutions, all its hesitations, doubts, and difficulties of choice will disclose their meaning to one who is familiar with stamps. Stamps introduce one to the complex game of morning diplomacy, to the prolonged negotiations and atmospheric deceits that precede the final version of any day. From the reddish mists of the ninth hour, the motley and spotted Mexico with a serpent wriggling in a condor's beak is trying to emerge, hot and parched by a bright rash, while in a gap of azure amid the greenery of tall trees a parrot is stubbornly repeating "Guatemala, Guatemala" at even intervals, with the same intonation, and that green word infects things that suddenly become fresh and leafy. Slowly, among difficulties and conflicts, a voting takes place, the order of ceremonies is established, the list of parades, the diplomatic protocol of the day.

In May the days were pink like Egyptian stamps. In the market square brightness shone and undulated. In the sky billows of summery clouds—volcanic, sharply outlined—folded under chinks of light (Barbados, Labrador, Trinidad), and everything was running with redness, as if seen through ruby glasses or the color of blood rushing to the head. There sailed across the sky the great corvette of Guiana, exploding with all its sails. Its bulging canvas towered amid taut ropes and the noise of tugboats, amid storms of gulls and the red glare of the sea. Then there rose to the sky and spread wide an enormous, tangled rigging of ropes, ladders, and masts and, with a full spread of canvas, a manifold, many-storied aerial spectacle of sails, yards, and braces, of holds from which small agile Negro boys shot out for a moment and were lost again in the labyrinths of canvas, among the signs and figures of the fantastic tropical sky.

Then the scenery changed in the sky: in massed clouds three simultaneous pink eclipses occurred, shiny lava began to smolder, outlining luminously the fierce contours of clouds (Cuba, Haiti, Jamaica), and the center of the world receded, its glaring colors became deeper. Roaring tropical oceans, with their azure archipelagoes, happy currents and tides and equatorial and salty monsoons made their appearance. With the stamp album in my hand, I was studying the spring. Was it not a great commentary on the times, the grammar of its days and nights?

The main thing was not to forget, like Alexander the Great, that no Mexico is final, that it is a point of passage which the world will cross, that beyond each Mexico there opens another, even brighter one, a Mexico of supercolors and hyperaromas . . .

20

Bianca is all gray. Her dark complexion has a tinge of burned-out ashes. The touch of her hand must be unimaginable.

The careful breeding of whole generations flows in her disciplined blood. Her resigned submission to the rules of tact, proof of conquered contrariness, broken rebellion, secret sobbing, and violence done to her pride, is quite touching. Every one of her gestures expresses submission, with good will and sad grace, to the prescribed forms. She does nothing that is unnecessary, each step is avariciously measured, just complying with the conventions, entering into their spirit without enthusiasm and only from a passive sense of duty. From these daily victories Bianca draws her premature experience and wisdom. Bianca knows what there is to know, and she does seem to enjoy her knowledge, which is serious and full of sadness. Her mouth is closed in lines of infinite beauty, her eyebrows traced with severe accuracy. No, her wisdom does not lead to relaxation of rules, to softness of self-indulgence. On the contrary. The truth, at which she gazes with her sad eyes, can only be borne by a tense attention to forms and their strictest observance. And that unfailing tact and loyalty to convention obscures a whole sea of sadness and suffering gallantly overcome.

And yet, although broken by form, she has emerged from it victorious. But with what sacrifice has that triumph been achieved!

When she walks—slim and straight—it is not clear what kind of pride she carries so simply in the unsophisticated rhythm of her walk, whether her own pride overcome, or the triumph of principles to which she has submitted.

But when she lifts her eyes and looks straight at you, nothing can be hidden from her. Her youth has not protected her from being able to guess the most secret things. Her quiet serenity has been achieved after long days of weeping and sobbing. This is why her eyes are deeply circled and have in them the moist, hot glow and that spare purposefulness that never misses anything.

21

Bianca, enchanting Bianca, is a mystery to me. I study her with obstinacy, passion, and despair—with the stamp album as my textbook. Why am I doing this? Can a stamp album serve as a textbook of psychology? What a naive question! A stamp album is a universal book, a compendium of knowledge about everything human. Naturally, only by allusion, implication, and hint. You need some perspicacity, some courage of the heart, some imagination in order to find the fiery thread that runs through the pages of the book.

One thing must be avoided at all costs: narrow-mindedness, pedantry, dull pettiness. Most things are interconnected, most threads lead to the same reel. Have you ever noticed swallows rising in flocks from between the lines of certain books, whole stanzas of quivering pointed swallows? One should read the flight of these birds . . .

But to return to Bianca. How movingly beautiful are her movements! Each is made with deliberation, determined centuries ago, begun with resignation, as if she knew in advance the course and the inevitable sequence of her destiny. It happens that I want to ask her something with my eyes, to beg for something in my thoughts, while I sit facing her in the park. And before I have formulated my plea, she has already answered. She has answered sadly by one short, penetrating look.

Why does she hold her head lowered? What is she gazing at with attention, with such thoughtfulness? Is her life so hopelessly sad? And yet, in spite of everything, doesn't she carry that resignation with dignity, with pride, as if things had to remain as they were, as if that knowledge, which deprives her of joy, had given her some untouchability instead, some higher freedom found only in voluntary submission? Her obedience has the grace of triumph and of victory.

With her governess she sits on a bench facing me, and both are reading. Her white dress—I have never seen her wear any other color—lies like an open flower on the seat. Her slim dark legs are crossed in front of her with indescribable grace. To touch her body must, I imagine, be painful from the sheer holiness of such a contact.

Then having closed their books, they both rise. With one quick look Bianca acknowledges and returns my ardent greeting and walks away, disengaged, weaving her feet, meandering, melodiously keeping pace with the rhythm of the long, elastic steps of her governess.

22

I have investigated the whole area around the estate. I have walked several times around the high fence that surrounds that vast terrain. I have seen the white walls of the villa with its terraces and broad verandas from all angles. Behind the villa spreads a park and, adjoining it, a large plot of land without any trees. Strange structures, partly factories, partly farm buildings, stand there. I put my eye against a chink in the fence, and what

I saw must have been an illusion. In the spring air, thinned by
the heat, you can sometimes see distant things mirrored through
miles of quivering air. All the same my head is splitting from
contradictory thoughts. I must consult the stamp album again.

23

Is it possible? Could Bianca's villa be an extraterritorial area
under the safeguard of international treaties? To what astonishing assumptions does the study of the stamp album lead me!
Am I alone in possession of this amazing truth? And yet one
cannot treat lightly the evidence and arguments provided on
this point by the stamp album.

Today I investigated the whole villa from nearby. For weeks
I have been hanging around the crested wrought-iron gate. My
opportunity came when two large empty carriages drove out of
the garden. The gates were left wide open and there was nobody
in sight. I entered nonchalantly, produced my drawing book
from my pocket, and, leaning against a pillar of the gate, pretended to draw some architectural detail. I stood on a graveled
path trod so many times by Bianca's light feet. My heart would
stop still from blissful anticipation at the thought that I might
see her emerging in a flimsy white dress from one of the French
windows. But all the windows and doors had green sunshades
drawn over them. Not even the slightest sound betrayed the life
hidden in that house. The sky on the horizon was overcast;
there was lightning in the distance. No breeze moved the warm
rarefied air. In the quietness of that gray day only the chalk
white walls of the villa spoke with the voiceless but expressive
eloquence of their ornate architecture. Its elegance was repeated
in pleonasms, in a hundred variations on the same motif. Along
a blindingly white frieze, bas-relief garlands ran in rhythmic cadenzas to the left and right and stopped undecided at the corners. From the height of the central terrace a marble staircase
descended, ceremonious and solemn, between smoothly running balusters and architectural vases, and, flowing broadly to
the ground, seemed to arrange its train with a deep curtsy.

I have quite an acute sense of style. The style of that building worried and irritated me, although I could not explain why. Behind its restrained classicism, behind a seemingly cool elegance, some other, elusive influences were hiding. The design was too intense, too sharply pointed, too full of unexpected adornments. A drop of an unknown poison inserted into the veins of the architect made his design recondite, explosive, and dangerous.

Inwardly disoriented, trembling from contradictory impulses, I walked on tiptoe along the front of the villa, scaring the lizards asleep on the steps.

By the round pool, now dry, the earth was parched from the sun and still bare; only here and there, from a crack in the ground, sprang a tuft of an impatient fantastical green. I pulled out some of these weeds and put them into my drawing book. I was shaking with excitement. Over the pool the air hung translucent and glossy, undulating from the heat. A barometer on a nearby post showed a catastrophic low. There was calm everywhere. Not a twig moved. The villa was asleep, its curtain drawn, and its chalky whiteness glared in the dullness of the gray air. Suddenly, as if the stagnation had reached its critical point, the air shook with a colored ferment.

Enormous, heavy butterflies coupling in amorous frolics appeared. The clumsy, vibrating fluttering continued for a moment in the dull air. The butterflies flew past, as if racing one another, then rejoined their partners, dealing out a flight like cards, whole packs of colorful shimmers. Was it only a quick decomposition of the overripe air, a mirage in an atmosphere that was full of hashish and visions? I waved my cap and a heavy, velvety butterfly fell to the ground, still fluttering its wings. I lifted it up and hid it. It was one more proof . . .

24

I have discovered the secret of the villa's style. The lines of its architecture repeated one incomprehensible pattern so many times and so insistently that I finally understood their mystifying code: the masquerade was really quite transparent. In those elaborate and mobile lines of exaggerated elegance there was too much spice, an excess of hot piquancy, something fidgety, too eager, too showy—something, in a word, colorful and colonial . . . Indeed, the style was in effect rather repulsive—lustful, overelaborate, tropical, and extremely cynical.

25

I need not say how this discovery shook me. The clues became clearer, the various reports and hints suddenly fitted. Most excited, I shared my discovery with Rudolph. He did not seem concerned. He even snorted angrily, accusing me of exaggeration and invention. He has been accusing me for some time of lying and willful mystification. I still had some remains of regard for him as the owner of the stamp album, but his envious and bitter outbursts set me more and more against him. I didn't show any resentment, as I was unfortunately dependent on him. What would I do without the stamp album? He knew this and exploited his advantage.

26

Too much has been happening during the spring. Too many aspirations, pretensions, and boundless ambitions are hidden in its dark depths. Its expansion knows no limits. The administration of that enormous, widespread, and overgrown enterprise is sapping my strength. Wishing to share part of the burden with Rudolph, I have nominated him co-regent. Anonymously of course. Together with the stamp album we form, we three, an unofficial triumvirate, on which rests the burden of responsibility for the whole impenetrable and convoluted affair of the spring.

27

I did not have enough courage to go round to the back of the villa. I should certainly have been noticed by someone. Why, in spite of this, did I have the feeling of having been there already— a long time ago? Don't we in fact know in advance all the landscapes we see in our life? Can anything occur that is entirely new, that in the depths of our being, we have not anticipated for a long time? I know, for instance, that one day at a late hour I shall stand on the threshold of these gardens, hand in hand with Bianca. We shall find forgotten corners where, between old walls, poisonous plants are growing, where Poe's artificial Edens, full of hemlock, poppies, and convolvuluses, glow under the grizzly sky of very old frescoes. We shall wake up the white marble statue sleeping with empty eyes in that marginal world beyond the limits of a wilting afternoon. We shall scare away its only lover, a red vampire bat with folded wings asleep on its lap. It will fly away soundlessly, soft and undulating, a helpless, disembodied, bright red scrap without bone or substance; it will circle, flutter, and dissolve without trace in the deadly air. Through a small gate we shall enter a completely empty clearing. Its vegetation will be charred like tobacco, like a prairie during an Indian summer. It will perhaps be in the state of New Orleans or Louisiana—countries are after all only a pretext. We shall sit on the stone wall of a square pond. Bianca will dip her white fingers in the warm water full of yellow leaves and will not lift her eyes. On the other side of the pond, a black, slim, veiled figure will be sitting. I shall ask about it in a whisper, and Bianca will shake her head and say softly: "Don't be afraid, she is not listening; this is my dead mother who lives here." Then she will talk to me about the sweetest, quietest, and saddest things. No comfort will be possible. Dusk will be falling . . .

28

Events are following one another at a mad pace. Bianca's father has arrived. I was standing today at the junction of Fountain and Scarab streets when a shining open landau as broad and shallow as a conch drove by. In that white silk-lined shell I saw Bianca, half-lying, in a tulle dress. Her gentle profile was shaded by the brim of her hat tied under her chin with ribbons. She was almost drowned in swathes of white satin. Next to her sat a gentleman in a black frock coat and a white piqué waistcoat, on which glistened a heavy gold chain with innumerable trinkets. Under his black bowler hat a grim, gray face with sideburns was visible. I shivered when I saw him. There could be no doubt. This was M. de V. . . .

As the elegant carriage passed me, discreetly rumbling with its well-sprung box, Bianca said something to her father, who turned back and stared at me through his large dark glasses. He had the face of a gray lion without a mane.

Excited, almost demented from contradictory feelings, I cried out: "Count on me!" and "Until the last drop of my blood . . ." and fired into the air a pistol produced from my breast pocket.

29

Many things seem to point to the fact that Franz Josef was in reality a powerful but sad Demiurge. His narrow eyes, dull like buttons embedded in triangular deltas of wrinkles, were not

human eyes. His face, with its milky white sideburns brushed back like those of Japanese demons, was the face of an old mopish fox. Seen from a distance, from the height of the terrace at Schönbrunn, that face, owing to a certain combination of wrinkles, seemed to smile. From nearby that smile unmasked itself as a grimace of bitterness and prosaic matter-of-factness, unrelieved by the spark of any idea. At that very moment when he appeared on the world stage in a general's green plumes, slightly hunched and saluting, his blue coat reaching to the ground, the world reached a happy point in its development. All the set forms, having exhausted their content in endless metamorphoses, hung loosely upon things, half-wilted, ready to flake off. The world was a chrysalis about to change violently, to disclose young, new, unheard-of colors and to stretch happily all its sinews and joints. It was touch and go, and the map of the world, that patchwork blanket, might float in the air, swelling like a sail. Franz Josef took this as a personal insult. His element was a world held by the rules of prose, by the pragmatism of boredom. The atmosphere of chanceries and police stations was the air he breathed. And, a strange thing, this dried-up dull man, with nothing attractive in his person, succeeded in pulling a great part of creation to his side. All the loyal and provident fathers of families felt threatened along with him and breathed with relief when this powerful demon laid his weight upon everything and checked the world's aspirations. Franz Josef squared the world like paper, regulated its course with the help of patents, held it within procedural bounds, and insured it against derailment into things unforeseen, adventurous, or simply unpredictable.

Franz Josef was not an enemy of godly and decent pleasures. It was he who invented, under the spur of kindliness of a sort, the imperial-and-royal lottery for the people, Egyptian dream books, illustrated calendars, and the imperial-and-royal tobacco shops. He standardized the servants of heaven, dressed them in symbolic blue uniforms, and let them loose upon the world, divided into ranks and divisions—angelic hordes in the shape of postmen, conductors, and tax collectors. The meanest of those heavenly messengers wore on his face a reflection of age-old wisdom borrowed from his Creator and a jovial, gracious smile framed by sideburns, even if his feet, as a result of his considerable earthly wanderings, reeked of sweat.

But has anyone ever heard of a frustrated conspiracy at the foot of the throne, of a great palace revolution nipped in the bud at the beginning of the glorious rule of the All-Powerful? Thrones wilt when they are not fed with blood, their vitality grows with the mass of wrongs committed, with life denials, with the crushing of all that is perpetually different and that has been ousted by them. We are disclosing here secret and forbidden things; we are touching upon state secrets hidden away and secured with a thousand seals of silence.

Demiurge had a younger brother of an entirely different cast of mind, with different ideas. Who hasn't a brother under one form or another who follows him like a shadow, an antithesis, the partner in an eternal dialogue? According to one version, he was only a cousin; according to another, he had never been born. He was only suggested by the fears and ravings of the Demiurge, overheard while he was asleep. Perhaps he had only invented him anyway, substituted someone else for him, in order to play out the symbolic drama, to repeat once more, for the thousandth time, ceremoniously and ritually that prelegal and fatal act that, in spite of the thousand repetitions, occurs again and again. The conditionally born, unfortunate antagonist, professionally wronged, as it were, because of his role, bore the name of Archduke Maximilian. The very sound of that name, mentioned in a whisper, renews our blood, makes it redder and brighter, makes it pulsate quickly in the clear colors of enthusiasm, of postal sealing wax, and of the red pencil in which happy messages are printed. Maximilian had pink swallows, squeaking with joy, cut across his path. The Demiurge himself loved him secretly while he plotted his downfall. First, he nominated him commander of the Levant Squadron in the hope that he would drown miserably on an expedition to the South Seas. Soon afterward he concluded a secret alliance with Napoléon III, who drew him by deceit into the Mexican adventure. Everything had been planned in advance. The young man, full of fantasy and imagination, enticed by the hope of creating a new, happier world on the Pacific, resigned all his rights as an agnate of the crown and heir to the Habsburgs. On the French liner *Le Cid* he sailed straight into a prepared ambush. The documents of that secret conspiracy have never seen the light of day.

Thus the last hope of the discontented was dashed. After Maximilian's tragic death, Franz Josef forbade the use of red under the pretext of court mourning. The black and yellow colors of mourning became official. The amaranth of enthusiasm has since been fluttering secretly only in the hearts of its adherents. But the Demiurge did not succeed in extirpating it completely from nature. After all, it is potentially present in sunlight. It is enough to close one's eyes in the spring sun in order to absorb it under one's eyelids in each wave of warmth. Photographic paper burns that same red in the spring glare. Bulls led along the sunny streets of the city with a cloth on their horns see it in bright patches and lower their heads, ready to attack imaginary toreros fleeing in panic in sun-drenched arenas.

Sometimes a whole bright day passes in explosions of the sun, in banks of clouds edged with a red glow. People walk about dizzy with light, with closed eyes that inwardly see rockets, Roman candles, and barrels of powder. Later, toward the evening, the hurricane fire of light abates, the horizon becomes rounder, more beautiful, and filled with azure like a glass globe with a miniature panorama of the world with happily arranged plans, over which clouds tower like a crown of gold medals or church bells ringing for evensong.

People gather in the market square, silent under the enormous cupola of light, and group themselves without thinking into a great, immobile finale, a concentrated scene of waiting; the clouds billow in ever-deepening pinks; in all eyes there is calm and the reflection of luminous distances. And suddenly, while they wait, the world reaches its zenith, achieves in a few heartbeats its highest perfection. The gardens arrange themselves on the crystal bowl of the horizon, the May greenery foams and overflows like wine about to spill, hills are formed in the shape of clouds; having passed its supreme peak, the beauty of the world dissolves and takes off to make an entry into eternity.

And while people remain immobile, lowering their heads still full of visions, bewitched by the great luminous ascent of the world, the man whom they had unconsciously all been waiting for runs out from among the crowd, a breathless messenger, pink of face, wearing raspberry-colored tights, and decorated with little bells, medals, and orders. He circles the square slowly six or seven times in order to be in everybody's view, his eyes downcast, as if ashamed, his hands on his hips. His rather heavy stomach is shaken by the rhythmical run. Red from exertion, the face shines with perspiration under the black Bosnian mustache, and the medals, orders, and bells jump up and down in time on his chest like a harness. One can see him from the distance as, turning the corner in a taut parabolic line, he approaches with the janissary band of his bells, handsome as a god, incredibly pink, with an immobile torso, and drives away with a short whip the pack of barking dogs that has been following him.

Then Franz Josef, disarmed by the universal harmony, discreetly proclaims an amnesty, concedes the use of red color, allows it for one May evening in a watered-down, candy shade, and reconciled with the world, appears in the open window of the Schönbrunn Palace; at that moment he is seen all over the world—wherever pink messengers are running on clean-swept market squares, bordered by silent crowds. One can see him in an enormous imperial-and-royal apotheosis against the background of cloud, leaning with gloved hands on the windowsill, clad in a turquoise coat with the ribbon of Commander Grand Cross of the Order of Malta; his eyes, blue buttons without kindness or grace, are narrowed in a kind of smile in the delta of wrinkles. Thus he stands, his snowy sideburns brushed back, made up to represent kindliness: an embittered fox who, for distant onlookers, fakes a smile without humor or genius.

30

After hesitating for a long time, I told Rudolph about the events of the last few days. I could no longer keep to myself the secret that weighed me down. His face darkened; he screamed, said I was lying, and finally burst out with an open show of jealousy. Everything was an invention, a complete lie, he shouted, running with his arms raised. Extraterritorialism! Maximilian! Mexico! Ha-ha! Cotton plantations! Enough of that, this is the end, he is not going to lend me his stamp album anymore. End of partnership. Cancellation of contract. He pulled his hair in agitation. He was completely out of control, ready for anything.

Very frightened, I began to plead with him. I admitted that my story seemed improbable on first hearing, even unbelievable. I myself, I agreed, was quite amazed. No wonder that it was difficult for him, unprepared as he was, to accept it at once. I appealed to his heart and honor. Would his conscience allow him to refuse me his help just when matters were about to reach a decisive stage? Would he now spoil everything by withdrawing his participation? At last I undertook to prove, on the basis of the stamp album, that everything was, word for word, the truth.

Somewhat mollified, Rudolph opened the album. Never before had I spoken with such force and enthusiasm. I outdid myself. Supporting my reasoning with the evidence of stamps, not only did I refute all his accusations and dispel his doubts, but what is more, I reached such revealing conclusions that I myself was amazed by the perspective that opened up. Rudolph remained silent and defeated, and no more was said about dissolving the partnership.

3 1

Can one consider it a coincidence that at about the same time a great theater of illusion, a magnificent wax figure exhibition, came to town and pitched its tent in Holy Trinity Square? I had been anticipating it for a long time and told Rudolph the news with great excitement.

The evening was windy; rain hung in the air. On the yellow and dull horizon the day was getting ready to depart, hastily putting weatherproof gray covers over the train of its carts, about to proceed in rows toward the cool beyond. Under a half-drawn, darker curtain the last streaks of sunset appeared for a moment, then sank into a flat, endless plain, a lakeland of watery reflections. A frightened, yellow, foredoomed glare shone from these streaks across half the sky; the curtain was falling quickly. The pale roofs of houses shone with a moist reflection; it was getting dark and the gutter pipes were beginning to sing in monotone.

The wax figure exhibition was already open. Crowds of people sheltering under umbrellas were outlined in the dim light of the sinking day in the forecourt of the tent, where they ceremoniously gave money for their tickets to a décolletaged lady, glittering with jewels and gold teeth: a live, laced-up, and painted torso, her lower extremities lost in the shadow of velvet curtains.

Through a half-open flap we entered a brightly lit space. It was full of people. Groups of them in wet overcoats with upturned collars ambled in silence from place to place, stopping in attentive semicircles. Without difficulty I recognized among them those who belonged to this world only in appearance, who in reality led a separate, dignified, and embalmed life on pedestals, a life on show, festively empty. They stood in grim silence, clad in somber made-to-measure frock coats and morning suits of good-quality cloth, very pale, and on their cheeks the feverish flush of the illnesses from which they had died. They had not had a single thought in their heads for quite a time, only the habit of showing themselves from every angle, of exhibiting the emptiness of their existence. They should have been in their beds a long time before, tucked under their cold sheets, their dose of medicine administered. It was a presumption to keep them up so late on their narrow pedestals and in chairs on which they sat so stiffly, in tight patent-leather footwear, miles from their previous existence, with glazed eyes entirely deprived of memory.

All of them had hanging from their lips, dead like the tongue of a strangled man, a last cry, uttered when they left the lunatic asylum where, taken for maniacs, they had spent some time in purgatory before entering this ultimate abode. No, they were not authentic Dreyfuses, Edisons, or Lucchenis; they were only pretenders. They may have been real madmen, caught red-handed at the precise moment a brilliant idée fixe had entered their heads; the moment of truth was skillfully distilled and became the crux of their new existence, pure as an element and unalterable. Ever since then, that one idea remained in their heads like an exclamation mark, and they clung to it, standing on one foot, suspended in midair, or stopped at half a gesture.

Passing anxiously from group to group, I looked in the crowd for Maximilian. At last I found him, not in the splendid uniform of admiral of the Levant Squadron, in which he sailed from Toulon on the way to Mexico in the flagship *Le Cid*, nor in the green tailcoat of cavalry general he wore in his last days. He was in an ordinary suit of clothes, a frock coat with long, folding skirts and light-colored trousers, his chin resting on a high collar with a cravat. Rudolph and I stopped reverently in the group of people forming a semicircle in front of him. Suddenly, I froze. A few steps from us, in the first row of the onlookers, stood Bianca in a white dress, accompanied by her governess. She stood there and looked. Her small face had become paler in the last few days, and her eyes, darkly circled and full of shadow, wore an expression of profound sadness.

She was standing immobile, with folded hands hidden in the pleats of her dress, looking from under her serious eyebrows with mournful eyes. My heart bled at the sight of her. Unconsciously I followed the direction of her gaze, and this is what I saw: Maximilian's features moved, as if awakened, the corner of his mouth curled up in a smile, his eyes shone and began to roll in their orbits, his breast covered with decorations heaved with a sigh. It was not a miracle, but a simple mechanical trick. Suitably wound up, the archduke held court in accordance with the principles of his mechanism, graciously and ceremoniously as he had done when alive. He was now scanning the spectators, his eyes looking attentively at everybody in turn.

His eyes rested on Bianca's for a moment. He winced, hesitated, swallowed hard, as if he had wanted to say something; but a moment later, obedient to his mechanism, he continued to run his eyes over other faces with the same inviting and radiant smile. Had he become aware of Bianca's presence, had it

reached his heart? Who could tell? He was not even fully himself, merely a distant double of his former being, much reduced
and in a state of deep prostration. On the basis of mere fact,
one must admit that in a way he was his own closest relative,
perhaps he was even as much himself as possible under the circumstances, so many years after his death. In that waxen resurrection it must have been very difficult to become one's real
self. Something quite new and frightening must have sneaked
into his being, something foreign must have detached itself
from the madness of the ingenious maniac who conceived him
in his megalomania—and this now seemed to be filling Bianca
with awe and horror. Even a very sick person changes and
becomes detached from his own self, let alone someone so
clumsily resuscitated. For how did he behave now toward his
own flesh and blood? With an assumed gaiety and bravado he
continued to play his clowning imperial comedy, magnificent

and smiling. Had he much to conceal, or was he perhaps afraid of the attendants who were watching him while he was on exhibition in that hospital of wax figures where he and the others stayed under hospital regulations? Distilled laboriously from somebody's madness; clean, cured, and saved at last—didn't he have to tremble at the possibility of being returned to chaos and turmoil?

When I turned to Bianca again, I saw that she had covered her face with a handkerchief. The governess put an arm around her, gazing inanely at her with her enamel blue eyes. I could not look any longer at Bianca's suffering and felt like sobbing. I pulled Rudolph's sleeve and we walked toward the exit.

Behind our backs, that made-up ancestor, that grandfather in the prime of life, continued to bestow on all and sundry his radiant imperial salutes: in an excess of zeal he even lifted his hand and was almost blowing kisses to us in the immobile silence, amid the hissing of acetylene lamps and the quiet dripping of rain on the canvas of the tent; he rose on tiptoe with the last remnants of his strength, mortally ill like the rest of them and longing for the death shroud.

In the vestibule the made-up torso of the lady cashier said something to us while her diamonds and gold teeth glittered against the black background of magic draperies. We went out into a dewy night, warm from rain. The roofs shone with water, the gutter pipes gurgled monotonously. We ran through the downpour, lit by streetlamps, jingling under the rain.

3 2

O abysmal human perversity, truly infernal intrigue! In whose mind could have arisen that venomous and devilish idea, bolder than the most elaborate flights of fancy? The deeper I penetrate its malevolence, the greater my wonder at the perfidy, the flash of evil genius, in that monstrous idea.

So my intuition has not led me astray. Here, at hand, in the midst of an apparent legality, in time of peace guaranteed by treaties, a crime was being committed that made one's hair stand on end. A somber drama was being enacted in complete silence, a drama so shrouded in secrecy that nobody could guess at it and detect it during the innocent aspects of that spring. Who could suspect that between that gagged, mute wax figure rolling its eyes and the delicate, carefully raised, and beautifully mannered Bianca a family tragedy was being enacted? Who really was Bianca? Are we to reveal the secret at last? What if she was not descended either from the legitimate empress of Mexico or even from the morganatic wife, Izabella d'Orgaz, who, from the stage of a touring opera, conquered Archduke Maximilian by her beauty?

What if her mother was the little Creole girl whom he called Conchita and who under that name has entered history through the back door as it were? Information about her that I have been able to collect with the help of the stamp album can be summarized in a few words.

After the Emperor's fall, Conchita left with her small daughter for Paris, where she lived on a widow's pension, keeping unbroken faith with the memory of her imperial lover. There, history lost track of that touching figure, giving way to hearsay and reconstruction. Nothing is known about the daughter's marriage and her subsequent fate. Instead, in 1900, a certain Mme de V., a lady of extraordinary and exotic beauty, left France with her small daughter and her husband on false passports and proceeded to Austria. At Salzburg, on the Austro-Bavarian frontier, when changing trains for Vienna, the family was stopped by the Austrian gendarmerie and arrested. It was remarkable that, after his false papers had been examined, M. de V. was freed but did not try to get his wife and daughter released. He returned the same day to France, and all trace of him has since been lost. Thereafter the story becomes very entangled. I was therefore very thrilled when the stamp album helped me to find the fugitives' trace. The discovery was entirely mine. I succeeded in identifying the said M. de V. as a highly suspect individual who appeared in a different country under a completely different name. But hush! . . . Nothing more can be said about it yet. Suffice it to say that Bianca's genealogy has been established beyond any doubt.

33

So much for canonical history. But the official history remains incomplete. There are in it intentional gaps, long pauses that spring fills swiftly with its fantasies. One needs a lot of patience to find a grain of truth in the tangle of springtime vagaries. This might be achieved by a careful grammatical analysis of the phrases and sentences of spring. Who? Whose? What? One must eliminate the seductive cross talk of birds—their pointed adverbs and prepositions, their skittish pronouns—and work oneself slowly to a healthy grain of sense. The stamp album serves as a compass in my search. Stupid, indiscriminating spring! It covers everything with growth, mingles sense with nonsense, cracking jokes, lighthearted to a degree. Could it be that it, too, is in league with Franz Josef, that it is tied to him by a bond of common conspiracy? Every ounce of sense breaking through is at once covered up by a hundred lies, by an avalanche of nonsense. The birds obliterate all evidence, obscure all traces by their family punctuation. Truth is cornered by the luxuriance that immediately fills each empty plot, each crevice, with its spreading foliage. Where is truth to shelter, where is it to find asylum if not in a place where nobody is looking for it: in fairground calendars and almanacs, in the canticles of beggars and tramps, which in direct line are derived from stamp albums?

34

After many sunny weeks came a period of hot and overcast days. The sky darkened as on old frescoes, and in the oppressive silence banks of clouds loomed like tragic battlefields in paintings of the Neapolitan school. Against the background of these leaden, ashen cumuli, the chalky whiteness of houses shone brightly, accentuated by the sharp shadows of cornices and pilasters. People walked with heads bowed, their mood dark and tense as before a storm charged with static electricity.

Bianca had not been seen again in the park. She was obviously closely supervised and not allowed out. They must have smelled danger.

I saw in town a group of gentlemen in black morning coats and top hats walking through the market square with the measured steps of diplomats. Their white shirt fronts glared in the leaden air. They looked in silence at the houses, as if valuing them, and walked with slow, rhythmic steps. They had coal black mustaches on carefully shaven faces with shining expressive eyes, which turned in their orbits smoothly, as if oiled. From time to time they doffed their hats and wiped their brows. They were all slim, tall, and middle aged, and they had the sultry faces of gangsters.

3 5

The days became dark, cloudy, and gray. A distant, potential storm lay in wait day and night over the horizon, not discharging itself in a downpour. In the great silence, a breath of ozone would pass at times through the steely air, with the smell of rain and a moist, fresh breeze.

Afterward the gardens filled the air with enormous sighs and grew their leaves hastily, doing overtime by day and by night. All flags hung down heavy and darkened, helplessly pouring out the last streaks of color into the dense aura. Sometimes at the opening of a street someone turned to the sky half a face, like a dark cutout with one frightened and shining eye, and listened to the rumble of space, to the electric silence of passing clouds while the air was cut by the flight of trembling, pointed, arrow-sharp, black-and-white swallows.

Ecuador and Colombia are mobilizing. In the ominous silence lines of infantry in white trousers, white straps crossed on their breasts, are crowding the quays. The Chilean unicorn is rearing. One can see it in the evening outlined against the sky, a pathetic animal, immobile with terror, its hoofs in the air.

36

The days are sinking ever deeper into shadow and melancholy. The sky has blocked itself and hangs low, swelled with a dark, threatening storm. The earth, parched and motley, is holding its breath; only the gardens, crazy and drunken, continue to grow, to sprout leaves and fill all their free spaces with a cool greenery. (The fat buds were sticky like an itchy rash, painful and festering; now they are healing with cool foliage, forming leafy scars, gaining green health, multiplied beyond measure and without count. They have already stifled under their greenness the forlorn call of the cuckoo, and its distant voice now rises faintly from deep thickets, dulled by the happy flood of leaves.)

Why are the houses shining so bright in that dusky landscape? As the rustling parks become darker, the whitewash on houses sharpens and glows in the sunless air with the hot reflection of burnt earth, as if it were to be spattered in a moment by the feverish spots of infectious disease.

Dogs run dizzily, their noses in the air. Crazed and excited, they sniff among the fluffy greenness. Something revealing and enormous prepares to spring forth from the closeness of these overcast days.

I am trying to guess what event could match the negative sum of expectations contained in this enormous load of electricity; what could equal this catastrophic barometrical low.

The thing that is growing is preparing nature for a trough that the gardens cannot fill although they are equipped with the most enchanting smell of lilac.

37

Negroes, crowds of Negroes, were in the city! People had seen them here and there, in many places at once. They were running in the streets in a noisy, ragged gang, rushing into grocery shops, and stealing food. They joked, nudged one another, laughed, rolled the whites of their eyes, chattered gutturally, and bared their white, shining teeth. Before the militia could be mobilized, they disappeared into thin air.

I have felt it coming; it was unavoidable. It was the natural consequence of meteorological tension. Only now do I realize what I have felt all along: that the spring was announcing the Negroes' arrival. Where had they come from? Why did the hordes of black men in striped cotton pajamas suddenly appear here? Was it the great Barnum who had opened his circus in the neighborhood, having traveled with an endless train of people, animals, and demons? Had his wagons, crowded with an endless chatter of beasts and acrobats, stopped anywhere near us? Not at all. Barnum was far away. I have my suspicions, but I won't breathe a word. For you, Bianca, I'll remain silent, and no torture will extract any confession from me.

38

On that day I dressed slowly and with great care. Finally, in front of the mirror, I composed my face into an expression of calm and relentless determination. I carefully loaded up my pistol, before slipping it in the back pocket of my trousers. I glanced into the mirror once more and with my hand patted the breast pocket of my jacket where I had hidden some documents. I was ready to face the man.

I felt completely calm and determined. Bianca's future was at stake, and for her I was prepared to do anything! I decided not to confide in Rudolph. The better I knew him, the stronger I felt that he was a prosaic fellow, unable to rise above triviality. I have had enough of his face, alternatively freezing in consternation and growing pale with envy at each of my new revelations.

Deep in thought, I quickly walked the short distance. When the great iron gates clanged shut behind me with suppressed vibrations, I at once entered a different climate, different currents of air, the cool and unfamiliar region of a great year. The black branches of trees pointed to another, abstract time; their bare forked tops were outlined against the white sky of another, foreign zone; the avenues closed in. The voices of birds, muted in

the vast spaces of the sky, cut the silence, a silence heavy and
loaded that spread into gray meditation, into a great, unsteady
paleness without end or goal.

With my head raised, cool and self-possessed, I asked to be
announced. I was admitted to a darkened hall that exuded an
aura of quiet luxury. Through a high open window the garden
air flowed in gentle, balmy waves. These soft influxes, penetrating across the gentle filter of billowing curtains, made objects
become alive; furtive chords resounded along rows of Venetian
tumblers in a glass-fronted cabinet, and the leaves on the wallpaper rustled, silvery and scared.

It is strange how old interiors reflect their dark turbulent past, how in their stillness bygone history tries to be reenacted, how the same situations repeat themselves with infinite variations, turned upside down and inside out by the fruitless dialectic of wallpapers and hangings. Silence, vitiated and demoralized, ferments into recriminations. Why hide it? The excessive excitements and paroxysms of fever have had to be soothed here, night after night by injections of secret drugs, and the wallpapers have provided imagined visions of gentle landscapes and of distant mirrored waters.

I heard a rustle. Preceded by a valet, a man was coming down the stairs, short but well built, economic of gesture, blinded by the light reflected on his large horn-rimmed spectacles. For the first time I faced him closely. He was inscrutable, but I noticed, not without satisfaction, that after my first words two furrows of worry and bitterness appeared on his face. While behind his spectacles he was composing his face into a mask of magnificent haughtiness, I could see panic slowly getting hold of him. As he gradually became more interested, it was obvious from his concentrated attention that at last he was beginning to take me seriously. He invited me into his study next door. When we entered it, a woman in a white dress leapt away from the door, as if she had been listening, and disappeared inside the house. Was it Bianca's governess? When I entered the room, I felt as if I were entering a jungle. The opaque greenish twilight was striped by the watery shadows of Venetian blinds drawn over the windows. The walls were hung with botanical prints; small colorful birds fluttered in large cages. Probably wishing to gain time, the man showed me specimens of primitive arms— jereeds, boomerangs, and tomahawks—which were displayed on the walls. My acute sense of smell detected the smell of curare. While he was handling a sort of primitive halberd, I suggested that he should be careful, and supported my warning by producing my pistol. He smiled wryly, a little put out, and put the weapon back in its place. We sat down at a very large ebony desk. I thanked him for the cigar he offered, saying that I did not smoke. My abstemiousness obviously impressed him. With a cigar in the corner of his hanging lips, he looked at me with a friendliness that did not inspire confidence. Then, turning the pages of his checkbook, he suddenly proposed a compromise, naming a four-figure sum while his pupils rolled into the corners of his eyes. My ironic smile made him abruptly change the subject. With a sigh he opened a large ledger. He began to explain the state of his affairs. Bianca's name was not mentioned even once, although every word we uttered concerned her. I looked at him without moving, and the ironic smile never left my lips. At last, quite exhausted, he leaned back in his chair.

"You are intractable," he said as if to himself. "What exactly do you want?"

I began to speak again. I spoke softly, with restrained passion. A flush came to my cheeks. Trembling, I mentioned several times the name Maximilian, stressing it, and observed how my adversary's face became successively paler. At last I finished, breathing heavily. He sat there shaken. He could not master the expression on his face, which suddenly became old and tired.

"Your decision will show me," I ended, "whether you have really understood the new state of affairs and whether you are ready to follow it by your actions. I demand facts, and nothing but facts . . ."

With a shaking hand he reached for the bell. I stopped him by raising my hand; with my finger on the trigger of the pistol, I withdrew backward from the room. At the door, the servant handed me my hat. I found myself on a terrace flooded by sunshine, my eyes still full of the eddying twilight. I walked downstairs, not turning my head, triumphant and now certain that no assassin's gun would be aimed at me from behind the drawn Venetian blinds of the mansion.

39

Important matters, highest affairs of state, force me now to have frequent confidential talks with Bianca. I prepare for them scrupulously, sitting at my desk late into the night, poring over genealogical details of a most delicate nature. Time goes by, the night stops softly outside the open window, matures, grows more solemn—suggesting deeper stages of initiation—and finally disarms itself with a helpless sigh. In long, slow gulps the dark room inhales the air of the park, its fluffy seeds and pollens, its silent plushy moths, that fly softly around the walls. The wallpaper bristles with fear, cool ecstasies and flights of fancy begin, the panic and the folly of a night in May, long after midnight. Its transparent and glassy fauna, the light plankton of gnats, falls on me as I lean over my papers and work far into the small hours. Grasshoppers and mosquitoes land on my papers—blown-glass squiggles, thin monograms, arabesques invented by the night—and grow larger and more fantastic, as large as bats or vampires.

On such extramarginal nights that know no limits, space loses its meaning. Surrounded by the bright circle of midges, with a sheaf of papers ready at last, I make a few steps into an unknown direction, into one of the blind alleys of the night that must end at a door, Bianca's white door. I press the handle and enter, as if from one room to another. When I cross the threshold, my black wide-brimmed hat flutters as if blown by the wind. My fantastically knotted tie rustles in the draft as I press to my heart an attaché case filled with most secret documents. It feels as if I have stepped from the vestibule of night into the night proper. How deeply one can breathe the nightly ozone! Here is the thicket, here is the core of the night scented with jasmine.

It is here that the night begins its real story. A large lamp with a pink shade is lighted at the head of the bed. In its pink glow Bianca rests on enormous pillows, sailing on the bedding like on a night tide, under a wide, open window. Bianca is reading, leaning on her white forearm. To my deep bow she replies with a quick look from over her book. Seen from nearby, her beauty is muted, not overwhelming. With sacrilegious pleasure I notice that her nose is not very nobly shaped and her complexion far from perfect. I notice it with a certain relief, although I know that she controls her glamour with a kind of pity in order that I do not become breathless and tongue-tied. Her beauty regenerates through the medium of distance and then becomes painful, peerless, and unbearable.

Emboldened by her nod, I sit down by her bed and begin my report, with the help of the documents prepared. Through the open window behind Bianca's head the crazy rustle of the trees is heard. Processions of trees pass by, penetrate through the walls, spread themselves, and become all-embracing. Bianca listens to me somewhat distractedly. It is quite irritating that she does not stop reading. She allows me to argue each matter thoroughly, to enumerate the pros and cons; then lifting her eyes from the book and fluttering her lids a little absently, she makes a quick, perfunctory, but astonishingly apt decision. Attentive and concentrating on her words, I listen carefully to the tone of her voice, so as to understand her hidden intentions. Then I humbly submit the papers for her signature; Bianca signs, with downcast eyes, her eyelashes casting long shadows, and watches me with slight irony as I countersign them.

Perhaps the late hour, past midnight, does not favor concentration on affairs of state. The night, having reached its last frontiers, leans toward dissolution. While we are talking, the illusion of a room fades; we are now practically in the middle of a forest. Tufts of fern grow in every corner; behind the bed a screen of bushes moves animated and entangled. From that leafy wall big-eyed squirrels, woodpeckers, and sundry night creatures materialize and look immobile at the lamplight with shining, bulging eyes. At a certain moment we have entered an illegal time, a night beyond control, liable to all kinds of excesses and crazes. What is happening now does not really count and consists of trifles, reckless misdemeanors, and nightly frolics. This must be the reason for the strange changes that occur in Bianca's behavior. She, always so self-possessed and serious, the personification of beautiful discipline, becomes now whimsical, contrary, and unpredictable. The papers are spread out on the great plain of her counterpane. Bianca picks them up nonchalantly, casts an eye on them, and lets them fall again from between her loosened fingers. Pouting, a pale arm laid under her head, she postpones her decisions and makes me wait. Or else she turns away from me, clamps her hands over her ears, and is deaf to my entreaties and persuasions. Then without a word, with one kick of her foot under the bedclothes, she makes all the papers slip to the floor, and with wide-open eyes she watches over her arm from the height of her pillows how, crouching, I pick them up carefully from the ground, blowing the pine needles from them. These whims, quite charming in themselves, do not make my difficult and responsible task as regent any easier.

During our conversation the rustle of the forest and the scent of jasmine evoke in the room visions of landscapes. Innumerable trees and bushes, whole woodland sceneries, move past us. And then it becomes clear that we find ourselves in a kind of train, a nightly forest train, rolling slowly along a ravine in the wooded outskirts of the city. Hence the delightful breeze that flows through the compartment. A conductor with a lantern appears from nowhere, emerges from among the trees, and punches our tickets with his machine. The darkness deepens, the draft becomes more piercing. Bianca's eyes shine, her cheeks are flushed, an enchanting smile opens her lips. Does she want to confide in me? Reveal a secret? Bianca talks of treason, and her face burns with ecstasy, her eyes narrow in a paroxysm of delight when, wriggling like a lizard under her counterpane, she accuses me of having betrayed my most sacred mission. She stubbornly fixes my face, now pale, with her sweet eyes, which are beginning to squint.

"Do it," she whispers intently, "do it. You will become one of them, one of the dark Negroes . . ."

And when in despair I put my finger to my lips in a gesture of entreaty, her little face suddenly becomes mean and venomous.

"You are ridiculous with your inflexible loyalty and your sense of mission. God knows why you imagine you are indispensable. And what if I should choose Rudolph? I prefer him to you, you boring pedant. Ah, he would be obedient and follow me into crime, into self-destruction!"

Then, with a triumphant expression she asks:

"Do you remember Lonka, the washerwoman Antonia's daughter, with whom you played when you were small?"

I look at her amazed.

"It was I," she says giggling, "only I was a boy at that time. Did you like me then?"

O there is something very rotten and dissolute at the very center of spring. Bianca, Bianca, must you disappoint me, even you?

40

I am afraid to reveal my trump card too soon. I am playing for too high a stake to risk it. It's a long time since I have ceased to report to Rudolph about developments. Besides, his behavior has recently undergone a change. Envy, which had been the dominant feature of his character, has given way to some sort of magnanimity. Whenever we meet by chance, an eager, rather embarrassed friendliness now shows in his gestures and clumsy remarks, whereas formerly, under the grumpy expression of a silent and expectant reserve, there was at least a devouring curiosity, a hunger for new details concerning the affair. Now he has become strangely calm and seems uninterested in what I might have to say. This suits me because every night I attend extremely important meetings at the Wax Figures Exhibition, meetings that must remain secret for the time being. The attendants, stupefied by drink, which I generously supply, sleep the sleep of the just in their closets, while I, in the light of a few smoking candles, confer with the distinguished company of exhibits. There are among them some Royals, and negotiations with them are never an easy matter. From their past they have preserved an instinctive gallantry now inapplicable, a readiness to burn in the fire of some principle, to put their lives at stake. The ideals that once guided their lives have been discredited one after another in the prose of daily life, their fires have burned out: here they stand, played out yet full of unspent energy, and, their eyes shining crazily, they await the cue for their last role. When they are so uncritical and defenseless, how easy it is to give them the wrong cue, to suggest any idea that comes along! This simplifies my task, of course. On the other hand, it is extremely difficult to reach them, to light in them the spark of interest, so empty have they become.

To wake them up at all has cost me a lot of effort. They were all in their beds, mortally pale and laboring for breath. I had to lean over each of them and whisper the vital words, words that should shock them like electric current. They would open one lazy eye. They were afraid of the attendants, pretended to be deaf or dead. Only when reassured that we were alone would they lift themselves up on their beds, bandaged, made of bits and pieces, feeling their wooden limbs, their false lungs and imitation livers. At first they were very mistrustful and wanted to recite the roles they had learned. They could not understand why anyone should ask them for anything different. And so they sat dully, groaning from time to time, these once-splendid men, the flower of mankind: Dreyfus and Garibaldi, Bismarck and Victor Emmanuel I, Gambetta, Mazzini, and many others. The most difficult to persuade was Archduke Maximilian himself. When, whispering in his ear, I kept repeating Bianca's name, he only blinked his eyes and no glimmer of understanding showed on his face. It's only when I uttered distinctly the name of Franz Josef that a wild grimace appeared on his face, a pure conditional reflex, in which his feelings were not involved. That particular complex had long ago been eliminated from his consciousness: how else could he live with it, with that burning hatred, he, who had been put together from pieces after the bloody execution at Querétaro? I had to teach him about his life from the beginning. His memory was very poor. I had to recur to the subconscious glimmers of feeling. I was implanting in him elements of love and hate, but already on the following night he did not remember anything. His more intelligent colleagues tried to help him, to prompt the reactions he should show; his reeducation advanced slowly, step-by-step. He had been very neglected, innerly ravaged by the attendants, yet in spite of this I finally succeeded in making him reach for his sword at the sound of Franz Josef's name. He very nearly stabbed Victor Emmanuel I, who did not give way to him quickly enough.

In fact, most of that splendid assembly absorbed my idea with much more eagerness and much quicker than the plodding, luckless Archduke. Their enthusiasm was boundless, and I had to use all my strength to restrain them. It is difficult to say whether they understood in all its implications the ideal for which they were to fight, but the merit of the case was not their concern. Destined to burn in the fire of some dogma, they were enchanted at having acquired, thanks to me, a catchword for which they could die fighting in exultation. I calmed them with hypnosis, taught them patiently how to keep a secret. I was proud of their progress. What leader had ever had under his command such illustrious subordinates, generals who were such fiery spirits, a guard composed of geniuses, cripples though they all might be!

At last the date came; on a stormy and windy night all that was being prepared had to happen. Lightning pierced the sky, opening up the gory, frightening interior of the earth and shutting it again. Yet the world continued to turn with the rustling of trees, processions of forests, shifting of horizons. Under cover of darkness we left the exhibition. I walked at the head of the inspired cohort, advancing among the violent limping and

rattling, the clatter of crutches and metal. Lightning licked the
bared blades of sabers. Stumbling, we reached the gate of the
villa. We found it open. Worried, anticipating treachery, I gave
the order to light flares. The air became red from burning
resinous chips, flocks of frightened birds shot up high into the
glare, and in this Bengal light we saw clearly the villa, its terraces and balconies illuminated by the flames. From the roof a
white flag was waving. Struck by a bad premonition, I marched
into the courtyard at the head of my warriors. The majordomo
appeared on the terrace. Bowing, he descended the monumental
staircase and approached hesitantly, with uncertain gestures. I
pointed my blade at him. My loyal troops stood immobile, lifting high their smoking flares: in the silence one could hear the
hissing of the flames.

"Where is M. de V.?" I asked.

He spread his hands helplessly.

"He has gone away, sir," he answered.

"We shall see if this is so. And where is the Infanta?"

"Her Highness has also left, they have all gone away . . ."

I had no reason to doubt his words. Someone must have betrayed me. There was no time to be lost.

"Company mount horse!" I cried. "We must cut off their flight!"

We broke into the stables. In the warm darkness we found the horses. Within a moment we were all mounted on the rearing and neighing steeds. Galloping, we formed a long cavalcade and reached the road.

"Through the woods toward the river," I commanded and turned into a forest path. The forest engulfed us. We rode amid waterfalls of noise, amid disturbed trees, the flares lighting the progress of our extended file. Confused thoughts rushed through my head. Had Bianca been kidnapped, or had her father's lowly ancestry overruled the voice of her mother's blood and the sense of mission I had been trying in vain to implant in her? The path became narrower and changed into a ravine, at the end of which there opened a large forest clearing. There at last we caught up with them. They saw us coming and stopped their carriage. M. de V. got out and crossed his arms on his breast. He was walking toward us, his glasses shining crimson in the light of the flares. Twelve bared blades were pointed at his breast. We approached in a large semicircle, in silence, the horses at a trot. I shielded my eyes in order to see better. The light of the flares now fell on the carriage, and inside it I saw Bianca, mortally pale, and, sitting next to her, Rudolph. He was holding her hand and pressing it against his breast. I slowly dismounted and advanced shakily toward the carriage. Rudolph rose as if wanting to get out and speak to me.

Stopping by the carriage, I turned to the cavalcade following me slowly, their sabers at the ready, and said:

"Gentlemen, I have troubled you unnecessarily. These people are free and can proceed if they wish, unmolested. No hair of their heads is to be touched. You have done your duty, gentlemen. Please sheathe your sabers. I don't know how completely you have understood the ideal that I engaged you to serve, and how profoundly it has fired your imagination. That ideal, as you can see, has now completely failed. I believe that, as far as you are concerned, you might survive its failure without much damage, for you have already survived once before the failure of your own ideals. You are indestructible now; as for me . . . but never mind that. I should not like you to think," and here I turned to those in the carriage, "that what has happened has found me entirely unprepared. This is not so. I have been anticipating it all for a long time. If I had persisted in my error for so long, not wishing to admit the truth to myself, it was only because it would not have been seemly for me to know things that exceed my competence, or openly to anticipate events. I wanted to remain in the role destiny had allotted to me, I wanted to fulfill my task and remain loyal to the position I had usurped. For, I must now confess with regret, despite the promptings of my ambition, I have only been a usurper. In my blindness, I undertook to comment on the text, to be the interpreter of God's will; I misunderstood the scanty traces and indications I believe I found in the pages of the stamp album. Unfortunately, I wove them into a fabric of my own making. I have imposed my own direction upon this spring, I devised my own program to explain its immense flourishing and wanted to harness it, to direct it according to my own ideas. The spring has carried me away for a time; it was patient and indifferent and hardly aware of me. I took its lack of response for tolerance, for solidarity, even for complicity. I thought that I could decipher, better than spring itself, its features, its deepest intentions, that I could read in its soul or anticipate what, overcome by its own immensity, it could not express. I ignored all the signs of its wild and unchecked independence, I overlooked its violent and incalculable perturbations.

"In my megalomania I went so far as to dare to pry into the dynastic affairs of the highest powers, and I have mobilized you, gentlemen, against the Demiurge. I have abused your receptiveness to ideas, your noble credulity, in order to implant in you a false and iconoclastic doctrine, to harness your fiery idealism for a wanton, inconsiderate action. I don't want to determine whether I have been suited to the highest duties to which my ambition has driven me. I was probably called only to initiate them, to be abandoned later. I have exceeded my competence, but even that has been foreseen. In reality, I have known my fate from the outset. As the fate of that luckless Maximilian, my fate was that of Abel. There was a moment when my sacrifice seemed sweet and pleasing to God, when your chances seemed nil, Rudolph. But Cain always wins. The dice were loaded against me."

At that moment a distant detonation shook the air, and a column of fire rose above the forests. All those present turned their heads.

"Stay calm," I said, "it is the Wax Figures Exhibition on fire. I left there, before our departure, a barrel of powder with a lighted fuse. You have lost your home, noble gentlemen, and now you are homeless. I hope that this does not affect you too much?"

But these once-powerful individuals, these leaders of mankind, stood silent, helplessly rolling their eyes, crazily keeping a battle formation in the distant glare of the fire. They looked at one another, blinking, without a thought.

"You, sire," I addressed myself to the Archduke, "were wrong. Perhaps you too were guilty of megalomania. I had no right to try to reform the world on your behalf. Perhaps this has never been your intention either. Red is, after all, only a color like all the others, and only all colors put together contribute to the wholeness of light. Forgive me for having misused your name for purposes that were alien to you. Long live Franz Josef the First!"

The Archduke shook at the sound of that name, reached for his saber, then hesitated and thought better of it; but a more vivid flush colored his painted cheeks, the corners of his mouth lifted, his eyes began to turn in their orbits, and in a measured step, with great distinction, he began to hold court, moving from one person to the other with a radiant smile. They moved away from him, scandalized. The revival of imperial manners at this unsuitable moment created the worst possible impression.

"Stop this, sire," I said. "I don't doubt that you know by heart the ceremonial of your court, but this is not the time for it. I want to read to you, noble gentlemen, and to you, Infanta, the act of my abdication. I am abdicating completely. I am dissolving the triumvirate. I am giving up the regency in favor of

Rudolph. You, noble gentlemen," here I turned to my staff, "are free to go now. Your intentions were excellent, and I thank you most sincerely in the name of our dethroned idea"—tears sprang to my eyes—"which, in spite of everything . . ."

Just then a shot was fired somewhere nearby. We all turned our heads in that direction. M. de V. stood with a smoking pistol in his hand, strangely stiff and leaning to one side. He grimaced, then staggered and fell on his face.

"Father, Father!" screamed Bianca and threw herself upon the prostrate man. Confusion followed. Garibaldi, an old hand who knew everything about wounds, leaned over him. The bullet had pierced his heart. The King of Piedmont and Mazzini lifted him carefully by the arms and laid him on a stretcher. Bianca was sobbing, supported by Rudolph. The Negroes who just then appeared under the trees crowded round their master. "Massa, Massa, our kind massa," they chanted in chorus.

"This night is truly fatal!" I cried. "This tragedy won't be the last. But I must confess that this is something I had not foreseen. I have wronged him. In reality, a noble heart beat in his breast. I hereby revoke my judgment of him, which has obviously been shortsighted and prejudiced. He must have been a good father, a good master to his slaves. My reasoning has failed even in this instance, but I admit it without regret. It is your duty, Rudolph, to comfort Bianca, to redouble your love, to replace her father. You will probably want to take his body on board; we shall therefore form a procession and march to the harbor. I can hear the siren of the steamship."

Bianca got back into the carriage; we mounted our horses. The Negroes took the stretcher on their shoulders and we all turned toward the harbor. The cavalcade of riders brought up the rear of that sorry procession. The storm had abated during my speech, the light of flares opened deep long cracks among the trees, and fleeting black shadows formed a semicircle behind our backs. At last we left the forest. We could see in the distance the steamship with its large paddles.

Not much remains to be added, the story is nearing its end. Accompanied by the sobbing of Bianca and the Negroes, the body of the dead man was taken aboard. For the last time we re-formed our ranks.

"One more thing, Rudolph," I said, taking hold of a button of his jacket. "You are leaving now as heir to an enormous fortune. I don't wish to make any suggestions, and it should be my task to provide for the old age of these homeless heroes, but, unfortunately, I am a pauper."

Rudolph at once reached for his checkbook. We conferred shortly and privately and quickly came to an agreement.

"Gentlemen," I exclaimed, addressing myself to my guard, "my generous friend here has decided to compensate you for my action, which has deprived you of your livelihood and a roof over your heads. After what has happened, no wax figure cabinet will ever admit you, especially since the competition is very great. You will have to give up some of your ambitions. Instead, you will become free men, which, I know, will appeal to you. As you have not been trained, unfortunately, for any practical work, having been destined for purely representative duties, my friend here has made a donation sufficient for the purchase of twelve barrel organs from the Black Forest. You will disperse all over the world, playing for people's pleasure. The choice of music is left to you. Why mince words, anyway, since you are not completely real Dreyfuses, Edisons, and Napoléons? You have assumed these names vicariously, for lack of anything better. Now you will swell the numbers of many of your predecessors, those anonymous Garibaldis, Bismarcks, and MacMahons who wander in their thousands, unacknowledged, all over the world. In the depths of your hearts you will remain forever what you are. And now, dear friends and noble gentlemen, let's wish together all happiness to the bridal pair. Long live Rudolph and Bianca!"

"Long live Rudolph and Bianca!" they cried in chorus.

The Negroes were singing a Negro spiritual. When they had finished, I regrouped them again with a wave of my hand, and then, producing my pistol, I cried:

"And now, farewell, gentlemen, and take warning from what you are about to see now and never attempt to guess at divine intentions. No one has ever penetrated the designs of the spring. *Ignorabimus*, gentlemen, *ignorabimus!*"

I lifted the pistol to my temple and was about to pull the trigger, when someone knocked it from my hand. An officer of the Feldjägers stood by me and, holding some papers in his hand, asked:

"Are you Joseph N.?"

"Yes," I answered.

"Haven't you some time ago," asked the officer, "dreamed the standard dream of the biblical Joseph?"

"Perhaps . . ."

"So you admit it," said the officer, consulting his papers. "Do you know that the dream has been noticed in the highest places and has been severely criticized?"

"I cannot answer for my dreams," I said.

"Yes, you can. I am arresting you in the name of His Majesty the Emperor-and-King!"

I smiled.

"How slow are the mills of justice. The bureaucracy of His Majesty the Emperor-and-King grinds rather slowly. I have outpaced that early dream by actions that are much more dangerous and that I wanted to expiate by taking my own life, yet it is this obsolete dream that has saved my life . . . I am at your disposal."

I saw an approaching column of troops. I stretched out my arms so that I could be handcuffed and turned my head once more. I saw Bianca for the last time. Standing on board the steamship, she was waving her handkerchief. The guard of veterans was saluting me in silence.

A NIGHT IN JULY

During the long holiday of my last year in school I became acquainted for the first time with summer nights. Our house, exposed all day long to the breezes and glares of the hot summer days that entered through the open windows, now contained a new lodger, my sister's small son, a tiny pouting, whimpering creature. He made our home revert to primitive conditions, he reduced us to the nomadic and haremlike existence of a matriarchal encampment where bedding, diapers, and sheets were forever being washed and dried, where a marked neglect of feminine appearance was accompanied by a predilection for frequent strippings of a would-be innocent character, an acid aura of infancy and of breasts swelling with milk.

After a very difficult confinement, my sister left to convalesce at a spa, my brother-in-law began to appear only at mealtimes, and my parents stayed in their shop until late at night. The household was ruled by the baby's wet nurse, whose expansive femininity was further enhanced by her role as mother-provider. That majestic dignity, coupled with her large and weighty presence, impressed a seal of gynecocracy on the whole house. It was a gynecocracy based on the natural advantages of a replete and fully grown carnality shared cleverly between herself and two servant girls, whose activities allowed them to display a whole gamut of feminine self-absorption. The blossoming and ripening of the garden full of rustling leaves, silvery flashes of light, and shadowy meditations was balanced inside the house by an aroma of femininity and maternity that floated over the white linen and the budding flesh. At the hotly glaring hour of noon all the curtains in the wide-open windows rose in fright and all the diapers drying on lines fluttered in a row: through this white avenue of linens and muslins feathery seeds, pollens, and lost petals flowed in; the garden tides of light and shadow, the intermittent rustle and calm slowly entered the rooms as if this hour of Pan had lifted all walls and partitions and allowed an all-embracing unity to rule the whole world.

I spent the evenings of that summer in the town's only cinema, staying there until the end of the last performance.

From the darkness of the cinema hall, with its fleeting lights and shadows, one entered a quiet, bright lobby like the haven of an inn on a stormy night.

After the fantastic adventures of the film, one's beating heart could calm down in the bright waiting room, shut off from the impact of the great pathetic night; in that safe shelter, where time stood still, the lightbulbs emitted waves of sterile light in a rhythm set by the dull rumbling of the projector, and kept by the shake of the cashier's box.

That lobby, plunged into the boredom of late hours like a railway waiting room after the departure of the last train, seemed at times to be the background for the final minutes of existence, something that would remain after all else had passed, after the tumult of life was exhausted. On a large colored poster, Asta Nielsen staggered forever with the black stigma of death on her forehead, her mouth open in a last scream, her eyes supremely beautiful and wide with superhuman effort.

The cashier had long since left for home. By now she was probably bustling by an unmade bed that was waiting in her small room like a boat to carry her off to the black lagoons of sleep, into the complicated world of dreams. The person sitting in the box office was only a wraith, an illusory phantom looking with tired, heavily made-up eyes at the emptiness of light, fluttering her lashes thoughtlessly to disperse the golden dust of drowsiness scattered by the electric bulbs. Occasionally she smiled palely to the sergeant of the fire brigade, who, himself empty of reality, stood leaning against the wall, forever immobile in his shining helmet, in the shallow splendor of his epaulettes, silver braids, and medals. The glass panes of the door leading into the late July night shook in time with the rhythm of the

projector, but the reflection of the electric lamp in the glass re-
futed the night, contributing to the illusion of a shelter safe
from the immense spreading darkness. Then at last the enchant-
ment of the lobby was broken: the glass door opened and the
red curtain swelled from the breath of night which overruled
everything.

Imagine the sense of adventure felt by a slim and sickly
schoolboy when he opens the glass door of a safe haven and
walks out all alone into the immensity of a July night. Will he
forever wade through the black morasses and quagmires of the
endless night, or will he come one morning to a safe harbor?
How many years will his lonely wanderings last?

No one has ever charted the topography of a July night. It remains unrecorded in the geography of one's inner cosmos.

A night in July! What can be likened to it? How can one describe it? Shall I compare it to the core of an enormous black
rose, covering us with the dreams of hundreds of velvety petals?
The night winds blow open its fluffy center, and in its scented
depth we can see the stars looking down on us.

Shall I compare it to the black firmament under our half-
closed eyelids, full of scattered speckles, white poppy seeds,
stars, rockets, and meteors? Or perhaps to a night train, long as
the world, driving through an endless black tunnel; walking
through a July night is like passing precariously from one coach
to another, between sleeping passengers, along narrow drafty
corridors, past stuffy compartments.

A night in July! The secret fluid of dusk, the living, watchful,
and mobile matter of darkness, ceaselessly shaping something
out of chaos and immediately rejecting every shape. Black timber out of which caves, vaults, nooks, and niches along the path
of a sleepy wanderer are constructed. Like an insistent talker,
the night accompanies a lonely pilgrim, shutting him within the
circle of its apparitions, indefatigable in invention and in fantasies, evoking for him starry distances, white Milky Ways, the
labyrinths of successive Colosseums and Forums. The night air,
that black Proteus playfully forming velvety densities streaked
with the scent of jasmine, cascades of ozone, sudden airless
wastes rising like black globes into the infinite, monstrous

grapes of darkness flowing with dark juice! I elbow my way along these tight passages, I lower my head to pass under arches and low vaults, and suddenly the ceiling breaks open with a starry sigh, a wide cupola slides away for a moment, and I am led again between narrow walls and passages. In these airless bays, in these nooks of darkness, scraps of conversation left by nightly wanderers hang in the air, fragments of inscriptions stick to posters, lost bars of laughter are heard, and skeins of whispers undispersed by the breeze of night unfold. Sometimes the night closes in around me like a small room without a door. I am overcome by drowsiness and cannot make out whether my legs are still carrying me forward or whether I am already at rest in that small chamber of the night. But then I feel again a velvety hot kiss left floating in space by some scented lips, some shutters open, I take a long step across a windowsill and continue to wander under the parabolas of falling stars.

From the labyrinth of night two wanderers emerge. They are weaving something together and pull from the darkness a long, hopeless plait of conversation. The umbrella of one of them knocks monotonously against the pavement (such umbrellas are carried as protection from the rain of stars and meteors), and large heads in globelike bowlers start rolling about. At other times I am stopped for a moment by the conspiratorial look of a black squinting eye, and a large bony hand with protruding joints limps through the night clutching the crutch of a stick, tightly grasping a handle made from a stag's horn (in such sticks long thin swords are sometimes hidden).

At last, at the city boundary the night gives up its games, removes its veil, discloses its serious and eternal face. It stops constructing around us illusory labyrinths of hallucination and nightmare and opens wide its starry eternity. The firmament grows into infinity, constellations glow in their splendor in time-hallowed positions, drawing magic figures in the sky as if they wanted to announce something, to proclaim something ultimate by their frightening silence. The shimmering of these distant worlds is a silvery starry chatter like the croaking of frogs. The July sky scatters an unbelievable dust of meteors, quietly soaked up by the cosmos.

At some hour of the night—the constellations still dreaming their eternal dreams—I found myself again in my own street. A star shone over the end of it, emitting an alien scent. When I opened the gate of the house, a draft could be felt like that in a dark tunnel. In the dining room the light was still on, four candles burned in a brass candelabrum. My brother-in-law was not yet in. Since my sister's departure, he had frequently been late for supper, sometimes not returning until late at night. Waking up from sleep, I often saw him undressing with a dull and meditative expression. Then he would blow out the candle, take all his clothes off, and, naked, lie for a long while sleepless on the cool bed. Sleep would only gradually overpower his large body. He would restlessly murmur something, breathe heavily, sigh, struggle with an imaginary burden on his breast. At times he would sob softly and drily. Frightened, I asked in the darkness: "Are you all right, Charles?" but in the meantime he was off on the steep path of his dreams, scrambling laboriously up some hill of snoring.

Through the open window the night was now breathing slowly. Into its large formless mass a cool, odorous fluid was being poured, the dark joints became looser, allowing thin rivulets of scent to seep through. The dead matter of darkness sought liberation in inspired flights of jasmine scent, but the unformed depths of the night remained still dead and unliberated.

The chink of light under the door to the next room shone like a golden string, sonorous and sensitive, like the sleep of the infant whining in his cradle. The chatter of caressing talk could be heard from there, an idyll between the wet nurse and the baby, the idyll of first love, in the midst of a circle of nightly demons that assembled in the darkness behind the window, lured by the warm spark of life glimmering inside.

On the other side was an empty room, and beyond it the bedroom of my parents. Straining my ear, I could hear how my father, on the threshold of sleep, glided in ecstasy over its aerial roads, wholly dedicated to this flight. His melodious and penetrating snoring told the story of his wandering along unknown impasses of sleep.

Thus did the souls slowly enter the aphelion, the sunless side of life, which no living creature has ever seen. They lay like people in the throes of death, rattling terribly and sobbing, while the black eclipse held their spirits in bond. And when at last they passed the black nadir, the deepest Orcus of the soul, when in mortal sweat they had fought their way through its strange promontories, the bellows of their lungs began to swell with a different tune, their inspired snores persisting until dawn.

A dense darkness still oppressed the earth when a different smell, a different color announced the slow approach of dawn. This was the moment when the most sober, sleepless head is visited for a time by the oblivion of sleep. The sick, the very sad, and those whose souls are torn apart have at that time a moment of relief. Who knows the length of time when night lowers the curtain on what is happening in its depth? That short interval is enough, however, to shift the scenery, to liquidate the great enterprise of the night and all its dark fantastic pomp. You wake up frightened, with the feeling of having overslept, and you see on the horizon the bright streak of dawn and the black, solidifying mass of the earth.

MY FATHER JOINS
THE FIRE BRIGADE

At the beginning of October my mother and I usually returned home from our holiday in the country. The place where we stayed was in a neighboring county, in a wooded valley of the River Slotvinka, which resounded with the murmur of innumerable underground springs. With our ears still filled with the rustle of beech trees and the chirping of birds, we rode in a large old landau, crowned with an enormous hood. We sat underneath it among numerous bundles in a kind of velvet-lined cavernous alcove, looking through the window at the changing landscape, colorful like pictures slowly dealt out from a pack.

At dusk we reached a plateau—the vast, startled crossroads of the country. The sky over it was deep, breathless, and windswept. Here was the farthest tollgate of the country, the last turning, beyond which the landscape of early autumn opened lower down. The frontier too was here, marked by an old, rotting frontier post with a faded inscription on a board that swayed in the wind.

The great wheels of the landau creaked as they sank in the sand, and the chattering spokes fell silent; only the large hood droned dully and flapped darkly in the crosswinds, like an ark that had landed in a desert.

Mother paid the toll, the bar of the turnpike squeaked when lifted, and the landau rolled heavily into the autumn.

We entered the wilted boredom of an enormous plain, an area of faded pale breezes that enveloped dully and lazily the yellow distance. A feeling of forlornness rose from the windswept space.

Like the yellowed pages of an old fable, the landscape became paler and more brittle as if it would disintegrate in an enormous emptiness. In that windy nowhere, in that yellow nirvana, we might have ridden to the limits of time and reality, or remained in it forever, amid the warm, sterile draftiness—an immobile coach on large wheels, stuck in the clouds of a parchment sky; an old illustration; a forgotten woodcut in an old-fashioned, moldy novel—when the coachman suddenly jerked the reins and from the lethargy of the crossroads pulled the landau into a forest.

We entered the thickets of dry fluff, a tobacco-colored wilting. Everything around us was sheltered and tawny like the inside of a box of trabucos. In that cedar semidarkness we passed tree trunks that were dry and odorous like cigars. We drove on and the forest became darker, smelling more aromatically of tobacco, until at last it enclosed us like a dry cello box, resounding faintly to its last tune. The coachman had no matches, so he could not light the lanterns. The horses, breathing heavily, found their way by instinct. The rattling of the spokes became less loud, the wheels began to turn softly in the sweet-smelling needles. My mother fell asleep. Time passed uncounted, making unfamiliar knots and abbreviations in its passage. The darkness was impenetrable; the dry rustle of the forest still resounded over the hood as the ground under the horses' hooves became solid and the carriages turned round and stopped, almost brushing a wall. Holding the door of the landau, my mother blindly felt for the gate to our house. The coachman was already unloading our bundles.

We entered a large vaulted hallway. It was dark, warm, and quiet like an old empty bakery at dawn, when the oven is cool, or like a Turkish bath late at night, when the forsaken tubs and basins grow cold in the darkness, in a silence measured by the dripping of taps. A cricket was patiently pulling from the darkness the tacking stitches of light, so fine that they could not lighten it at all. We groped around blindly until we found the stairs.

When we reached the creaking landing, my mother said:

"Wake up, Joseph, you are dropping off; only a few more steps to go."

But, almost unconscious with drowsiness, I clung closer to her and fell completely asleep.

Afterward, I never could learn from my mother how real were the things that I saw that night through my closed eyelids, overwhelmed as I was by tiredness and falling again and again into dull oblivion, and how much of it was the product of my imagination.

A great debate was taking place between my father, my mother, and Adela, the chief protagonist of that scene—a debate, I now realize, of capital importance. The gaps in my memory must be at fault if I cannot reconstruct its sense, also the blind spots of sleep I am now trying to fill with guesswork, supposition, and hypothesis. Inert and unconscious, I swam away again and again while the breezes of the starry nights coming from the open windows swept over my closed eyes. The night's breathing was regular and pure; as if uncovered by removing a transparent curtain, the stars appeared at times to look at my sleep. From under my eyelids I saw a room lighted by a candle, its glow casting a pattern of golden lines and curlicues.

It is possible, of course, that the scene took place at some other time. Many things seem to indicate that I had been its witness much later, when with my mother and the shop assistant I returned home late one day, after the shop had been closed.

On entering our apartment, my mother exclaimed in amazement and wonder and the shop assistants stopped still, transfixed. In the middle of the room stood a splendid knight clad in brass, a veritable St. George, looming large in a cuirass of polished golden tinplate, a sonorous armor complete with golden armlets. With astonishment and pleasure I recognized my father's bristling mustache and beard, which could be seen from under the heavy praetorian helmet. The armor was undulating on his breast, its strips of metal heaving like the scales on the abdomen of some huge insect. Looking tall in that armor, Father, in the glare of golden metal resembled the arch-strategist of a heavenly host.

"Alas, Adela," my father was saying, "you have never been able to understand matters of a higher order. Over and over again you have frustrated my activities with outbursts of senseless anger. But encased in armor, I am now impervious to the tickling with which you had driven me to despair when I was

bedridden and helpless. An impotent rage has now taken hold
of your tongue, and the vulgarity and grossness of your language is only matched by its stupidity. Believe me, I am full of
sorrow and pity for you. Unable to experience noble flights of
fancy, you bear an unconscious grudge against everything that
rises above the commonplace."

Adela directed at my father a look of utter contempt and,
turning to my mother, said in an angry voice, while shedding
tears of irritation: "He pinches all our raspberry syrup! He has
already taken away from the larder all the bottles of syrup we
made last summer! He wants to give it all to these good-for-
nothing firemen. And, what is more, he is being rude to me!"
Adela sobbed.

"Captain of the fire brigade, captain of some crowd of
layabouts!" she continued, looking at Father with loathing.
"The house is full of them. In the morning, when I want to
fetch the rolls, I cannot open the front door. Two of them are
lying asleep in the hallway barring it. On the staircase a few
more are spread on the steps, asleep in their brass helmets.
They force their way into my kitchen; they push in their rabbit
faces, lift up two fingers like schoolboys in class, and beg plaintively: 'Sugar, sugar, please . . .' They snatch the bucket from
my hands and run to the pump to get water for me; they dance
around me, smile at me, very nearly wag their tails. And all the
time they leer at me and odiously lick their lips. If I glance at
any one of them, he immediately becomes red in the face like an
obscene turkey. And to that horrible lot I am supposed to give
our raspberry syrup?"

"Your vulgarity," said my father, "defiles everything it comes
into contact with. You have given us a picture of these sons of
fire as seen by your profane eyes. As to me, all my sympathy is
with that unfortunate tribe of salamanders, those poor, disin-
herited creatures of fire. The mistake committed by that once-
so-splendid tribe was that they devoted themselves to the
service of mankind, that they sold themselves to man for a
spoonful of miserable broth. They have been repaid by scorn
because the stupidity of plebeians is boundless. Now these
once-so-sensitive creatures have to live in degradation. Can one

wonder that they don't like their dull and coarse fare, cooked by the wife of the beadle of the city school in a communal pot that they have to share with men under arrest? Their palates, the delicate and refined palates of fiery spirits, crave noble and dark balms, aromatic and colorful potions. Therefore, on the festive night when we shall all sit in the great city hall at tables covered with white cloth and when the light of a thousand illuminations will sparkle over the city, each of us will dip his roll of bread in a beaker of raspberry juice and slowly sip that noble liquor. This is the way to fortify the firemen, to regenerate all the energy they squander under the guise of fireworks, rockets, and Bengal fires. My heart is full of fellow feeling for their misery and undeserved abasement. I have accepted from their hands the saber of a captain in the hope that I might lead them from their present degradation to a future pledged to new ideas."

"You are completely transformed, Jacob," said my mother, "you are magnificent! All the same, I hope that you will stay at home tonight. Don't forget that we have not had a chance to talk seriously since my return from the country. And as for the firemen," she added, turning to Adela, "I really think that you are a little prejudiced. Though ne'er-do-wells, they are decent boys. I always look with pleasure at those slim young men in their shapely uniforms; I must say, though, that their belts are drawn in a shade too tightly at the waist. They have a natural elegance, and their eagerness and readiness to serve the ladies at any time is really touching. Whenever I drop my umbrella in the street or stop to tie a bootlace, there is always one of them at hand, ready to help and to please. I daren't disappoint them so I always wait patiently for one of them to appear and to perform the little service that seems to make them so happy. When, having performed his duty, he walks away, he is at once surrounded by a group of his colleagues who discuss the event with him eagerly, while the hero illustrates with gestures what actually happened. If I were you, Adela, I would willingly make use of their gallantry."

"I think they are nothing but a bunch of loafers," said Theodore, the senior shop assistant. "We don't even let them fight fires anymore because they are as irresponsible as children. It is enough to see how enviously they watch groups of boys throwing buttons against a wall to understand that they have brains like hares. Whenever you look out a window at boys playing in the street, you are sure to see among them one of these large chaps breathlessly running about, almost crazy with pleasure at the boys' game. At the sight of a fire, they jump for joy, clap their hands, and dance like savages. No, one cannot rely on them to put out the fires. Chimney sweeps and city militiamen are the people to use. This would leave fairs and popular festivals to the firemen. For instance, at the so-called storming of the Capitol on a dark morning last autumn, they dressed up as Carthaginians and lay siege, with a devilish noise, at the Basilian Hill, while the people, who watched them, sang: 'Hannibal, Hannibal, ante portas!' Toward the end of autumn, they become lazy and somnolent, fall asleep standing up, and with the first snows disappear completely from sight. I have been told by an old stove fitter that when he repairs chimneys, he often finds firemen clinging to the air duct, immobile like pupae and still in their scarlet uniforms and shiny helmets. They sleep upright, drunk with raspberry syrup, filled up with its sticky sweetness and fire. You must pull them out by their ears and take them back to their barracks, sleep drunk and semiconscious, along morning streets whitened by hoarfrost, while street urchins throw stones at them, and they, in return, smile the embarrassed smiles of guilt and bad conscience and sway about like drunkards."

"Be that as it may," said Adela, "they can't have any of my syrup. I did not spend hours at the hot kitchen range making syrup and spoiling my complexion so that these idlers should drink it now."

Instead of answering, my father produced a tin whistle and blew a piercing note. At once, four slim young men rushed into the room and arranged themselves in a row against the wall. The room brightened from the glare of their helmets, and they, dark and sunburnt under their hats, having adopted a military posture, waited for Father's orders. At a sign from my father, two of them got hold of a large carboy, full of raspberry syrup, and before Adela could stop them, ran downstairs with their precious loot. The two remaining men gave a smart military salute and followed suit.

For a moment it seemed that Adela would throw a fit: her beautiful eyes blazed with rage. But Father did not wait for her outburst. With one leap, he reached the windowsill and spread his arms wide. We rushed after him. The market square, brightly lit, was crowded. Under our house, eight firemen held fully extended a large sheet of canvas. Father turned round, the plate of his armor flashing in the light; he saluted us silently, then, with arms outspread, bright like a meteor, he leaped into the night sparkling with a thousand lights. The sight was so beautiful that we all began to cheer in delight. Even Adela forgot her grievance and clapped and cheered. Meanwhile, my father jumped onto the ground from the canvas sheet and, having shaken his clanking breastplate into position, went to the head of his detachment, which, two by two, slowly marched in formation past the dark lines of the watching crowd, lights playing on the brass of their helmets.

A SECOND AUTUMN

Among the many scientific researches undertaken by my father in rare periods of peace and inner serenity between the blows of disasters and catastrophes in which his adventurous and stormy life abounded, studies of comparative meteorology were nearest to his heart, particularly those of the climate of our province, which had many peculiarities. It was my father who laid the foundations of a skillful analysis of climatic trends. His *Outline of General Systematics of the Autumn* explained once and for all the essence of that season, which in our provincial climate assumed a prolonged, parasitical, and overgrown form known also by the name of "Chinese summer," extending far into the depths of our colorful winters. What more can I say? My father was the first to explain the secondary, derivative character of that late season, which is nothing other than the result of our climate having been poisoned by the miasmas exuded by degenerate specimens of baroque art crowded in our museums. That museum art, rotting in boredom and oblivion and shut in without an outlet, ferments like old preserves, oversugars our climate, and is the cause of this beautiful malarial fever, this extraordinary delirium, to which our prolonged autumn is so agonizingly prone. For beauty is a disease, as my father maintained; it is the result of a mysterious infection, a dark forerunner of decomposition, which rises from the depth of perfection and is saluted by perfection with signs of the deepest bliss.

A few factual remarks about our provincial museum might be apposite here. Its origins go back to the eighteenth century, and it stems from the admirable collecting zeal of the Order of Saint Basil, whose monks bestowed their treasure on the city, thus burdening its budget with an excessive and unproductive expense. For a number of years the Treasury of the Republic, having purchased the collection for next to nothing from the impoverished order, ruined itself grandly by artistic patronage, a pursuit worthy of some royal house. But already the next generation of city fathers, more practical and mindful of economic necessities, after fruitless negotiations with the curators of an archducal collection to whom they had tried to sell the museum, closed it down, dismissed its trustees, and granted the last keeper a pension for life. During these negotiations, it has been authoritatively stated by experts, the value of the collection had been greatly exaggerated by local patriots. The kindly Fathers of Saint Basil had, in their praiseworthy enthusiasm, bought more than a few fakes. The museum did not contain even a single painting by a master's hand but owned the whole oeuvre of third- and fourth-rate painters, whole provincial schools, known only to specialist art historians.

A strange thing: the kindly monks had militaristic inclinations, and the majority of the paintings represented battle scenes. A burnt, golden dusk darkened these canvases decayed with age. Fleets of galleons and caravels and old forgotten armadas moldered in enclosed bays, their swelled sails carrying the majestic emblems of remote republics. Under smoky and blackened varnishes, hardly visible outlines of equestrian engagements could be discerned. Across the emptiness of sunscorched plains under a dark and tragic sky, cavalcades passed in an ominous silence balanced on the left and right by the distant flashes and smoke of artillery.

In paintings of the Neapolitan school a sultry, cloudy afternoon grows old in perpetuity, as if seen through a bottle darkly. A pale sun seems to wilt under one's eyes in those landscapes, forlorn as if on the eve of a cosmic catastrophe. And this is why the ingratiating smiles and gestures of dusky fisherwomen, selling bundles of fish to wandering comedians, seem so futile. All that world has been condemned and forgotten a long time ago. Hence the infinite sweetness of the last gestures that alone remain, frozen forever. And deeper still in that country, inhabited by a carefree race of merrymakers, harlequins, and birdmen with cages, in that country without any reality or earnestness, small Turkish girls with fat little hands pat honey cakes lying in rows on wooden boards; two boys in Neapolitan hats carry a basket of noisy pigeons on a pole that sways slightly under the burden of its cooing, feathered load. And still further in the background, on the very edge of the evening, on the last plot of soil where a wilting bunch of acanthus sways on the border of nothingness, a last game of cards is still being played before the arrival of the already looming darkness.

That whole lumber room of ancient beauty has been subjected to painful distillation under the pressure of years of boredom.

"Can you understand," my father used to ask, "the despair of that condemned beauty, of its days and nights?" Over and over again it had to rouse itself to fictitious auctions, stage successful sales and noisy, crowded exhibitions, become inflamed with wild gambling passions, await a slump, scatter riches, squander them like a maniac, only to realize on sobering up that all this was in vain, that it could not get anywhere beyond a self-centered perfection, that it could not relieve the pain of excess. No wonder that the impatience and helplessness of beauty had at last to find its reflection in our sky, that it therefore glows over our horizon, degenerates into atmospheric displays, into these enormous arrangements of fantastic clouds I call our second or spurious autumn. That second autumn of our province is nothing but a sick mirage projected through an expanse of radiation into our sky by the dying, shut-in beauty in our museums. Autumn is a great touring show, poetically deceptive, an enormous purple-skinned onion disclosing ever new panoramas under each of its skins. No center can ever be reached. Behind each wing that is moved and stored away new and radiant scenes open up, true and alive for a moment, until you realize that they are made of cardboard. All perspectives are painted, all the panoramas made of board, and only the smell is authentic, the smell of wilting scenery, of theatrical dressing rooms, redolent of greasepaint and scent. And at dusk there is disorder and chaos in the wings, a pileup of discarded costumes, among which you can wade endlessly as if through yellowed fallen leaves. There is great confusion: everybody is pulling at the curtain ropes, and the sky, a great autumnal sky, hangs in tatters and is filled with the screeching of pulleys. And there is an atmosphere of feverish haste, of belated carnival, a ballroom about to empty in the small hours, a panic of masked people who cannot find their real clothes.

Autumn, the Alexandrian time of the year, collecting in its enormous library the sterile wisdom of three hundred and sixty-five days of the sun's race. Oh, those elderly mornings, yellow like parchment, sweet with wisdom like late evenings! Those forenoons smiling slyly like wise palimpsests, the many-layered texts of yellowed books! Ah, days of autumn, that old crafty librarian, groping his way up ladders in a faded dressing gown and trying spoonfuls of sweet preserves from all the centuries and cultures! Each landscape is for him like the opening chapter of an old novel. What fun he has letting loose the heroes of old stories under that misty, honey-colored sky into an opaque and sad late sweetness of light! What new adventures will Don Quixote find at Soplicowo?* How will Robinson Crusoe fare upon his return to his native Drohobycz?

On close, immobile evenings, golden after fiery sunsets, my father read us extracts from his manuscript. The flow of ideas allowed him sometimes to forget about Adela's ominous presence.

Then came the warm winds from Romania, establishing an enormous yellow monotony, a feel of the south. The autumn would not end. Like soap bubbles, days rose ever more beautiful and ethereal, and each of them seemed so perfect that every moment of its duration was like a miracle extended beyond measure and almost painful.

In the stillness of those deep and beautiful days, the consistency of leaves changed imperceptibly, until one day all the trees stood in the straw fire of completely dematerialized leaves, in a light redness like a coating of colored confetti, magnificent peacocks and phoenixes; the slightest move or flutter would cause them to shed the splendor of their plumage—the light, molted, superfluous leafy feathers.

*Name of the estate in Lithuania where the action of *Pan Tadeusz* (*Master Thaddeus,* 1834) by Adam Mickiewicz takes place.

DEAD SEASON

I

At five o'clock in the morning, an hour glaring with early sunshine, our house was already enveloped in an ardent but quiet brightness. At that solemn hour, unobserved by anyone—while the rooms in the semidarkness of drawn blinds were still filled with the harmonious breathing of sleeping people—its facade bathed in the sun, in the silence of the early haze, as if its surface were decorated by blissfully sleeping eyelids. Thus, in the stillness of these early hours, it absorbed the first fires of the morning with a sleepy face melting in brilliance, its features slightly twitching from intense dreams. The shadow of the acacia in front of the house slid in waves down the hot surface, trying in vain to penetrate into the depth of golden sleep. The linen blinds absorbed the morning heat, portion after portion, and sunbathed fainting in the glare.

At that early hour, my father, unable to sleep any longer, went downstairs loaded with books and ledgers, in order to open the shop, which was on the street level of the building. For a moment he stood still in the gateway, sustaining with half-closed eyes the powerful onslaught of the sun. The sun-drenched wall of the house pulled him tenderly into its blissfully leveled, smooth surface. For a moment Father became flat, grown into the facade, and felt his outstretched hands, quivering and warm, merging into its golden stucco. (How many other fathers have grown forever into the facades of houses at five o'clock in the morning, while on the last step of the staircase? How many fathers have thus become the concierges of their own gateways, flatly sculpted into the embrasure with a hand on the door handle and a face dissolved into parallel and blissful furrows, over which the fingers of their sons would wander, later, reminiscing about their parent, now incorporated forever into the universal smile of the housefront?) But soon he wrenched himself away, regained a third dimension and, made human once more, freed the metal-framed door of the shop from its bolts, bars, and padlocks.

While he was opening the heavy ironclad door, the grumbling dusk took a step back from the entrance, moved a few inches deeper, changed position and lay down again inside. The morning freshness, rising like smoke from the cool tiles of the pavement, stood shyly on the threshold in a tiny, trembling stream of air. Inside the shop the darkness of many preceding days and nights lurked in the unopened bales of cloth, arranged itself in layers, then spent itself at the very heart of the shop—in the storeroom—where it dissolved, undifferentiated and self-saturated, into a dully looming arch-matter of cloth.

My father walked along that high wall of cheviots and cords, passing his hand caressingly along the upright bales. Under his touch the rows of blind torsos ever ready to fall over or break order, calmed down and entrenched themselves in their cloth hierarchy and precedence.

For my father our shop was the place of eternal anguish and torment. This creature of his hands had for some time, in the years of its growth, been pushing against him ever more violently from day to day, and it had finally outgrown him. The shop became for him a task beyond his strength, at once immense and sublime. The immensity of its claims frightened him. Even his life could not satisfy their awful extent. He looked with despair at the frivolity of his shop assistants, their silly, carefree optimism, their jokes and thoughtless manipulations, occurring at the margins, as it were, of that great business enterprise. With bitter irony he watched that gallery of faces undisturbed by any worry, those foreheads innocent of any idea; he looked into the depths of those trusting eyes never troubled by even the slightest shadow of doubt. For all her loyalty and devotion, how could my mother help him? The realization of matters of a higher order was outside the scope of her simple and uncomplicated mind. She was not created for heroic tasks. For he did notice that behind his back she occasionally exchanged quick and understanding looks with the shop assistants, glad of any moment without supervision, when she could take part in their fatuous clowning.

My father separated himself more and more from that world of lightheartedness and escaped into the hard discipline of total dedication. Horrified by the laxity spreading everywhere, he shut himself off in the lonely service of his high ideal. His hand never strayed from the reins, he never allowed himself a relaxation of rules or the comfort of facile solutions.

That was good enough for Balanda & Co. and these other dilettanti of the trade, who knew not the hunger for perfection nor the asceticism of high priesthood. My father suffered when he saw the downfall of the retail textile trade. Who of the present generation of textile merchants remembered the good traditions of their ancient art? Which of them knew, for instance, that pieces of cloth, laid in a stack on display shelves in accordance with the principles of textile art, could emit under the touch of a finger running downward a sound like a descending scale? Which among his contemporaries was conversant with the finer points of style in the exchange of notes, memos, and letters? How many still remembered the charm of merchant diplomacy, the diplomacy of the good old school, the exciting stages of negotiation: beginning with irreconcilable stiffness and intransigent reserve at the visit of the representative of a foreign firm, through gradual thaw under the influence of the indefatigable persuasions and blandishments of that envoy, until the invitation to a working supper with wine—served at the desk, on top of papers, in an exalted mood, with some pinching of Adela's bottom while she served the meal, amid peppery jokes and a free flow of talk, as behooves gentlemen who know what is expected in the circumstances—was crowned with a mutually profitable business deal?

In the quietness of the morning hours, while the heat was slowly rising, my father expected to find a happy and inspired phrase that would give the required weight to his letter to

Messrs. Christian Seipel & Sons, Spinners and Mechanical Weavers. It was to be a cutting riposte to the unfounded demands of these gentlemen, the reply ad rem, concise at the decisive point, so that the letter could rise to a strong and witty final plea to produce the desired shock effect and could then be rounded off with one energetic, elegant, and final irrevocable sentence. He could almost feel the form of that phrase that had been eluding him for many days, he could almost touch it with his fingertips, but he could not lay his hands on it. He waited for a flash of carefree humor to take by storm the obstacle that stubbornly barred his way. He reached for yet another clean sheet of paper, in order to give fresh impetus to the conquest of the obstacle that had been defying all his efforts.

Meanwhile the shop became gradually peopled with his assistants. They entered flushed from the early morning heat and avoided Father's desk, at which they cast frightened and guilt-ridden looks.

Exhausted after the night and conscious of it, they felt the weight of his silent disapproval, which nothing they did could dispel. Nothing could placate the master, brooding over his worries; no show of eagerness could pacify him as he sat lurking like a scorpion behind his desk, his glasses flashing ominously as he foraged like a mouse among his papers. His excitement increased, his latent temper intensified in step with the heat. The square patch of sunlight on the floor glared. Shiny, metallic flies flashed like lightning in the entrance to the shop, settling for a moment on the sides of the door, glass bubbles blown from the hot pipe of the sun, from the glassworks of that radiant day: they sat with wings outspread, full of flight and swiftness, then changed places in furious zigzags. Through the bright quadrilateral of the doorway one could see the lime trees of the city park fainting in the sunlight, the distant bell tower of the church outlined clearly in the translucent and shimmering air, as if in the lenses of binoculars. The tin-plated roofs were burning; the enormous, golden globe of heat was swelling all over the world.

Father's irritation grew. He looked round helplessly, doubled up with pain, exhausted by diarrhea. He felt in his mouth a taste more bitter than wormwood.

The heat intensified, sharpening the fury of the flies, making the metal on their abdomens shine. The quadrilateral of light now reached Father's desk and the papers burned like the Apocalypse. Father's eyes, blinded by the sunlight, could not stand their white uniformity. Through his thick glasses he saw everything he looked at in crimson, greenish, or purple frames and was filled with despair at this explosion of color, the anarchy raging over the world in an orgy of brightness. His hands shook. His palate was bitter and dry, heralding an attack of sickness. His eyes, embedded in the furrows of wrinkles, watched with attention the development of events in the depth of the shop.

2

When, at noon, my father, exhausted by the heat, trembling with futile excitement and almost on the verge of madness, retreated upstairs and the ceilings of the floor above cracked here and there under his skulking step, the shop experienced a momentary pause and relaxation: the hour of the afternoon siesta.

The shop assistants turned somersaults on the bales of cloth, pitched tents of fabric on the shelves, made swings from draperies. They unwound the cloth, set free the smooth, tightly rolled ancient darkness. The shopworn, felted dusk, now liberated, filled the spaces under the ceiling with the smell of another time, with the odor of past days patiently arranged in innumerable layers during the cool autumns of long ago. Blind moths scattered in the darkened air, fluffs of feathers and wool circled with them all over the shop, and the smell of finishing, deep and autumnal, filled this dark encampment of cloth and velvet. Picnicking in that camp the shop assistants devised practical jokes. They let their colleagues wrap them tightly up to their ears in dark, cool cloth and lay in a row blissfully immobile under the stack of bales—living bolts of cloth like mummies, rolling their eyes with an assumed fear at their own immobility. Or else they let themselves be swung up to the ceiling on enormous, outspread blankets of cloth. The dull thudding of these blankets and the current of air that arose made them mad with joy. It seemed as if the whole shop was taking off in flight, the fabrics rising in inspiration, the shop assistants, with their coattails flowing, swinging upward like prophets on short ascensions. My mother looked indulgently at these games; the relaxation due in the hours of siesta justified in her eyes even the worst transgressions.

In the summer the back of the shop was dark because of the weeds growing in the courtyard. The storeroom window overlooking it became all green and iridescent like submarine depths from the movement of leaves and their undulating reflections. Flies buzzed there monotonously in their semiobscurity of long afternoons; they were monstrous specimens bred on Father's sweet wine, hairy hermits lamenting their accursed fate day in, day out in long, monotonous sagas. These flies, inclined to wild and unexpected mutations, abounded in unnatural specimens, bred from incestuous unions, degenerated into a superrace of top-heavy giants, of veterans emitting a deep melancholy buzz. Toward the end of the summer some specimens were posthumously hatched out with wasted wings—mute and voiceless, the last of their race, resembling large, bluish beetles—and ended their sad lives running up and down the green windowpanes on busy, futile errands.

The rarely opened door became covered with cobwebs. My mother slept behind the desk, in a cloth hammock swinging between the shelves. The shop assistants, bothered by flies, winced and grimaced, stirring in an uneasy sleep. Meanwhile, the weeds took over the courtyard. Under the ruthless heat of the sun the rubbish heap sprouted enormous nettles and mallows.

The heat of the sun falling on the subterranean water on this plot of soil produced a fermentation of venomous substances, some poisonous derivatives of chlorophyll. This morbid process brought forth malformed wrinkled leaves of astonishing lightness that spread until the space under the window was filled with a tissue-thin tangle of green pleonasms, of weedy rubbish degenerating into a papery, tawdry patchwork clinging to the walls of the storeroom. The shop assistants woke with flushed faces from a quick nap. Strangely excited they got up with feverish energy, ready for even more heroic buffooneries; corroded by boredom, they climbed on tall shelves and drummed with their feet, looking fixedly at the empty expanse of the market square, longing for any kind of diversion.

Once a peasant from the country, barefoot and smock clad, stopped in the doorway of the shop and looked in shyly. For the bored shop assistants this was a heaven-sent opportunity. They quickly swept down the ladders, like spiders at the sight of a fly; the peasant, surrounded, pulled, and pushed, was asked a hundred questions, which he tried to parry with a bashful smile. He scratched his head, smiled, and looked with suspicion at the assiduous young men. So he wanted tobacco? But what kind? The best, Macedonian, golden as amber? Not that kind? Would ordinary pipe tobacco do? Shag perhaps? Would he care to step in? To come inside? There was nothing to fear. The shop assistants prodded him gently deeper into the shop, toward a side counter. Leon went behind the counter and pretended to pull out a nonexistent drawer. Oh, how he worked at it, how he bit his lip with effort! It was stuck and would not move. One had to thump the top of the counter with one's fists, with all one's might. The peasant, encouraged by the young men, did it with concentration, with proper attention. At last, when there was no result, he climbed, hunched and gray haired, on top of the counter and stamped it with his bare feet. He had us all in fits of laughter.

It was then that the regrettable incident occurred that filled us all with sadness and shame. Although we did not act in bad faith, we were all equally to blame. It was all due to our frivolity, our lack of seriousness and understanding for Father's worries. Given the unpredictable, insecure, and volatile nature of my father, our thoughtlessness produced consequences that were truly fatal.

While we were all standing in a semicircle, enjoying our little joke, my father quietly entered the shop.

We did not see him come in. We noticed him only when the sudden understanding of our little game distorted his face in a grimace of wild horror. My mother came running, very frightened:

"What is the matter, Jacob?" she asked breathlessly.

She began to slap him on the back as one would a person who is choking. It was too late. My father was bristling all over, his face was decomposing quickly, falling apart, changing under our eyes, struck by the burden of an inexplicable calamity. Before we could understand what was happening, he shook himself violently, buzzed, and rose in flight before our eyes, transformed into a monstrous, hairy, steel blue horsefly, furiously circling and knocking blindly against the walls of the shop. Transfixed, we listened to the hopeless lament, the expressively modulated dull plaint, running up and down the registers of boundless pain—an unrelieved suffering under the dark ceiling of the shop.

We stood unmoving, deeply shamed, unable to look at one another. In the depth of our hearts we felt a certain relief that at a critical moment my father had found a way out of an impossible situation. We admired the courage with which he threw himself recklessly into a blind alley of desperation from which, as it seemed, there was no return.

Yet, looking at it dispassionately, one had to take my father's transformation *cum grano salis*. It was much more the symbol of an inner protest, a violent and desperate demonstration from which, however, reality was not absolutely absent. One has to keep in mind that most of the events described here suffer from summer aberrations, the canicular semireality, the marginal time running irresponsibly along—the borderline of the dead season.

We listened in silence. My father's revenge was particularly cunning: it was a kind of reprisal. From then on we were condemned to hearing forever that baleful low buzzing—a persistent, doleful complaint, which rose to a pitch and then suddenly stopped. For a moment, we savored the silence with relief, a beneficent respite during which a glimmer of hope arose in us. But after a while the buzzing began again, ever more insistent and plaintive, and we realized that there was no end to that suffering, to that curse, to the homeless beating against all the walls. That monologue of complaint and silence, each time rising even louder and angrier, as if it wanted to cancel the previous moment of short appeasement, jarred on our nerves. Suffering that is limitless, suffering that is stubbornly enclosed within the circle of its own mania, suffering to the point of distraction, of self-mutilation, becomes in the end unbearable for the helpless witnesses of misfortune. That incessant, angry appeal for our sympathy contained too obvious a reproach, too glaring an accusation against our own well-being, not to make us rebellious. We all inwardly writhed, full of protest and fury instead of contrition. Was there really no other way out for him but to throw himself blindly into that pitiful and hopeless condition, and, having fallen into it, no matter whether by his own fault or by ours, couldn't he find more strength of spirit or more dignity to bear it without complaint? My mother could only check her anger with difficulty. The shop assistants, sitting on their ladders in dull amazement, had dreams of retaliation and thought of reckless pursuit along the shelves with a leather flyswatter, and their eyes became bloodshot. The canvas blind over the shop entrance was flapping furiously, the afternoon heat hung over miles of sun-drenched plain and devastated the distant world underneath it, and in the semiobscurity of the shop, under the dark ceiling, my father hopelessly circled and circled, enmeshing himself tighter and tighter in the desperate zigzags of his flight.

3

Yet, in spite of all the evidence to the contrary, such episodes were of no great importance, for, that same evening, my father was poring as usual over his papers and the incident seemed to be long forgotten, the deep grudge overcome and erased. We, of course, refrained from any allusion to it. We looked with pleasure as, with seeming equanimity, in peaceful concentration, he industriously covered page after page with his calligraphically precise writing. Instead, it became ever more difficult to forget the compromising presence of the poor peasant. It is well known how stubbornly such unfinished business becomes rooted in certain minds. We ignored him on purpose during these empty weeks, leaving him to stamp on the counter in the dark corner, daily becoming smaller and grayer. Almost unnoticeable now, he was still stamping away on the same spot, smiling benevolently, hunched over the counter, indefatigable, chattering softly to himself. The stamping and knocking became his true vocation, in which he was completely engrossed. We did not interfere with him. He had gone too far, we could not reach him now.

Summer days have no dusk. Before we knew where we were, night would come to the shop, a large oil lamp was lighted, and shop affairs continued. During these short summer nights it was not worth returning home. My father usually sat at his desk in apparent concentration and marked the margins of letters with black scattered stars, ink spots, hairlines that circled in his field of vision, atoms of darkness detached from the great summer night behind the windows. The night meanwhile scattered like a puffball a microcosm of shadows under the globe of the lamp. Father was blinded as his spectacles reflected the lamp. He was waiting, waiting with impatience and listening while he stared at the whiteness of the paper through which flowed the dark galaxies of black stars and dust specks. Behind his back, without his participation, as it were, the great battle for the shop was being fought. Oddly enough, it was fought on a painting hanging behind his head, between the filing cabinet and the mirror, in the bright circle of the lamplight. It was a magic painting, a talisman, a riddle of a picture, endlessly interpreted and passed on from one generation to the next. What did it represent? That was the subject of unending disputations conducted for years, a never-ending quarrel between two opposing points of view. The painting represented two merchants facing one another, two opposites, two worlds.

"I gave credit," cried the slim, down-at-heel little fellow, his voice breaking in despair.

"I sold for cash," answered the fat man in the armchair, crossing his legs and twiddling his thumbs above his stomach.

How my father hated the fat one! He had known both since his childhood. Even as a schoolboy, he was full of contempt for any fat egoist who devoured innumerable buttered rolls in the middle of the morning. But he did not quite support the slim one either. Now he looked amazed as all initiative slipped from his hands, taken over by the two men at loggerheads. With bated breath, blinking his eyes from which the spectacles had slipped, my father now tensely awaited the result of the dispute.

The shop itself was a perpetual mystery. It was the center of all Father's thoughts, of his nightly cogitations, of his frightening silences. Inscrutable and all-embracing, it stood in the background of daily events. In daytime, the generations of fabrics, full of patriarchal dignity, lay in order of precedence, segregated according to their ancestry and origins. But at night the rebellious blackness of the materials broke out and stormed about with silent tirades and hellish improvisations. In the autumn the shop bustled, overflowing with the dark stock of winter merchandise, as if whole acres of forest had been uprooted and were marching through a windswept landscape. In the summer, in the dead season, the shop retreated to its dark reservations, inapproachable in its thickets of cloth. The shop assistants banged at night with their wooden yardsticks at the dull wall of bales, listening as the shop roared with pain, immured in the cave of cloth.

In the surrounding darkness my father harked back to the past, to the abyss of time. He was the last of his line, he was Atlas on whose shoulders rested the burden of an enormous legacy. By day and by night, my father thought about the meaning of it all and tried to understand its hidden intention. He often looked askance, full of expectation, at his assistants. Not himself receiving any secret signs, any enlightenment, any directives, he expected that these young and naive men, just emerging from their cocoons, might suddenly realize the meaning of his trade that stubbornly evaded him. He pestered them with persistent questioning, but they, stupid and inarticulate, avoided his looks, turned their eyes away, and mumbled some confused nonsense. In the mornings, using a walking stick for support, my father wandered like a shepherd among his blind, woolly flock, among the bleating headless rumps crowded around the drinking trough. He was still waiting, postponing the moment when he would have to move his tribe and go out into the night burdened with responsibility for that swarming, homeless Israel . . .

The night behind the door was leaden—close, without a breeze. After a few steps it became impassable. One walked without moving forward as in a dream, and while one's feet stuck to the ground, one's thoughts continued to run forward endlessly, incessantly questioning, led astray by the dialectical byways of the night. The differential calculus of the night continued. At last, one's feet stopped moving, and one stood riveted to the spot, at the darkest, most intimate corner of the night, as in front of a privy, in dead silence, for long hours, with a feeling of blissful shame. Only thought, left to itself, slowly made an about-turn, the complex anatomy of the brain unwound itself like a reel, and the abstract treatise of the summer night continued its venomous dialectic, turning logical somersaults, inventing new sophisticated questions to which there was no answer. Thus one debated with oneself through the speculative vastness of the night and entered, disembodied, into ultimate nothingness.

It was long after midnight when my father abruptly lifted his head from his pile of papers. He stood up, full of self-importance, with dilated eyes, listening intently.

"He is coming," he said with a radiant face, "open the door."

Almost before Theodore, the senior assistant, could open the glass door, which had been bolted for the night, a man had already squeezed himself in, loaded with bundles, black haired, bearded, splendid, and smiling: the long awaited guest. Mr. Jacob, deeply moved, hurried to greet him, bowing, both his hands outstretched in greeting. They embraced. It seemed for a moment as if the black shining engine of a train had voicelessly driven up to the very door of the shop. A porter in a railwayman's hat came in carrying an enormous trunk on his back.

We never learned who this distinguished visitor really was. Theodore firmly maintained that he was Christian Seipel & Sons (Spinners and Mechanical Weavers) in person, but there was little evidence for it, and my mother did not subscribe to this theory. There was no doubt, though, that the man must have been a powerful demon, one of the pillars of the County

Creditors' Union. A black, carefully trimmed beard surrounded his fat, shiny, and most dignified face. With Father's arm around him, he proceeded, bowing, toward the desk.

Unable to understand the conversation, which was in a foreign language, we nonetheless listened to it with respect, and watched the smiles, the closing of the eyes, the delicate and tender mutual self-congratulations. After the exchange of preliminary courtesies, the gentlemen proceeded to the crux of the matter. Ledgers and papers were spread out on the desk, a bottle of white wine was uncorked. With strong cigars in the corners of their mouths, with faces folded into grimaces of gruff contentment, the gentlemen exchanged short one-syllable code words, spasmodically pointing their fingers at an appropriate entry in the ledgers with a humorous flash of villainy in their eyes. Slowly the discussion became more heated; one could perceive a mounting, barely suppressed, excitement. They bit their lips, the cigars hung down, now bitter and cold, from mouths suddenly disappointed and hostile. They were trembling with inner irritation. My father was breathing through the nose, red flushes under his eyes, his hair bristling over his perspiring brow. The situation became inflammable. A moment came when both men got up from their chairs and stood almost blind with anger, breathing heavily and glaring from under their spectacles. Mother, frightened, began to pat Father imploringly on his back, wanting to prevent a catastrophe. At the sight of a lady, both gentlemen came to their senses, recalled the rules of etiquette, bowed, smiling, to one another, and sat down to a further spell of work.

At about two o'clock in the morning, Father banged shut the heavy cover of the main ledger. We looked anxiously into the faces of both men to discern who had won the battle. My father's apparent good humor seemed to be artificial and forced, while the black-bearded man was leaning back in his armchair, with legs crossed, and breathing kindness and optimism. With ostentatious generosity he began to distribute gratuities among the shop assistants.

Having tidied up the papers and invoices, the gentlemen now rose from behind the desk. Winking to the shop assistants with implied anticipation, they silently intimated that they were now ready for new initiatives. They suggested behind Mother's back that the time had come for a little celebration. This was empty talk, and the shop assistants knew what to make of it. That night did not lead anywhere. It had to end in the gutter, at a certain place by the blind wall of nothingness and secret shame. All the paths leading into the night turned back to the shop. All sorties attempted into the depth of it were doomed from the outset. The shop assistants winked back only from politeness.

The black-bearded man and my father, arm in arm, left the shop full of energy, followed by the tolerant looks of the young men. Immediately outside the door, darkness obliterated their heads at a stroke, and they plunged into the black waters of the night.

Who has ever plumbed the depths of a July night, who has ever measured how many fathoms of emptiness there are in which nothing happens? Having crossed that black infinity, the two men again stood in front of the door as if they had just left it, having regained their heads with yesterday's words still unused on their lips. Standing thus for a long time, they conversed in monotones, as if they had just returned from a distant expedition. They were now bound by the comradeship of alleged adventures and nighttime excesses. They pushed back their hats as drunks do and rocked on unsteady legs.

Avoiding the lighted front of the shop, they stealthily entered the porch of the house and began to walk quietly up the creaking steps to the first floor. They crept out onto the balcony and stood in front of Adela's window trying to look at the sleeping girl. They could not see her; she lay in shadow and sobbed unconsciously in her sleep, her mouth slightly open, her head thrown back and burning, fanatically engrossed in her dreams. They knocked at the black windowpanes and sang dirty songs. But Adela, a lethargic smile on her half-opened lips, was wandering, numb and hypnotized, on her distant roads, miles away, outside their reach.

Then, propping themselves up against the rail of the balcony, they yawned broadly and loudly in resignation and began to kick their feet against the balustrade. At some late and unknown hour of the night, they found their bodies again on two narrow beds, floating on high mountains of bedding. They swam on them side by side, racing one another in a gallop of snoring.

At some still more distant mile of sleep—had the flow of sleep joined their bodies, or had their dreams imperceptibly merged into one?—they felt that lying in each other's arms they were still fighting a difficult, unconscious duel. They were panting face-to-face in sterile effort. The black-bearded man lay on top of my father like the angel on top of Jacob. My father pressed against him with all the strength of his knees and, stiffly floating away into numbness, stole another short spell of fortifying sleep between one round of wrestling and another. So they fought: what for? For their good name? For God? For a contract? They grappled in mortal sweat, to their last ounce of strength, while the waves of sleep carried them away into ever more distant and stranger areas of the night.

4

The next day my father walked with a slight limp. His face was radiant. At dawn a splendid phrase for his letter had come to him, a formulation he had been trying in vain to find for many days and nights. We never saw the black-bearded gentleman again. He left before daybreak with his trunk and bundles, without taking leave of us. That was the last night of the dead season. From that summer night onward seven long years of prosperity began for the shop.

SANATORIUM UNDER THE SIGN OF THE HOURGLASS

I

The journey was long. The train, which ran only once a week on that forgotten branch line, carried no more than a few passengers. Never before had I seen such archaic coaches; withdrawn from other lines long before, they were spacious as living rooms, dark, and with many recesses. Corridors crossed the empty compartments at various angles; labyrinthine and cold, they exuded an air of strange and frightening neglect. I moved from coach to coach, looking for a comfortable corner. Drafts were everywhere: cold currents of air shooting through the interiors, piercing the whole train from end to end. Here and there a few people sat on the floor, surrounded by their bundles, not daring to occupy the empty seats. Besides, those high, convex oilcloth-covered seats were cold as ice and sticky with age. At the deserted stations no passengers boarded the train. Without a whistle, without a groan, the train would slowly start again, as if lost in meditation.

For a time I had the company of a man in a ragged railway man's uniform—silent, engrossed in his thoughts. He pressed a handkerchief to his swollen, aching face. Later even he disappeared, having slipped out unobserved at some stop. He left behind him the mark of his body in the straw that lay on the floor, and a shabby black suitcase he had forgotten.

Wading in straw and rubbish, I walked shakily from coach to coach. The open doors of the compartments were swinging in the drafts. There was not a single passenger left on the train. At last, I met a conductor, in the black uniform of that line. He was wrapping a thick scarf around his neck and collecting his things—a lantern, an official logbook.

"We are nearly there, sir," he said, looking at me with washed-out eyes.

The train was coming slowly to a halt, without puffing, without rattling, as if, together with the last breath of steam, life were slowly escaping from it. We stopped. Everything was empty and still, with no station buildings in sight. The conductor showed me the direction of the Sanatorium. Carrying my suitcase, I started walking along a narrow white road toward the dark trees of a park. With some curiosity, I looked at the

landscape. The road along which I was walking led up to the brow of a gentle hill, from which a wide expanse of country could be seen. The day was uniformly gray, extinguished, without contrasts. And perhaps under the influence of that heavy and colorless aura, the great basin of the valley, in which a vast wooded landscape was arranged like theatrical scenery, seemed very dark. The rows of trees, one behind the other, ever grayer and more distant, descended the gentle slopes to the left and right. The whole landscape, somber and grave, seemed almost imperceptibly to float, to shift slightly like a sky full of billowing, stealthily moving clouds. The fluid strips and bands of forest seemed to rustle and grow with rustling like a tide that swells gradually toward the shore. The rising white road wound itself dramatically through the darkness of that woody terrain. I broke a twig from a roadside tree. The leaves were dark, almost black. It was a strangely charged blackness, deep and benevolent, like restful sleep. All the different shades of gray in the landscape derived from that one color. It was the color of a cloudy summer dusk in our part of the country, when the landscape has become saturated with water after a long period of rain and exudes a feeling of self-denial, a resigned and ultimate numbness that does not need the consolation of color.

It was completely dark among the trees of the parkland. I groped my way blindly on a carpet of soft needles. When the trees thinned, the planks of a footbridge resounded under my feet. Beyond it, against the blackness of the trees, loomed the gray walls of the many-windowed hotel that advertised itself as the Sanatorium. The double glass door of the entrance stood open. The little footbridge, with shaky handrails made of birch branches, led straight to it.

In the hallway there was semidarkness and a solemn silence. I moved on tiptoe from door to door, trying to see the numbers on them. Rounding a corner, I at last met a chambermaid. She had run out of a room, as if having torn herself from someone's importuning arms, and was breathless and excited. She could hardly understand what I was saying. I had to repeat it. She was fidgeting helplessly.

Had my telegram reached them? She spread her arms, her eyes

moved sideways. She was only awaiting an opportunity to leap
back behind the half-opened door, at which she kept squinting.

"I have come a long way. I booked a room here by telegram,"
I said with some impatience. "Whom shall I see about it?"

She did not know. "Perhaps you could wait in the restaurant," she babbled. "Everybody is asleep just now. When the
doctor gets up, I shall announce you."

"They are asleep? But it is daytime, not night."

"Here everybody is asleep all the time. Didn't you know?"
she said, looking at me with interest now. "Besides, it is never
night here," she added coyly.

She had obviously given up the idea of escape, for she was now
picking fussily at the lace of her apron. I left her there and entered
the half-lit restaurant. There were some tables, and a large buffet
ran the length of one wall. I was now feeling a little hungry and
was pleased to see some pastries and a cake on the buffet.

I placed my suitcase on one of the tables. They were all un-
occupied. I clapped my hands. No response. I looked into the
next room, which was larger and brighter. That room had a
wide window or loggia overlooking the landscape I already
knew, which, framed by the window, seemed like a constant re-
minder of mourning, suggestive of deep sorrow and resignation. On some of the tables stood the remains of recent meals,
uncorked bottles, half-empty glasses. Here and there lay the
tips, not yet picked up by the waiters. I returned to the buffet
and looked at the pastries and cake. They looked most appetiz-
ing. I wondered whether I should help myself; I suddenly felt
extremely greedy. There was a particular kind of apple flan that
made my mouth water. I was about to lift a piece of it with a silver knife when I felt somebody behind me. The chambermaid
had entered the room in her soft slippers and was touching my
back lightly.

"The doctor will see you now," she said, looking at her fin-
gernails.

She stood facing me and, conscious of the magnetism of her
wriggling hips, did not turn away. She provoked me, increasing
and decreasing the distance between our bodies as, having left
the restaurant, we passed many numbered doors. The passage

became ever darker. In almost complete darkness, she brushed against me fleetingly.

"Here is the doctor's door," she whispered. "Please go in."

Dr. Gotard was standing in the middle of the room to receive me. He was a short, broad-shouldered man with a dark beard.

"We received your telegram yesterday," he said. "We sent our carriage to the station, but you must have arrived by another train. Unfortunately, the railway connections are not very good. Are you well?"

"Is my father alive?" I asked, staring anxiously into his calm face.

"Yes, of course," he answered, calmly meeting my questioning eyes. "That is, within the limits imposed by the situation," he added, half-closing his eyes. "You know as well as I that from the point of view of your home, from the perspective of your own country, your father is dead. This cannot be entirely remedied. That death throws a certain shadow on his existence here."

"But does Father himself know it, does he guess?" I asked him in a whisper.

He shook his head with deep conviction. "Don't worry," he said in a low voice. "None of our patients know it, or can guess. The whole secret of the operation," he added, ready to demonstrate its mechanism on his fingers, "is that we have put back the clock. Here we are always late by a certain interval of time of which we cannot define the length. The whole thing is a matter of simple relativity. Here your father's death, the death that has already struck him in your country, has not occurred yet."

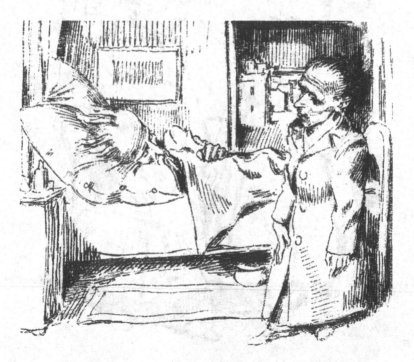

"In that case," I said, "my father must be on his deathbed or about to die."

"You don't understand me," he said in a tone of tolerant impatience. "Here we reactivate time past, with all its possibilities, therefore also including the possibility of a recovery." He looked at me with a smile, stroking his beard. "But now you probably want to see your father. According to your request, we have reserved for you the other bed in your father's room. I shall take you there."

When we were out in the dark passage, Dr. Gotard spoke in a whisper. I noticed that he was wearing felt slippers, like the chambermaid. "We allow our patients to sleep long hours to spare their vitality. Besides, there is nothing better to do."

At last, we stopped in front of one of the doors, and he put a finger to his lips. "Enter quietly. Your father is asleep. Settle down to sleep, too. This is the best thing for you to do. Good-bye for now."

"Good-bye," I whispered, my heart beating fast.

I pressed the handle, and the door opened, like unresisting lips that part in sleep. I went in. The room was almost empty, gray and bare.

Under a small window, my father was lying on an ordinary wooden bed, covered by a pile of bedding, fast asleep. His breathing extracted layers of snoring from the depths of his breast. The whole room seemed to be lined with snores from floor to ceiling, and yet new layers were being added all the time. With deep emotion, I looked at Father's thin, emaciated face, now completely engrossed in the activity of snoring—a remote, trancelike face, which, having left its earthly aspect, was confessing its existence somewhere on a distant shore by solemnly telling its minutes.

There was no second bed in the room. Piercingly cold air blew in through the window. The stove had not been lit.

They don't seem to care much for patients here, I thought. To expose such a sick man to such drafts! And no one seems to do any cleaning here, either. A thick layer of dust covered the floor and the bedside table, on which stood medicine bottles and a cup of cold coffee. Stacks of pastries in the restaurant, yet they give the patients black coffee instead of anything more nourishing!

But perhaps this is a detail compared with the benefits of having the clock put back.

I slowly undressed and climbed onto Father's bed. He did not wake up, but his snoring, having probably been pitched too high, fell an octave lower, forsaking its high declamatory tone. It became, as it were, more private, for his own use. I tucked Father in under his eiderdown, to protect him as much as possible from the drafts in the room. Soon I fell asleep by his side.

2

The room was in twilight when I woke up. Father was dressed and sitting at the table drinking tea, dunking sugar-coated biscuits in it. He was wearing a black suit of English cloth, which he had had made only the previous summer. His tie was rather loose.

Seeing that I was awake, he said with a pleasant smile on his pale face, "I am extremely pleased that you have come, Joseph. It was a real surprise! I feel so lonely here. But I suppose one should not complain in my situation. I have been through worse things, and if one were to itemize them all—but never mind. Imagine, on my very first day here they served an excellent fillet of beef with mushrooms. It was a hell of a piece of meat, Joseph. I must warn you most emphatically—beware if they should ever serve you fillet of beef! I can still feel the fire in my stomach. And the diarrhea—I could hardly cope with it. But I must tell you a piece of news," he continued. "Don't laugh. I have rented premises for a shop here. Yes, I have. And I congratulate myself for having had that bright idea. I have been bored most terribly, I must say. You cannot imagine the boredom. And so I at least have a pleasant occupation. Don't imagine anything grand. Nothing of the kind. A much more modest place than our old store. It is a booth compared with the previous one. Back home I would be ashamed of such a stall, but here, where we have had to give up so many of our pretensions—don't you agree, Joseph?" He laughed bitterly. "And so one manages somehow to live."

The wrong word—I was embarrassed by Father's confusion when he realized that he had used it.

"I see you are sleepy," he continued after a while. "Go back to sleep, and then you can visit me in the shop if you want. I am going there now to see how things are. You cannot imagine how difficult it has been to get credit, how mistrustful they are here of old merchants, of merchants with a reputable past. Do you recall the optician's shop in the market square? Well, our shop is right next door to it. There is still no sign over it, but you will find your way, I am sure. You can't miss it."

"Are you going out without a coat?" I asked anxiously.

"They have forgotten to pack it. Imagine, I could not find it in my trunk. But I don't really need it. That mild climate, that sweet air—"

"Please take my coat, Father," I insisted. "You must."

But Father was already putting on his hat. He waved to me and slipped out of the room.

I did not feel sleepy anymore. I felt rested and hungry. With pleasant anticipation I thought of the buffet. I dressed, wondering how many pastries to sample. I decided to start with the apple flan but did not forget the sponge cake with orange peel, which had caught my eye, too. I stood in front of the mirror to fix my tie, but the surface was like bottle glass: it secreted my reflection somewhere in its depth, and only an opaque blur was visible. I tried in vain to adjust the distance—approaching the mirror, then retreating from it—but no reflection would emerge from the silvery, fluid mist. I must ask for another looking glass, I thought, and left the room.

The corridor was completely dark. In one corner a tiny gas lamp flickered with a bluish flame, intensifying the impression of solemn silence. In that labyrinth of rooms, archways, and niches, I had difficulty remembering which door led to the restaurant.

I'll go out, I thought with sudden decision. I'll eat in the town. There must be a good café somewhere.

Beyond the gate, I plunged into the heavy, damp, sweet air of that peculiar climate. The grayness of the aura had become somewhat deeper; now it seemed to me that I was seeing daylight through mourning crepe.

I feasted my eyes on the velvety, succulent blackness of the darkest spots, on passages of dull grays and ashen, muted tones—that nocturne of a landscape. Waves of air fluttered softly around my face. They smelled of the sickly sweetness of stale rainwater.

And again that perpetual rustle of black forests—dull chords disturbing space beyond the limits of audibility! I was in the backyard of the Sanatorium. I turned to look at the rear of the main building, which was shaped like a horseshoe around a courtyard. All the windows were shuttered in black. The Sanatorium was in deep sleep. I went out by a gate in an iron fence. Nearby stood a dog kennel of extraordinary size, empty. Again I was engulfed and embraced by the black trees. Then it became somewhat lighter, and I saw outlines of houses between the trees. A few more steps and I found myself in a large town square.

What a strange, misleading resemblance it bore to the central square of our native city! How similar, in fact, are all the market squares in the world! Almost identical houses and shops!

The pavements were nearly empty. The mournful semidarkness of an undefined time descended from a sky of an indeterminable grayness. I could easily read all the shop signs and posters, yet it would not have surprised me to learn that it was the middle of the night. Only some of the shops were open. Others, their iron shutters pulled halfway down, were being hurriedly closed. A heady, rich, and inebriating air seemed to obscure some parts of the view, to wash away like a wet sponge some of the houses, a streetlamp, a section of signboard. At times it was difficult to keep one's eyes open, overcome as one was by a strange indolence or sleepiness. I began to look for the optician's shop that my father had mentioned. He had spoken of it as of something I knew, and he seemed to assume that I was familiar with local conditions. Didn't he remember that I had just come here for the first time? No doubt his mind was confused. Yet what could one expect of Father, who was only half-real, who lived a relative and conditional life, circumscribed by so many limitations! I cannot deny that much goodwill was needed to believe in his kind of existence. What he experienced was a pitiful substitute for life, depending on the indulgence of others, on a *consensus omnium* from which he drew his faint strength. It was clear that only by the solidarity of forbearance, by a communal averting of eyes from the obvious and shocking shortcomings of his condition, could this pitiful semblance of life maintain itself, for however short a moment, within the tissue of reality. The slightest doubt could undermine it, the faintest breeze of skepticism destroy it. Could Dr. Gotard's Sanatorium provide for Father this hothouse atmosphere of friendly indulgence and guard him from the cold winds of sober analysis? It was astonishing that in this insecure and questionable state of affairs, Father was capable of behaving so admirably.

I was glad when I saw a shop window full of cakes and pastries. My appetite revived. I opened the glass door, with the inscription "Ices" on it, and entered the dark interior. It smelled of coffee and vanilla. From the depths of the shop a girl appeared, her face misted over by dusk, and took my order. At last, after waiting so long, I could eat my fill of excellent doughnuts, which I dipped in my coffee. Surrounded by the dancing arabesques of dusk, I devoured pastries one after another, feeling darkness creep under my eyelids and stealthily fill me with its warm pulsations, its thousand delicate touches. In the end, only the window shone, like a gray rectangle, in the otherwise complete darkness. I knocked with my spoon on the tabletop, but in vain; no one appeared to take money for my refreshment. I left a silver coin on the table and walked out into the street.

In the bookshop next door, the light was still on. The shop assistants were busy sorting books. I asked for my father's shop. "It is next door to ours," one of them explained. A helpful boy even went with me to the door, to show me the way.

Father's shop had a glass pane in the door, the display window was not ready and was covered with a gray paper. On entering, I was astonished to see that the shop was full of customers. My father was standing behind the counter and adding a long row of figures on an invoice, repeatedly licking his pencil. The man for whom the invoice was being prepared was leaning over the counter and moving his index finger down the column of figures, counting softly. The rest of the customers looked on in silence.

My father gave me a look from over his spectacles and, marking his place on the invoice, said, "There is a letter for you. It is on the desk among all the papers." He went back to his sums. Meanwhile, the shop assistants were taking pieces of cloth bought by the customers, wrapping them in paper, and tying them with string. The shelves were only half-filled with cloth; some of them were still empty.

"Why don't you sit down, Father?" I asked softly, going behind the counter. "You don't take enough care of yourself, although you are very sick."

Father lifted his hand, as if wanting to reject my pleas, and did not stop counting. He looked very pale. It was obvious that only the excitement of his feverish activity sustained him and postponed the moment of complete collapse.

I went up to the desk and found not a letter but a parcel. A few days earlier, I had written to a bookshop about a pornographic

book, and here it was already. They had found my address, or
rather, Father's address, although he had only just opened a
new shop here that had neither a name nor a signboard! What
amazing efficiency in collecting information, what astounding
delivery methods! And what incredible speed!

"You may read it in the office at the back," said my father,
looking at me with displeasure. "As you can see, there is no
room here."

The room behind the shop was still empty. Through a glass
door some light filtered in from the shop. On the walls the shop
assistants' overcoats hung from hooks. I opened the parcel and,
by the faint light from the door, read the enclosed letter.

The letter informed me that the book I had ordered was
unfortunately out of stock. They would look out for it, although
the result of the search was uncertain; meanwhile, they were
sending me, without obligation, a certain object, which, they
were sure, would interest me. There followed a complicated description of a folding telescope with great refractive power and
many other virtues. Interested, I took the instrument out of the
wrapping. It was made of black oilcloth or canvas and was folded
into the shape of a flattened accordion. I have always had a
weakness for telescopes. I began to unfold the pleats of the instrument. Stiffened with thin rods, it rose under my fingers until
it almost filled the room; a kind of enormous bellows, a labyrinth
of black chambers, a long complex of camera obscuras, one
within another. It looked, too, like a long-bodied model automo-
bile made of patent leather, a theatrical prop, its lightweight paper
and stiff canvas imitating the bulkiness of reality. I looked into
the black funnel of the instrument and saw deep inside the vague
outline of the back of the Sanatorium. Intrigued, I put my head
deeper into the rear chamber of the apparatus. I could now see in
my field of vision the maid walking along the darkened corridor
of the Sanatorium, carrying a tray. She turned round and smiled.
"Can you see me?" I asked myself. An overwhelming drowsiness
misted my eyes. I was sitting, as it were, in the rear chamber of
the telescope as if in the back seat of a limousine. A light touch on
a lever and the apparatus began to rustle like a paper butterfly; I
felt that it was moving and turning toward the door.

Like a large black caterpillar, the telescope crept into the
lighted shop—an enormous paper arthropod with two imitation headlights on the front. The customers clustered together,
retreating before this blind paper dragon; the shop assistants
flung open the door to the street, and I rode slowly in my paper
car amid rows of onlookers, who followed with scandalized
eyes my truly outrageous exit.

3

That is how one lives in this town, and how time goes by. The
greater part of the day is spent in sleeping—and not only in
bed. No one is very particular when it comes to sleep. At any
place, at any time, one is ready for a quiet snooze: with one's
head propped on a restaurant table, in a horse-drawn cab, even
standing up when, out for a walk, one looks into the hall of an
apartment house for a moment and succumbs to the irrepress-
ible need for sleep.

Waking up, still dazed and shaky, one continues the interrupted conversation or the wearisome walk, carries on complicated discussions without beginning or end. In this way, whole chunks of time are casually lost somewhere; control over the continuity of the day is loosened until it finally ceases to matter; and the framework of uninterrupted chronology that one has been disciplined to notice every day is given up without regret. The compulsive readiness to account for the passage of time, the scrupulous penny-wise habit of reporting on the used-up hours—the pride and ambition of our economic system—are forsaken. Those cardinal virtues, which in the past one never dared to question, have long ago been abandoned.

A few examples will illustrate this state of affairs. At a certain time of day or night—a hardly perceptible difference in the color of the sky allows one to tell which it is—I wake up in twilight at the railings of the footbridge leading to the Sanatorium. Overpowered by sleep, I must have wandered unconsciously for a long time all over the town before, mortally tired, I dragged myself to the bridge. I cannot say whether Dr. Gotard accompanied me on that walk, but now he stands in front of me, finishing a long tirade and drawing conclusions. Carried away by his own eloquence, he slips his hand under my arm and leads me somewhere. I walk on, with him, and even before we have crossed the bridge, I am asleep again. Through my closed eyelids I can vaguely see the Doctor's expressive gestures, the smile under his black beard, and I try to understand, without success, his ultimate point—which he must have triumphantly revealed, for he now stands with arms outstretched. We have been walking side by side for I don't know how long, engrossed in a conversation at cross-purposes, when all of a sudden I wake up completely. Dr. Gotard has gone; it is quite dark, but only because my eyes are shut. When I open them, I find that I am in our room and don't know how I got there.

An even more dramatic example: at lunchtime, I enter a restaurant in town, which is full and very noisy. Whom do I meet in the middle of it, at a table sagging under the weight of dishes? My father. All eyes are on him, while he, animated, almost ecstatic with pleasure, his diamond tiepin shining, turns

in all directions, making fulsome conversation with everybody
at once. With false bravado, which I observe with the greatest
misgivings, he keeps ordering new dishes, which are then
stacked on the table. He gathers them around him with glee,
chewing and speaking at the same time, he mimes his great satisfaction with this feast and follows with adoring eyes Adam,
the waiter, to whom, with an ingratiating smile, he gives more
orders. And when the waiter, waving his napkin, rushes to get
them, Father turns to the company and calls them to witness the
irresistible charm of Adam, the Ganymede.

"A boy in a million," Father exclaims with a happy smile,
half-closing his eyes, "a ministering angel! You must agree, gentlemen, that he is a charmer!"

I leave in disgust, unnoticed by Father. Had he been put there

by the management of the restaurant in order to amuse the guests, he could not behave in a more ostentatious way. My head heavy with drowsiness, I stumble through the streets toward the Sanatorium. On a pillar box I rest my head and take a short siesta. At last, groping in darkness, I find the gate and go in. Our room is dark. I press the light switch, but there is no current. A cold draft comes from the window. The bed creaks in the darkness.

My father lifts his head from the pillows and says, "Ah, Joseph, Joseph! I have been lying here for two days without any attention. The bells are out of order, no one has been to see me, and my own son has left me, a very sick man, to run after girls in the town. Look how my heart is thumping!"

How do I reconcile all this? Has Father been sitting in the restaurant, driven there by an unhealthy greed, or has he been lying in bed feeling very ill? Are there two fathers? Nothing of the kind. The problem is the quick decomposition of time no longer watched with incessant vigilance.

We all know that time, this undisciplined element, holds itself within bounds but precariously, thanks to unceasing cultivation, meticulous care, and a continuous regulation and correction of its excesses. Free of this vigilance, it immediately begins to do tricks, run wild, play irresponsible practical jokes, and indulge in crazy clowning. The incongruity of our private times becomes evident. My father's time and my own no longer coincide.

Incidentally, the accusation that my father has made is completely groundless. I have not been chasing after girls. Swaying like a drunkard from one bout of sleep to another, I can hardly pay attention, even in my more wakeful moments, to the local ladies.

Moreover, the chronic darkness in the streets does not allow me to see faces clearly. What I have been able to observe— being a young man who still has a certain amount of interest in such things—is the peculiar way in which these girls walk.

Heedless of obstacles, obeying only some inner rhythm, each one walks in an inexorably straight line, as if along a thread that she seems to unwind from an invisible skein. This linear trot is full of mincing accuracy and measured grace. Each girl seems to carry inside her an individual rule, wound tight like a spring.

Walking thus, straight ahead, with concentration and dignity, they seem to have only one worry—not to break the rule, not to make any mistake, not to stray either to the right or to the left. And then it becomes clear to me that what they so conscientiously carry within themselves is an idée fixe of their own excellence, which the strength of their conviction almost transforms into reality. It is risked anticipation, without any guarantee: an untouchable dogma, held high, impervious to doubt.

What imperfections and blemishes, what retroussé or flat noses, what freckles or spots are smuggled under the bold flag of that fiction! There is no ugliness or vulgarity that cannot be lifted up to a fictional heaven of perfection by the flight of such a belief.

Sanctified by it, bodies become distinctly more beautiful, and feet, already shapely and graceful in their spotless footwear, speak eloquently, their fluid, shiny pacing monologue explaining the greatness of an idea that the closed faces are too proud to express. The girls keep their hands in the pockets of their short, tight jackets. In the cafés and in the theater, they cross their legs, uncovered to the knee, and hold them in provocative silence.

So much for one of the peculiarities of this town. I have already mentioned the black vegetation of the region. A certain kind of black fern deserves special mention: enormous bunches of it in vases are in the windows of every apartment here, and every public place. The fern is almost the symbol of mourning, the town's funeral crest.

4

Conditions in the Sanatorium are becoming daily more insufferable. It has to be admitted that we have fallen into a trap. Since my arrival, when a semblance of hospitable care was displayed for the newcomer, the management of the Sanatorium has not taken the trouble to give us even the illusion of any kind of professional supervision. We are simply left to our own devices. Nobody caters to our needs. I have noticed, for instance, that the wires of the electric bells have been cut just behind the doors and lead nowhere. There is no service. The corridors are dark and silent by day and by night. I have a strong suspicion that we are the only guests in this Sanatorium and that the mysterious or discreet looks with which the chambermaid closes the doors of the rooms on entering or leaving are simply mystification.

I sometimes feel a strong desire to open each door wide and leave it ajar, so that the miserable intrigue in which we have got ourselves involved can be exposed.

And yet I am not quite convinced that my suspicions are justified. Sometimes, late at night, I meet Dr. Gotard in a corridor, hurrying somewhere in a white coverall, with an enema bottle in his hand, preceded by the chambermaid. It would be difficult to stop him then and demand an explanation.

Were it not for the restaurant and pastry shop in town, one might starve to death. So far, I have not succeeded in getting a second bed for our room. There is no question of the sheets being changed.

One has to admit that the general neglect of civilized habits has affected both of us, too. To get into bed dressed and with shoes on was once, for me—a civilized person—unthinkable. Yet now, when I return home late, sleep drunk, the room is in semidarkness and the curtains at the window billow in a cold breeze. Half-dazed, I tumble onto the bed and bury myself in the eiderdown. Thus I sleep for irregular stretches of time, for days or weeks, wandering through empty landscapes of sleep, always on the way, always on the steep roads of respiration, sometimes sliding lightly and gracefully from gentle slopes, then climbing laboriously up the cliffs of snoring. At their summit I embrace the horizons of the rocky and empty desert of sleep. At some point, somewhere on the sharp turn of a snore, I wake up half-conscious and feel the body of my father at the foot of the bed. He lies there curled up, small as a kitten. I fall asleep again, with my mouth open, and the vast panorama of mountain landscape glides past me majestically.

In the shop, my father displays an energetic activity, transacting business and straining all his capacities to attract customers. His cheeks are flushed with animation, his eyes shine. In the Sanatorium he is very sick, as sick as during his last weeks at home. It is obvious that the end must be imminent. In a weak voice he addresses me: "You should look into the store more often, Joseph. The shop assistants are robbing us. You can see that I am no longer equal to the task. I have been lying here sick for weeks, and the shop is being neglected, left to run itself. Was there any mail from home?"

I begin to regret this whole undertaking. Perhaps we were misled by skillful advertising when we decided to send Father here. Time put back—it sounded good, but what does it come to in reality? Does anyone here get time at its full value, a true time, time cut off from a fresh bolt of cloth, smelling of newness and dye? Quite the contrary. It is used-up time, worn out by other people, a shabby time full of holes, like a sieve.

No wonder. It is time, as it were, regurgitated—if I may be forgiven this expression: secondhand time. God help us all!

And then there is the matter of the highly improper manipulation of time. The shameful tricks, the penetration of time's mechanism from behind, the hazardous fingering of its wicked secrets! Sometimes one feels like banging the table and exclaiming, "Enough of this! Keep off time, time is untouchable, one must not provoke it! Isn't it enough for you to have space? Space is for human beings, you can swing about in space, turn somersaults, fall down, jump from star to star, but for goodness' sake, don't tamper with time!"

On the other hand, can I be expected to give notice to Dr. Gotard? However miserable Father's existence, I am able to see him, to be with him, to talk to him. In fact, I should be infinitely grateful to Dr. Gotard.

Several times, I have wanted to speak openly to Dr. Gotard, but
he is elusive. He has just gone to the restaurant, says the chambermaid. I turn to go there, when she runs after me to say that she
was wrong, that Dr. Gotard is in the operating theater. Hurrying
upstairs, I wonder what kind of operations can be performed
here; I enter the anteroom and am told to wait. Dr. Gotard will be
with me in a moment, he had just finished the operation, he is
washing his hands. I can almost visualize him: short, taking long
steps, his coat open, hurrying through a succession of hospital
wards. After a while, what am I told? Dr. Gotard had not been
there at all, no operation has been performed there for many
years. Dr. Gotard is asleep in his room, his black beard sticking
up into the air. The room fills with his snores as if with clouds
that lift him in his bed, ever higher and higher—a great pathetic
ascension on waves of snores and voluminous bedding.

Even stranger things happen here—things that I try to conceal from myself and that are quite fantastic in their absurdity. Whenever I leave our room, I have the impression that someone who has been standing behind the door moves quickly away and turns a corner. Or somebody seems to be walking in front of me, not looking back. It is not a nurse. I know who it is! "Mother!" I exclaim, in a voice trembling with excitement, and my mother turns her face to me and looks at me for a moment with a pleading smile. Where am I? What is happening here? What maze have I become entangled in?

5

I don't know why—it may be the time of year—but the days are growing more severe in color, darker and blacker. It seems as if one were looking at the world through black glasses.

The landscape is now like the bottom of an enormous aquarium full of watery ink. Trees, people, and houses merge, swaying like underwater plants against the background of the inky deep.

Packs of black dogs are often seen in the vicinity of the Sanatorium. Of all shapes and sizes, they run at dusk along the roads and paths, engrossed in their own affairs, silent, tense, and alert.

They run in twos and threes, with outstretched necks, their ears pricked up, whining softly in plaintive tones that escape from their throats as if against their will—signals of the highest nervousness. Absorbed in running, hurrying, always on their way somewhere, always pursuing some mysterious goal, they hardly notice the passersby. Occasionally one shoots out a glance while running past, and then the black and intelligent eyes are full of a rage contained only by haste. At times the dogs even rush at one's feet, succumbing to their anger, with heads held low and ominous snarls, but soon think better of it and turn away.

Nothing is to be done about this plague of dogs, but why does the management of the Sanatorium keep an enormous Alsatian on a chain—a terror of a beast, a werewolf of truly demoniacal ferocity? I shiver with fear whenever I pass his kennel, by which he stands immobile on his short chain, a halo of matted hair

bristling around his head, bewhiskered and bearded, his powerful jaws displaying the whole apparatus of his long teeth. He
does not bark, but his wild face contorts at the sight of a human
being. He stiffens with an expression of boundless fury and,
slowly raising his horrible muzzle, breaks into a low, fervent,
convulsive howl that comes from the very depths of his hatred—
a howl of despair and lament of his temporary impotence.

My father walks past the beast with indifference whenever
we go out together. As for myself, I am deeply shaken when
confronted by the dog's impotent hatred. I am now some two
heads taller than Father who, small and thin, trots at my side
with the mincing gait of a very old man.

Approaching the city square one day, we noticed an extraordinary commotion. Crowds of people filled the streets. We heard the incredible news that an enemy army had entered the town.

In consternation, people exchanged alarmist and contradictory news that was hard to credit. A war not preceded by diplomatic activity? A war amid blissful peace? A war against whom and for what reason? We were told that the enemy incursion gave heart to a group of discontented townspeople, who have come out in the open, armed, to terrorize the peaceful inhabitants. We noticed, in fact, a group of these activists, in black civilian clothing with white straps across their breasts, advancing in silence, their guns at the ready. The crowd fell back onto the pavements, as they marched by, flashing from under their hats ironic dark looks, in which there was a touch of superiority, a glimmer of malicious and perverse enjoyment, as if they could hardly stop themselves from bursting into laughter. Some of them were recognized by the crowd, but the exclamations of relief were at once stilled by the sight of rifle barrels. They passed by, not challenging anybody. All the streets filled at once with a frightened, grimly silent crowd. A dull hubbub floated over the city. We seemed to hear a distant rumble of artillery and the rattle of gun carriages.

"I must get to the shop," said my father, pale but determined. "You need not come with me," he added. "You will be in my way. Go back to the Sanatorium."

The pull of cowardice made me obey him. I saw my father trying to squeeze himself through the compact wall of bodies in the crowd and lost sight of him.

I broke into a run along side streets and alleys, and hurried toward the upper part of the town. I realized that by going uphill I might be able to avoid the center, now packed solid by people.

Farther up, the crowd thinned and at last completely disappeared. I walked quietly along empty streets to the municipal park. Streetlamps were lit there and burned with a dark bluish flame, the color of asphodels, the flowers of mourning. Each light was surrounded by a swarm of dancing june bugs, heavy as bullets, carried on their slanting flight by vibrating wings.

The fallen were struggling clumsily in the sand, their backs arched, hunched beneath the hard shields under which they were trying to fold the delicate membranes of their wings. On grassy plots and paths people were walking along, engrossed in carefree conversation.

The trees at the far end of the park drooped into the courtyards of houses that were built on lower ground on the other side of the park wall. I strolled along that wall on the park side, where it reached only to my breast; on the other side, it fell in escarpments to the level of courtyards. In one place, a ramp of firm soil rose from the courtyards to the top of the wall. There I crossed the wall without difficulty and squeezed between houses into a street. As I had expected, I found myself almost facing the Sanatorium; its back was outlined clearly in a black frame of trees. As usual, I opened the gate in the iron fence and saw from a distance the watchdog at his post. As usual, I shivered with aversion and wished to pass by him as quickly as possible, so as not to have to listen to his howl of hatred; but I suddenly noticed that he was unchained and was circling toward the courtyard, barking hollowly and trying to cut me off.

Rigid with fright, I retreated and, instinctively looking for shelter, crept into a small arbor, sure that all my efforts to evade the beast would be in vain. The shaggy animal was leaping toward me, his muzzle already pushing into the arbor. I was trapped. Horror-struck, I then saw that the dog was on a long chain that he had unwound to its full length, and that the inside of the arbor was beyond the reach of his claws. Sick with fear, I was too weak to feel any relief. Reeling, almost fainting, I raised my eyes. I had never before seen the beast from so near, and only now did I see him clearly. How great is the power of prejudice! How powerful the hold of fear! How blind had I been! It was not a dog, it was a man. A chained man, whom, by a simplifying metaphoric wholesale error, I had taken for a dog. I don't want to be misunderstood. He was a dog, certainly, but a dog in human shape. The quality of a dog is an inner quality and can be manifested as well in human as in animal shape. He who was standing in front of me in the entrance to the arbor, his jaws wide open, his teeth bared in a terrible growl, was a man of middle height,

with a black beard. His face was yellow, bony; his eyes were
black, evil, and unhappy. Judging by his black suit and the shape
of his beard, one might take him for an intellectual or a scholar.
He might have been Dr. Gotard's unsuccessful elder brother. But
that first impression was false. The large hands stained with glue,
the two brutal and cynical furrows running down from his nostrils and disappearing into his beard, the vulgar horizontal wrinkles on the low forehead quickly dispelled that first impression.
He looked more like a bookbinder, a tub-thumper, a vocal party
member—a violent man, given to dark, sudden passions. And it
was this—the passionate depth, the convulsive bristling of all his
fibers, the mad fury of his barking when the end of a stick was
pointed at him—that made him a hundred percent dog.

   If I tried to escape through the back of the arbor, I thought,
I would completely elude his reach and could walk along a side

path to the gate of the Sanatorium. I was about to put my leg over the railing when I suddenly stopped. I felt it would be too cruel simply to go away and leave the dog behind, possessed by his helpless and boundless fury. I could imagine his terrible disappointment, his inexpressible pain as I escaped from his trap, free once and for all from his clutches. I decided to stay.

I stepped forward and said quietly, "Please calm down. I shall unchain you."

His face, distorted by spasms of growling, became whole again, smooth and almost human. I went up to him without fear and unfastened the buckle of his collar. We walked side by side. The bookbinder was wearing a decent black suit but had bare feet. I tried to talk to him, but a confused babble was all I heard in reply. Only his eyes, black and eloquent, expressed a wild spurt of gratitude, of submission, which filled me with awe. Whenever he stumbled on a stone or a clod of earth, the shock made his face shrivel and contract with fear, and that expression was followed by one of rage. I would then bring him to order with a harsh comradely rebuke. I even patted him on the back. An astonished, suspicious, unbelieving smile tried to form on his face. Ah, how hard to bear was this terrible friendship! How frightening was this uncanny sympathy! How could I get rid of this man striding along with me, his eyes expressing his total submission, following the slightest changes in my face? I could not show impatience.

I pulled out my wallet and said in a matter-of-fact tone, "You probably need some money. I will lend you some with pleasure." But at the sight of my wallet his look became so unexpectedly wild that I put it away again as quickly as I could. For quite some time afterward, he could not calm himself and his features continued to be distorted by more spasms of growling. No, I could not stand this any longer. Anything, but not this. Matters were already confused and entangled enough.

I then noticed the glare of fire over the town: my father was somewhere in the thick of a revolution or in a burning shop. Dr. Gotard was unavailable. And to cap it all, my mother had appeared, incognito, on that mysterious errand! These were the elements of some great and obscure intrigue, which was hemming me in. I must escape, I thought, escape at any cost. Anywhere. I

must drop this horrible friendship with a bookbinder who smells of dog and who is watching me all the time. We were now standing in front of the Sanatorium.

"Come to my room, please," I said with a polite gesture. Civilized gestures fascinated him, soothed his wildness. I let him enter my room first and gave him a chair.

"I'll go to the restaurant and get some brandy," I said.

He got up, terrified, and wanted to follow me.

I calmed his fears with a gentle firmness. "You will sit here and wait for me," I said in a deep, sonorous voice, which concealed fear. He sat down again with a tentative smile.

I went out and walked slowly along the corridor, then down-stairs and across the hall leading to the entrance door; I passed the gate, strode across the courtyard, banged the iron gate shut, and only then began to run, breathlessly, my heart thumping, my temples throbbing, along the dark avenue leading to the railway station.

Images raced through my head, each more horrible than the next. The impatience of the monster dog; his fear and despair when he realized that I had cheated him; another attack of fury, another bout of rage breaking out with unchecked force. My father's return to the Sanatorium, his unsuspecting knock at the door, and his confrontation with the terrible beast.

Luckily, in fact, Father was no longer alive; he could not really be reached, I thought with relief, and saw in front of me the black row of railway carriages ready to depart.

I got into one of them, and the train, as if it had been waiting for me, slowly started to move, without a whistle.

Through the window the great valley, filled with dark rustling forests—against which the walls of the Sanatorium seemed white—moved and turned slowly once again. Farewell, Father. Farewell, town that I shall never see again.

Since then, I have traveled continuously. I have made my home in that train, and everybody puts up with me as I wander from coach to coach. The compartments, enormous as rooms, are full of rubbish and straw, and cold drafts pierce them on gray, colorless days.

My suit became torn and ragged. I have been given the shabby uniform of a railway man. My face is bandaged with a dirty rag, because one of my cheeks is swollen. I sit on the straw, dozing, and when hungry, I stand in the corridor outside a second-class compartment and sing. People throw small coins into my hat: a black railway-man's hat, its visor half-torn away.

DODO

He usually visited us on Saturday afternoons wearing a dark suit, a white piqué waistcoat, and a bowler hat that he had to have specially made to fit his head. He would stay for a quarter of an hour or so and sip a drink of raspberry syrup with soda, his chin propped on the bone handle of a walking stick planted between his knees, or else he would quietly contemplate the blue smoke of his cigarette.

Other relatives usually called on us at the same time, and then, as the conversation became general, Dodo withdrew and assumed the passive role of an extra. He would not say a word during these animated meetings, but his expressive eyes under his magnificent eyebrows would rest in turn on each person, while his jaw dropped and his face became elongated, unable to control its muscles in the act of passionate listening.

Dodo spoke only when spoken to—and then he answered in monosyllables, grudgingly, looking away—and only if the questions were easy ones dealing with simple matters. Sometimes he succeeded in keeping the conversation going beyond these elementary questions by resorting to a stock of expressive gestures and grimaces that were most useful because they could be interpreted in many different ways, filling the gaps in articulate talk and creating an impression of sensible response. This, however, was an illusion that was quickly dispelled; the conversation would break down completely; and while the interlocutor's gaze wandered slowly and pensively away from Dodo, he, left to himself, reverted once more to his proper role as an outsider, a passive observer of other people's social intercourse.

How could one talk to him when, to the question whether he had been in the country with his mother, he would answer softly: "I don't know." And this was the sad and embarrassing truth, for Dodo's mind did not register anything but the present.

During his childhood, a long time before, Dodo had suffered a serious brain disease during which he had been unconscious for many months, more dead than alive. When his condition had finally improved, it became obvious that he had been withdrawn from circulation and that he no longer belonged to the community of sensible people. His education had to be private, for the sake of form, and taken in tiny doses. The demands of convention, harsh and unyielding where other people were concerned, lost their sternness and gave way to tolerance with regard to Dodo.

A zone of special privilege was created around Dodo for his own protection, a no-man's-land unaffected by the pressures of life. Everyone outside it was subjected to the buffeting of events, waded in them noisily, let himself be carried away, absorbed, and engrossed; within the zone there was calm and stillness, a caesura in the general tumult.

Thus Dodo lived and grew, and his exceptional destiny grew

together with him, taken for granted, without protest from anyone.

Dodo was never given a new suit; he always wore the cast-off clothes of his elder brother. While the life of his peers was divided into phases and periods, marked by notable events, sublime and symbolic moments—birthdays, exams, engagements, promotions—his life passed in a level monotony, undisturbed by anything pleasant or painful, and his future, too, appeared as a completely straight, smooth path without surprises.

It would be wrong to think that Dodo protested inwardly against such a state of affairs. He accepted it with simplicity and without astonishment as a life that was suited to him. He managed his existence and arranged details of it within the confines of that eventless monotony with sober and dignified optimism.

Every morning he went for a walk along three streets and, having come to the end of the third, he returned the same way. Clad in an elegantly cut but rather shabby suit passed on by his brother, he proceeded with unhurried dignity, holding his walking stick behind his back. He might have been a gentleman walking about the city for pleasure. This lack of haste, of any direction or purpose, sometimes became quite embarrassing, for Dodo was inclined to stand gaping in front of shops, outside workshops where people were hard at work, and even joined groups of people engaged in conversation.

His face matured early, and, strange to say, while experience and the trials of living spared the empty inviolability, the strange marginality of his life, his features reflected experiences that had passed him by, elements in a biography never to be fulfilled; these experiences, although completely illusory, modeled and sculpted his face into the mask of a great tragedian, which expressed the wisdom and sadness of existence. His eyebrows were arched magnificently, shadowing his large, sad, darkly circled eyes. On both sides of his nose two furrows, marks of spurious suffering and wisdom, ran toward the corners of his lips. The small full mouth was shut tight in pain, and a coquettishly pointed beard on a protruding Bourbon chin gave him the appearance of an elderly *bon viveur*.

It was inevitable that Dodo's privileged strangeness should be detected by the lurking and always hungry malice of the human race.

Thus, with increased frequency, Dodo would get company on his morning walks: one of the penalties of not being an ordinary person was that these companions were of a special kind, and not colleagues sharing communal interests. They were individuals of much younger years who clung to the dignified and serious Dodo; the conversations they conducted were in a gay and bantering tone that might have been agreeable to Dodo.

As he walked, towering by a head over that merry and carefree gang, he looked like a peripatetic philosopher surrounded by his disciples, and his face, under its mask of seriousness and sadness, broke into frivolous smiles that fought against its usually tragic expression.

Dodo now began to return late from his morning walks, to come home with tousled hair, his clothes in some disarray, but animated and inclined to tease Caroline, a poor cousin given a home by Aunt Retitia.

Fully aware of the fact that the company he was keeping was perhaps of no great consequence, Dodo maintained at home a complete silence on the subject.

Very occasionally, events occurred in his monotonous life that stood out by their importance. Once, having left in the morning, Dodo did not return to lunch. Nor did he return to supper, nor to lunch the following day. Aunt Retitia was in despair. But in the evening of the second day he returned somewhat the worse for wear, his bowler hat crushed and awry, but otherwise in good health and full of spiritual calm.

It was difficult to reconstruct the history of that escapade, as Dodo kept completely silent about it. Most probably, having extended the course of his daily walk, he had wandered off to an unfamiliar area of the city, perhaps helped in it by the young peripatetics who were not averse to exposing Dodo to new and unfamiliar conditions of life.

Maybe it was one of the occasions when Dodo's poor, overburdened memory had a day off, and he forgot his address and even his name, details he somehow usually managed to remember, but we never did learn the details of his adventure.

When Dodo's elder brother went abroad, the family shrank to four members. Apart from Uncle Jerome and Aunt Retitia, there was only Caroline, who played the part of lady housekeeper in that patrician establishment.

Uncle Jerome had been confined to his room for many years. From the moment when Providence gently eased from his hand the steering of the battered ship of his life, he had led the existence of a pensioner in the narrow space allotted to him between the hallway and the dark alcove of his apartment.

In a long housecoat reaching down to his ankles, he used to sit in the darkest corner of the alcove, his facial hair growing daily longer. A beard the color of pepper, with long strands of hair almost completely white at the ends, surrounded his face and spread halfway up his cheeks, leaving free only a hawk's nose and eyes, rolling their whites under the shadow of shaggy eyebrows.

In this windowless room—a narrow prison in which, like a large cat, he was condemned to walk up and down in front of the glass door leading to the drawing room—stood two enormous oak beds. Uncle's and Aunt's nightly abode. The whole back wall of the room was covered with a large tapestry, the indistinct woven figures of which loomed through the darkness. When one's eyes became accustomed to the dark, one could see on it, among bamboos and palms, an enormous lion, powerful and forbidding as a prophet, majestic as a patriarch.

Sitting back-to-back, the lion and Uncle Jerome felt each other's presence and loathed it. Without looking, they growled at each other, bared their evil teeth, and muttered threats. Sometimes the lion in an excess of irritation would rise on his forelegs, his mane bristling, and fill the overcast tapestry sky with his roaring. Sometimes Uncle Jerome would tower over the lion and deliver a prophetic tirade, frowning under the weight of the great words, his beard waving in inspiration. Then the lion would narrow his eyes in pain and, slowly turning his head, cringe under the lash of divine words.

The lion and Jerome transformed the dark alcove in my uncle's apartment into a perpetual battlefield.

Uncle Jerome and Dodo lived in the small apartment

independently from each other, in two different dimensions that never coincided. Their eyes, whenever they met, wandered on without focusing, like the eyes of animals of two unrelated and distant species that are incapable of retaining the picture of anything unfamiliar.

They never spoke to each other.

At table, Aunt Retitia, sitting between her husband and her son, formed a buffer between two worlds, an isthmus between two oceans of madness.

Uncle Jerome ate jerkily, his long beard dipping into his plate. When the kitchen door creaked, he half rose from his chair and grabbed his plate of soup, ready to flee with it to the alcove should a stranger enter the room. Aunt Retitia would reassure him, saying:

"Don't be afraid, no one is there; it is only the maid."

Then Dodo would cast an angry and indignant look at his frightened father and mumble to himself with great displeasure: "He's off his head."

Before Uncle Jerome accepted absolution from the complex and difficult affairs of life and got permission to retreat into his refuge in the alcove, he was a man of quite a different stamp. Those who knew him in his youth said that his reckless temperament knew no restraints, considerations, or scruples. With great satisfaction he spoke to mortally sick people about the death that awaited them. Visits of condolence provided him with an opportunity for sharply criticizing the life of the deceased, still being mourned by his family. About the unpleasant or intimate incidents in people's private lives that they wanted to conceal, he spoke to them loudly and with sarcasm. Then one night he returned from a business trip completely transformed and, shaking with fear, tried to hide under his bed. A few days later news was spread in the family that Uncle Jerome had given up all the complicated, dubious, and risky business affairs that had threatened to submerge him, had abdicated, and had begun a new life, regulated by strict, although to us somewhat obscure, principles.

On Sunday afternoons when we were usually invited by Aunt Retitia to a small family tea party, Uncle Jerome did not recognize us. Sitting in the alcove, he looked through the glass door at the company with wild and frightened eyes. Sometimes, however, he unexpectedly left his hermitage, still in his long housecoat, his beard waving round his face, and, spreading his hands as if he wanted to separate us, he would say:

"And now, I beg you, all you that are here, disperse, run along, but quietly, stealthily, on tiptoe . . ."

Then, waving his finger mysteriously at us, he would add in a low voice:

"Everybody is talking about it: Dee-da . . ."

My aunt would push him gently back to the alcove, but he would turn at the door and grimly, with raised finger, repeat: "Dee-da."

Dodo's understanding was a little slow, and he needed a few moments of silence and concentration before a situation became clear to him. When it did, his eyes wandered from one person to another, as if to make sure that something very funny had really happened. He then burst into noisy laughter, and,

with great satisfaction, shaking his head in derision, he repeated amid the bursts of laughter: "He's off his head!"

Night fell on Aunt Retitia's house. The servant girl went to bed in the kitchen; bubbles of night air floated from the garden and burst against the window. Aunt Retitia slept in the depths of her large bed; on the other, Uncle Jerome sat upright among the bedclothes, like a tawny owl, his eyes shining in the darkness, his beard flowing over his knees, which were drawn up to his chin.

He slowly climbed down from his bed and walked on tiptoe to my aunt's bed. He stood over the sleeping woman, like a cat ready to leap, eyebrows and beard abristle. The lion on the wall tapestry gave a short yawn and turned his head away. My aunt, awakened, was alarmed by that head with its shining eyes and spitting mouth.

"Go back to bed at once," she said, shooing him away as one would shoo a hen.

Jerome retreated spitting and looking back with nervous movements of his head.

In the next room Dodo lay on his bed. Dodo never slept. The center of sleep in his diseased brain did not function correctly, so he wriggled and tossed and turned from side to side all night long.

The mattress groaned. Dodo sighed heavily, wheezed, sat up, lay down again.

His unlived life worried him, tortured him, turning round and round inside him like an animal in a cage. In Dodo's body, the body of a half-wit, somebody was growing old, although he had not lived; somebody was maturing to a death that had no meaning at all.

Then suddenly, he sobbed loudly in the darkness.

Aunt Retitia leapt from her bed.

"What is it, Dodo, are you in pain?"

Dodo turned to her amazed.

"Who?" he asked.

"Why are you sobbing?" asked my aunt.

"It's not I, it's he . . ."

"Which he?"

"The one inside . . ."

"Who is he?"

Dodo waved his hand resignedly. "Eh . . ." he said and turned on his other side.

Aunt Retitia returned to bed on tiptoe. As she passed Uncle Jerome's bed, he waved a threatening finger at her.

"Everybody is talking about it: Dee-da . . ."

EDDIE

I

On the same floor as our family, in a long and narrow wing of the house overlooking the courtyard, Eddie lives with his.

Eddie has long ago stopped being a small boy. Eddie is a grown-up man with a full, manly voice who sometimes sings arias from operas.

Eddie is inclined to obesity, not to its spongelike and flabby form, but rather to the athletic and muscular variety. His shoulders are strong and powerful like a bear's, but what of it? He had no use of his legs, which are completely degenerate and shapeless. Looking at his legs, it is difficult to determine the reason for his strange infirmity. It looks as if his legs had too many joints between the knee and the ankle; at least two more joints than normal legs. No wonder that they bend pitifully at those supernumerary joints, not only to the side but also forward and indeed in all possible directions.

Thus, Eddie can move only with the help of two crutches, which are remarkably well made and polished to resemble mahogany. On these he walks downstairs every day to buy a newspaper: this is his only walk and his only diversion. It is painful to look at his progress down the stairs. His legs sway irregularly to one side, then back, bending in unexpected places; and his feet, like horses' hooves, small but thick, knock like sticks on the wooden planks. But having reached street level, Eddie unexpectedly changes. He straightens himself up, pushes out his chest grandly, and makes his body swing. Taking his weight on his crutches as if on parallel bars, he throws his legs far to the front. When they hit the ground with an uneven thud, Eddie moves the crutches forward and with a new impetus swings his body again. With these forward swings, he conquers space. Often, maneuvering his crutches in the courtyard, he can, with the excess of strength gathered during long hours of rest, demonstrate with truly magnificent gusto this heroic method of locomotion, to the amazement of servant girls from the first and the second floors. The back of his neck swells, two folds of flesh form under his chin, and on his face held aslant appears a grimace of pain when he clenches his teeth in effort. Eddie does no work, as if fate, having saddled him with the burden of infirmity, had in exchange freed him from that curse of Adam's breed. In the shadow of his disability Eddie exploits to the full his exceptional right to idleness and deep at heart is not displeased at that private transaction, individually negotiated with fate.

Nonetheless, we have often wondered how such a young man in his twenties can fill his time. The reading of the newspaper provides a lot of work, for Eddie is a careful reader. No advertisement or announcement in small print escapes his notice. And when he finally gets to the last page of the journal, he is not condemned to boredom for the rest of the day—not at all. Only then does Eddie get down to the hobby to which he looks forward with pleasure. In the afternoon, when other people take a short siesta, Eddie gets out his large, fat scrapbooks, spreads them on the table under the window, prepares glue, sets out a brush and a pair of scissors, and begins the pleasant and rewarding job of cutting out the most interesting articles and pasting them in, according to a certain rigid system. The crutches are at his side, prepared for any eventuality, standing propped against the windowsill, but Eddie does not need them, for everything is within his reach. Thus busily occupied, he fills the few hours until teatime. Every third day Eddie shaves himself. He likes this activity and all the paraphernalia associated with it: hot water, shaving soap, and the smooth, gentle cutthroat razor. While mixing soap with water and stropping the razor on a leather strap, Eddie sings. His voice is not trained, nor is it very tuneful, so he sings loudly without any pretensions, and Adela maintains that his voice is pleasant.

However, Eddie's home life is not entirely harmonious. Unfortunately there seems to be a very serious conflict between him and his parents, the reason and background to which we do not know. We shan't repeat the gossip or hearsay; we shall limit ourselves to facts empirically confirmed.

It is usually toward the evening during the warm season, when Eddie's window is open, that we hear the echoes of these altercations. We hear, to be precise, only one half of the dialogue, Eddie's part, because the replies of his antagonists, hidden in the farther parts of the apartment, cannot reach our ears.

It is difficult, therefore, to guess what Eddie is accused of, but from the tone of his retorts one can only deduce that he is cut to the quick, almost at his wits' end. His words are violent and injudicious, obviously dictated by great agitation, but his tone, although indignant, is rather whining and miserable.

"Yes, indeed," he calls in a plaintive voice, "and so what? . . . What time yesterday? . . . It is not true! . . . And what if it were? . . . Then Dad is lying!"

And so it continues for whole stretches of time, diversified only by outbursts of Eddie's anger and by his attempts to tear out his reddish hair in helpless fury.

But sometimes—and this is the climax of these scenes that gives them a specific appeal—there follows what we have been waiting for with bated breath. In the depth of the apartment there is a loud crash, a door is opened with a bang, pieces of furniture are thrown to the floor, and lastly Eddie emits a heartrending scream.

We listen to it shaken and embarrassed, but also morbidly excited at the thought of the savage and fantastic violence being wrought on an athletic full-blooded youth, however crippled in his legs.

2

At dusk, when the washing up after an early supper is finished, Adela usually sits on one of the balconies overlooking the courtyard, not far from Eddie's window. Two long balconies in the form of a squared horseshoe overlook the courtyard, one on the first floor and one on the second floor. In the cracks of their wooden planks bits of grass are growing, and from one crack even a small acacia tree waves high above the courtyard.

Apart from Adela, one or two neighbors sit on these balconies in front of their doors sprawled on chairs or squatting on stools, wilting faintly in the dusk; they rest after the toil of their day, mute as tied-up sacks, waiting for the night to untie them gently.

Down below, the courtyard quickly fills with darkness, but the air above it does not yet relinquish its light and seems to become steadily lighter as everything below gradually turns pitch dark; it shimmers and trembles from the sudden, furtive flights of bats.

Down below, the quick and silent work of night now begins in earnest. Greedy ants swarm everywhere, decomposing into atoms the substance of things, eating them down to their white bones, to their ribs and skeletons, which phosphoresce in the nightmare of this sad battlefield. White papers, in tatters on the rubbish heap, survive longest, like undigested rays of brightness in the worm-ridden darkness, and cannot completely dissolve. At times they seem engulfed by darkness, then they emerge again, but in the end it is impossible to say whether one sees anything or whether these are illusions that begin their nightly ravings; in the end people sit in their own aura under stars projected by their own pulsating brains, by the phantoms of hallucinations.

And then thin veins of breezes rise from the bottom of the courtyard, hesitant and uncertain, streaks of freshness, which line like silt the folds of summer nights. And while the first shimmering stars appear in the sky, the summer night emerges with a sigh—deep, full of starry dust and the distant croaking of frogs.

Without putting on the light, Adela goes to bed and sinks into the tired bedding of the previous night; hardly has she closed her eyes when the race on all floors and in all apartments of the house begins.

Only for the uninitiated is the summer night a time of rest and forgetfulness. Once the activities of the day have finished and the tired brains long for sleep, the confused to-ing and fro-ing, the enormous tangled hubbub of a July night begins. All the apartments of the house, all rooms and alcoves, are full of noise, of wanderings, enterings and leavings. In all windows lamps with milky shades can be seen, even passages are brightly lit and doors never stop being opened and shut. A great, disorderly, half-ironic conversation is conducted with constant misunderstandings in all the chambers of the human hive. On the second floor people misunderstand what those from the first floor have said and send emissaries with urgent instructions. Couriers run through all the apartments, upstairs and downstairs, forget their instructions on their way and are repeatedly called back. And there is always something to add, nothing is ever fully explained, and all that bustle among the laughter and the jokes leads to nothing.

The back rooms, which do not participate in this great muddle of the night, have their separate time, measured by the ticking of clocks, by monologues of silence, by the deep breathing of the sleepers. Enormous wet nurses swollen with milk sleep there, clinging greedily to the lap of night, their cheeks burning in ecstasy. Small babies wander with closed eyelids on the surface of their nurses' sleep, crawl delicately like ferreting animals over the blue map of veins on the white plains of their breasts, searching with blind faces the warm opening, the entry into the depths of sleep, and find at last with their tender lips the source of sleep: the trusted nipple filled with sweet forgetfulness.

And those in their beds who have already caught sleep will not let go of it; they fight with it as with an angel that is trying to escape until they conquer it and press it to the pillow. Then they snore intermittently as if quarreling and reminding themselves of the angry history of their hatreds. And when the grumbles and recriminations have ceased and the struggle with sleep is over and every room in turn has sunk into stillness and nonexistence, Leon the shop assistant climbs blindly and slowly up the stairs, his boots in his hand, and in darkness tries to find the keyhole of the door. He returns thus nightly from the brothel, with bloodshot eyes, shaken by hiccups and with a thread of saliva trailing down his half-opened lips.

In Mr. Jacob's room a lamp is alight on the table, over which he sits hunched, writing a long letter to Christian Seipel & Sons (Spinners and Mechanical Weavers). On the floor lies a whole stack of papers covered with his writing, but the end of the letter is not yet in sight. Every now and then he rises from the table and runs round the room, his hands in his windswept hair, and as he circles thus, he occasionally climbs a wall, flies along the wallpaper like a large gnat blindly hitting the arabesques of design, and descends again to the floor to continue his inspired circling.

Adela is fast asleep, her mouth half open, her face relaxed and absent; but her closed lids are transparent, and on their thin parchment the night is writing its pact with the devil, half text, half picture, full of erasures, corrections, and scribbles.

Eddie stands undressed in his room and exercises with dumbbells. He needs a lot of strength in his shoulders, twice as much as a normal man, for shoulders replace his useless legs, and, therefore, he exercises every night, zealously and in secret.

Adela is flowing backward into oblivion and cannot shout or call, nor can she stop Eddie from trying to climb out of his window.

Eddie crawls out onto the balcony without his crutches, and one wonders if his stumps would carry him. But Eddie is not attempting to walk. Like a large white dog, he approaches in four-legged squat jumps, in great shuffling leaps on the resounding planks of the balcony, until he has reached Adela's window. Every night, grimacing with pain, he presses his white, fat face to the windowpane shining in the moonlight, and plaintively and eagerly he tells her, crying, that his crutches have been locked in a cupboard for the night and that now he must run about like a dog, on all fours.

But Adela is completely limp, completely surrendered to the deep rhythm of sleep. She has no strength even to pull up the blanket over her bare thighs and cannot prevent the columns of bedbugs from wandering over her body. These light and thin, leaflike insects run over her so delicately that she does not feel their touch. They are flat receptacles for blood, reddish blood bags without eyes or faces, now on the march in whole clans on a migration of the species subdivided into generations and tribes. They run up from her feet in scores, a never-ending procession, they are larger now, as large as moths, flat red vampires without heads, lightweight as if cut out of paper, on legs more delicate than the web of spiders.

And when the last laggard bedbugs have come and gone, with an enormous one bringing up the rear, complete silence comes at last. Deep sleep fills the empty passages and apartments, while the rooms slowly begin to absorb the grayness of the hours before dawn.

In all the beds people lie with their knees drawn up, with faces violently thrown to one side, in deep concentration, immersed in sleep and given to it wholly.

And the process of sleeping is, in fact, one great story, divided into chapters and sections, into parts distributed among sleepers. When one of them stops and grows silent, another takes up his cue so that the story can proceed in broad, epic zigzags while they all lie in the separate rooms of that house, motionless and inert like poppy seed within the partitions of a large, dried-up poppy.

THE OLD-AGE PENSIONER

I am an old-age pensioner in the true and full meaning of the word, very far advanced in that estate, an old pensioner of high proof. It may be that I have even exceeded the definite and allotted limits of my new status. I don't wish to hide it. There is nothing extraordinary about it. Why cast wondering looks and stare at me with hypocritical respect and solemn seriousness that conceal a lot of secret pleasure at one's neighbor's misfortune? How little elementary tact most people have! Facts of this kind should be accepted with a certain nonchalance. One must take these things as they come, just as I have accepted them

lightly and without care. Perhaps this is why I am a little shaky
on my feet and must put one before the other slowly and cautiously and watch where I go. It is so easy to stray under such
circumstances. The reader will understand that I cannot be too
explicit. My form of existence depends to a large degree on
conjecture and requires a fair amount of goodwill. I will now
have to appeal to this goodwill frequently by discreet winks,
which don't come easily to me because of the stiffening of my
facial muscles unused to mimic expressions. On the whole I
don't force myself on anyone. I don't want to dissolve in gratitude for the sanctuary kindly provided for me by anyone's
quick understanding. I acknowledge kindness without emotion,
coolly and with complete indifference. I don't like to receive,
along with the bonus of understanding, a heavy account for
gratitude. The best thing is to treat me offhandedly, with a dose
of healthy ruthlessness, with camaraderie and a sense of humor.
In this respect, my good simpleminded colleagues from the office, all younger than myself, have found the proper tone.

I sometimes call at the office by force of habit, around the
first of each month, and stand quietly at the counter waiting to
be noticed. The following scene then takes place: at a given
time, the head of the office, Mr. Filer, puts away his pen, winks
at his subordinates, and says suddenly, looking past me into
space, his hand cupping his ear:

"If my hearing doesn't deceive me, it must be you, Councillor,
somewhere amongst us!"

His eyes, looking over my head into emptiness, begin to
squint as he says this, and a humorous smile lights his face.

"I heard a voice somewhere and I at once thought it must be
you, dear Councillor!" he exclaims loudly, articulating distinctly
as if he were speaking to a deaf person. "Please do make a sign,
disturb the air at least in the place where you are floating!"

"Don't pull my leg, Mr. Filer," I say softly. "I have come to
collect my pension."

"Your pension?" Mr. Filer exclaims, again squinting into the
air. "Did you say your pension? You can't be serious, dear Councillor. Your name has been removed from the list of pensioners.
Do you still expect to receive a pension, dear Councillor?"

Thus they joke with me, in a warm, sympathetic, and humane way. The roughness, that direct jocularity, gives me a certain comfort. I leave the place more cheerful and hurry home quickly, in order to take with me indoors some of the pleasant warmth before it all evaporates.

But as to other people . . . An insistent questioning, never voiced aloud, which I can read in their eyes. It is difficult to avoid it. Supposing things are as they suspect—why immediately make these long faces, put on these solemn expressions, fall into uninvited silences, be both embarrassed and overcautious? Anything in order not to mention my condition . . . How well can I see through that game! It is no more than a kind of sybaritic self-indulgence and delight at their being different, a complete detachment from my condition, masked with hypocrisy. They exchange telltale looks but don't speak, and allow the thing to grow bigger in silence. Perhaps my condition is not quite as it should be. Perhaps it is even due to a small basic disability? Goodness gracious, so what? Is this a reason for that quick and frightened eagerness to please? Sometimes I want to burst out laughing when I see the recognition they show me, a kind of deference. Why do they insist so, why stress it, and why does doing it give them the profound satisfaction, which they try to conceal behind a mask of scared devotion?

Let's assume that I am a passenger of light weight, even of excessively light weight; let's assume that I am embarrassed by certain questions such as how old I am, when is my birthday, and so on—is that a reason for incessantly touching upon the subjects as if they were very relevant? Not that I am in the least ashamed of my condition. Not at all. But I cannot bear the exaggeration with which they magnify the importance of a certain fact, a certain difference, no bigger really than a hair's breadth. I am amused by the false theatricality and the solemn pathos that surrounds this matter, by the tragic costumes and gloomy pomp that drape this fact. While in reality? . . . Nothing pathetic at all, nothing more natural and commonplace. Lightness, independence, irresponsibility . . . And an increased ear for music, a most extraordinary musicality of one's limbs, as it were. It is impossible to pass by a barrel organ and not dance to it. Not because you feel happy, but because you don't care, and the tune has its own will, its own stubborn rhythm. So you give in. "Maggie, Maggie, treasure of my soul . . ." You are too light, too agile to protest; and besides, why protest against such an unpretentious and enticing proposal? Therefore I dance, or rather trot, in time with the tune, with the tiny steps of an old-age pensioner, and from time to time I give a little skip. Few people notice it, they are too busy rushing about their daily affairs.

I am anxious to avoid one thing: that the reader should have exaggerated ideas about my situation. I must warn him against it both in the positive and negative sense. No sentimentality, please. It is a condition like any other, and therefore capable of being understood and treated naturally. Any strangeness disappears once you have crossed to the other side. You sober up—this is what is characteristic of my situation: you are unburdened, feel light, empty, irresponsible, without respect for class, for personal ties, for conventions. Nothing holds me and nothing fetters me. I am boundlessly free. The strange indifference with which I move lightly through all the dimensions of being should be pleasurable in itself. But . . . that lack of anchorage, the would-be careless animation and lightheartedness—but I must not complain . . . There is a saying: gather no moss. That is exactly it: I stopped gathering moss a long time ago.

From the window of my room, which is high up, I have a bird's-eye view of the city, its walls, its roofs and chimneys in the gray light of a fall dawn—the whole densely built-up panorama just unwrapped from the night, palely lighted at the yellow horizon, cut into light strips by the black scissors of cawing crows. I feel: this is life. Everyone is stuck within himself, within the day to which he wakes up, the hour which belongs to him, or the moment. Somewhere in the semidarkness of a kitchen coffee is brewing, the cook is not there, the dirty glare of a flame dances on the floor. Time deceived by silence flows backward for a while, retreats, and in these uncounted moments night returns and swells the undulating fur of a cat. Kathy from the first floor yawns and stretches languorously for long minutes before she opens the windows and starts sweeping and dusting. The night air, saturated with sleep and snoring, lazily wafts toward the window, gets out, and slowly enters the dun and smoky grayness of the day. Kathy dips her hands reluctantly into the dough of bedding, warm and sour from sleep. At last, with a shiver, with eyes full of night, she shakes from the window a large, heavy feather bed, and scatters over the city particles of feathers, stars of down, the lazy seed of night dreams.

At such a time I would dream of being a baker who delivers bread, a fitter from the electric company, or an insurance man collecting the weekly installments. Or at least a chimney sweep. In the morning, at dawn, I would enter some half-opened gateway, still lit by the watchman's lantern. I would put two fingers to my hat, crack a joke, and enter the labyrinth to leave late in the evening, at the other end of the city. I would spend all day going from apartment to apartment, conducting one neverending conversation from one end of the city to the other, divided into parts among the householders; I would ask something in one apartment and receive a reply in another, make a joke in one place and collect the fruits of laughter in the third or fourth. Among the banging of doors I would squeeze through narrow passages, through bedrooms full of furniture, I would upset chamber pots, walk into squeaking perambulators in which babies cry, pick up rattles dropped by infants. I would stop for longer than necessary in kitchens and hallways, where servant girls were tidying up. The girls, busy, would stretch their young legs, tauten their high insteps, play with their cheap shining shoes, or clack around in loose slippers.

Such are my dreams during the irresponsible, extramarginal hours. I don't deny them, although I see their lack of sense. Everybody should be aware of his condition and know how to accept it.

For us old-age pensioners, autumn is on the whole a dangerous season. He who knows how difficult it is for us to achieve any stability at all, how difficult it is to avoid distraction or destruction by one's own hand, will understand that autumn, its winds, disturbances, and atmospheric confusions, does not favor our existence, which is precarious anyway.

There are, however, some days during autumn that are calm, contemplative, and kind to us. Days sometimes occur without sun, but warm, misty, and amber colored on their edges. In the gap between the houses, a view suddenly opens on a stretch of sky moving low, ever lower, toward the last windswept yellowness of the distant horizon. The perspectives opening into the depth of day seem like the archives of the calendar, the cross section of days, the endless files of time, floating in tiers into a bright eternity. The tiers order themselves in the fawn sky, while the present moment remains in the foreground and only a few people ever lift their eyes to the distant shelves of this illusory calendar. Eyes on the ground, everybody rushes somewhere, impatiently avoiding others; the street is cut by the invisible paths of these comings and goings, meetings and avoidings. But in the gap between the houses, where one can see the lower part of the city and its whole architectural panorama, lit from the back by a streak of sun, there is a gap in the hubbub. On a small square, wood is being cut for the city school. Cords of healthy, crisp timber are piled high and melt slowly, one log after another, under the saws and axes of workmen. Ah, timber, trustworthy, honest, true matter of reality, bright and completely decent, the embodiment of the decency and prose of life! However deep you look into its core, you cannot find anything that is not apparent on its evenly smiling surface, shining with that warm, assured glow of its fibrous pulp woven in a likeness of the human body. In each fresh section of a cut log a new face appears, always smiling and golden. Oh, the strange complexion of timber, warm without exaltation, completely sound, fragrant, and pleasant!

The sawing of wood is a truly sacramental function, symbolic and dignified. I could stand for hours on a late afternoon watching the melodious play of saws, the rhythmical work of axes. Here is a tradition as old as the human race. In that bright gap of the day, in that hiatus of time opened onto a yellow and wilting eternity, beech logs have been sawed since Noah's day, with the same patriarchal and eternal movements, the same strokes and the same bent backs. The workmen stand up to their armpits in the golden shavings and slowly cut into the logs and cords of wood; covered with sawdust, with a tiny spark of light in their eyes, they cut ever deeper into the warm healthy pulp, into the solid mass; with each stroke a reflection sparks in their eyes, as if they were looking for something in the core of the timber: a golden salamander, a screaming fiery creature, that burrows deeper and deeper under their cutting. Perhaps they are simply dividing time into small splinters of wood. They husband time, they fill the cellars with an evenly sawed future for their winter months.

Oh, to endure that critical period, those few weeks, until the morning frosts begin and winter starts in earnest. How I like the prelude to winter, still without snow but with the smell of frost and smoke in the air. I remember Sunday afternoons in the late autumn. Let us assume that it has been raining for a whole week, that a long downpour has saturated the earth with water, and that now the surface begins to dry out, exuding a hearty, healthy cold. The week-old sky with a cover of tattered clouds has been raked up, like mud, to one side of the firmament, where it looms dark in a folded compressed heap, while from the west the hale, healthy colors of an autumn evening begin to spread and slowly fill the cloudy landscape. And while the sky clears gradually from the west and becomes translucent, servant girls walk out in their Sunday best, in threes, in fours, holding hands. They walk in the empty, Sunday-clean and drying street between the suburban houses bright in the tartness of the air which now turns crimson before dusk; rosy and round-faced from the cold, they walk with elastic steps in their new, too tight shoes. A pleasant, touching memory, brought up from a dark corner of the mind!

Recently, I have been calling almost daily at the office. It sometimes happens that someone is sick and they allow me to work in his place. Or somebody has something urgent to do in town and lets me deputize for him. Unfortunately, this is not regular work. It is pleasant to have, even for a few hours, a chair of one's own with a leather cushion, one's own rulers, pencils, and pens. It is pleasant to run into or even be rebuked by one's fellow workers. Someone addresses you, makes a joke, pulls your leg, and you blossom forth for a moment. You rub

against somebody, attach your homelessness and nothingness to
something alive and warm. The other person walks away and
does not feel your burden, does not notice that he is carrying
you on his shoulders, that like a parasite you cling momentarily
to his life . . .

But since the appointment of a new head of department, even
this has come to an end.

Quite often now, if the weather is good, I sit out on a bench
in a small square that faces the city school. From the street
nearby comes the sound of wood being cut. Girls and young
women return from the market. Some have serious and regular
eyebrows and walk looking sternly from under them, slim and
glum—angels with basketfuls of vegetables and meat. Sometimes they stop in front of shops and look at their reflections in
the shop window. Then they walk away turning their heads,
casting a proud and mustering eye on the backs of their shoes.
At ten o'clock the beadle appears at the school gate and fills the
street with the shrill ringing of his bell. Then the inside of the
school seems to swell with a violent tumult that almost wrecks
the building. Fugitives from the general commotion, small
ragamuffins appear in the gateway, rush screaming down the
stone steps and, finding themselves free, undertake some crazy
leaps, and, between two mad looks of their rolling eyes, they
throw themselves blindly into improvised games. Sometimes
they venture up to my bench in their lunatic chases, throwing
over their shoulders some obscure abuse at me. Their faces
seem to come off their hinges in the violent grimaces that they
make at me. Like a pack of busy monkeys, in a self-parody of
clowning, this bunch of children run past me, gesticulating
with a hellish noise. I can see their upturned, unformed, running noses, their mouths torn by shouting, their cheeks covered
with spots, their small tight fists. Sometimes they stop near me.
Strange to say, they treat me as if I were their age. True, I have
been growing smaller for a long time. My face, wilted and
flabby, has assumed the appearance of a child's face. I am
slightly embarrassed when they address me as "thou." When
one day one of them suddenly struck me across my chest, I
rolled under the bench. I was not offended. They pulled me out,

enchanted by this rather unexpected but refreshing behavior. The fact that I take no offense however violent and impetuous their conduct has gradually won me a measure of popularity. From then on, I have carried a supply of stones, buttons, empty cotton reels, and pieces of rubber in my pockets. This has enormously facilitated exchanges of ideas and made a natural bridge for starting friendships. Moreover, engrossed in factual interests, they pay less attention to me as a person. Under the cover of the arsenal produced from my pockets, I need not fear anymore that their curiosity and inquisitiveness will be directed at me.

One day I decided to translate into action a certain idea that had been worrying me more and more insistently.

The day was mild, dreamy, and calm—one of those late autumn days when the year, having exhausted all the colors and nuances of that season, seems to revert to the springtime pages of the calendar. The sunless sky had settled itself into colored streaks, gentle strips of cobalt, verdigris, and celadon, framed at the edges with whiteness as clear as water—the colors of April, inexpressible and long forgotten. I had put on my best suit and went out not without some misgivings. I walked quickly, effortlessly in the calm aura of the day, straying neither to the left nor right. Breathless, I ran up the stone steps. *Alea jacta est*, I said to myself, knocking at the door of the office. I stood in a modest posture in front of the headmaster's desk, as befitted my new role. I was slightly embarrassed.

The headmaster produced from a glass-topped box a cockchafer on a pin and lifting it aslant to his eye, looked at it against the light. His fingers were stained with ink, the nails were short and cut straight. He looked at me from behind his glasses.

"So you wish to enroll in the first form, Councillor?" he said. "This is praiseworthy and admirable. I understand that you would like to refresh your education from the foundations, from the beginnings. I always repeat: grammar and the tables are foundations of all learning. Of course, we cannot consider you, Councillor, as a schoolboy to whom compulsory education applies. Rather as a volunteer, a veteran of the alphabet, to coin a phrase, who after long years of wandering has called again at the haven of the school, who has brought his distressed ship to a safe port, as it were. Yes, yes, Councillor, very few people show us gratitude and recognition for our work, and few return to us after a lifetime of toil and settle down here permanently as a voluntary, life pupil. You shall enjoy special privileges, Councillor. I have always thought—"

"Excuse me," I interrupted, "but I should like to say that, as far as special privileges are concerned, I would like to renounce them completely . . . I don't want any. On the contrary, I should not like to be treated differently in any way; I wish to merge completely, to disappear in the gray mass of the class. My plan would fail if I were to be privileged. Even with regard to corporal punishment," here I lifted my finger, "and I completely recognize its beneficial and educational importance—I insist that no exception should be made for me."

"Most praiseworthy, most thoughtful," said the headmaster with respect. "Come to think of it, your education might reveal certain gaps through the long years of nonusage. We all have in this respect some optimistic illusions, which can easily be dispelled. Do you remember, for instance, how much is five times seven?"

"Five times seven," I repeated, embarrassed, feeling confusion flowing in a warm and blissful wave to my head, creating a mist that obscured the clarity of my thoughts. Enchanted by my own ignorance, I began to stammer and repeat over and over again: "Five times seven, five times seven . . ." enormously pleased that I was really reverting to childlike ignorance.

"There you are," said the headmaster, "it is high time for you to enroll in school once more."

Then, taking me by the hand, he led me to the form where a class was being held.

Again, as half a century ago, I found myself in the tumult of a room swarming and dark from a multitude of mobile heads. I stood, very small, in the center holding the tail of the headmaster's coat, while fifty pairs of young eyes looked at me with the indifferent, cruel matter-of-factness of young animals confronted with a specimen of the same race. From all sides faces were made at me, grimaces of instant token enmity, tongues stuck out. I did not react to these provocations, remembering the good upbringing I had once received. Looking round the mobile, awkwardly grimacing faces, I recalled the same situation fifty years before. At that time I had stood next to my mother, while she talked to the lady teacher. Now, instead of my mother, it was the headmaster whispering something into the ear of the instructor, who was nodding his head and staring at me attentively.

"He is an orphan," the instructor said at last to the class, "he has no father or mother, so don't be unkind to him."

Tears came to my eyes after that short address, real tears of emotion, and the headmaster, himself moved, placed me on the bench nearest the rostrum.

A new life thus began for me. The school at once absorbed me completely. Never in my earlier life had I been so engrossed in a thousand affairs, intrigues, and interests. I lived a life of incessant excitement. Over my head the lines of multiple and complicated messages were crossing. I was on the receiving end of signals, telegrams, signs of understanding. I was hissed at, winked at, and reminded in all manner of ways about a hundred promises which I had sworn to fulfill. I could hardly wait for the end of the lesson, during which out of inborn decency I sustained with stoicism all attacks and tried not to miss a single one of the instructor's words. But hardly had the bell been rung than the whole shouting gang fell upon me, surrounding me with an elemental impetus, and almost tearing me to pieces. They came from behind, or, stamping across the benches, they jumped over my head and turned somersaults over me. Each of them shouted his demands into my ears. I became the center of all interests, and the most important transactions, the most complicated and doubtful deals, could not take place without my participation. In the street, I walked surrounded by a noisy, violently gesticulating gang. Dogs passed us at a distance, with tails between their legs, cats jumped onto roofs when they saw us approaching, and lonely small boys, met in the street, with passive fatalism hunched their heads between their shoulders, preparing for the worst.

Tuition at school had lost none of the charm of novelty, as, for instance, the art of spelling. The instructor appealed to our ignorance very skillfully and cunningly, he drew it forth until he reached that tabula rasa on which the seeds of all teaching must fall. Having thus eradicated all our prejudices and habits, he taught us from the very start. With difficulty and with concentration we melodiously spelled and divided words into syllables, sniffing in the intervals and pointing with our fingers at each new letter in our book. My primer had the same traces of my index finger, thicker at the more difficult letters, as the primers of my schoolmates.

One day, I cannot remember why, the headmaster entered the room and in the sudden silence pointed his finger at three of us, one of whom was myself. We were to follow him to his study at once. We knew what was in store, and my two fellow culprits began to cry in advance. I looked with indifference at their premature contrition, at their faces deformed by sudden weeping as if with the onset of tears the human mask had fallen off and disclosed a formless pulp of weeping flesh. I myself was calm: with the stoicism of fair and moral natures I submitted myself to the course of events, ready to face the consequence of my actions. That strength of character, which resembled obstinacy, did not please the headmaster, as we three culprits stood facing him in his study, the instructor standing by with a cane in his hand. I undid my belt with indifference, but the headmaster, looking at me, exclaimed:

"Shame on you! How is it possible, at your age?" and looked indignantly at the instructor.

"A strange freak of nature," he added with a look of disgust. Then, having sent the two small boys away, he made a long and earnest speech, full of regrets and disapproval. But I did not understand him. Biting my nails, I looked stupidly ahead of me and then said lisping:

"Please, shir, it was Andy who shpat at the other shir's roll."
I had become a complete child.

For gymnastics and art we went to another school building, which had a special room and equipment for these subjects. We marched in pairs, talking passionately, filling every street we passed with the sudden tumult of our mingled sopranos.

The other school was in a large wooden building, recon-structed from an old theater hall, and with many outhouses. The art class resembled an enormous bathhouse; the ceiling rested on wooden pillars, and there was a gallery all around the room, to which we climbed at once, storming the stairs, which resounded thunderously under our feet. The numerous smaller rooms and recesses were wonderfully well suited to the game of hide-and-seek. The art master never appeared, so we could play to our heart's content. From time to time the headmaster of that other school rushed into the hall, put the noisiest boys into cor-ners, and pulled the ears of the wildest. Hardly had his back been turned than the noise began anew.

We did not hear the bell announcing the end of the class. The afternoon came, short and colorful as usual in autumn. Some boys were fetched by their mothers, who, scolding and smack-ing them, carried them off home. But for the others and those deprived of such solicitous care, the proper playtime only started at that moment. It was late evening before the old beadle who came to lock up the school finally chased us away.

At that time of the year, there was dense darkness in the mornings when we walked to school, and the city was still asleep. We moved blindly with outstretched hands, dragging our feet in the rustling leaves that lay thick on the pavements. We groped along the walls of houses so as not to lose our way. Unexpectedly in a window recess we would feel under our hands the face of one of our mates, coming from the opposite direction. How we laughed, guessing whom it might be, how many surprises we had! Some boys would carry lighted bits of tallow candle, and the city was punctuated with these wander-ing lights, advancing low above ground in a trembling zigzag, meeting, then stopping to shed light on a tree, a clump of earth, a pile of yellow leaves among which very small boys looked for horse chestnuts. In some houses the first lamps were lit, and the hazy glow from the upper floors, magnified by the squares of windows, fell in irregular patches on the pavements, on the town hall, on the blind facades of houses. And when somebody, lamp in hand, walked from one room to another, enormous rectangles of light outside would turn like the pages of a colossal book and the market square seemed to shift the houses and shadows and pick them up as if it were playing patience with an outsize pack of cards.

At last we reached school. The candles were extinguished, darkness surrounded us as we groped for our places. Then the instructor entered, put an end of a tallow candle into a bottle, and the boring questions about declension of the irregular verbs would begin. As there was not yet sufficient light, the lesson remained oral and had to be memorized. While one of us was reciting monotonously, we looked, blinking, at the golden arrows shooting up from the candle, at lines that cut across one another like blades of straw on our half-closed eyelashes. The instructor poured ink into inkwells, yawned, looked out through the low window into the blackness. Under the seats it was completely dark. We dived there, giggling, walked on all fours, smelling one another like animals, and performing blindly and in whispers the usual transactions. I shall never forget those blissful early morning hours at school while a slow dawn matured beyond the windowpanes.

At last came the season of autumnal winds. On its first day, early in the morning, the sky became yellow and modeled itself against that background in dirty gray lines of imaginary landscapes, of great misty wastes, receding in an eastward direction into a perspective of diminishing hills and folds, more numerous as they became smaller, until the sky tore itself off like the wavy edges of a rising curtain and disclosed a further plan, a deeper sky, a gap of frightened whiteness, a pale and scared light of remote distance, discolored and watery, that like final amazement closed the horizon. As in Rembrandt's etchings one could see on such a day distant microscopic regions that, under the streak of brightness usually hard to locate, now rose from beyond the horizon under that clear crevice of sky.

In that miniature landscape, one could see with sharp precision a railway train usually not visible at that distance, moving on a wavy track and crowned with a plume of silvery white smoke, which in turn dissolved into bright nothingness.

And then, the wind rose. As if thrown from the clear gap in

the sky, it circled and spread all over the city. It was woven of softness and gentleness, but it pretended to be brutal and fierce. It kneaded, turned over, and tortured the air until it felt like dying from bliss. Then it stiffened in space and reared, spread itself like canvas sails—enormous, taut, flapping like drying sheets—tangled itself in hard knots, trembling with tension, as if it wanted to move the whole atmosphere into a higher space; and then it pulled and untied the false knot and, a mile further away, threw again its hissing lasso, that lariat which could catch nothing.

And the dance the wind led the chimney smoke! The smoke did not know how to avoid its scolding, how to turn, whether left or right, how to escape its blows. Thus the wind lorded it over the city as if on that memorable day it had wanted to give a telling example of its infinite willfulness.

From early in the morning, I had a premonition of disaster. I made my way in the gale only with difficulty. On street corners, where the crosswinds met, my schoolmates held me by my coattails. So I sailed across the city and all was well. Later we went for gymnastics to the other school. On our way we bought some crescent rolls. Talking incessantly, our long crocodile wound through the gate and into the courtyard. One more minute and I should have been safe, in a secure spot, safe until the evening. If need be, I might have spent the night in the hall. My loyal friends would have stayed with me. But as fate had it, Vicky had that day been given a new top as a present, and he let it spin in front of the school. The top spun, a crowd formed at the entrance, I was pushed outside the gate and was immediately swept away.

"Boys, help, help!" I shouted, already suspended in the air. I could still see their outstretched arms and their shouting, open mouths, but the next moment, I turned a somersault and ascended in a magnificent parabola. I was flying high above the roofs. Breathless I saw in my mind's eye how my schoolmates raised their arms, and called out to the instructor, "Please, sir, please. Simon has been swept away!"

The instructor looked at them from under his spectacles. He

went slowly over to the window and, screening his eyes with his hands, scanned the horizon. But he could not see me. In the dull glare of the pale sky, his face had the color of parchment.

"We must cross his name off the register," he said with a bitter smile and returned to the rostrum. I was carried higher and higher into the unexplored yellow space.

LONELINESS

It is with great relief that I feel able to go out again. But for what a long time was I confined to my room! These have been bitter months and years.

I cannot explain why I have been living in my old nursery—the back room of the apartment, with access from the balcony—which was rarely used in the past, forgotten, as if it did not belong to us. I cannot remember how I got there. I believe it was during a bright watery white moonless night. I could see every detail in the dim light. The bed was unmade, as if someone had just left it, and I listened in the stillness for the breathing of people asleep. But who was likely to be breathing here? Since then, this has been my home. I have been here for years and am rather bored. Why didn't I think in advance about stocking up! Ah, you who still can do it, who still are given the time, make provisions, save up grain—good, nourishing, sweet grain—for a great winter of lean and hungry years lies ahead, and the earth will not bear fruit in the land of Egypt. Alas, I was not provident, like a hamster. I have always been a lighthearted field mouse, I have lived from day to day without a care for the morrow, trusting in my starveling's talent. Like a mouse, I thought, What do I care about hunger? If worst comes to worst, I can gnaw wood or nibble paper. The poorest of animals, a gray church mouse, at the tail end of the Book of Creation, I can exist on nothing. And so I live in this dead room. Many flies died in it a long time ago. I put my ear against wood, to hear the sound of a woodworm. Deadly silence. Only I, the immortal mouse, lonely and posthumous, rustle in this room, running endlessly on the table, on the shelf, on the chairs. I run around resembling Aunt Thecla in a long gray frock reaching to the ground—agile, quick, and small, pulling behind me a mobile tail. I am now sitting in bright daylight on the table, immobile, as if stuffed, my eyes like two protruding shiny beads. Only the end of my muzzle pulsates imperceptibly, by force of habit, in minute chewing movements.

This, of course, is to be understood as a metaphor. I am really an old-age pensioner, not a mouse. It is part of my existence to be the parasite of metaphors, so easily am I carried away by the first simile that comes along. Having been carried away, I have to find my difficult way back, and slowly return to my senses.

What do I look like? Sometimes I see myself in the mirror. A strange, ridiculous, and painful thing! I am ashamed to admit it: I never look at myself full face. Somewhat deeper, somewhat farther away I stand inside the mirror a little off center, slightly in profile, thoughtful and glancing sideways. Our looks have stopped meeting. When I move, my reflection moves too, but half-turned back, as if it did not know about me, as if it had got behind a number of mirrors and could not come back. My heart bleeds when I see it so distant and indifferent. It is you, I want to exclaim; you have always been my faithful reflection, you have accompanied me for so many years and now you don't recognize me! Oh, my God! Unfamiliar and looking to one side, my reflection stands there and seems to be listening for something, awaiting a word from the mirrored depths, obedient to someone else, waiting for orders from another place.

Mostly I sit at the table and turn the pages of my yellowed university notes—my only reading.

I look at the sun-bleached curtain, stiff with dust, waving slightly in the cold breeze from the window. I could do exercises on the curtain rod, an excellent bar. How lightly one could turn somersaults on it in the sterile, tired air. Almost casually one could make an elegant *salto mortale*, coolly, without too much involvement—a speculative exercise, as it were. When one stands on tiptoe, balancing oneself on the bar, with one's head touching the ceiling, one has the impression that it is slightly warmer higher up—the illusion of being in a warmer zone. Ever since my childhood, I have liked to have a bird's-eye view of my room.

So I sit and listen to the silence. The room is whitewashed. Sometimes on the white ceiling a wrinklelike crack appears, sometimes a flake of plaster breaks off with a click. Am I to reveal that the room is walled in? How can that be? Walled in? How could I leave it? That is just it: where there is a will, there is a way; a passionate determination can conquer all. I must only imagine a door, a good old door, like the one in the kitchen of my childhood, with an iron handle and a bolt. There is no walled-in room that could not be opened by such a trusted door, provided one were strong enough to suggest that such a door exists.

FATHER'S LAST ESCAPE

It happened in the late and forlorn period of complete disruption, at the time of the liquidation of our business. The signboard had been removed from over our shop, the shutters were halfway down, and inside the shop my mother was conducting an unauthorized trade in remnants. Adela had gone to America, and it was said that the boat on which she had sailed had sunk and that all the passengers had lost their lives. We were unable to verify this rumor, but all trace of the girl was lost and we never heard of her again.

A new age began—empty, sober, and joyless, like a sheet of white paper. A new servant girl, Genya, anemic, pale, and boneless, mooned about the rooms. When one patted her on the back, she wriggled, stretched like a snake, or purred like a cat. She had a dull white complexion, and even the insides of her eyelids were white. She was so absentminded that she sometimes made a white sauce from old letters and invoices: it was sickly and inedible.

At that time, my father was definitely dead. He had been dying a number of times, always with some reservations that forced us to revise our attitude toward the fact of his death. This had its advantages. By dividing his death into installments, Father had familiarized us with his demise. We became gradually indifferent to his returns—each one shorter, each one more pitiful. His features were already dispersed throughout the room in which he had lived, and were sprouting in it, creating at some points strange knots of likeness that were most expressive. The wallpaper began in certain places to initiate his habitual nervous tic; the flower designs arranged themselves into the doleful elements of his smile, symmetrical as the fossilized imprint of a trilobite. For a time, we gave a wide berth to his fur coat lined with polecat skins. The fur coat breathed. The panic of small animals sewn together and biting into one another passed through it in helpless currents and lost itself in the folds of the fur. Putting one's ear against it, one could hear the melodious purring unison of the animals' sleep. In this well-tanned form, amid the faint smell of polecat, murder, and nighttime matings, my father might have lasted for many years. But he did not last.

One day, Mother returned home from town with a preoccupied face.

"Look, Joseph," she said, "what a lucky coincidence. I caught him on the stairs, jumping from step to step—" and she lifted a handkerchief that covered something on a plate. I recognized him at once. The resemblance was striking, although now he was a crab or a large scorpion. Mother and I exchanged looks: in spite of the metamorphosis, the resemblance was incredible.

"Is he alive?" I asked.

"Of course. I can hardly hold him," Mother said. "Shall I place him on the floor?"

She put the plate down, and leaning over him, we observed him closely. There was a hollow place between his numerous curved legs, which he was moving slightly. His uplifted pincers and feelers seemed to be listening. I tipped the plate, and Father moved cautiously and with a certain hesitation onto the floor. Upon touching the flat surface under him, he gave a sudden start with all of his legs, while his hard arthropod joints made a clacking sound. I barred his way. He hesitated, investigated the obstacle with his feelers, then lifted his pincers and turned aside. We let him run in his chosen direction, where there was no furniture to give him shelter. Running in wavy jerks on his many legs, he reached the wall and, before we could stop him, ran lightly up it, not pausing anywhere. I shuddered with instinctive revulsion as I watched his progress up the wallpaper. Meanwhile, Father reached a small built-in kitchen cupboard, hung for a moment on its edge, testing the terrain with his pincers, and then crawled into it.

He was discovering the apartment afresh from the new point

of view of a crab; evidently, he perceived all objects by his sense of smell, for, in spite of careful checking, I could not find on him any organ of sight. He seemed to consider carefully the objects he encountered in his path, stopping and feeling them with his antennae, then embracing them with his pincers, as if to test them and make their acquaintance; after a time, he left them and continued on his run, pulling his abdomen behind him, lifted slightly from the floor. He acted the same way with the pieces of bread and meat that we threw on the floor for him, hoping he would eat them. He gave them a perfunctory examination and ran on, not recognizing that they were edible.

Watching these patient surveys of the room, one could assume that he was obstinately and indefatigably looking for something. From time to time, he ran to a corner of the kitchen, crept under a barrel of water that was leaking and, upon reaching the puddle, seemed to drink.

Sometimes he disappeared for days on end. He seemed to manage perfectly well without food, but this did not seem to affect his vitality. With mixed feelings of shame and repugnance, we concealed by day our secret fear that he might visit us in bed during the night. But this never occurred, although in the daytime he would wander all over the furniture. He particularly liked to stay in the spaces between the wardrobes and the wall.

We could not discount certain manifestations of reason and even a sense of humor. For instance, Father never failed to appear in the dining room during mealtimes, although his participation in them was purely symbolic. If the dining-room door was by chance closed during dinner and he had been left in the next room, he scratched at the bottom of the door, running up and down along the crack, until we opened it for him. In time, he learned how to insert his pincers and legs under the door, and after some elaborate maneuvers he finally succeeded in insinuating his body through it sideways into the dining room. This seemed to give him pleasure. He would then stop under the table, lying quite still, his abdomen slightly pulsating. What the meaning of these rhythmic pulsations was, we could not imagine. They seemed obscene and malicious, but at the same time expressed a rather gross and lustful satisfaction. Our dog, Nimrod, would approach him slowly and, without conviction, sniff at him cautiously, sneeze, and turn away indifferently, not having reached any conclusions.

Meanwhile, the demoralization in our household was increasing. Genya slept all day long, her slim body bonelessly undulating with her deep breaths. We often found in the soup reels of cotton, which she had thrown in unthinkingly with the vegetables. Our shop was open nonstop, day and night. A continuous sale took place amid complicated bargainings and discussions. To crown it all, Uncle Charles came to stay.

He was strangely depressed and silent. He declared with a sigh that after his recent unfortunate experiences he had decided to change his way of life and devote himself to the study of languages. He never went out but remained locked in the most remote room—from which Genya had removed all the carpets and curtains, as she did not approve of our visitor. There he spent his time reading old price lists. Several times he tried viciously to step on Father. Screaming with horror, we told him to stop it. Afterward he only smiled wryly to himself, while Father, not realizing the danger he had been in, hung around and studied some spots on the floor.

My father, quick and mobile as long as he was on his feet, shared with all crustaceans the characteristic that when turned on his back he became largely immobile. It was sad and pitiful to see him desperately moving all his limbs and rotating helplessly around his own axis. We could hardly force ourselves to look at the conspicuous, almost shameless mechanism of his anatomy, completely exposed under the bare articulated belly. At such moments, Uncle Charles could hardly restrain himself from stamping on Father. We ran to his rescue with some object at hand, which he caught tightly with his pincers, quickly regaining his normal position; then at once he started a lightning, zigzag run at double speed, as if wanting to obliterate the memory of his unsightly fall.

I must force myself to report truthfully the unbelievable deed, from which my memory recoils even now. To this day I cannot understand how we became the conscious perpetrators of it. A strange fatality must have been driving us to it; for fate does not evade consciousness or will but engulfs them in its mechanism, so that we are able to admit and accept, as in a hypnotic trance, things that under normal circumstances would fill us with horror.

Shaken badly, I asked my mother in despair, again and again, "How could you have done it? If it were Genya who had done it—but you yourself." Mother cried, wrung her hands, and could find no answer. Had she thought that Father would be better off? Had she seen in that act the only solution to a hopeless situation, or did she do it out of inconceivable thoughtlessness and frivolity? Fate has a thousand wiles when it chooses to impose on us its incomprehensible whims. A temporary blackout, a moment of inattention or blindness, is enough to insinuate an act between the Scylla and Charybdis of decision. Afterward, with hindsight, we may endlessly ponder that act, explain our motives, try to discover our true intentions; but the act remains irrevocable.

When Father was brought in on a dish, we came to our senses and understood fully what had happened. He lay large and swollen from the boiling, pale gray and jellified. We sat in silence, dumbfounded. Only Uncle Charles lifted his fork toward the dish, but at once he put it down uncertainly, looking at us askance. Mother ordered it to be taken to the sitting room. It stood there afterward on a table covered with a velvet cloth, next to the album of family photographs and a musical cigarette box. Avoided by us all, it just stood there.

But my father's earthly wanderings were not yet at an end, and the next installment—the extension of the story beyond permissible limits—is the most painful of all. Why didn't he give up, why didn't he admit that he was beaten when there was every reason to do so and when even Fate could go no further in utterly confounding him? After several weeks of immobility in the sitting room, he somehow rallied and seemed to be slowly recovering. One morning, we found the plate empty. One leg lay on the edge of the dish, in some congealed tomato sauce and aspic that bore the traces of his escape. Although boiled and shedding his legs on the way, with his remaining strength he had dragged himself somewhere to begin a homeless wandering, and we never saw him again.

THE REPUBLIC OF DREAMS

AUTUMN

FATHERLAND

THE REPUBLIC OF DREAMS

Here on the Warsaw pavement in these days of tumult, heat, and dazzle I retreat in my mind to the remote city of my dreams, I let my vision rise to command that low, sprawling, polymorphic countryside, that greatcoat of God flung down at the sills of heaven like a mottled sheet. For that country submits utterly to heaven, holds heaven over itself in vaulted colors, variform, intricate with cloisters, triforia, stained-glass roses, windows opening onto eternity. Year after year that country grows up into the sky, merges with the dawn redness, turns angelic in the reflected light of the greater atmosphere.

A good way to the south, where the mapped land shifts—fallow from the sun, bronzed and singed by the glow of summer like a ripe pear—there it stretches like a cat in the sun, that chosen land, that peculiar province, the town unique in all the world. There is no point in speaking of this place to the profane—no point in explaining it is from that long tongue of rolling land over there lapping up breath for the countryside in the summer conflagrations, that boiling island of land facing south, that lone spur sticking up among swarthy Hungarian vineyards, that this one particle of earth detaches itself out of the collective landscape and, tramping alone down an untried path, attempts to be a world in itself. Sealed in a self-sufficient microcosm, that town and its countryside have boldly installed themselves at the very brink of eternity.

The garden plots at the outskirts of town are planted as if at the world's edge and look across their fences into the infinity of the anonymous plain. Just beyond the tollgates the map of the region turns nameless and cosmic like Canaan. Above that thin

forlorn snippet of land a sky deeper and broader than anywhere
else, a sky like a vast gaping dome many stories high, full of unfinished frescoes and improvisations, swirling draperies and violent ascensions, opens up once again.

How to express this in words? Where other towns developed
into economies, evolved into statistics, quantified themselves—
ours regressed into essence. Nothing happens here by chance,
nothing results without deep motive and premeditation. Here
events are not ephemeral surface phantoms; they have roots
sunk into the deep of things and penetrate the essence. Here decisions take place every moment, laying down precedents once
and for all. Everything that happens here happens only once
and is irrevocable. This is why such weightiness, such heavy
emphasis, such sadness inheres in what takes place.

Just now, for example, the yards are drowning in nettles and
weeds, tumbledown moss-grown sheds and outbuildings are up
to their armpits in enormous bristly burdocks that grow right
to the eaves of the shingled roofs. The town lives under the sign
of the Weed, of wild, avid, fanatical plant life bursting out in
cheap, coarse greenery—toxic, rank, parasitic. That greenery
glows under the sun's conjury, the maws of the leaves suck in
seething chlorophyll; armies of nettles, rampant, voracious, de-
vour the flower plantings, break into the gardens, spread over
the unguarded back walls of houses and barns overnight, run
wild in the roadside ditches. It is amazing what insane vitality,
feckless and unproductive, lives in this fervid dab of green, this
distillate of sun and groundwater. From a pinch of chlorophyll
it draws out and extrapolates under the blaze of these summer
days that luxuriant texture of emptiness, a green pith replicated
a hundred times onto millions of leaf surfaces, downy or
furred, of veined translucent verdure pulsing with watery plant
blood, giving off the pungent herbal smell of the open fields.

In that season the rear window of the shop's storage room
overlooking the yard was blinded by a diaphragm of green glit-
ter from leaf reflections, gauzy flutterings, wavy foliated greenery, all the monstrous excesses of this hideous backyard
fecundity. Sunk in deep shade, the storeroom riffled through all
shades of virescence, green reflections spread in undulating

paths through its vaulted length like the sibilant murmur of a forest.

The town had fallen into that wild luxuriance as into a sleep raised to the hundredth power, supine in a daze from the summer's heat and glare, in a thick maze of cobwebs and greenery, empty and shallow of breath. In rooms greenly lit to underwater opacity by the morning glory over the windows, platoons of flies struggled on their last wings, imprisoned forever as in the bottom of a forgotten bottle and locked in a dolorous agony that they proclaimed by drawn-out monotonous lamentations or trumpetings of fury and grief. In time, the window became the gathering place of all that lacework of scattered insectdom for one last premortal sojourn: huge crane flies, which had long bumped against the walls with a subdued drumming of misdirected flight and made a final torpid landing on a pane; whole genealogies of flies and moths, rooted and branching out from this window and spread by slow migration across the glass; pullulating generations of meager winglings, sky blue, metallic, glassy.

Over the shop displays, great bright opaque awnings flap lazily in the hot breeze, wavy stripes baking in the blaze. The dead season lords it over the empty squares, the wind-scoured streets. Distant prospects gathered up and shirred by gardens lie in a dazzled faint in the heat-glazed sky, as if they had only just fluttered down, a vast garish cloth, from the hollows of heaven, bright, glowing, rumpled from the flight, and were waiting, already spent, for a new charge of brilliance in which to renew themselves.

What to do on those days, where to flee from the conflagration, from the incubus lying heavy on the chest in a torrid noontime nightmare? On such days, Mother might hire a cab and, jammed together in its black body, the shop assistants up on the box with the bundles or clutching onto the springs, we would all ride out of town to Little Hill. We rode into the rolling, hill-studded landscape. The vehicle toiled its long, lonesome way among humped fields, rooting through the hot golden dust of the highway.

The convex necks of the horses bulged tensely, their glistening hindquarters knotted with honest toil, swept every so often by bushy slaps of the tail. The wheels turned slowly, squeaking on their axles. The old hack passed flat pastures dotted with molehills and broadly humped with reclining cattle, forked and horned, prodigious shapeless lumps of bones, knots, and ridges. There they lay, monumental as barrows, their quiet gaze mirroring remote and shifting horizons.

We came to a halt at last on Little Hill, next to the squat masonwork tavern. It stood alone, its roof spread out against the sky, on the watershed, the high spine between two opposed territories. The horses strained to struggle up the high edge, then stopped on their own, as if in bemusement, at the pike gate dividing two worlds. This gate commanded a wide sweep of landscape seamed by highways, pale and opalescent like faded tapestry, breathed on by a vast afflatus of air, sky blue and vacant. From that distant rolling plain a breeze rose, lifting the horses' manes and floating past under a high clear sky.

Here we might stop for the night, or Father might make a sign for us to forge on into that landscape, capacious as a map and webbed with highways. Barely visible in the distance before us on the winding roads crawled the vehicles that had come before us, making their way on the bright macadam lined by cherry trees straight to what was then a small inn, wedged in a narrow glen full of the chatter of springs and tumbling waters and muttering leaves.

In those far-off days our gang of boys first hit on the outlandish and impossible notion of straying even farther, beyond that inn, into no-man's- or God's-land, of patrolling borders both neutral and disputed, where boundary lines petered out and the compass rose of the winds skittered erratically under a high-arching sky. There we meant to dig in, raise ramparts around us, make ourselves independent of the grown-ups, pass completely out of the realm of their authority, proclaim the Republic of the Young. Here we would form a new and autonomous legislature, erect a new hierarchy of standards and values. It was to be a life under the aegis of poetry and adventure, never-ending signs and portents. All we needed to do, or so it seemed to us, was push apart the barriers and limits of convention, the old markers imprisoning the course of human affairs, for our lives to be invaded by an elemental power, a great inundation of the unforeseen, a flood of romantic adventures and fabulous happenings. We wanted to surrender our lives to this torrent of the fabulating element, this inspired onrush of historical events, be carried away by its surging waves without a will of our own. The spirit of nature was by its very essence a great storyteller. Out of its core the honeyed discourse of fables and novels, romances and epics, flowed in an irresistible stream. The whole atmosphere was absolutely stuffed full of stories. You only needed to lay a trap under this sky full of ghosts to catch one, set a wooden post upright in the wind for strips of narrative to be caught fluttering on its tip.

We resolved to become self-sufficient, create a new life principle, establish a new age, reconstitute the world—on a small scale, to be sure, for ourselves alone, but after our own tastes and pleasures.

This was going to be a stronghold, a blockhouse, a fortified base ruling the neighborhood; part fortress, part theater, part laboratory of visions. All nature would be yoked to its purpose. As in Shakespeare, this unleashed theater spilled over into nature, expanding into reality, soaking up impulses and inspiration from all elements, undulating with the great tidal ebb and flow of natural currents. Here we were going to locate the node of all processes that course through the body of nature, the point of entry to all story threads and fables shimmering in her great misty soul. Like Don Quixote, we wanted to divert the channel of all those histories and romances into our lives, throw open the frontiers to all those intrigues, convolutions, and intricate ventures that are spun in the great ether when it overreaches itself in the fantastical.

We dreamed the region was being threatened by an unknown danger, was permeated by a mysterious menace. Against this peril and hazard we would find safe refuge and shelter in our fortress. The countryside was crisscrossed by packs of wolves, bands of highwaymen infested the forest. We constructed shelters and bulwarks and, shaken by not unpleasant forebodings and delicious shudders, made ready for sieges. Our gates drew fugitives out from under the knives of brigands, and they found haven and sanctuary with us. Carriages chased by wild beasts flew up to our gates at a dead gallop. We played host to mysterious distinguished strangers and lost ourselves in conjectures in our desire to penetrate their disguises. In the evenings everyone gathered in the great hall, where, by flickering candlelight, we listened to one tale or revelation after another. There were times when the plot spun through these stories jumped out of the narrative frame and stepped among us, live and hungry for prey, and tangled us up in its perilous whorl. Sudden recognitions, unexpected disclosures, an improbable encounter pushed their way into our private lives. We lost the ground beneath our feet, placed in jeopardy by contingencies we ourselves had unleashed. From far away the howling of wolves was carried on the air, we brooded over romantic entanglements, ourselves halfway caught up in their coils, while an inscrutable night rustled on the other side of the window, fraught with shapeless aspirations, ardent, incomprehensible confidences, unplumbed, inexhaustible, itself knotted into labyrinthine convolutions.

Today those remote dreams come back, and not without reason. The possibility suggests itself that no dreams, however absurd or senseless, are wasted in the universe. Embedded in the dream is a hunger for its own reification, a demand that imposes an obligation on reality and that grows imperceptibly into a bona fide claim, an IOU clamoring for payment. We have long since abandoned our dreams of that fortress, but here, years later, someone turns up who picks them up and takes them seriously, someone ingenuous and true of heart who understood them literally, took them for coin of the realm, and treated them as things that were plain, unproblematic. I have seen this person, I have spoken with him. His eyes were an improbably vivid sky blue, not made for looking outward but for steeping themselves in the cerulean essence of dreams. He told me that when he came to the neighborhood I am referring to, that anonymous, virginal no-man's-land, he caught the scent of poetry and adventure at once, perceived the ready contours of myth suspended over the site. He discovered in the atmosphere the preformed outlines of this concept, the planes, elevations, and stone tablets of data. He heard a summons, an inner voice, like Noah did when he received his orders and instructions.

He was visited by the spirit of this design, which wandered at large in the atmosphere. He proclaimed a Republic of Dreams, a sovereign realm of poetry. On so many acres of land, on a surface sheet of landscape flung down in the woods, he established the exclusive domain of the fictive. He staked out its borders, laid down the foundations for a fortress, converted the realm into a single great rose garden. Guest apartments took shape, cells for solitary contemplation, refectories, dormitories, libraries, cabins tucked away in the park, arbors, pavilions, and scenic vistas . . .

That man who drags himself to the gates of this fortress, wolves or brigands hot on his trail, is saved. In triumphant procession they usher him in, relieve him of his dusty clothing. Festive, joyous, exhilarated, he enters the Elysian ambience and breathes in the rose-laden sweetness of the air. Off behind him cities and worldly affairs, the days and their fevers, dwindle. He has entered a radiant new holiday regularity, has cast off his own body like a bony carapace, has shed the grimacing mask that had grown onto his face, has completed the liberating metamorphosis.

The man with the sky blue eyes is no architect. He is, rather, a director, a director of cosmic landscapes and sceneries. His art consists in catching nature's intentions in midair, knowing how to read her arcane ambitions. For nature is full of potential architecture, rife with plans and construction. Did the master builders of the great ages behave any differently? They eavesdropped on the immense pathos of great squares, the dynamic perspectives of distance, the silent pantomime of symmetrical lanes. Long before Versailles, clouds in the immense skies of summer evenings arranged themselves into the kinds of spacious compounds that religious orders live and worship in, ethereal megalomaniacal residences, had tried their hand at stage setting, piling up towering structures, oversized and world-scale layouts. The grand theater of uncircumscribed airspace is inexhaustible in its ideas, its projects, its aerial preliminaries; it hallucinates an architecture of grandiose inspiration, an ethereal, transcendental brand of urbanistics.

Human works have the peculiarity that, once completed, they become hermetic, cut off from nature, consolidated on a base of their own. The work of the Blue-eyed One, in contrast, has not cut itself off from the great cosmic contexts; it is immersed in them half-humanized like a centaur, harnessed to the sublime processes of nature, still unfinished and growing. The man with the sky blue eyes invites everyone to keep on working, fabricating, jointly creating: we are all of us dreamers by nature, after all, brothers under the sign of the trowel, destined to be master builders.

AUTUMN

You know that moment when summer, so recently buoyant and vigorous, universal summer hugging to itself all things imaginable—people, events, objects—one day sustains a barely perceptible injury. The sun still blazes dense and copious, the landscape still wields the classic magisterial flourish bequeathed to this season by the genius of Poussin, but, strange to report, we return from a morning stroll oddly wearied and jejune: was there something to be ashamed of? We feel a bit out of sorts, avoid looking at each other—why? And we know that at dusk someone or other will take himself with a worried smile to a remote corner of summer and knock, knock at the wall to check if, in fact, the sound is still full and genuine. This testing carries with it a perverse relish in treacherous unmasking, a small frisson of scandal. But officially we are still full of respect and loyalty: we are dealing with a solid firm, an enterprise with sound financial backing . . . And yet, if the next day brings tidings of summer's bankruptcy, it seems like day-before-yesterday's news and no longer has the explosive impact of a scandal. And as the auction of assets takes its sober and revitalizing course, and the desecrated apartments, stripped and empty, fill with luminous sober echoes, this rouses no regret or sentiment: all this liquidating of summer displays the same languor, irrelevance, casual spirit of a belated carnival that has run on into Ash Wednesday.

On the other hand, indulging in pessimism is perhaps premature. Negotiations are still going on, the summer's reserves not yet exhausted, full rehabilitation is yet in the cards . . . But deliberation and cool heads are not what summer people are known for. Even the hotel-keepers, who have invested over their heads in the stock market of summer, are capitulating. Really—such lack of loyalty and proper feeling toward a faithful ally shows little trace of the royal merchant! They are shopkeepers—petty, craven souls incapable of taking the long view. One and all, they hug to their bellies what they have scraped together. Cynically they take off the mask of courtesy and the cutaway suit to reveal . . . the cashier.

And we, too, pack our luggage. I am fifteen years old and quite unburdened by mundane duties. Since an hour remains before our departure, I run outdoors once more to say good-bye to the summer place, check out the season's yield, decide what may be taken along and what will have to be relinquished for good in these doomed surroundings. But at the little round plaza in the park, empty now and bright in the afternoon sun, next to the Mickiewicz monument, the truth about the crisis of summer dawns in my soul. In the euphoria of this revelation I climb up the two steps of the pedestal and, drawing an impassioned arc with my eyes and outspread arms as if addressing the entire resort, I say: "Farewell, Season! You were very beautiful and rich. No other summer can compare with you. Today I recognize this even though there have been times when you made me terribly unhappy and sad. As something to remember me by, I leave you my adventures, littered all over the park and the lanes and gardens. I can't take my age fifteen back with me, that will have to stay behind here for good. I've slipped a drawing I did for you into a crack between two beams on the porch of the bungalow where I stayed as another souvenir. Now you're sinking among the shades, and down to the underworld along with you goes all this town full of cottages and gardens, too. You have no offspring. You and this town are dying, the last of your kind.

"But you're not guiltless, O Season! Let me tell you wherein your guilt lies. You did not want to stay, O Season, within the bounds of the given. No reality satisfied you; you broke out beyond the realm of what can be realized. Finding no surcease in reality, you created a superstructure out of the figurative stuff of metaphor, you moved among associations and allusions, the imponderables between things. All things referred to other things, which in turn called further things to witness, and so on ad infinitum. In the end your honeyed words grew cloying. People wearied of rocking on the billows of an unending rhetoric. Yes, rhetoric—pardon the expression. This became clear when, in many imaginations, in one place and another, a longing for the genuine and essential welled up. That moment already spelled your defeat. The borders of your universality became visible; your grand style, your splendid baroque, which satisfied the needs of reality when you were in your prime, now turned out to be a mannered trick. Your dulcitudes and reveries bore the stamp of childish inflation. Your nights were vast and boundless like the megalomanic aspirations of lovers, or they were swirling spectacles like the hallucinations of feverish patients. Your perfumes were extravagant, beyond the ability of human delight to absorb them. Under the magic of your touch everything dematerialized, grew toward ever further, higher forms. Eating your apples one dreamed of fruit from the territory of Paradise, your peaches brought up the image of ethereal fruit that is consumed by smell alone. Your palette held only the highest registers of color, you didn't know the saturation and pith of the dark, earthy, greasy browns. Autumn is the human soul's yearning for matter, essence, boundary. When for unexplored reasons human metaphors, projects, dreams begin to hanker for realization, the time of autumn is at hand. Those phantoms that, formerly spread out over the furthest reaches of the human cosmos, lent its high vaults the colors of their spectra now return to man, seeking the warmth of his breath, the cozy narrow shelter of his home, the niche that holds his bed. Man's house becomes like the little stable of Bethlehem, the core around which all demons, all spirits of the upper and lower spheres, condense. The time of beautiful classical gestures, Latinate rhetoric, the histrionic roundedness of the south, is over. Autumn looks for herself in the sap and primitive vigor of the Dürers and Brueghels. That form bursts from the overflow of material, hardens into whorls and knots, seizes matter in its jaws and talons, squeezes, ravishes, deforms, and dismisses it from its clutches imprinted with the marks of this struggle as half-formed hunks, with the brand of uncanny life stamped in the grimaces extruded from their wooden faces."

All this and more I said to the empty half-circle of the park, which seemed to recede before me. Only some fragments of this soliloquy issued from my mouth, partly because I couldn't find the proper words, partly because I was only miming my oration, eking out words with gesticulation. I made reference to nuts, the classic fruits of autumn, kindred to house furnishings, nourishing, tasty, and durable. I mentioned chestnuts, those polished models of fruit, cup-and-ball toys made for children to play with; I spoke of autumn apples on windowsills flushed an honest, homey, prosaic red.

Dusk was fumigating the air by the time I returned to the boardinghouse. Two large carriages were already drawn up in the courtyard against our leave-taking. The horses, not yet harnessed, snorted with their heads buried in feed bags. The doors all stood wide open, the candles burning on the table in our room flickered in the draft. The fast-descending gloom, the people grown faceless in the dusk who were hurrying out with luggage, the disorder in the ravished opened room, all this held a dismal suggestion of haste and belated panic, intimations of terror and disaster. Finally we took our places in the deep caverns of the carriages and started off. The dark, dense, deep air of the fields blew over us. The coachmen drew vigorous cracks from this intoxicating ether with their long whips and took pains to steady the gaits of the horses, whose powerful, splendidly sculptured withers rocked in the darkness between bushy slaps of their tails. Thus the two masses of horseflesh, rattling trunks, and creaking leather shells shifted through the dark, starless, solitary landscape of night. At times they seemed to disintegrate, come apart like crabs separating and scuttling away. Then the coachmen would take the reins more firmly in hand, reassemble the scattered hoofbeats and gather them into regular disciplined patterns. The lighted carriage lanterns sent long shafts into the deep of the night that telescoped out, broke off, and fled in great leaps into wild vague voids. They slunk off on their long legs just to be able to mock the coachmen with derisive gestures far off somewhere at the edge of the woods. Unperturbed, the coachmen swept them with broadsides of whip cracking. The town lay sleeping when we drove in among its houses. Streetlights shone here and there in empty streets, as if created simply for the purpose of illuminating a low-slung house or balcony, or to rivet to one's memory a number over a closed gate. Caught by surprise at this late hour, heavy-lidded padlocked shops, gates with prolapsed sills, signs jerked by the night wind displayed the hopeless desolation, the profound orphanhood of objects left to themselves, objects forgotten by people. My sister's carriage turned into a side street while we drove on to the marketplace. The horses changed their gait when we entered the deep shade of the square. On the threshold of his open hallway the barefoot baker stabbed us with a glance of dark eyes, the apothecary widow, still wide awake, proffered and withdrew raspberry balsam from a great jar. The pavement thickened under the horses' feet, single and paired clinks of iron separated out of the clatter of hoofbeats more and more slowly and distinctly, and the scored facade of our house gradually drew out of the darkness and stopped beside the carriage. A maid opened the gate for us, a kerosene lamp with a reflector in her hand. Our enormous shadows grew up over the stairs and skewed off at the arches of the stairway. The apartment was lit by a single candle, which dipped its flame to the draft from the open window. The dark wallpaper was mildewed with the sorrows and afflictions of many ailing generations. Roused from its slumber and released from long solitude, the old furniture seemed to gaze at the returning family with wry knowingness and patient wisdom. You can't escape from us, they seemed to be saying; in the end you have to reenter the realm of our magic, because we've long since divided up among ourselves all your movements and gestures, risings up and settlings down, all your future days and nights. We can wait, we know . . . The vast cavernous beds, piled high with chilly layers of sheets and blankets, waited for our bodies. The night's floodgates groaned under the rising pressure of dark masses of slumber, a dense lava that was just about to erupt and pour over its dams, over the doors, the old wardrobes, the stoves where the wind sighed.

FATHERLAND

After a great many of fate's capricious ups and downs, which
I have no intention of going into here, I found myself abroad at
last, in that realm of my youthful dreams I once ardently
yearned for. Fulfillment came too late, though, and in circumstances vastly different from those I had fondly imagined. I
made my return not as a conqueror but as one of life's derelicts.
The intended domain of my triumphs was now the scene of
wretched, inglorious, petty defeats in which I lost, one after the
next, my proud and lofty aspirations. By now I was fighting for
mere survival; battered, trying as best I could to save my flimsy
shell from shipwreck, blown here and there by the whims of
fate, I finally came upon that middle-sized provincial town
where, in the dreams of my youth, a certain country house was
to stand, the famous old master's refuge from the world's turmoil. Unconscious even of the irony involved in the coincidence, I now intended to hunker down and stay there some little
time, hibernate maybe, until the next windy burst of events. I
didn't care where chance might carry me. The glamour of the
landscape had faded irrevocably for me; now, harassed, worn
out, I wanted only peace.

But things took a different turn. Evidently I had reached
some fork in my road, a peculiar twist of my personal fate, for
unexpectedly my existence began to stabilize. I had a sense of
having passed into a favoring current. Wherever I turned I met
a situation that seemed tailored for me, people dropped everything as if they had been waiting for me, I spotted that sponta-
neous glint of attention in their eyes, that instant decision to put
themselves at my service, as though at the dictate of some

higher authority. This was illusion, of course, produced by the
deft interaction of circumstances, the dexterous meshing of the
gears of my destiny by the clever hands of chance, which led me
from event to event in what seemed like a sleepwalker's trance.
There was scarcely time for astonishment: the happy turn in my
fortunes went hand in hand with a complaisant fatalism, a
blithe passivity and trust that bade me submit to the gravita-
tional pull of events with no resistance. I had barely registered
all this as the fulfillment of a long-unsatisfied need, the profound gratification of the unrecognized and rejected artist's
perennial hunger, when my gifts found appreciation at long
last. From a café fiddler eager for any kind of job, I rapidly advanced to concertmaster of the local opera; the exclusive circles
of amateurs of the arts opened before me and I entered the best
society by what seemed like long-standing privilege—I, who
had been halfway domiciled in the underworld of the déclassé,
the between-decks stowaways and freeloaders of society's ship.
Aspirations that had led a tormenting subconscious existence in
the depth of my soul as smothered, mutinous pretensions
swiftly gained legitimacy and embarked on a life of their own.
The mark of usurper and vain pretender faded from my brow.

I recount all this in abridged form, in the context of a general
outline of my fortunes, not permitting myself to delve into details of this odd career, since all those events really belong to
the prehistory of occurrences already reported. No—my happiness had absolutely no element of excess or unbridled abandon
in it, as might have been suspected. I was utterly possessed by a
feeling of deep calm and certainty—a sign by which (sensitized
by life to every tremor of its countenance, seasoned physiogno-
mist of destiny) I recognized with profound relief that this time
it hid no malign intent. The quality of my happiness was endur-
ing and genuine.

My whole past of homeless wandering, the submerged misery
of my former existence, separated itself from me and floated
back like a stretch of country positioned crosswise against the
rays of the setting sun, rising one more time over distant horizons, while the train that bore me away rounded the last curve
and headed straight into the night, full-breasted with the future

that thrust against its face, a swelling, intoxicating, future slightly seasoned with smoke. This is the place for me to introduce the cardinal fact, the fact closing and crowning that age of prosperity and happiness: Eliza, whom I met at that stage of my pilgrimage, and whom after a brief rapturous engagement I made my wife.

The measure of my good fortune is ample and full. My position with the opera is unassailable. The conductor of the philharmonic orchestra, Maestro Pellegrini, values me and seeks my opinion on all decisions of importance. He is a dear old man on the verge of retirement, and there is a tacit three-way understanding among him, the opera management, and the town's Philharmonic Society that on his departure the conductor's baton will devolve upon me with no further ado. I have already held it in my hand more than once, conducting the monthly philharmonic concerts or in the orchestra pit of the opera, standing in for the maestro when he was ill or did not feel up to the demands of a modern piece of music alien to his spirit.

The opera is among the best endowed in the country. My salary is ample to sustain a comfortable style of life, even a certain gilding of luxury. Our lodgings have been furnished and arranged by Eliza in accordance with her taste, since I am quite without ambitions or enterprise in that direction. By contrast, Eliza has very decided (though constantly changing) ideas, which she puts into practice with an energy worthy of a better cause. She is forever embroiled with suppliers, battling vigorously over quality and price and bringing off exploits on these lines in which she takes no little pride. I watch her bustling with a tender indulgence tinged with some apprehension, as one might witness a child playing carelessly near the brink of an abyss. What innocence to imagine that we shape our destiny by struggling with a thousand mundane trifles!

Happily come to anchor in this calm bay, I want no more now than to cheat fate's vigilance, not to thrust myself upon its attention, to cling unobserved to my good fortune and be unnoticeable.

The city where fate has granted me to find such quiet and

serene refuge is famous for its venerable cathedral, situated on a
high bluff some way distant from the boundary of the residen-
tial quarters. Here the town comes to an abrupt stop, the terrain breaks off into steep battlements and promontories
covered with stands of mulberry and walnut and commanding a
sweeping view. This is the last outcropping of a high Creta-
ceous massif that stands guard over the broad clear plain of the
province, which is open all along its width to the warm breath
of the west. Under the caress of these mild currents the town
has wrapped itself in a calm, sweet climatic zone, creating as it
were a miniature meteorological orbit of its own within the
larger one containing it. All the year round, mild and barely
perceptible breezes wander through, gradually fusing toward
autumn into one steady harmonious current that resembles a
bright Gulf Stream of the air, a universal monotone of wind
that is gentle to the point of oblivion and blissful dissolution.

The cathedral, chiseled and chased over the centuries in the
precious twilight of its endlessly swelling hoard of stained glass,
jewel grafted on jewel over the generations, now draws throngs
of tourists from all over the world. During any season one can
find them roaming our streets, clutching guidebooks. They take
up the lion's share of our hotel space, comb our shops and antique stores for curios, fill up our places of amusement. From the
far-off outer world they bring the smell of the sea, sometimes the
zest and verve of great projects, the broad élan of big business.
Some, charmed by the climate, the cathedral, the pace of life,
have been known to settle down for a longer stay, adjust to the
environment, and remain for good. Others carry off wives when
they leave, the fair daughters of our merchants, manufacturers,
and restaurateurs. Thanks to these ties, outside capital is often invested in our enterprises and strengthens our industrial plant.

The town's economic life, for that matter, has been running a
placid course for years, free of shocks and crises. The highly developed sugar industry feeds three-quarters of the population at
its sweet artery; the town boasts as well a celebrated porcelain
factory that carries on a fine old tradition. It produces for ex-
port, but every Briton returning to his country makes a point of
ordering a set of so many pieces of ivory-colored china featuring

views of the cathedral and town as created by the young ladies of our art academy.

Generally speaking, this is a liberally and efficiently managed town, like many others in this country—moderately bustling and business minded, moderately fond of its comfort and civic well-being, also moderately given to snobbish ambition and social climbing. The ladies display an almost metropolitan sartorial extravagance, the gentlemen emulate the lifestyle of the capital, laboring with the help of a few cabarets and clubs to keep a marginal sort of nightlife alive. Card playing is very popular, even the ladies indulge in it; and for us too hardly a day goes by that does not end, sometimes deep into the night, over cards at the elegant quarters of one of our friends. The initiative in this matter lies once again with Eliza, who in justifying her fervor to me cites her concern for our social standing, which she claims makes it necessary for us to go out more in order to remain part of the scene. But in fact she is simply addicted to the charm of this mindless and lightly stimulating waste of time.

Sometimes I watch her excitement as she gives herself over heart and soul to the mutable nature of gaming, eyes shining, a hectic flush spreading over her cheeks. The shaded lamp casts mild light on the table around which a group of deeply absorbed people, cards fanning out from their hands, run their imaginary race on the trail of treacherous fortune. I catch glimpses of her, an elusive figure tense with the challenge of the séance, fleetingly revealed behind the back of this player or that. Into the reigning silence remarks are dropped in undertones that mark the varied and winding itinerary of luck. For my part, I wait for the moment when the silent fervid trance has enveloped all their senses, when, oblivious of all else, they are stooped in a cataleptic crouch over a whirling disc, to withdraw unnoticed from that realm of magic arts to the solitude of my thoughts. Sometimes, dropping out of the game, I manage to leave the table without attracting notice and move quietly into another room. The space is dark, lit only by a distant streetlight. With my head resting against a windowpane I stand there for a long time, meditating.

Above the autumnal opacity of the park the night is flushed by a vague reddish glow. In the ravaged upholstery of the tree-tops crows wake with caws of mindless alarm and, deceived by the false dawn, take off in noisy squads; their yawping, wheeling disarray throws tumult and vibrations into the murky redness tartly redolent of herbage and fallen leaves. Eventually the great flurry of loops and turns all over the sky subsides; calming gradually, it descends, lighting in the combed-out tangle of trees in a ragged, provisional file that still shows signs of unrest, rife with misgivings, chatter falling silent, plaintive queries. At last the swarm settles down for good and becomes part of the sibilant stillness of the surrounding languor. And night, deep and late, resumes its sway. Hours pass. Hot forehead pressed against the pane, I sense and know: from now on no harm may come to me, I have found a peaceful haven. A long succession of years heavy with happiness and fulfillment now lies ahead, an unending mathematical progression of joyful good times. The last few sighs, shallow and sweet, fill my breast utterly with happiness. I stop breathing. I know one day death will take me into her open arms, as she does all life, bountiful and benign. I will lie, entirely sated, among the green undergrowth of the beautifully manicured local cemetery. My wife—how beautiful she'll look in her widow's veil—will bring me flowers on those bright, calm midmornings we enjoy here. Out of the depth of this boundless plenitude a ponderous full-throated music, the solemn, mournful, resonant bars of a majestic overture, seems to rise. I sense the powerful pulsing of its rhythms as it thrusts upward from the deep. Eyebrows rising, my gaze riveted on a distant point, I feel the hair stand up on my head. I freeze, listening . . .

A louder babble of conversation wakes me from my torpor. People are asking about me and laughing. I hear my wife's voice. From my place of retreat I come back into the bright room, rubbing eyes still steeped in darkness. By now the party is breaking up. The host and hostess are standing in the doorway, chatting with their departing guests and exchanging valedictory courtesies. Finally we are alone in the dark street. My wife adjusts her free, buoyant steps to mine. We walk well together; going up a

hill with her head slightly bent, she kicks at the whispering carpet of dead leaves that covers the pavement. Still keyed up by
the gambling, the luck that favored her, the wine she has drunk,
she is full of little feminine schemes. By a tacit covenant between
us, she exacts absolute tolerance on my part for this sort of non-
committal fantasizing and takes sharp offense at any sober critical comments. A green smudge of dawn already shows above the
dark horizon as we enter our apartment. The good smell of a
heated and well-groomed interior envelops us. We don't turn on
the light. A distant lantern traces the silvery pattern of the curtains onto the opposite wall. Still dressed, sitting on the bed, I
silently take Eliza's hand and hold it awhile in mine.